Immortal Alexandros

By Alexander Geiger

Prime Directive (2013)
Flood Tide (2019)
Conquest of Persia (2019)
Immortal Alexandros (2021)
Funeral Games (2023)

Book Four of the Ptolemaios Saga

Immortal Alexandros

*An Epic Novel of the Decline and
Death of Alexander the Great*

Alexander Geiger

Requests for permission to make copies of any part of the work may be sent to:

Permissions Department
Ptolemaios Publishing & Entertainment, LLC
668 Stony Hill Road, Suite 150
Yardley, PA 19067

www.PtolemaiosPublishing.com

ISBN-13: 978-0-9892584-8-7

Library of Congress Control Number: 2021916746

Cover Design: Scott Schmeer, The Fierce Pixel, LLC

The author of this work is available to speak at live events. For further information, please contact the author at Alex@AlexanderGeiger.com

First Edition

Published in New York, New York, USA
Manufactured in the United States of America

To the Memory of all the Victims of the Holocaust

Table of Contents

"To win eternal mention in the deathless roll of fame."

Plato, Symposium, 208[1]

---

[1] From *The Dialogues of Plato,* translated by B. Jowett (3rd ed., Oxford University Press, 1892)

Maps and Animated Battle Depictions[2]

Map 1 – Ancient Macedonia and its Environs

Map 2 – Mainland Greece in 336 B.C.E.

Map 3 – Lands Traversed by Alexandros in 335 and early 334 B.C.E.

Map 4 - Lands Traversed by Alexandros, May 334 -- November 333 B.C.E.

Map 5 - Miletos and its Environs, c. 334 B.C.E.

Map 6 – Halikarnassos, c. 334 B.C.E.

Map 7 - Movements of Persian and Pan-Hellenic Armies Prior to Issos

Map 8 - Lands Traversed by Alexandros, November 333 – May 330 B.C.E.

Map 9 – Siege of Tyros, 332 B.C.E.

Map 10 – Egypt, 4th Century B.C.E.

Map 11 – Babylon, c. 331 B.C.E.

Map 12 – Persian Satrapies, 4th Century B.C.E.

---

[2] In lieu of black-and-white maps and static battle depictions in this book, color maps and animated depictions of battles are available at AlexanderGeiger.com.

Immortal Alexandros

List of Principal Characters[3]

Abisares (unk-325) – Indian raja

Alexandros Aniketos (356-323) – King of Macedonia (336-323); Persian Emperor (330-323)

Antigone (unk-unk) – Philotas's mistress

Antigonos Monophthalmos (c. 382-301) – Military commander under both Philippos and Alexandros; appointed satrap of Phrygia by Alexandros

Antipatros (397-319) – Macedonian nobleman; served as regent under both Philippos and Alexandros

---

[3] Each of the following characters is an actual historical figure. The numbers in parentheses refer to the year of birth and death of that figure, to the extent these dates are known. All years are B.C.E. In some cases, the actual dates are either uncertain or in dispute. In those cases, the year in question is preceded by a c. In a few cases, the actual dates are simply lost to the shifting sands of time.

It is important to remember, however, that this is a work of fiction. The author has taken some liberties with a few of his characters. For example, the date of Kleitos's birth is uncertain but he was probably several years older than depicted in this book. The reader should not draw any conclusions from the dates of death listed here about the lifespan, fate, date of death, or manner of demise of any character. To find the answers to all those questions, the reader should read the book. Simply looking at a List of Principal Characters would be just too easy.

Apame (c.340-unk) – Daughter of Spitamenes; Seleukos's 1st wife

Artabazos (c.387-c.328) – Persian nobleman; father of Barsine and Artakama, among others

Artakama (347-unk) – Artabazos's daughter; Barsine's sister; Ptolemaios's 1st wife

Barsine (355-309) – Alexandros's mistress; mother of his first child, Herakles

Bessos (unk-329) – Satrap of Baktria

Dareios (c.380-330) – Persian Emperor (336-330)

Drypetis (c.343-c.322) – Daughter of Dareios and Stateira(1); Hephaistion's wife

Harpalos (361-323) – Alexandros's childhood companion; became treasurer in Babylon

Hephaistion (356-324) – Alexandros's closest friend

Kallisthenes (c.368-327) – Aristoteles's great nephew; accompanied Alexandros as campaign historian

Kassandros (358-297) – Antipatros's son

Kleandros (c.365-324) – A commander in Alexandros's army; Koinos's brother

Kleitos Melas (c.357-327) – A commander in Alexandros's army

Kleopatra (354-308) – Daughter of Philippos and

Immortal Alexandros

Olympias; Alexandros's sister

Koinos (370-325) – A commander in Alexandros's army; Kleandros's brother; Parmenion's son-in-law

Krateros (365-320) – A commander in Alexandros's army

Lysimachos (360-282) – A commander in Alexandros's army

Nikanoros (358-331) – A commander in Alexandros's army; Parmenion's son

Olympias (a/k/a Myrtale) (377-314) – Philippos's 4th wife; Alexandros's mother

Omphis (unk-unk) – Indian raja; ruler of Taxila

Oxyartes (unk-unk) – Prominent warlord in Sogdiana; Roxane's father

Parmenion (400-330) – Leading Macedonian general; served both Philippos and Alexandros

Parysatis (340-unk) – Daughter of Artaxerxes Ochos; Alexandros's 3rd wife

Perdikkas (359-321) – A commander in Alexandros's army

Philippos Amyntou Makedonios (382-336) – King of Macedonia (359-336); Alexandros's father

Philippos of Akarnia (unk-unk) – Alexandros's physician

Philotas (360-330) – A commander in Alexandros's army; Parmenion's son

Polyperchon (c.380-c.295) – A commander in Alexandros's army

Poros (unk-317) – Indian raja; ruler of Paurava

Ptolemaios Metoikos (c.364-282) – One of Alexandros's bodyguards

Roxane (342-315) – Alexandros's 1st wife

Seleukos (358-281) – A commander in Alexandros's army

Sisikottos (unk-unk) – Indian raja

Sisygambis (unk-323) – Dareios's mother

Spitamenes (370-328) – Prominent warlord in Sogdiana

Stateira(1) (c.365-331) – Dareios's 1st wife

Stateira(2) (c.345-c.342) – Daughter of Dareios and Stateira(1); Alexandros's 2nd wife

Thais (unk-unk) – Famous Athenian hetaira

Place Name Glossary[4]

Alexandria Eschate (Alexandria the Farthest) – A garrison city founded by Alexandros on the southern bank of the Jaxartes River. The city, which still exists, is now called Khujand and is situated on both banks of the Syr Darya at the entrance to the Fergana Valley. It eventually became an important stop on the Silk Road. Today, it is the second largest city in Tajikistan and lies close to the current Tajik border with both Uzbekistan and Kyrgyzstan.

Alexandria-in-Arakhosia – Another garrison city founded by Alexandros, it has evolved into the present-day city of Kandahar in Afghanistan. Remains of ancient fortress walls have been excavated during more peaceful times in the 1960's and 1970's in a large mound located in the western quarter of Kandahar. Because the fortress was rebuilt many times before, during, and after Alexandros's lifetime, it is difficult to tell due to the current incomplete state of archaeological research which remnants, if any, can be attributed directly to Alexandros.

Alexandria-in-Areia – The new capital of Areia, founded by Alexandros, was located a few miles to the south of the existing capital of Artakoana. Its exact location has been the subject of some debate among scholars but was probably near present-day Herat in Afghanistan.

---

[4] Many of these places are shown on Maps 13, 14, and 15 at AlexanderGeiger.com

Alexandria-in-the-Caucasus – A garrison city founded by Alexandros in preparation for his crossing of the Hindu Kush. Remains of the city, including some finds that may date to the time of Alexandros, have been excavated on a hill near Begram, a town located approximately 50 miles north of Kabul, Afghanistan.

Artakoana (Artacoana) – The capital of Areia when it was conquered by Alexandros. He moved the capital to a new city called Alexandria-in-Areia, located a few miles to the south.

Babylon – One of the four capitals of the Persian Empire. Prior to its conquest, it had been the capital of two successive Babylonian Empires. The city straddled the Euphrates River. Remnants of the ancient city lie approximately 50 miles south of Baghdad, Iraq.

Baktra (Bactra) – Capital of Baktria. Present-day town of Balkh sits on the ancient site of Baktra. It is located near the provincial capital of Mazar-e Sharif in Afghanistan, approximately 46 miles south of the Amu Darya and the border with Uzbekistan.

Boukephala (Bucephala) – A city founded by Alexandros in memory of his beloved horse Boukephalas, who died of injuries sustained in a battle fought nearby. It was located on the Hydaspes River, now known as the Jhelum River, somewhere in present-day Punjab. The exact location is subject to dispute.

Ekbatana (Ecbatana) – One of the four capitals of the Persian Empire. Prior to its conquest, it had been the capital of Media. Remnants of the Ekbatana Royal Palace may be buried in Hagmatana Hill near modern Hamadan in the Zagros Mountains of western Iran.

Marakanda (Maracanda) – Capital of Sogdiana, it corresponds to present-day Samarkand, which is located in the Zeravshan River valley in northeastern Uzbekistan, near the Uzbek border with Tajikistan. According to archaeologists, it is one of the oldest continuously inhabited settlements in Central Asia, with some remains dating back 40,000 years. It too became a stop on the Silk Road a few centuries after Alexandros's time.

Opis – An ancient city located on the east bank of the Tigris River approximately 50 miles northeast of ancient Babylon and 20 miles southeast of present-day Baghdad.

Pattala – An ancient city located at the apex of the Indos delta. Because the course of the river has shifted over the centuries, the exact location of the city is in dispute but it was somewhere in present-day Sindh Province of Pakistan.

Persepolis – Principal capital of the Persian Empire until its destruction by Alexandros. Ruins of Dareios's capital have been unearthed near modern Marvdasht, Fars Province, Iran.

Phrada – Capital of Drangiana, it corresponds to present-day Farah, the capital and largest city of Farah Province in western Afghanistan, close to the border with Iran.

Prophthasia (a/k/a Alexandria Prophthasia) – Another garrison city founded by Alexandros, its precise location is unknown but it is believed to be at or near present-day

Farah. There are scholars who believe that some of the fortification remnants found at the citadel of Farah date back to Alexandros's time.

Pura – The old capital of Gedrosia, before Alexandros moved it to Rhambakia. It is located in the Sistan and Baluchestan Province, Iran.

Rhambakia (Rhambacia) – The new capital of Gedrosia, established by Alexandros during his crossing of the Gedrosian desert. Its exact location is unknown but is believed to be in Balochistan Province, Pakistan.

Salmous – Capital of Karmania. This city ceased to be inhabited in the third century B.C.E. It is currently an archaeological site called Tapeh Yahya, which is located 140 miles south of Kerman City, in Kerman Province, Iran.

Sousa (Susa) – One of the four capitals of the Persian Empire. Prior to its conquest, it had been the capital of Elam. It is mentioned under the name Shushan several times in the Hebrew Bible, especially in the Book of Esther. The site of the ancient city, located near the modern Iranian town of Shush, has been extensively excavated. Shush is located in the lower Zagros Mountains, not far from the northern tip of the Persian Gulf. Ancient Sousa was much closer to the Gulf than modern Shush; the coast has receded as a result of silting, changes in sea level, and land reclamation projects.

Susia – A crossroads city located in eastern Parthia. Today, the Iranian city of Tus sits on the site. It is situated approximately 50 miles from the Iran-Turkmenistan border.

Taxila – This city continues to exist to this day and is still called Taxila. It is located approximately 20 miles north-west of Islamabad and Rawalpindi in Pakistan. The vast archaeological sites at Taxila include remains dating from the 2nd millennium B.C.E. to the two centuries immediately following Alexandros's visit. Taxila was designated a UNESCO World Heritage Site in 1980.

Zadrakarta (Zadracarta) – Capital of Hyrkania, it is now known as Sari, which is the provincial capital of Mazandaran Province, Iran. It is located in the north of Iran, between the northern slopes of the Alborz Mountains and the southern coast of the Caspian Sea.

Chapter 1 – Whither Now?

"Hey, Ptolemaios, we've known each other for thirteen years and I still have no idea where're you're from."

"That's true," I agreed, "although you've asked me approximately eight hundred and fifty-seven times."

Kleitos shook his head. "Nah, it's gotta be closer to a thousand."

I laughed. "Didn't realize you were counting."

In the murky light of dawn, we were gingerly slip-sliding toward Alexandros's tent through the thick, sucking mud. It was the day after Alexandros, with the assistance of his troops, had burned down most of Persepolis. Neither Kleitos nor I had gotten much sleep during the night. As a result, our banter was even more lame than usual.

The fires, both the normal camp variety and the spectacular conflagration kind, had sputtered into oblivion under the relentless rain. Only the barest tendrils of lavender, creeping timidly above the ridges of the eastern mountains, illuminated our way.

Kleitos changed the subject. "What do you think he'll have to say for himself this morning?"

I shrugged. "Maybe he'll tell us where we're going next."

"Oh, that's a no-brainer. Even I can figure that much out. I'm just wondering what his ultimate goal is."

"Who knows?" Even though I'd lost my ability to know the future, I still possessed sufficient insight into our leader's psyche to make a fairly good guess about our next destination, as well as Alexandros's ultimate objective. However, I chose to keep my surmises to myself.

****

The road to immortality went through Ekbatana. After that, all bets were off. Oh, there were omens aplenty, even before we'd left Persepolis, if only we'd paid attention. But Alexandros had bigger swords to whet, we were all distracted by the recent inferno, and, in any event, there wasn't a soothsayer among us.

Immortal Alexandros

As we gathered at the entrance to the command tent, awaiting our leader's emergence, each of us had a different excuse for our lack of foresight. Parmenion, who would've normally spent his time worrying about Alexandros's next impulsive move, was instead basking in the company of his two surviving sons, Philotas and Nikanoros. Even though the three of them served in the same army, they were rarely able to spend much time together. Perdikkas, as dour as the weather, was too busy pondering his next intrigue to consider any troubles that might lie ahead. Then there was Hephaistion, who'd spent so much time brown-nosing Alexandros, his vision was effectively blocked by our leader's rippling nether cheeks. And I was too busy wrestling, for the umpteenth time, with the implications of the Prime Directive to consider what the Fates had in store for us.

As we shivered and stamped our feet, Kleitos attempted to pierce the miasma of a sodden day. "You boys look like a litter of drowned rats." Then, realizing that Parmenion was standing in our midst, he wiped the smile off his face. "Begging your pardon, sir. Didn't mean to imply you look like a drowned rat, sir."

For once, even the usually humorless Parmenion played along. "That's alright, Kleitos. At least this rain will wash all the rejectamenta from our camp."

"Reject a what?"

But Parmenion had already turned back to his boys and Kleitos gave up his efforts to cheer us up. "You guys should've stayed in your tents."

"Speaking of which, where is he?" This from Krateros, who'd managed to join our group unobserved. "Isn't he up yet?"

"He had a tough night," I said. "And besides, who wants to rush on a morning like this?"

"I do." Alexandros poked his head out. "Take every day by storm is my motto."

"In that case, sire, the gods have stolen a march on you today." Kleitos's wit was, as usual, even quicker than his sword.

For a split second, the air crackled with menace but, with a hearty laugh, Alexandros cut through the tension like sunshine dispersing fog. "The day is still young, my friend. Now let's get moving." He parted the flaps and joined us.

There was something about the king, as he emerged from his tent, that struck me as odd. I searched his face for some telltale sign of regret for the wanton destruction he had wreaked the day before or chagrin at his nocturnal misadventures but he seemed well-rested and relaxed. He was dressed in Persian garb, which we were still trying to get used to, but that wasn't it, either.

Immortal Alexandros

Ah, he's no longer a callow youth, I thought. *He's twenty-six by now and the presumptive emperor of Persia. That must be it.* Looking at my fellow commanders, I imagined similar questions coursing through their minds.

Alexandros set off at a brisk pace and we fell in around him, forming an honor guard. In case of need, we were quite capable of protecting his physical safety but, on this day, he was invulnerable. We proceeded in silence, each of us lost in our own thoughts.

I was busy gawking at our newly altered surroundings. A pall cast by smoldering ruins hung over the great platform upon which a succession of Persian emperors had erected their splendid royal palace. The soaring halls, adorned by colorful murals, finely woven Persian rugs and tapestries, priceless art and furniture, had all been destroyed by the implacable flames. Where marvelous marble statues had stood the day before only small heaps of melted quicklime remained. Decapitated columns, ashen floors, shattered tiles, and hard-baked cuneiform tablets were the sole, mute, accusing survivors of the formerly imposing imperial complex.

Since our capture of Persepolis, some four months earlier, Alexandros had been using the apadana, the great reception hall adjoining the royal palace, for his daily audiences. This morning, unfortunately, the apadana was gone, burnt to the ground by the caprice of an outraged Alexandros. As a result, we all headed for the mustering ground in the middle of our military camp, a small square of oozing mud, trampled weeds, and buzzing flies.

By the time we arrived, a temporary throne had been set up at the eastern edge of the square, balanced precariously atop two large tables. The skies were still threatening but the rain had stopped. People stood around in small clusters, marking time, awaiting the entrance of the putative new emperor of Persia.

Macedonian commanders, doing double duty as bodyguards, searched the Persian noblemen, courtiers, and eunuchs for concealed weapons. Our erstwhile enemies, risible in their resplendent robes amidst the squalor of a military encampment, were clotted in tight knots near the empty throne. Eddies of unctuous priests and oleaginous soothsayers swirled around the periphery, emitting whiffs of smoke, hard-to-identify odors, and unintelligible incantations. Among the surrounding tents, ordinary soldiers, going about their quotidian tasks, eyed the crowd curiously while staying well clear of the square.

All conversation and movement within the various groups ceased when the squishing sound of boots alerted them to our arrival. Alexandros was wearing one of Dareios's imperial robes, cut down to suit his smaller frame. Anyone else might have felt self-conscious but he exuded an air of easy confidence, as if he'd been sporting Persian attire all his life.

Immortal Alexandros

He clambered up the rickety structure to his throne, sure-footed as a mountain goat, smiling and waving to his friends. His entrance had its usual effect. The Macedonian commanders faced the throne, their attentive expressions glowing with eagerness. The Persian courtiers, after a barely perceptible moment of hesitation while they searched for a dry patch of ground, prostrated themselves as per protocol. The sight of those splendidly dressed men and almost-men, wallowing on their bellies in the mud, did detract a bit from the solemnity of the moment. Kleitos burst out laughing, as was his wont, but quickly controlled himself. Alexandros, too, fought to suppress the smile tugging at the corners of his mouth. The priests and soothsayers paid various degrees of obeisance, depending on the norms of their faiths, some bowing, others kneeling; some touching their foreheads to the mud, others sprawling in it. Only the magoi of Ahura Mazda remained rigidly erect. Even the common soldiers milling among the tents, although well out of earshot, ceased their movement. As if on cue, the threatening clouds parted and a shaft of sunlight illuminated the makeshift throne. *Professional courtesy*, I thought.

Alexandros raised his hand. "We're leaving for Ekbatana tomorrow." His order arrived, like a heart attack, without preamble, apology, or explanation. All of us, including Alexandros, knew it wasn't possible for the army to march out in less than a week. Even absent the chaos caused by the destruction of the palace complex, it would take days and days to carry out all the organizational, administrative, and logistical arrangements required to get an army of close to 50,000 men on the march in a day – assuming the men were willing to go.

Two days later, on the first day of June, 256 Z.E.[5], we were on the road to Ekbatana.

****

The contrast to Dareios's morning audience, taking place in the Ekbatana royal palace at that very moment, couldn't have been starker. For one thing, the incumbent emperor of Persia was sitting alone. Gone were the days when his audience halls – whether in Persepolis, Sousa, Babylon, or Ekbatana – were packed with supplicants, courtiers, and sycophants, days when he would make a grand entrance, accompanied by his bodyguard, and all the great and mighty assembled before him would fall on their bellies.

Dareios climbed down from the oversized throne, built just for him, and stood on the elevated platform,

---

[5] Zoroaster Era, calculated from the great prophet's purported date of birth. Ptolemaios, the narrator of this tale, was a time traveler from a future that used the Zoroastrian calendar. Writing for an audience in his native era, Ptolemaios naturally retained their method for keeping track of dates. Had he been composing his memoirs for our edification, he would've written 330 B.C.E. instead.

gazing at the empty hall. It was smaller than the Sousa and Persepolis audience halls, which had been built by Achaemenid emperors. This one had been designed and erected by Median kings before the great Persian emperor Kyros conquered Media. The columns were fashioned from huge tree trunks, cedar and cypress mostly, and then covered in silver and gold. The foil was beginning to peel. The walls were painted a garish red, which must have been vivid once but had lost its shimmer. The roof leaked in a few places. *I should've made some repairs,* Dareios thought, *while I had the chance.*

A few short months earlier, this historic hall; the adjoining palace; the harem, with its fragrant paradeisos and alluring inmates; the entire akropolis, with its temples of Zoroaster and Ahura Mazda, imperial mint and treasury, paved parade grounds, statuary, and imposing battlements; and the city beyond, with its countless temples, sacred precincts, municipal buildings, and entertainment venues; all that had been his. In fact, it still was – if he could keep it.

Skipping down the steps from the raised platform to the granite floor of the apadana with an easy grace that belied his fifty years, he strode between the columns as if inspecting his Immortals before an engagement. Of course, the Immortals were gone, killed in battle, or dead of disease, or simply lost to desertion. His current bodyguard was made up of Baktrian savages, with whom he could barely communicate and whose loyalty he seriously doubted.

How had it come to this? Dareios had started life as the bastard son of a royal chambermaid named Sisygambis. His name at birth was Artashata. The identity of his father was always subject to debate. According to his mother, the sperm donor was the grandson of the brother of the then-emperor of Persia, Artaxerxes Deuteros.[6] Artashata never quite believed the story. As a youngster, he once caught a glimpse of his alleged father. The strutting philanderer was short and ugly; Artashata was already tall and handsome. Fortunately for Artashata, nobody else believed his mother's story either. Members of the royal family, no matter how remote the connection, tended to die upon the accession of each new emperor but no one ever thought it necessary to dispose of Sisygambis's young bastard son.

By inclination and physique, Artashata was meant to be a soldier. He spent his youth practicing the martial arts. Finally, just before he turned eighteen, he caught the eye of a commander of the palace guard. Before long, he

---

[6] The relevant Persian emperors were: Artaxerxes Deuteros (reigned 404-358); Artaxerxes Tritos Ochos (r. 358-338); Artaxerxes Tetratos Arses (r. 338-336); Dareios Tritos Kodomannos (r. 336-330); Artaxerxes Pemptos Bessos (never actually reigned); and Alexandros Tritos of Macedonia (r. 330-323).

was leading his own platoon into combat. In action, he dazzled his fellow soldiers and impressed his commanders. More importantly, on the battlefield, he mesmerized the enemy.

He had become a battalion commander by the time the new emperor, Artaxerxes Tritos Ochos (who was supposedly Artashata's second cousin once removed), decided personally to lead a punitive expedition against the Kadousians. They were one of the most violent and mercurial tribes under the nominal control of the Persian Empire, allies of the emperor one moment, breaking into rebellion the next. The mountainous terrain of western Media, which was their ancestral home, helped them to shrug off imperial control at will. This time, Ochos intended to teach them a lesson they would long remember. Instead, the Kadousians schooled Ochos.

They lured his entire army into a deep valley guarded at both ends by serpentine defiles and then cut off all avenues of escape. That left Ochos with two unpalatable choices: He could try to fight his way out of the trap at the cost of horrendous casualties or he could sit back and await reinforcements, while the Kadousians, who held the high ground, picked off a few dozen of his men every night. Ochos chose to wait. Days passed, men perished, and no relief force ever came.

Eventually, watching his fellow soldiers die of injuries, disease, and starvation, Artashata decided to take matters into his own hands. He requested an audience with Ochos. When the emperor granted the request, Artashata made a bold proposal. He offered to fight, as the designated champion of the Persians, against the Kadousians' champion in single combat. If he won, the Kadousians would let the Persians go home. If he lost, the Persians would surrender to the Kadousians without a fight.

It's a measure of Ochos's desperation that he chose to give this proposal serious consideration. Eventually, he dispatched an emissary to the Kadousians' leader proposing a resolution of the conflict through the ancient expedient of single combat. The Kadousians, confident in the undefeated record of their champion, accepted the proposal.

On the appointed day, the twenty-six-year-old Artashata, magnificently arrayed in the emperor's own armor, faced off against a man even larger than he was, encumbered by nothing heavier than a thick felt tunic and a leather apron. Artashata carried a wicker shield and was armed with a curved Persian sword and a jewel-encrusted dagger. The Kadousians' champion had no shield and carried nothing but a long spear. Attached to his waist was an ominous knife whose only function was to cut off his opponent's head after victory. The edge of the knife was pitted, despite the champion's compulsive whetting, as a result of sawing through so many gullets, carotid arteries, sinews, and vertebrae.

Their field of combat was a fairly large meadow halfway between the valley floor and the ridgeline. The Kadousians, massed on the uphill side of the meadow, kept themselves busy sharpening their weapons and champing at the bit. The Persians, assembled in orderly, serried ranks below the meadow, watched the fight with the fascination of men eyeing the arrival of their executioner. Neither side thought Artashata had a chance.

The fight started at dawn. The Kadousian champion was able to run circles around his opponent, poking and probing with his long spear. Artashata, evidently the quicker and more agile of the two, patiently parried the thrusts with his shield but couldn't find a way to get close enough to inflict any injury with his sword.

They were still jousting when the sun reached high noon. The Kadousian was slowing down; the Persian continued to plod. And then, like a thunderbolt on a cloudless day, Artashata struck. Tossing aside his shield, he lunged at his surprised opponent, brushing the long spear aside with his sword and plunging his dagger into the exposed chest of the massive, stupefied warrior. The Kadousian was dead before he hit the ground.

Remarkably, the Kadousians accepted the defeat of their champion with good grace. They permitted the Persian army to depart unmolested. And Ochos wasted no time decamping, leaving most of their equipment behind. The only Persian enriched by the experience was Artashata, who acquired a new name – Kodomannos, meaning 'bellicose-minded.'

Once safely back in his nearest capital, which happened to be Ekbatana, the grateful emperor named young Kodomannos satrap of Greater Armenia. The young man formerly known as Artashata promptly took up his new duties in the somewhat remote satrapy and stayed there, except when summoned by Ochos to assist in military campaigns. The satrapy was extraordinarily well run. Internal rebellions and upheavals were forcefully suppressed; taxes fairly collected; amounts owed to the central government punctually transmitted. However, all those achievements didn't keep Kodomannos from also assembling, equipping, and training a substantial infantry force of native Armenian fighters, augmented by a few hundred Greek mercenaries.

Despite his remote location, Kodomannos was soon one of the most powerful satraps in the empire. However, he religiously refrained from flaunting his military resources. When called by the emperor, he showed up at the head of his battalions of native fighters, careful to bring only a fraction of his forces, and fought with distinction against whatever enemy was placed in front of him. When the campaign was over, he and his troops retired to his satrapy. He never caused any trouble and his loyalty was never in question.

On the personal front, he took only one wife, a well-born woman named Stateira, who was fifteen years his junior. She was also said to be the most beautiful woman in Asia, although perhaps that appellation wasn't applied until after he'd gained considerable power. In any event, quite unusually for Persian nobility, their marriage was a successful one and they remained loyal to each other for as long as they both lived, even after he eventually acquired a harem of dozens of younger and (contrary to the sycophants' claims) even more beautiful women. The marriage produced three children: A daughter named Stateira (known as Little Stateira while her mother was alive); a daughter named Drypetis; and a son named Ochos, in honor of the emperor.

After a twenty-one-year reign, Emperor Artaxerxes Tritos Ochos ran afoul of his castrated grand vizier Bagoas and died. The venomous eunuch, having grabbed a tiger by the tail, found it difficult to let go. Out of a sense of self-preservation, if for no other reason, he proceeded to poison every other member of the royal family, as well as anyone else with a colorable claim to the throne. The only survivors were Ochos's two youngest children. Realizing that he himself could never become emperor, Bagoas spared Ochos's son Arses, a callow, malleable youth, whom he installed as Emperor Artaxerxes Tetratos Arses. The youngest girl, named Parysatis, who was only two years old at the time, was hidden by a wet nurse in the harem and forgotten.

Unexpectedly, after two years on the throne, Arses started showing worrisome signs of independence. Bagoas promptly poisoned him as well. The only problem was that now there really was no one left with a legitimate claim to the throne. This caused a certain amount of chaos in the empire. Kodomannos, then aged forty-four, stepped forward to fill the vacuum. He was probably the strongest of the satraps, with a distinguished military record, a small army of his own, and a reputation for competence and probity. And, of course, there was the story of his connection, tenuous though it might have been, to the royal house. He became Emperor Dareios Tritos Kodomannos. His first act as emperor was to force Bagoas to imbibe a generous cocktail of his own fatal potions.

Dareios smiled at the recollection. *Those were heady days.* His reverie was interrupted by a noise at the back of the audience hall. He spun on his heels to confront the intruder. "Who's there?"

"It's me, your celestial majesty – Artabazos. Where is everybody?"

Dareios did his best to hide his embarrassment. He couldn't decide which was worse, being caught away from his throne, wandering the apadana like a naïve provincial, or presiding at an imperial audience with no one in attendance. "Of course, Artabazos. I know who you are. Come closer. The rest, I'm sure, are coming soon."

Artabazos caught himself, suddenly realizing he was in the apadana, approaching his emperor. He sank to the hard granite floor as quickly as he could without inflicting grievous injury to his kneecaps and touched his forehead to the ground. "A thousand pardons, your exalted highness."

"No, no, stand up!" Dareios had few friends left. He wasn't sure whether Artabazos was one of them but, as long as the elderly noble was willing to observe the traditional formalities, Dareios was happy to confer friendship upon him.

He helped Artabazos to his feet. "Come here, my friend!" Leaning down, he bestowed the high honor of kissing the older man on both cheeks. Artabazos, momentarily forgetting their current circumstances, beamed. He returned the compliment by kissing Dareios's hand.

"Walk with me," the emperor said, "since we're both early." The two men set off on the first of many circuits around the perimeter of the apadana. They were actually fairly close in age. Dareios was fifty and Artabazos fifty-seven but Dareios, despite his recent reverses, was in the prime of life, tall, powerful, and nimble, while Artabazos was an old man, prematurely stooped by a lifetime of struggle and frequent bouts of illness.

Their starts in life couldn't have been more different. Artabazos was the scion of one of the oldest noble families of Persia. Emperor Artaxerxes Deuteros was his grandfather. His father was satrap of Hellespontine Phrygia, a post young Artabazos inherited upon his father's death. In keeping with Persian custom, he had several wives and twenty-one children. (At least two of his daughters were being held in captivity by Alexandros at that very moment, as were all three of Dareios's children.) He managed to assemble the largest mercenary army of any satrap, commanded by two Rhodian brothers, Mentor and Memnon.

As long as his grandfather remained in power, Artabazos remained a loyal supporter of the emperor. However, when Artaxerxes Deuteros was succeeded by Artaxerxes Tritos Ochos, Artabazos disagreed with the choice of emperor, deeming himself better qualified for the post than his uncle.[7] He led a rebellion of satraps against the new emperor. Ochos defeated the rebels in battle and a thirty-one-year-old Artabazos had to flee for his life.

The safe haven he chose for himself, his large and growing family, and his entourage, was, of all places,

---

[7] Artabazos's mother was Artaxerxes Tritos Ochos's sister.

Macedonia. Even back then, King Philippos Deuteros of Macedonia was nurturing dreams of defeating the great Persian Empire one day. Therefore, he welcomed the exiles, both to tweak Ochos and to gain valuable intelligence about his realm. Philippos's son Alexandros was a baby when the exotic refugees arrived and close to twelve by the time they left.

Eventually, Artabazos's mercenary commander Mentor, who was part of the entourage, grew tired of exile and asked Artabazos for permission to return to Persia and throw himself on Ochos's mercy. This was a fairly risky gambit, since Persian emperors were known for long memories and a notable lack of clemency. Nevertheless, Artabazos acceded to his commander's request and Mentor made his way back to the Persian royal court. By coincidence, just then Emperor Ochos was licking his wounds after several military reverses. Uncharacteristically, but perhaps predictably, he discovered a wellspring of forgiveness bursting from his bosom. He pardoned Mentor and appointed him commander of one of his expeditionary armies. Mentor marched from victory to victory. In recognition of his services, Ochos named Mentor commander of all imperial mercenary forces. In addition, as a token of his gratitude, Ochos pardoned the entire Artabazos clan, allowed them to return to Persia, and reappointed Artabazos satrap of Hellespontine Phrygia. And Artabazos, whose great wealth included a surfeit of daughters, expressed his gratitude by giving one of them to Mentor as a future bride.

When Mentor died, a couple of years later, Ochos appointed Mentor's younger brother Memnon commander of the imperial mercenary corps. In addition to his military position, Memnon also inherited Mentor's wife. A little while later, Mentor was followed into the afterworld by Ochos himself, who in turn was followed by his son Arses, which brought us to Dareios Tritos Kodomannos. Memnon, however, remained commander of the imperial mercenary corps throughout all the turmoil. And Artabazos, having grown older in years and wiser in experience, decided to throw his support behind Dareios and served him loyally throughout the six-year period between Kodomannos's accession to the throne and their solitary walk around the Ekbatana royal audience hall.

After a long period of silent circumlocomotion, Artabazos finally worked up his courage. "Your highness, when exactly is this morning's audience supposed to start?"

"Oh, it was supposed to start some time ago but the invitations must have gotten lost in transit."

Artabazos managed to keep a straight face. He actually knew what the rest of the satraps and nobles were doing, having been invited to their conclave himself. He alone had declined to participate.

Dareios had a good idea as well but chose to suppress his suspicions. Instead, he stopped walking and turned to the old satrap. "Tell me, my friend, how did we come to this?"

Artabazos could've hazarded an educated guess but tactfully chose to keep it to himself. "I don't know, your highness. What do you think?"

Dareios resumed their stroll. "I know they blame me for our setbacks." There was no response. "I did everything in my power to defeat that insolent upstart from Macedonia. But there's something about him. He refuses to lose."

"I've met him, your highness."

Dareios arched an eyebrow. "Have you? When?"

"When I was in exile in Macedonia. Before you became emperor. But he was just an ordinary boy then. I venture to say, he's not much more than that now."

"Oh no, he's not a boy anymore. And he certainly isn't ordinary. I've looked into his eyes. Trust me when I tell you, he was more than human when he was slicing his way through my Immortals, trying to get to me."

Artabazos could contain his tongue no longer. "Is that why you chose to depart the field of battle at Gaugamela, your celestial majesty?"

Dareios took no offense. "I know what the men are saying. That I abandoned the troops in mid-fight and cost us the victory; that I'm a coward who ran away from a fight; that I should've stood my ground and died fighting, if it came to that."

"I didn't say that, your highness."

"But you were thinking it. And you, and the rest of your fellow satraps and nobles, are wrong on all three counts. I didn't cost us the victory at Gaugamela. I was there. I know. The battle was lost long before I signaled for retreat. And I'm no coward; I have the scars and military record to prove it. And it would've done us no good if I'd chosen to die on that battlefield. I'm the only man in this empire who can organize a resistance movement that will eventually win our country back for us. Which is exactly what I intend to tell my commanders if and when they finally choose to show up this morning."

As if on cue, the doors to the apadana burst open and a flood of men poured in, led by several high-ranking satraps and commanders. Many of them carried arms. In the past, if anyone had entered the audience hall with a weapon, the emperor's bodyguards would have killed him on the spot. And a few of the sentries guarding the entrance would've been executed for good measure as well, for allowing an armed intruder to get that far. Unfortunately for Dareios, there were no bodyguards, there were no sentries, and there was precious little decorum.

Dareios flew to his throne, reared himself to his full height atop the platform, and roared. "To the ground! You're in the presence of the emperor."

The rafters shook and a few of the intruders quaked but nobody sank to the floor. If Dareios's eyes could've hurled lightning bolts, several men would've gone up in flames. Alas, Dareios was no god and no one was incinerated. Whether he was still the emperor was not entirely clear.

Bessos, striding at the head of the mob, stopped just short of the first step to the platform, contempt dripping from his countenance. At twenty-nine, he was almost as young as Alexandros. He was uncouth, uneducated, violent, and ambitious. Unlike Dareios, he was impulsive and reckless. He was also the unquestioned leader of the most feared, most savage, most effective mounted warriors of the Central Asian steppes. He saw himself as the only man capable of saving the empire.

Standing defiantly erect, Bessos glared at his nominal commander-in-chief. "It's time to shit or get off the pot, Artashata. Either you start fighting back or we'll do it for you."

"I'm pursuing my strategy, you insolent bastard. Now get down on the floor!"

"Make me," Bessos sneered.

Dareios couldn't make him do anything and both of them knew it. They stared at each other for a long moment while everyone else in the apadana held his breath. This showdown had been coming for eight months, ever since the two men had made their separate escapes from the battle that had changed everything.

At Gaugamela, Dareios fielded the largest army ever assembled by the Persian Empire against a much smaller pan-Hellenic army led by Alexandros.[8] Almost without exception, every satrapy in the empire had contributed contingents to the Persian army. The tribute-paying but untamed, semi-autonomous satrapy of Baktria had sent 12,000 tough, fearless, and effective mounted warriors, known as the savage scrappers of the steppes, led by the satrap himself, Bessos.

The battle was fought on terrain chosen and prepared by Dareios. His intent was to use his cavalry, which was his strongest arm, to spearhead the assault on the numerically inferior and mostly infantry troops of the enemy. Bessos and his savages were tasked with outflanking, overwhelming, and annihilating the veteran

---

[8] For a more complete description of the Battle of Gaugamela, see the third volume of this series, **Conquest of Persia**, pp. 215-258. For an animated depiction of this battle, visit AlexanderGeiger.com.

Macedonian foot soldiers who comprised the right wing of Alexandros's battle line. The hardened phalanxes proved to be a tough nut to crack but Bessos's men went about their sanguinary work with their customary zeal.

Dareios, surrounded by his Immortals and by the best Greek mercenaries money could buy, stood atop his oversized chariot in the middle of the Persian line, observing the unfolding clash of arms and issuing orders as necessary. At the height of the battle, Alexandros, charging at the head of his elite Companion Cavalry, mounted a counterattack aimed directly at Dareios's post. As an incredulous, mesmerized Dareios watched, Alexandros and his horsemen sliced steadily through the proficient Greek mercenaries and the vaunted Persian Immortals. When Alexandros got close enough for Dareios to look directly into his eyes, the Persian emperor lost his nerve. He leapt from his chariot onto a nearby horse and departed the field of battle.

Seeing their leader fleeing had an understandably demoralizing effect on the Persian army. Although the battle continued to rage for some time after Dareios's departure, the pan-Hellenic army eventually carried the day, killing tens of thousands of soldiers in the process, from noble Persian knights to lowly conscripts of many subject nations. Those who could, escaped from the battlefield and headed to their homes in faraway satrapies.

A small group of bodyguards, led by Dareios, made it to the nearest imperial capital of Ekbatana. Bessos and his 12,000 Baktrian fighters, who'd lost very few men before following Dareios's lead and abandoning the field, arrived in the same city, in good order, the next day. (Ekbatana was on the way to Baktria.) More survivors of the battle continued to stream in for the next two weeks. Now, eight months later, they were all still in Ekbatana, waiting to find out what came next.

Immediately upon his arrival in Ekbatana, Dareios formulated a plan. He was going to assemble an even larger army, find even more favorable terrain, and this time defeat the insolent invaders. After all, Alexandros's logistical lines were becoming more and more stretched, his manpower resources were limited, and his veteran soldiers had to be getting homesick. So, Dareios continued to hold briefings at the palace, attended by surly satraps, contemptuous courtiers, and commanders whose insubordination grew by the day. He hectored them on the bright prospects of victory, if only they would supply additional troops from their provinces. He also sent countless letters to all the other satraps who remained under his nominal authority, requisitioning fresh troops. Precious few troops and no satraps beyond those already present ever showed up. As a result, Dareios was forced to devise a new plan.

Bessos, who was the only satrap in Ekbatana in command of an actual fighting force, seldom attended the briefings, despite being repeatedly summoned by Dareios. He had retired from the battlefield at Gaugamela in a state of rage, convinced that Dareios's cowardice had deprived his fighters, and all the other warriors on the Persian side, of certain victory. And he continued to nurse his grievance during the long months in Ekbatana like a falconer raising the perfect bird of prey from an eyas taken out of its nest before fledging.

Bessos finally broke the minatory silence. "Let's get a couple things straight. First, you are the only bastard here. My mother was married to my father when I was born. Second, I've got the only viable fighting force in Ekbatana. And third, we're out of time. Alexandros will be here before you know it."

Dareios grew beet red. "I'm still the emperor and I'm in charge here – "

"Could've fooled me," someone yelled from the back of the hall.

" – and it was the failure of your so-called fighting force to accomplish its limited mission at Gaugamela that cost us the victory. So, you can take your crap and shove it up your ass." A juicy shower of imperial spittle, arcing dangerously close to Bessos's face, added an exclamation point to Dareios's outburst.

Bessos stepped back, to get out of the line of fire, and opened his mouth for some telling riposte, but

Dareios beat him to the punch. "A good general always has a backup plan, in case something goes wrong. If you'd deigned to show up for my briefings, you would have realized that I've been preparing for this contingency ever since we arrived here in Ekbatana." This last part was a temporary detour into the realm of fiction because Dareios's current strategy was at least plan number three since his arrival in Ekbatana but one can't let minor details get in the way of a rhetorical outburst.

"You have a backup plan?" Bessos sounded genuinely shocked. "And here I thought you were simply trying to figure out which ceremonial robe to wear when you surrendered our empire to Alexandros."

Dareios ignored the interruption. "My primary objective has always been to kill this invader in a set piece battle. And I would've done it, too, but for the fecklessness of commanders like you. Still, I never lost sight of our greatest strategic asset."

"What's that, your ability to crawl on your belly?"

"No, our greatest strategic asset are the rugged mountains, desolate deserts, and untamed wilderness that make up our eastern satrapies, your savage homeland included. We're going to lure Alexandros and his army into this trap. Even without any help from us, this vast expanse of barely habitable land, filled with ferocious native tribes, would swallow any invading army whole, an army ten times the size of Alexandros's pathetic horde.

But we are going to help nature take its course. We will stoke rebellions and tribal resistance movements wherever we go; we'll convince the natives to destroy any food, fodder, or provisions that may be useful to the enemy; we'll stage night raids and ambushes when they least expect them; we'll destroy their lines of communication, their supplies, their will to fight. They'll be begging us to finish them off by the time we're done."

"And how exactly are we going to accomplish all that?"

"Just wait and see." And with that, Dareios seemingly lost interest in any further debate. "Now get out of my sight."

The assembled satraps, nobles, courtiers, and commanders reluctantly started backing out, buzzing among themselves. Dareios, as he was stepping off the platform, stopped them one more time. "And by the way, in case any of you are still wondering, as this addle-brained moron did," he pointed at Bessos, "the reason we had to linger here in Ekbatana was precisely to lure Alexandros to follow us. If you want your hounds to chase the fox, you can't give the fox too much of a head start. The trail must be fresh in their nostrils."

"Yeah, but the hounds usually get the fox," Bessos muttered to the satraps next to him, too quietly for Dareios to hear.

****

In the steaming heat and humidity of the Sousa harem, Barsine was in high dudgeon. "You're not the queen, you know."

Sisygambis's countenance glowed with anger, sweat, and contempt. "So, what's it to you?"

"You've got no business occupying the Queen's Suite."

"Why? You think you should have it?"

Barsine, who was forty-five years younger and a head taller, took another step forward, threatening to smother the dowager's face in her ample cleavage. "As a matter of fact, I do."

Sisygambis, trying to gain a little breathing space, rammed her head into Barsine's sternum. "Why should you have it? What are you?" She didn't wait for an answer. "You're a turd on the bottom of my sandals. You're just some savage's whore. *I* am the mother of the emperor."

Barsine, surprised by the physical turn their argument had taken and momentarily blinded by the reflected sunshine coruscating from the enormous bald spot that covered the crown of the older woman's head, started to laugh. "That's rich, my lady." She grabbed

Sisygambis by the shoulders and pushed her away. She almost felt sorry for the old crone. "You were never anything but a chambermaid who got accidently impregnated by some man who didn't even know your name. The fact that the issue of that unintended pregnancy became emperor of Persia makes no difference any more. He's nothing now, having had his ass whipped by that man you call a savage. Whipped not once but three times."

Sisygambis began to cry. Barsine let go of her shoulders and started patting her on the back, as if dealing with a child. "That man you call a savage has been incredibly kind to you and your grandchildren. You know, and I know, that it's your son who's been the real savage and who is nothing but a pathetic loser now. So, keep the Queen's Suite. You won't be able to enjoy it much longer."

Thus, for the umpteenth time, the two leaders of the opposing factions in the harem parted company, having failed to resolve their differences. Sisygambis returned to the Queen's Suite and Barsine retired to her nearly-as-sumptuous first concubine's apartment.

Although neither woman would've ever admitted it, even to herself, the truth was that they had much in common. For a start, they were both inmates of the hellish paradise that was the Sousa harem.

Physically, the harem adjoined the imperial palace. Psychologically, it could just as well have been on another planet. The harem's tall, thick walls shut out the hubbub, bustle, and sheer vitality of the outside world. Enclosed within was a complex of buildings, including large, airy common rooms, luxurious apartments for the most important residents, and fairly utilitarian accommodations for everybody else. These buildings were set in a lush, languid landscape of flowering meadows, exotic trees, aromatic bushes, murmuring brooks, cooling ponds, and soft, carefully tended walking paths. Each imperial harem had its own paradeisos but the one in Sousa, thanks to the local climate, surpassed them all in prodigal profusion. It had an aura of eternal peace or perhaps, depending on one's point of view, terminal ennui. It was also incredibly hot and humid in the summer months.

For more than two centuries, Persian emperors had progressed from one capital to the next, as dictated by the seasons. Babylon was most enjoyable in autumn, when temperatures were moderate and there was some cloud cover. Sousa was glorious in wintertime, pleasantly warm and relatively dry. Spring was the ideal season to visit Persepolis. Situated on the Persian plateau, its mile-high altitude provided the perfect antidote to the rising temperatures of the Mesopotamian plain, while the surrounding mountains wrung out the rain clouds and provided shelter from the worst of the winds. And finally, summer was a good time to visit Ekbatana, located even higher up in the mountains than Persepolis. It goes without saying that when the emperor moved his court to the next capital on the itinerary, the inhabitants of the harem accompanied the wagon train, along with an army of courtiers, viziers, magoi, eunuchs, servants, slaves, soldiers, porters, and a couple of thousand other hangers-on.

The emperors didn't visit every capital every year and sometimes external events, such as wars, interfered with the normal schedule. However, no sensible person who had a choice in the matter wanted to be caught in Babylon or Sousa at the height of the summer or in Persepolis or Ekbatana in the middle of winter. Of course, when Alexandros and his army invaded the Persian Empire, four years earlier, all routines went out the window.

At first, Dareios hadn't taken Alexandros seriously. He sent an army to take care of him but didn't think it necessary to lead the army in person, putting a committee of satraps in charge instead. The satraps failed in their assignment; their forces were thoroughly defeated near the Propontis coast, on the banks of the Granikos River.[9]

---

[9] For a description of the Battle of Granikos, see the first volume of this series, **Prime Directive**, pp. 401-416. For related maps and an animated depiction of the battle, visit AlexanderGeiger.com.

At that point, Dareios decided he'd better take charge of repelling the invaders personally. He set out from Babylon, with his usual massive train, but this time, instead of heading toward Sousa, they traveled to a dusty little town in Lowland Assyria called Damaskos, which was near the place where he thought the next, and final, battle against Alexandros would be fought. Naturally, Dareios didn't wish to be deprived of his customary court services during this extended expedition; therefore, he brought the harem with him, as part of his baggage train. Which is how, instead of strolling the soft paths of one of the imperial paradeisoi, the ladies of the harem found themselves housed in tents, enclosed within the walls of an old fort on the outskirts of Damaskos.

Eventually, the two armies found each other on the Mediterranean coast, some three hundred miles north of Damaskos, and prepared for a pitched contest. So confident was Dareios of victory that, when he traveled from Damaskos to join his army, already in the field, he took his mother, wife, children, and a few other women of the harem with him in order to afford them the opportunity to witness his triumph.

The two armies met on the shores of the Gulf of Issos. Things didn't go as expected, the Persian army was defeated, and Dareios barely escaped with his life. All the ladies he had brought along to observe the battle were captured by Alexandros's soldiers. In due course, the rest of the harem, left behind in Damaskos, was captured as well.[10]

There was yet another defeat in store for Dareios near a small village called Gaugamela, which is how Dareios found himself in Ekbatana, having lost his legitimacy and the best part of his empire. All those ladies of the harem, plus a few other high-ranking women captured along the way, had remained in Alexandros's custody ever since. They'd traveled as part of the baggage train with Alexandros's army for more than two years until being finally left behind in Sousa while Alexandros resumed his pursuit of Dareios.

Now, almost three years after the Battle of Issos and eight months since Gaugamela, Dareios and Alexandros were too preoccupied with the final stages of their epochal struggle to give the captives a second thought. As the sidereal calendar slowly turned toward the summer solstice and as temperatures soared, the ladies of the harem remained sequestered amidst the stifling splendors of the Sousa paradeisos, hoping for a change of scenery or, at the very least, something new to talk about.

---

[10] For a description of the Battle of Issos, see the second volume of this series, **Flood Tide**, pp. 322-360. For related maps and an animated depiction of the battle, visit AlexanderGeiger.com.

One morning, as the inmates' communal breakfast was winding down, Dilshad, the principal eunuch, entered the dining hall. This was an unusual occurrence, signaling that something was afoot. A sudden silence replaced the usual din of dozens of women talking at once.

After months of isolation, the ladies craved any morsel of news like dungeoned convicts yearning for a ray of sunshine. As a matter of protocol, the eunuchs, who were simultaneously their prison guards and their only contact with the outside world, were instructed to remain tightlipped. But this time Dilshad evidently had something to say.

"Ladies," he announced, "may I have your attention, please. We're expecting a new arrival from Persepolis later today. Please make yourselves presentable." And with that, he stepped off the raised dais and disappeared, leaving the hall in an uproar.

Eager speculation among the inmates as to the identity of the visitor displaced, at least for a few hours, the endemic, internecine strife that was the usual way of life in the harem. The women lived in splendid luxury, lacking only freedom and anything meaningful to do. As a result, they devoted their energies to gossip, backbiting, prurience, and pecking-order tilts.

"Who do you think is coming?" Artakama asked her older sister.

Barsine shrugged. "It's not Alexandros and it's not Dareios, I can promise you that."

"But no other man would be allowed to enter."

"Oh, don't be so naïve. The world is changing."

Before Dareios had suffered his military reverses at Granikos, Issos, and Gaugamela, he was the only intact adult male permitted to visit the harem. The female denizens included his mother, his wife, his concubines, young girls being groomed to become his concubines, superannuated dowagers who had once been concubines of previous emperors, an occasional high-ranking female hostage, and female servants and slaves of all these people. In addition, there were a few children of both sexes and, of course, the eunuchs who were theoretically sexless.

Housing was assigned strictly by rank. In Dareios's time, his wife Stateira and their three children occupied the most spectacular suite of rooms, decorated with colorful glazed tiles and intricate mosaics, known as the Queen's Suite. Also occupying the same set of lavish chambers was Stateira's mother-in-law, Sisygambis, whose sole purpose in life was to do what she could to turn Stateira's privileged existence into hell on Earth. In fairness, Stateira was more than able to reciprocate.

After his family, along with the rest of the harem, were captured by Alexandros's soldiers, Dareios sent several letters to Alexandros offering huge sums of money in order to ransom his family. Alexandros, who had greater objectives in mind than the mere accumulation of wealth, refused to entertain these offers.

As it turned out, Stateira succumbed to illness shortly before the battle of Gaugamela, despite extraordinary efforts by Alexandros to maintain Dareios's family in the lifestyle to which they had become accustomed. Even after Stateira's death, however, the Queen's Suite continued to be occupied by Sisygambis and her three grandchildren, Little Stateira, Drypetis, and Ochos.

This arrangement caused ongoing friction among the inmates. In addition to the usual cliques and cat fights that were a way of life in any harem, there was an unbridgeable chasm of resentment between the women who had been part of the harem all along and the small but assertive group of newcomers. These new ladies were the mistresses of some of Alexandros's leading commanders.

When Alexandros set out from Sousa, in the middle of the previous winter, to conquer Persepolis and get himself crowned emperor of Persia, he decreed that all women accompanying his army, even the mistresses of high-ranking officers, had to stay behind in Sousa lest they slow the progress of the campaign. For their comfort and safety, these privileged ladies were installed in the harem, alongside Dareios's ladies. In theory, their stay in the Sousa harem would be short and pleasant. In fact, it turned out to be neither.

The two groups mixed as well as oil and vinegar. The invaders' paramours viewed themselves as free women, enjoying a luxurious vacation from the sexual demands of their men. They looked down on the original inhabitants of Dareios's harem as slaves, captives, and hostages. The Persian ladies, led by Sisygambis, looked down on everyone else from force of habit. They might have been some man's property all their lives but their man was more important than the men who owned the other women. And in the case of the newcomers, the men who owned them were uncivilized savages to boot.

Barsine found herself the leader of the newcomers, even though she herself was a longtime denizen of the harem. By ethnicity, parentage, and upbringing, she had a foot in each camp. At one time, by dint of marriage and family, she had thought of herself as mostly Persian. More recently, because her own fate, and the fate of her youngest son, had become inextricably tied to Alexandros's success, she had rediscovered her Greek roots.

In her twenty-five short years, she had already experienced enough peaks and valleys to rival the formidable mountain ranges of the Persian Plateau. She entered life at the pinnacle of fortune. Thanks to her father Artabazos, she carried the genes of Persian nobility. Her father was the satrap of Hellespontine Phrygia, as had been her grandfather. Her great grandfather had been Emperor Artaxerxes Deuteros. On her mother's side, she was a Greek patrician, the granddaughter of the leading oligarch of the Island of Rhodos. More importantly, she inherited from her mother intelligence, grit, and beguiling good looks. If she had been a boy, she would have been a candidate to become emperor of Persia one day. Since she was a girl, she could expect to become the bride of some rich and powerful potentate. In the meantime, she lived in the lap of luxury in Artabazos's harem.

Her good luck didn't last. When she was three, her father lost out in a dynastic struggle and the entire family had to flee. She grew up as an exile living in backward, provincial, barbaric Macedonia. By the time the family returned to Persia, Barsine was twelve years old. She had received a good education, could read and write in two languages, Greek and Persian, and was fluent in three more. She was also pledged in marriage, by her father and without her consent, to a Greek mercenary commander. The fact that her intended was forty-one and happened to be the brother of Barsine's mother and thus Barsine's uncle was not deemed an obstacle.

Mentor was too busy fighting wars to consummate the marriage but his younger brother Memnon, who was "only" thirty-six at the time, took a fraternal interest in his young sister-in-law. When Barsine was fourteen, Memnon consummated the marriage on behalf of his older brother. As usual, no one had bothered to solicit the young girl's views concerning these matters.

Barsine soon became pregnant, creating a possibly sticky situation for the two brothers. Fortunately, Mentor conveniently died of what could have been natural causes before he found out about the pregnancy. At that point, custom, decency, and lust all dictated that Memnon marry Barsine, which he promptly did. Contrary to most people's expectations, though, the marriage proved to be a happy one, perhaps because Memnon was too busy with his military duties to spend much time at home. He did make good use of what little time he had with Barsine. She had her first child at age fifteen. By the time she was twenty-one, she was the mother of three girls and one boy.

When Dareios became emperor, he kept Memnon on as the commander of the mercenary corps. However, to guarantee Memnon's faithful performance of his military duties, Dareios graciously offered to house Barsine and their children in his harem. It was not an offer subject to negotiation.

Shortly before the Battle of Issos, while the harem was housed in their temporary quarters in Damaskos, Dareios came to see Barsine personally to inform her that her husband had died of some unexplained illness. He didn't offer to release her from the harem, though. When Barsine asked what would happen to her and the children, Dareios assured her that she was the most beautiful woman in the harem and he would see to it that a place would be found for her.

Then, when Dareios arranged to have the special women in his life transported to the battlefield on the eve of the clash in order to observe his inevitable triumph, Barsine was surprised to see herself included in this select group. After Dareios ignominiously fled the field and all the women were captured, Barsine became one of the spoils of victory. Alexandros generously distributed his share of the loot among his troops, keeping only one item as his personal booty: The alluring captive woman whose name he didn't know.

Of course, Barsine knew exactly who Alexandros was. When he came to visit her, she made full use of her charms, of her fluency in the Macedonian dialect, and of their previous acquaintance as children. (The only thing she neglected to mention was the existence of her four children.) By the end of that first visit, he was smitten. The two remained inseparable – except when military necessity called – for the next two years. When Barsine became pregnant, Alexandros's advisors urged him to marry her to legitimize the child, which, according to the omens, was likely to be a boy. Alexandros, despite his infatuation, declined to make her more than his mistress.

Immortal Alexandros

By the time the child was born – and it was indeed a boy – Alexandros was following up his victory at Gaugamela by accepting the surrender of Babylon. When they were reunited in that notoriously dissolute city, Barsine showed off their three-week-old baby. After their extended separation, Alexandros was more interested in Barsine than the child but, in due course, he succumbed to the irresistible attraction babies exert on their parents. He chose the name Herakles for his firstborn son, in honor of the mythical founder of the Macedonian royal line. No one could predict the little boy's future but, if Barsine had any say in the matter, she was determined to make sure that her youngest child would grow up to be king of Macedonia and emperor of Persia.

In the meantime, however, she was stuck in the Sousa harem, trying to assert her right to occupy the Queen's Suite, if only because she was the mother of the next emperor. Sisygambis, of course, saw it differently. She considered herself the mother of the current emperor. Each of them was busy lobbying for her cause when the great gates creaked open and an unusual procession made its way in.

Eight robust young men, naked to the waist, marched in, carrying an ornate palanquin on their shoulders. Several of the younger women shrieked, whether in delight or consternation at the sight of so much masculine flesh, it was hard to tell. And, of course, the main attraction, the person riding in the litter, remained concealed behind the curtains.

Several guardian eunuchs came running, not sure whether they should draw their daggers or prostrate themselves. Some attempted to do both simultaneously, falling to the ground with their daggers clattering to the pavement in front of them.

Dilshad, who had received advance notice of the identity of the visitor, strolled up to the unusual conveyance and motioned to the porters to put it down. However, before they could carry out his order, a heavy wagon, laden with furniture, trunks, and chests trundled in and the porters had to keep moving to make room for the wagon. And then a second wagon, carrying dozens of amphorae, clattered through the gate. There were six wagons in all. When the last one made it inside the wall and the great gates were once again shut, the entire train came to a halt and the porters finally placed the palanquin on the ground.

By now, every single denizen of the harem had come out to witness the spectacle. Some oldtimers, deprived of any news of the outside world and lacking any appreciation of the military realities on the ground, expected Dareios to step out. The newcomers, letting hope race ahead of reason, were convinced that one of the Macedonian commanders, or perhaps Alexandros himself, would emerge. Only Sisygambis remained focused on the breach of protocol represented by the entrance of so many half-naked men within the sacred precincts of the harem. "Get these men out of here right now!" she barked. In the swirl of excitement and speculation, no one paid her the slightest attention.

Dilshad, having caught up to the palanquin once again, got down to one knee in order to help pull the curtain aside. "Welcome to the Sousa harem, madam."

The surrounding clamor came to an abrupt halt as a tall woman dressed in a flowing white chiton emerged through the vehicle's opening. "Who are you?" someone called out.

The woman ignored the crowd's curiosity. "See to it that my possessions are properly installed in the Queen's Suite," she said to Dilshad.

By virtue of repeated practice, the old eunuch started to nod, then caught himself. "But madam, the Queen's Suite is currently occupied."

"Well, have their possessions moved out. And tell my men to be careful. I don't want any of my stuff broken."

"Madam, I have a perfectly nice suite prepared for you. You wouldn't know what to do with the Queen's Suite anyway. It's too big for one person."

"Listen my man … er, my … what's your name?"

"Dilshad, Madam."

"Listen, Dilshad. I want the Queen's Suite. And, as you can see, I have more than enough possessions to fill it. Now, find a nice young eunuch to take me to the bathhouse. And, by the time I get out, I want everything ready for me – in the Queen's Suite."

"Madam, the mother of the emperor has the Queen's Suite."

Thais arched an eyebrow. "Alexandros's mother is here?"

"No, no," Dilshad quickly corrected himself. "The mother of the former emperor."

"Do you know the difference between a former emperor and a dead man?"

The old eunuch shrugged.

"A very brief interval of time." Thais laughed. "Now, let's stop this chitchat. It's been a long trip. I need a bath and I need to use the facilities. And if Dareios's mother says anything, tell her she's lucky to be alive. If need be, we can arrange to have her moved directly into a coffin."

Immortal Alexandros

By the time Thais emerged from her bath, her pink skin glowing through her sheer chiton, all her possessions were ready and waiting in the Queen's Suite.

****

Alexandros was in a buoyant mood. The march from Persepolis toward Ekbatana couldn't have gone any better. Even the veterans forgot their discontent. The royal road was broad and smooth, the early summer weather in the highlands of Persia glorious, and nary an enemy in sight. Without much effort, we were still making an easy fifteen miles a day. And we all believed that, once we reached Ekbatana, our long journey would be at an end.

We would besiege the fourth, and last, of the Persian capitals, sack it, if necessary, kill or capture the defenders, including their leader Dareios, and thus complete our conquest of the Persian Empire. For those of us who had crossed the Hellespont with Alexandros, some four years earlier, it was an unimaginable achievement: A ragtag army, composed of fighters from places no one had ever heard of, defeating the greatest military power in history, whose hegemony over most of the known world had stood unchallenged for more than two hundred years.

Alexandros, having started the expedition with the modest, and rather farfetched, goal of liberating the Greek-speaking cities of Ionia, would become the unchallenged ruler of Persia and all its possessions, acknowledged as the new emperor even by the stiff-necked magoi. He could travel the circuit of Persian capitals, as other Persian emperors had done before him, perhaps adding an occasional visit to his ancestral capital of Pella in Macedonia or a swing through Egypt to soak up the sun and the adoration of his subjects. His power, wealth, and everlasting fame would be assured.

Any lingering doubts as to the triumphant conclusion of his campaign were dispelled by the arrival of reinforcements. Although we'd thought we were marching at a fairly good clip, two weeks out of Persepolis a force of 5,000 foot and 1,000 horse soldiers overtook us. They'd been sent from Macedonia but recruited all over Greece and led by a Greek mercenary commander. They had barely missed catching up to us in Persepolis, having been on the march from Macedonia for months. They were young, fresh, and eager to get in on the loot before the fighting ended for good. And we were glad to have them, although they did present a nomenclatural challenge.

The Macedonian long-timers, who'd been with Alexandros for years, zealously guarded their 'veteran' appellation. The men joining us now were 'newbies,' 'mercenaries,' or, if they were not Greek, 'barbarians.' Even years later, and after many additional waves of reinforcements, the best these newbies could hope to achieve was the oxymoronic title of 'old newbies.'

As soon as our rearguard reported the arrival of the reinforcements, Alexandros halted the march and declared a two-day rest stop to give the troops a chance to get acquainted, to realign the organizational and command structure of his newly enlarged army, and – most important – to give everyone time to read (or have read to them) the mail brought by the newcomers from home.

That evening, Alexandros called me to his tent. "Here, Ptolemaios, let's see how smart you are."

This was part of our usual repartee. Over the years he'd developed trust, even respect, for my acumen, which he demonstrated by needling me about my alleged intellectual shortcomings. I was expected to repay him in kind, especially if he was in a good mood. And provided I didn't push it too far. He took it for granted that he excelled us all in mental and physical gifts and attainments; he wouldn't have appreciated any demonstration to the contrary. But he was a good sport about it.

I walked up to the table where he was reading some scrolls. "What have you got, sire?"

"What I got, my friend, is a bunch of letters from my mother. Your challenge, should you decide to accept it, is to tell which of them were forged by Antipatros and which are genuine. We can even wager a gold daric on it."

"And who's going to decide whether my determinations are right or wrong?"

"I am, of course. Don't you think I can tell a genuine letter from my mother from a forgery?"

"Well, yes, I think you can. But then, so can I. You've let me read enough of her letters over the years to let me become an expert on her handwriting and her modes of expression."

"Ah-ha! That's where we're going to make this a sporting proposition. I've read them and I can tell you three are legitimate and three are forgeries. As you say, it's easy to pick out Antipatros's and Kassandros's handiwork. They're laughably inept in their deceptions. But I'll make it a little tougher on you. You can only look at the letters upside down, so you can't actually read them. If you pick out the three forgeries, I'll give you a daric. If you get it wrong, you'll owe one to me. What do you say, is it a bet?"

I nodded, suppressing a smile. What Alexandros didn't know was that I could read upside down with almost the same facility as right-side up. "You've got yourself a bet, Aniketos[11]."

---

[11] "Aniketos" was Alexandros's nickname. It meant "invincible."

Immortal Alexandros

I read the six letters, upside down, quickly but thoroughly. The differences between the forgeries and the real articles were almost comical. Perhaps, if the letters had arrived singly, with big time gaps in between, the contrast wouldn't have been so obvious.

Each of the letters began more or less the same, telling Alexandros that his mother, sister, niece, and nephew were healthy and doing well. Since this pro forma first paragraph never changed, the forgers managed to reproduce it perfectly every time.

The next few paragraphs usually contained a concise summary of the geopolitical situation in Greece. There was an interesting divergence in these paragraphs. The events recounted tended to be the same but the ultimate conclusions drawn by the writer were like night and day. The genuine Olympias sought to put Alexandros's mind at ease that things in Macedonia and on the Greek mainland were well in hand and urged him to take all the time he needed to fulfill his destiny in Asia. The fake Olympias, by contrast, fretted about the constant mortal threats facing Macedonia, bewailed the burden imposed on the country by Alexandros's ongoing campaigns in faraway lands, and predicted imminent doom unless he and his army returned home immediately.

The closing paragraphs provided an amusing contrast. Olympias invariably complained that Antipatros and his snotty son were arrogant, insolent, and disloyal but reassured Alexandros that they were too incompetent to pose any threat. The forgers, on the other hand, praised Antipatros and Kassandros to the sky but urged Alexandros to return home as soon as possible because his mother missed him terribly.

As soon as I had finished reading, I sorted the scrolls into two neat piles and pointed to the one on the left. "These are the forgeries."

"That's amazing! How d'ya do that?"

I smiled modestly. "A soothsayer never reveals his tricks."

At that point, Hephaistion, who had been observing the proceedings from the corner of the tent, piped up. "Soothsayers don't have tricks; they have a gift."

Alexandros waved away the objection. "Never mind that. Just give the man his gold daric."

"Aye, aye, sire. I'll send it over as soon as I get my hands on one."

I guess that means never. Hephaistion would rather make love to a duck than part with an obol.

As if reading my thoughts, Alexandros interrupted. "Don't worry, Ptolemaios. You'll get your daric. But I have one more letter I want to show you. And this time, you can read it right side up."

He handed me the scroll. It was from Antipatros, Alexandros's regent in Macedonia. When Alexandros crossed into Asia, he had left Antipatros behind to administer the ancestral kingdom, to suppress any revolts among the restless barbarians in our rear, to maintain Macedonian hegemony over the city-states of the Greek mainland, and to keep a steady stream of reinforcements flowing our way. He was also supposed to keep Alexandros's imperious mother Olympias, who had remained in Pella, happy and contented. It was an impossible assignment.

If anyone could pull it off, though, it was Antipatros. He was sixty-eight years old, head of an ancient noble family, and loyal servant of five Macedonian kings. When Alexandros's father was assassinated and the army assembled to elect, or at least ratify the ascension of, his successor, Antipatros was the first to call out, "Long live King Alexandros of Macedonia!" He was first to jump off his charger, approach the mounted Alexandros, pay homage, and pledge his personal allegiance and loyalty. A long procession of commanders followed his example. The army confirmed Alexandros as the new king by acclamation.

On the day of Philippos's assassination, Parmenion was already in Asia, having been sent there by Alexandros's father three months earlier to prepare the ground for the main-force invasion. As a result, Antipatros became, at age sixty-two, the unquestioned second-in-command in Macedonia.

When Alexandros finally launched the invasion envisioned by his father two years later, he left Antipatros behind as regent. He did take with him Antipatros's two youngest sons, named Iolaos and Philippos, to serve as pages. (Antipatros had a total of six sons and four daughters.) Pages were young sons of Macedonian nobility who accompanied the army in order to learn the military trade from seasoned veterans, to be groomed as future commanders, to act as squires to the king and his senior staff, and, incidentally, to serve as convenient hostages for the good behavior of their fathers back home in Macedonia. Their brother Kassandros, who was only slightly older than Alexandros and had been his classmate when they both attended the royal preparatory school in Mieza, was left behind because of ill health. He eventually recovered well enough to become his father's ruthless right-hand man.

"Well, are you going to read it or are you just going to stand there?"

I returned my gaze to the scroll in my hands. It was a bracing read. Seemingly, all of Macedonia's historical enemies took the protracted absence of the king as a signal to attack. The most serious threat was an uprising of Peloponnesian city-states, led by Sparta and funded by Persian money sent by Dareios before Gaugamela. In addition, the untamed, belligerent tribes of barbarians on Macedonia's eastern and northern frontiers sensed an opportunity for mischief. Finally, menacing hordes of fierce, mounted, nomadic warriors, known collectively as the Skythians, appeared on the faraway steppes to the north of the Black Sea, endangering Macedonia's trading interests in that part of the world.

Theoretically, almost all the Greek city-states, with the notable exception of Sparta, were members of the Hellenic League and treaty-bound to support Macedonia. To keep these nominal allies in line, Antipatros had stationed a garrison of 10,000 men in Megalopolis, the largest city in the Peloponnese, to serve as a counterweight to Sparta. When King Agis of Sparta laid siege to Megalopolis with a force of 30,000 men, comprised of elite Spartan warriors, soldiers sent by other rebellious cities in the Peloponnese, and mercenaries recruited with Persian money, the Macedonian commander of the Megalopolis garrison, named Korrhagos, sent an urgent message to Antipatros seeking reinforcements. At the same time, another of Antipatros's generals, by the name of Zopyrion, who had been dispatched with a force of 30,000 men to deal with the various barbarian tribes, also ran into trouble and was desperately pleading for help. Antipatros scraped together a force of 20,000 men and set off to relieve Korrhagos, leaving his son Kassandros with but a token force in charge of Macedonia. Regretfully, he informed Zopyrion to expect no further help from the fatherland; there were no additional troops to be had.

While marching to the Peloponnese, Antipatros put out a call to the nominal allies of the Hellenic League, asking for reinforcements. By the time this relief force reached Megalopolis, they numbered 40,000 men. Unfortunately, they arrived a couple of days too late. Korrhagos, whose men were out of food and out of hope, decided it was better to die fighting than to starve to death. He and his emaciated men rushed out of their fortified stronghold and attacked the besiegers. They were slaughtered to a man. A neat circle of enemy dead marked the place of Korrhagos's last stand.

Agis's army was still in place, maintaining its siege of Megalopolis and holding the high ground, when the pan-Hellenic army arrived. Without hesitation, Antipatros ordered an all-out attack the morning after their arrival. The outcome hung in the balance during an entire day of vicious fighting. Eventually, Antipatros's men managed to kill Agis and force the remnants of his army to withdraw from the battlefield. The Spartans, who could ill afford it, lost more than 5,000 warriors in the battle. The pan-Hellenic army lost 3,500 men as well, including 1,000 Macedonians. However, Antipatros's hard-fought and costly victory effectively saved Macedonian hegemony over mainland Greece.

Zopyrion, left to his own devices, didn't fare nearly as well. Having taken his army all the way to the north coast of the Black Sea, he finally encountered the fearsome Skythians. The bellicose nomads, who learned to ride their large and fast horses before they learned to walk, materialized seemingly out of nowhere, launched their cloudbursts of arrows before the Macedonians could even grab their shields or mount their horses, inflicted heavy casualties, and vanished into the boundless grasslands of Central Eurasia. Eventually, Zopyrion concluded that his army had no chance of defeating these fierce and mobile warriors, especially without additional men and resources, and ordered a retreat back to Macedonia.

It proved to be a death march. The Skythians, having tasted blood, attacked the retreating column night after night, killing men and destroying supplies. The Macedonians, marching through uncharted lands, lost their way, ran out of food, contracted diseases, drowned in hidden bogs and marshes, and were picked off by silent assassins belonging to various insect, animal, and human species. When they finally reached Thrake, the remnants of the Macedonian army were ambushed by a coalition of hostile Thrakian tribes. Not a single man returned from Zopyrion's ill-fated expedition.

The letter struck me as painfully honest. Antipatros didn't try to sugarcoat the setbacks. On the other hand, he also took full credit for the signal victory over Sparta, which was arguably as important to the survival of Macedonia as Alexandros's victories against the Persian Empire. He concluded by observing that the resources of Macedonia were stretched to the breaking point and urged Alexandros to bring back his troops at the earliest opportunity.

Seeing I had finished reading, Alexandros reached for the scroll. "So, what do you think?"

I tried to put the best face on it. "Wasn't that a great victory Antipatros achieved against Agis and Sparta? If the Spartans had won, all of Greece would have risen against Macedonia and you would have been obliged to return home just to salvage your country."

The corners of Alexandros's lips descended into a smirk. "You call that a victory? When I defeated the Persians, not once but three times, I was fighting against men; Antipatros fought against mice."

I remained silent, sensing there was more vitriol to come.

"If he had sent reinforcements to Zopyrion, he wouldn't have lost us 30,000 men. For that matter, if he weren't so stingy and tardy in sending reinforcements to me, we'd be done here in Persia already. And now he tells me, before I even ask, that he intends to ignore my future orders for reinforcements. Unbelievable. Let me tell you something, Metoikos[12]. All Antipatros wants is to hoard our resources so he can establish himself as the actual king, rather than my regent."

I couldn't hold my tongue any longer. "If he really wanted to usurp your throne, Aniketos, why would he urge you to return home with all your troops as soon as possible?"

Hephaistion spoke up from his corner again. "That's all part of Antipatros's master plan. He's hoping that through enemy attacks and attrition, by the time we returned to Macedonia we would have so little fighting power left, he could mop us up with all the troops he's withholding from us."

Alexandros shook his head. "We're not going back until all of Persia acknowledges me as emperor and submits to my authority. Speaking of which, Antipatros forgets that he serves as regent at my pleasure. If I recall him tomorrow, there won't be a single Macedonian soldier willing to follow his orders. They all know I'm

---

[12] "Metoikos" was Ptolemaios's nickname. It meant "traveler, alien, stranger, outsider."

their king and they're all willing to lay down their lives for me."

Hephaistion nodded vigorously. "How true."

Fortuitously, I was saved from digging myself into a deeper hole by two sentries dragging a man in Persian garb into the tent. "We caught him trying to sneak into our camp, sire."

Alexandros took one look at the man. "You can let go of him."

As soon as he was free, the man prostrated himself in front of Alexandros and stayed there. Even after Alexandros gave him permission to rise, he didn't move. After a moment, Alexandros poked him with his foot to get the man's attention and motioned for him to rise. The man struggled to his knees. It wasn't clear whether he was overawed to be in the presence of the king or exhausted from his journey or both.

Alexandros was losing patience. "Well, man, speak!"

"My name Orophernes," he stammered. "I last surviving member ancient Persian family. I surrender." His Greek was borderline unintelligible.

"This isn't going to work." Alexandros sat down. "Somebody, go get Seleukos!"

With Seleukos acting as interpreter, Orophernes was finally able to spit out his story. He was a descendant of an ancient noble family that had fallen on hard times. He feared for his survival if he had stayed in Dareios's service. He wished to pledge his life and loyalty to Alexandros.

"He undoubtedly also expects a generous reward," Seleukos added in an aside.

The words started to pour out. "There is utter chaos and disfunction in Ekbatana, your celestial mightiness. Dareios is on the verge of running away with his last remaining troops. All you have to do is wait a week or so and you'll find no resistance when you arrive at the city. You'll be welcomed with open arms."

To Orophernes's evident surprise, Alexandros greeted his report with barely contained fury. "Why would he leave the city undefended?"

"He doesn't have enough loyal soldiers to withstand a siege."

"In that case, why doesn't he open the gates and surrender?"

Orophernes hesitated. "Despite your well-known and well-deserved reputation for clemency, your celestial mightiness, Dareios is afraid to surrender."

Alexandros exploded. "Get him out of here! Shackle him to the execution post! And summon my command staff! Right now!"

When the commanders were assembled in the tent, Seleukos repeated the defector's story.

"That's great news, sire," Kleitos called out.

"No, it isn't. Dareios is simply trying to deprive me of legitimacy. You all know that to be recognized as the next emperor, I need three things. I must hold the imperial scepter; I have to possess the imperial tiara; and the previous incumbent must be dead or, at a minimum, he must abdicate. I have the scepter but the tiara is missing. And, most vexing, that coward Dareios refuses to surrender or die."

Alexandros paused to catch his breath. "We've got to capture him before he leaves Ekbatana. We're leaving tonight."

His outburst was met with stunned silence. Finally, Philotas spoke up. "If he's flown the coop, sire, riding through the night won't accomplish anything."

"We don't actually know that he's left Ekbatana," Hephaistion observed. "All we know is that he's getting ready to leave."

"Well, to be completely accurate," Seleukos said, "Dareios was getting ready to leave when the traitor left Ekbatana. That must have been a few days ago. A lot can change in a few days."

"When did the traitor leave Ekbatana?" somebody asked. Nobody knew.

"Let's get him back in here," Alexandros ordered.

When Orophernes stumbled back into the tent, still wearing his shackles, Alexandros immediately turned on him. "When did you leave Ekbatana and what was going on at the time?"

Seleukos served as both interpreter and moderator. He slowed the flood of Alexandros's questions, broke them down into discrete parts, and patiently elicited the whole story.

Ekbatana was three-days' march away. He, Orophernes, had ridden the distance in a day and a half, at the cost of his horse's life. When he left, Dareios was still in the city. However, the baggage train, most of the soldiers, and all the courtiers had departed two weeks earlier. All that Dareios had left were the Baktrian cavalry, numbering around 12,000 horsemen, 6,000 Persian and Greek mercenary infantry, and whatever gold coins remained in the Ekbatana treasury. Preparations for departure had reached the final stage. Orophernes couldn't say whether Dareios was still in the city or not.

"Ask him what route Dareios was planning to take."

"He says he doesn't know but thinks the remnants of Dareios's army are planning to march toward Baktria, via the Caspian Gates."

"Well, I don't believe a word this man says." This from Perdikkas. "How do we know this isn't an elaborate ruse, intended to lure us into a trap?"

"What trap would that be?" Hephaistion asked. "Are they planning to lure us into attacking Ekbatana? We're going to do that anyway. Or are they planning to lure us into the city by opening the gates? That'd be fine, too."

Perdikkas shrugged. "I don't know. It just smells bad."

"Enough," Alexandros interrupted. "This man doesn't know whether Dareios has left already or not. We ride out tonight. If he managed to get here in a day and a half, we can get there in a day."

"But sire," Philotas wouldn't let it rest. "That makes no sense. We'll simply break our horses, and possibly our necks, riding through the dark. And when we reach Ekbatana, after riding all night and all day, it will be dark once again. And we'll be exhausted and easy pickings for any defenders left in the city. And there is obviously no way the infantry, and our siege engines, and the baggage train can keep up with us. It's just crazy."

At that point Parmenion jumped in. "He didn't mean that, sire. He just got carried away."

"That no problem, Parmenion," Alexandros said. "We encourage full and frank discussion." It didn't sound like he meant it.

"But my son's basic point is sound, sire. It makes more sense to take a day to make preparations for breaking down the camp and resuming the march and then setting off, as an organized unit, prepared to take on whatever may await us at Ekbatana."

"I understand," Alexandros said with minatory patience. "This is what we will do. The Companion Cavalry will set off within the hour, led by me. Those of you in this tent who command Companion squadrons will get your men mounted and ready to ride on my signal. Don't worry about taking too much equipment. We'll be riding light and fast.

"Parmenion will stay behind to organize the breaking down of the camp and the departure of everybody else. They'll catch up to us at Ekbatana as soon as they can.

"Now, let's see whether we can capture that bastard before he slips through our fingers."

****

Kleitos and I were riding in the rear, responsible for sweeping up any stragglers. Thus far, we hadn't lost any men, either to mishap or sluggishness, but the night was still young. When the moon broke through the cloud cover and our eyes adjusted to the dim light, it became almost a comfortable ride.

Kleitos was in a chatty mood. "So, Ptolemaios, this seems like a great time for you to tell me where you came from."

"That's eight hundred and fifty-eight, my friend."

Kleitos laughed. "Seems closer to a thousand to me."

"You keep this up and you'll reach a thousand in no time. By the way, have I mentioned that I can't answer that question?"

"Why not?"

"Because I don't want to lie and, if I told you the truth, you wouldn't believe me."

The truth, which I could never disclose to anyone, was that I had arrived in this era thirteen years earlier as a naive twenty-one-year-old time traveler, intending to observe a Dionysian initiation ceremony. It was supposed to be the field research portion of my senior thesis project at the Academy. I should have been home, in my own native time, within a few days. Things hadn't gone as planned.

While observing the initiation ceremony, I happened to be watching as a fourteen-year-old boy found himself in imminent peril. None of the people on the scene seemed inclined to save him. On impulse, and contrary to all my training, I jumped in and rescued him, in clear violation of the Prime Directive. Of course, I should've known better but I told myself that it would be all right, that no one would ever be the wiser.

The Prime Directive was the paramount commandment drummed into the heads of all time travelers, to do nothing that might influence, interfere with, or change the future course of events. We all believed, almost as an article of faith, that we held the fates of countless generations yet unborn in our hands. By the same token, however, we also knew that some small deviations were self-correcting and would dampen out over time.

I couldn't simply stand by and watch a small boy get killed. I assumed that my intervention would be one of those small, self-correcting deviations. It turned out that I was wrong.

The boy whose life I'd saved was named Kleitos. In short order, Kleitos returned the favor. We became fast friends.

We both fought at Granikos, Kleitos with greater distinction than I. In fact, Kleitos saved Alexandros's life in the course of that battle, which is when I began to realize the extent of the perturbation in the torrent of time that I'd caused.

According to the history I'd been taught in school, the Battle of Granikos was won by Persia. It was the opening salvo of the final stage of the showdown between the Achaemenid Empire and mainland Greece that had started a century and a half earlier at the Battle of Marathon. The flood tide of victory gained at Granikos carried the Persian Empire to the eventual conquest of the entire Greek-speaking world and thus to the unchallenged control of most of Asia and the entire Mediterranean basin. As a result, twenty-six centuries later, we were all Zoroastrians and our history textbooks were written in Persian.

Alexandros was a minor footnote in those history books. He was the leader of the pan-Hellenic army who was killed during the battle, along with most of his soldiers. Yet, I'd seen with my own eyes that Alexandros not only didn't die at Granikos, he actually led his troops to victory. He should've died, and would've died, but for the last-minute intervention of my friend Kleitos Melas. And Kleitos wouldn't have been around to save Alexandros's life if I hadn't, in contravention of the Prime Directive, saved his life nine years earlier.

Immortal Alexandros

After the battle, it took some time for the ramifications of the pan-Hellenic victory to manifest themselves. Some consequences were immediately apparent. Alexandros's improbable triumph boosted the faith of his soldiers in their own abilities and in their commander's leadership qualities. Ironically, Alexandros's near-death experience during the fight did nothing to diminish his own confidence. On the contrary, as I've learned the hard way, few things in life are as exhilarating as escaping – in the nick of time – from the greedy maw of certain death. In Alexandros's case, he emerged from his ordeal more certain than ever that he was destiny's darling. Carried by the resulting wave of euphoria, Alexandros and his army marched from victory to victory. The hegemony of the Persian Empire was destroyed once and for all.

On a personal level, the repercussions dawned on me immediately. Prior to the Battle of Granikos, I had known, from my reading of history books, what would happen next. That certainty went out the window the moment the tide of battle turned. I also understood in a flash why the artificial time portal intended to facilitate my return home never materialized. And, last but perhaps most important, my implicit, unquestioning, quasi-religious faith in the Prime Directive took a hit, too.

During the period of my exile, I had learned two things about this unforgiving imperative of time travel: First, no matter what they taught us at the Academy, punctilious compliance with the Prime Directive for a day or two was quite a challenge. Chances of not committing a violation over a period of years, intentionally or by accident, were nil. Second, I'd paid a heavy price trying to comply.

It's hard to be a soldier, especially in a time of war, if you're not allowed to kill or even injure anyone. Eventually, in the heat of battle, trying to save my own life as well as the lives of my comrades, I did kill some people. How much of a disruption those violations caused only time would tell. Ironically, in the calculus of time travel, saving the life of someone meant to die was just as bad as killing someone else who was meant to live. And the one didn't cancel out the other. On the contrary, in terms of potential disruption of the future, the violations were cumulative.

During the interminable lectures we had endured at the Academy, the most frequently mentioned illustration of this quandary was the case of a time traveler bringing into existence, during his or her visit into the past, a life that wouldn't have been created otherwise. We were told to imagine all the different ways a newborn could change history in the course of its lifetime. I'd hated those exercises. In fact, it was during one of those sessions, trying to envisage all the dire consequences that might result from conceiving a child that I came up with my belief in reverse premonition: "If you can see it coming, it won't happen. It's what you don't anticipate that'll kill you."

I got very good at anticipating disasters. So good, in fact, that I almost quit the time traveler corps, paralyzed by the prospect of all the disasters which I might cause during a trip into the past. *I should've followed my first instinct and quit the corps when I had the chance*, I found myself thinking more than once.

But I didn't quit the corps. I negotiated an internal compromise instead. I would continue trying to anticipate calamities in order to avoid them but I would not stop living. And I would go ahead with this little trip into ancient Macedonia that I needed to complete my senior thesis.

The crimp imposed on my military career by my reluctance to kill people was bad enough. My proclivity to save people's lives was demonstrably worse. And my impulse to create new life was worst of all.

Even before I had fully internalized the realization that I would be stranded in this ancient world for a good long time, I developed a bad habit of falling in love with attractive, intelligent, admirable young women. I was, after all, a normal, young, red-blooded male. And some of those women even liked me. There was Kleitos's sister Lanike, with whom I fell in love at first sight, within days of my arrival in this time. I was desperate to spend the rest of my life with her and she wanted to marry me, too.

In the end, driven by the dictates of the Prime Directive, I broke her heart.

And then there was Barsine, the most beautiful and accomplished woman I'd ever met. She and I were still friends but, in her case, Alexandros had saved me from my perpetual predicament by claiming her for himself. Finally, there was Barsine's sister Artakama. She was as beautiful as her older sister; she was incredibly alluring; she was available; and I couldn't stop thinking about her.

You are a glutton for punishment, aren't you? Even though she was far away in Sousa, I could feel her warm skin, I could taste her delectable lips, I could imagine fathering a child with her. *If you can see it coming, it won't happen. And lucky for you, because there couldn't be a bigger Prime Directive violation than marrying Artakama and starting a family.*

Kleitos broke the silence once again. "So, Ptolemaios, what do you think tomorrow will bring?"

"I wish I knew, my friend, I wish I knew."

.

Chapter 2 – Ekbatana

By the time we reached the summit of Mount Orontes, the sun was setting behind our backs. The city below us, at the foot of the mountain, was lost in deep shadow. We could still make out, but only barely, the multiple walls encircling the city. The imperial complex, built on a high platform carved into the mountainside, appeared as little more than variations in the texture of darkness.

In the penumbral region beyond the city walls, we could see huts, cultivated plots, and irrigation ditches, but no movement. Farther out, the broad valley was still sunlit but curiously dark. There were fields, streams, and stands of trees, but nothing green, only shades of umber, taupe, and black. The entire forlorn panorama was framed by thin wisps of smoke floating on a gentle breeze.

"Can you make out whether the walls are manned?" Alexandros wanted to know.

Perdikkas, who had the sharpest eyes among us, could only shrug. "Can't make out any details, sire."

"Well, we might as well settle down for the night here at the summit. No fires, no noise, nothing to warn them of our presence. And Hephaistion, organize a scouting party to take a closer look, while the rest of us get some sleep. Have them descend through the woods, not on the road, and without horses. And maintain absolute silence. I don't want them to so much as break a twig. Just take a look and report. We'll attack at sunup."

We tied up our horses, ate some hard bread dipped in wine, and slipped into sleep without removing our armor. In what seemed like a blink of an eye, we were being kicked awake by the returning scouts.

They hadn't seen or heard a soul, they said. The city gates were shut but no sentries posted. Something was amiss but they couldn't tell us what.

We dispensed with breakfast, since we had already consumed whatever little food we had managed to grab during our precipitous departure a day and a half earlier. Against our better judgment, we drank some water from a nearby spring and were aboard our mounts while the stars still sparkled overhead. At this hour and altitude, the air was fragrant and bracingly crisp, even in midsummer.

******

We approached the outermost wall without opposition. The gates yielded at the slightest pressure, swinging wide open. As we rode in, we were met by ominous silence. There were no people to be seen; no animals roamed the streets and alleys; even the birds seemed to have taken flight. We scanned in vain for telltale smoke of cooking fires. Yet, the city had a lived-in smell.

Fearing a trap, Alexandros ordered a house-to-house search, starting with a large warehouse near the gate. The warehouse was a jumble of disorganized wares. Someone's half-eaten meal lay scattered on the floor. A tiny flame still guttered in an oil lamp left untended in a corner. There were no people around but an army of rats scattered at our approach. "Make sure you climb to the roof," Alexandros yelled. "We don't want anybody pelting us from above." But the roof was empty as well.

The building across the street, which appeared to be a guardhouse, was similarly deserted. Some furniture remained, a set of gaming bones lay on the table, a shattered bowl had been swept into a corner. *Not much dust,* I thought. *This place was occupied quite recently.*

Repeated calls of "empty" sounded from soldiers as they searched room after room, building after building.

"These are all public buildings," Seleukos said. "We should be searching private dwellings."

I nodded. "OK, let's go." We took a dozen troopers with us as we veered off into an alley. The entrance door to the first house we reached was locked and barred. We smashed through without difficulty, finding ourselves in a colonnaded courtyard, with doorways leading to various rooms and a staircase to an upper floor. I could tell there were people here but couldn't see anyone. And then we heard the cry of a baby.

With my sword drawn, I rushed toward the sound but Seleukos stopped me. "Wait! Let them come out."

He yelled a few words of Persian. Then he yelled again, this time with a little more conviction. Finally, an old man appeared in one of the doorways. Seeing a dozen armed men, he threw himself to the ground, face down, arms stretched out to the side.

Seleukos, who was the only one among us with a decent command of Persian,[13] said something that caused the man to rise and eye us warily. A brief conversation ensued between them. After a moment, the man turned around and disappeared into what looked like a small reception room with a door at the far end leading to a second courtyard.

"What's going on?" I wanted to know.

---

[13] Ptolemaios knew Persian, of course, from his native era, but it was Persian as it had evolved over 2,600 years. This ancient version of the language was scarcely intelligible to him.

Seleukos made a calming gesture with his hand. "They're coming. But, just in case, let's fall back against the wall, draw our swords, and stay on our toes."

Soon enough, people came streaming out, old men, women, and children. "Where are the young men?" I asked.

Seleukos resumed his interrogation of the old man. Quickly, the entire story emerged. A mass evacuation of the palace took place a couple of weeks earlier. All the infantry soldiers, courtiers, servants, slaves, women, children, and domesticated pets left in a huge caravan. They took with them as many possessions as their wagons could carry. The only people to stay behind were the emperor, a few noblemen, and the mounted soldiers.

"The former emperor," Seleukos corrected him.

The old man seemed startled and Seleukos let the matter drop. With a little prodding, the rest of the story dribbled out. The day before, Dareios and his soldiers rode out, taking only their weapons.

"What about the young men of this household?" Seleukos asked.

"Oh yes, Dareios also conscripted all the young men in the city. They left with the caravan two weeks ago."

"That last bit sounded a little funny," Seleukos added after translating this latest intelligence. "Take a couple of men and search the house. I suspect there may be a few more people here than this guy is letting on. But be careful. They're probably able-bodied and armed."

We found them cowering under the stinking straw in the stable. Whether they were able-bodied was subject to debate; they certainly weren't armed. Eight young men, scared out of their wits.

As we led them out, the women let out a tremendous keening wail.

I raised an eyebrow. "What's the matter with them?"

"They think we're going to slaughter them."

Seleukos assured the old man that we would not kill, rape, or enslave anyone. Instead, he asked that the young men go house to house and inform every resident remaining in the city to appear at the palace gate at dawn of the next day. "Anyone who fails to show up will be killed," he added.

"Why did you say that?" I asked.

Seleukos smiled. "For authenticity. We're in the Persian Empire, after all."

****

"Dareios's bed is still warm," an excited soldier reported to Alexandros. "These guys left in a hurry."

Our occupation of Ekbatana, and of the palace complex on the akropolis, had been swift and uneventful. A few hundred defenders could have easily held off our small cavalry force, at least until the rest of our army arrived. And even then, it would have taken a laborious siege to take the city. In the event, it took us less than a day, a feat facilitated by the absence of a single defender.

Alexandros was less than overjoyed. "The bastard has slipped through our fingers again. We resume the chase tomorrow."

Once again, it fell to Philotas to be the voice of reason. "We can't, sire. Just stop a minute and think about it."

This time, there was no Parmenion to back up his son, the old general having been left behind. Finally, the one man who had a chance of cooling the ardor of our leader spoke up. "I hate to say it, Aniketos, but he's right," Hephaistion said. "We have to consolidate our gains here in Ekbatana, before we can press on."

Alexandros just shook his head, refusing to acknowledge the obvious. After a long silence, he cut loose with a loud, frustrated grunt, drew his sword, decapitated a nearby statue with a single stroke, spun on his heels, and departed in search of Dareios's bed. When we saw him again in the morning, he looked rested, cheerful, and ready to conquer the world.

******

Seleukos's arrangements worked out better than expected. When Alexandros, wearing armor and his trademark helmet with the unmistakable white plume, sitting aboard his imposing charger, skipped his way down the broad ceremonial staircase that led from the palace complex to the parade grounds below, he was greeted by a great outcry. Seemingly every remaining inhabitant of Ekbatana turned out as ordered. Now, looking at this apparition that was said to be their new emperor, they were seized by a collective impulse to roar, forgetting their duty to prostrate themselves.

While the rest of us attempted to follow his example and gingerly rode down the steps, trying not to break our necks, Alexandros alighted from his horse and waded into the throng. Those closest to him shrank back, as if scorched by flames, and sank to their knees. Those farther back stopped screaming and simply stared, unable to move, as if transfixed by the sight of a deity.

From somewhere behind me, Seleukos's voice cut through the overawed silence. "Get down!" he yelled in Persian. A great sigh rose from the crowd as they collapsed in unison to the ground.

Alexandros laughed. "That's fine, Seleukos. I want them to see their new emperor. Tell them to get up."

Upon command, the great crowd rose like an army of zombies, their eyes bulging, mouths agape, hands reaching out and then quickly shrinking back in terror as this man of modest stature made great by the aura he exuded, walked among them. Several of us dismounted and tried to form a protective envelope around him but he waved us back, drinking in the adulation of the crowd.

When one man failed to jerk his hand back fast enough as Alexandros approached, Kleitos, quick as a cat, leapt into the gap and slapped down the man's arm with the flat of his sword. *Lucky he didn't use the edge,* I thought. *Otherwise, that man would be going home short one arm.*

Finally, Hephaistion caught up to his friend and leaned into his ear. "Aniketos, I think it's time to return to the palace."

Reluctantly, Alexandros remounted Boukephalas and, with one final wave, departed the scene of his latest conquest.

****

As soon as the rest of the army caught up and settled in, the grumbling started anew. Many of the troops supplied by members of the Hellenic League pursuant to their treaty obligations had wanted to go home even before we'd left Persepolis. They missed their wives, wanted to see their children grow up, and looked forward to enjoying the fruits of their victories. Most of them had accumulated enough loot and had managed to save enough of their pay to make them rich men back home. Assuming they lived long enough to return.

Soldiers on campaign tend not to dwell on the hazards of their chosen occupation. But, in an odd way, the longer they survive the perils of military life, the more wealth they amass, and the farther they travel, the more they miss home. Spending four months in Persepolis with little to do except daydream about discharge and repatriation didn't help their morale.

When the troops received the order to march on Ekbatana, they'd been told this would be their final engagement. Once the last capital of the Persian Empire had been taken and Dareios killed or captured, once Alexandros was crowned the undisputed new emperor of Persia, once the riches of Ekbatana had been distributed among them, once they received their final pay and bonuses, they'd be released from service.

Much to their disappointment, Ekbatana surrendered without a fight. That meant, in keeping with Alexandros's usual policies, that there would be no plunder. To make matters worse, Dareios had gotten away, which brought the prospect of more marching, more fighting, and more years away from home. Sitting in their tents outside Ekbatana's city walls, they were not happy campers.

The newcomers, who had joined us after we'd left Persepolis, didn't feel the same way; they still yearned for their chance to throw the dice. And some oldtimers, although disappointed by the absence of loot in Ekbatana, were ready to press on. Some were mercenaries who couldn't imagine any other way of life. Some, for one reason or another, had no home or family awaiting them. And for some, the army was their family; the peripatetic camp was their home.

The Macedonian veterans were a special case. They had been with Alexandros since the beginning; they had shared his triumphs; they believed he was destiny's darling. But even their attitudes were starting to shift. In the beginning, they worshipped Alexandros and willingly sacrificed their lives for him. They loved him because he knew every soldier's name, because he fought in the front line of every battle, and because he won. Lately, though, like children sitting on a seesaw, the higher he rose in his own estimation, the less enamored they became.

Alexandros, always attuned to the mood of his soldiers, was acutely aware of the discontent brewing in the ranks. After considering the matter for a few days, he called a general assembly of the army and announced his plans.

He told the men assembled on the parade ground beneath the palace wall that he had decided to discharge all Hellenic League troops. The separation terms were generous indeed. Cavalrymen would be paid 6,000 drachmai each, equal to more than 8 years' pay. Infantrymen would receive 1,000 drachmai each, equal to a little less than 3 years' pay. Since most of these Hellenic League soldiers were desperate to go home, they greeted Alexandros's announcement with loud, sustained cheering that proved to be almost impossible to stop. The Macedonian veterans, some of whom would have been happy to receive the same separation offer, stood in sullen silence through the prolonged ovation.

Alexandros was willing to release the Hellenic League troops for a number of reasons. He understood, having observed the performance of Dareios's conscripts, that soldiers compelled to serve against their wishes made for poor fighters. He was also not entirely convinced of the loyalty of the Hellenic League troops. He thought he could manage with a smaller, elite, all-volunteer army devoted to him personally. Finally, he expected these discharged Greek soldiers, who were suddenly the richest people in their respective city-states, to spread word of Alexandros's success and beneficence and become a font of pro-Alexandros and pro-Macedonian propaganda in their homeland.

On the other hand, Alexandros was desperate to retain the support of his Macedonian veterans and he could see that some of them were disgruntled as a result of the separation offer he had just extended to the Hellenic League troops. Improvising on the spot, he raised his hands and made it clear he had an additional announcement to make.

When the uproar subsided, he announced that all Macedonian veterans who'd been with him since the outset of the invasion would receive an immediate reenlistment bonus of three talents each (equal to 18,000 drachmai). An infantryman would've had to toil almost fifty years to earn that much pay. It was now the Macedonian veterans' turn to cheer. And everyone else assembled on the parade grounds that morning could look forward to the day when he too would be the recipient of the great man's munificence.

In the end, Alexandros's extravagant gestures cost perhaps 20,000 talents – an enormous amount that exceeded the total accumulated treasuries of all the Hellenic League cities combined.[14] But Alexandros liked grandiose gestures and, having seized most of the treasure accumulated by the Persian Empire over two hundred years of conquest and avarice, he could afford it.

****

---

[14] An infantryman was paid one drachma per day; cavalrymen were paid two drachmai. 20,000 talents equaled 120,000,000 drachmai, enough to keep a 50,000-man army in the field for more than six years.

Inevitably, all that talk of home reminded me of my own. Although I steadfastly refused to disclose my origins to Kleitos, or to anyone else, for that matter, I had come from a place and time that I still considered home.

The reason I'd become marooned in this ancient era in the first place was that the portal meant to take me back home never appeared. Eventually, after the Battle of Granikos, I realized that it was my own violation of the Prime Directive that must have caused the glitch.

Fortunately, all was not lost. Prior to my departure, I had been informed of the next available, naturally occurring "escape hatch," which I could use in the extremely unlikely event that my artificial portal failed to materialize and no extraction team showed up to rescue me. Trouble was, escape hatches were few and far between. As luck would have it, my first opportunity to catch a spontaneous portal was slated to take place, according to those brilliant chronoscientists who trained me, on the Mediterranean coast of Egypt, near the Nile delta, in 266 Z.E.

Initially, the idea that I could stay alive in this foreign land for twenty-three years, comply with the Prime Directive during all that time, and be at the escape hatch on the appointed day seemed fairly farfetched. But here I was, thirteen years later, still kicking. I'd managed to comply, more or less, with the paramount commandment, and I'd even visited the site of the portal's projected appearance near the Nile delta. Alas, I'd gotten there way too early. Still, if I could do it once, I should be able to repeat the feat, except with better timing.

Only ten years to go.

****

"Gentlemen, we have no choice." This was our first briefing in the Ekbatana apadana. The large hall was mostly empty, with only senior officers present. For once, there were no Persian courtiers, noblemen, priests, or hangers-on. For a change, Alexandros wore the clothes he used to wear when he was just the king of Macedonia. Seated on Dareios's vacated throne, he was all business. "We have to hunt Dareios down. He's only a few days ahead of us and we all know he's not as fast as we are. If we leave tomorrow and if we maintain double-time pace, we'll catch up to him within a week."

"It's the middle of summer, sire, and we're at altitude. The men can't maintain a double-time pace for a day, much less a week." Parmenion was saying aloud what each of us was thinking.

"You're underestimating our men. They tend to be younger than you are." Alexandros's smile failed to conceal the implicit barb.

Philotas, as was his wont, sprang to his father's defense. "You're doing Dareios's work. Our men will be dead before we catch him."

"Oh, shut up." Alexandros was losing patience. "We've done it before. The men will have plenty to eat and drink and I will see to it that they get adequate rest."

"That could be another problem, sire." This time, it was Koinos's turn to speak. At forty, he was a proven commander, frequently entrusted by Alexandros with missions requiring independent judgment, such as foraging expeditions. He also happened to be married to one of Parmenion's daughters and thus Philotas's brother-in-law. "We've searched every house in this city and have found precious little food. When Dareios's army left, they took all available provisions with them. And, as we saw on our way into Ekbatana, what they couldn't carry, they destroyed. All livestock has been killed and left to putrefy. Every hut, storage shed, and cultivated field along the route of their withdrawal has been burnt to the ground. There will be no harvest this year. They've done us a favor, in a way, because we won't have any trouble determining which way they went. On the other hand, keeping up our own supplies won't be easy and the necessary foraging will slow us down."

"I've considered all that." Alexandros's tone was sharp. "We have sufficient supplies for a week, which is all we need. After we catch the bastard, we'll have plenty of time to forage."

Several people tried to speak at once. Alexandros's voice cut through the hubbub. "Enough already! This is not a debate; this is a briefing. Now, listen up!

"I'm leaving a garrison of 6,000 mercenaries to hold the city and control Media." *He's unloading another contingent of potentially disloyal soldiers.* As if reading my thoughts, Alexandros hastened to explain. "This is an important assignment. We can't afford any unrest behind us while we pursue Dareios and the Medians are a notoriously rebellious lot. This will be our biggest garrison in any of the Persian capitals. And besides, we'll all be reunited here in Ekbatana soon enough."

Had the 6,000 mercenaries been present in the apadana, they would have undoubtedly expressed their displeasure at missing out on all the loot that was sure to come our way as we rampaged through the eastern satrapies of the Persian Empire. As it was, nobody in the hall was anxious to get into another dispute with Alexandros just then.

In any event, before anyone had a chance to object, Alexandros dropped another bombshell. "To underline the importance of this force, I'm leaving Parmenion behind as garrison commander and as satrap of Media."

This time, there was only stunned silence. To leave his leading general behind, the man who had commanded the expeditionary corps sent across the Hellespont by Alexandros's father to prepare the ground for the main-force invasion and who had acted as Alexandros's second-in-command ever since we commenced our Asian campaign, was truly astonishing.

Alexandros feigned puzzlement. "What's the matter with you? This is a crucial command, as I've explained. Plus, you've all been busy telling me what a killer pace I'm planning to impose. Well, it's not a killer pace but it might be a bit too much for a seventy-year-old man. And, as I've just finished saying, we'll all be back here in Ekbatana soon enough."

As the silence turned sullen, Alexandros, ever the great tactician, temporized. He jolted us with another surprise announcement, presumably to take our minds off the previous stunner. "I'm also leaving behind my friend Harpalos as tax collector and treasurer and one of my most trusted officers, Kleandros, as Parmenion's second-in-command."

It was Alexandros's usual practice, after taking control of a satrapy, to split up the jobs of satrap, treasurer, and garrison commander among different men, so they could keep an eye on each other. Thus, appointing someone tax collector and treasurer was not surprising in itself; what was surprising was the identity of the person chosen for the post.

Harpalos had been with us since the start of the invasion but it was hard to define what exactly he did. Having been born with one leg shorter than the other, he was certainly not a soldier. Calling him the staff clown might have been a bit too harsh. He was charming, witty, and an inveterate prankster. He performed no useful function from what I could see but Alexandros enjoyed having him around. Naming him tax collector and treasurer for an important satrapy, however, was beyond surprising.

Naming Kleandros as Parmenion's deputy commander was unusual as well. Normally, someone as senior as Parmenion would be trusted to choose his own staff. And Alexandros wasn't done yet. After naming Kleandros deputy commander, he proceeded to undermine Parmenion's authority even further. "Because we're leaving behind an unusually large contingent, I thought it prudent to divide the garrison brigade into three battalions of two thousand men, each with their own commander. The men I've chosen are Sitalkes, Herakon, and Agathon. All three of them will report to Kleandros, who will, of course, report to Parmenion."

There was a lot of muttering but Alexandros didn't seem too receptive to further discussion.

"Now, get out of here and get busy organizing your troops. Do I even have to say it – we march out before dawn."

And, before dawn, at least the lead elements of Alexandros's army set off in pursuit of Dareios, marching double-time.

Chapter 3 – The Chase

It happened so quickly, Dareios didn't even have time to draw his sword. One minute, he was surrounded by his satraps, chatting amicably; the next, he was lying face down in the dirt, a sharp rock stabbing his left cheek, strong hands and knees holding him down, shackles being hammered shut on his ankles.

With so much weight pressing on his back and neck, he was finding it difficult to breathe. Finally, once the shackles were in place, the pressure eased and he was able gulp some dust-laden air. He wanted to scream but all he could do was gasp and cough.

Eventually, they raised him to his feet, disarmed him, and bound his wrists. No one was willing to look him in the eyes. He felt a trickle of blood coursing down his face and into his beard. Someone picked up his tiara, which had fallen into the dust, and mockingly placed it on his head.

"What is this?" he was finally able to spit out.

No one answered. Instead, they urged him with their sword points to hobble over to a nearby wagon and climb in. After he was seated in the smelly straw, they fastened the chain running from his leg irons to the slats on which he sat. The teamster sitting up front whipped the yoked oxen into motion.

Unbeknownst to Dareios, it had all been a carefully choreographed dance. Dareios's plan, after his repeated calls for reinforcements fell on deaf ears, was to evacuate what was left of his army into the vast, untamed, inhospitable expanses of the eastern satrapies; lure Alexandros to chase after him; and then make the pursuit as difficult as possible by destroying forageable provisions, interrupting lines of communication, inspiring guerilla attacks, and fomenting disaffection within Alexandros's army. At the same time, he hoped to attract fresh recruits while Alexandros's army lost men and lost its will to fight. Then, when the time and terrain were right, he would inflict the coup de grâce.

Ironically, the handful of satraps who had gathered in Ekbatana agreed with this strategy. All of them, with the exception of Artabazos, governed eastern satrapies. The governors of western satrapies, when faced with the arrival of Alexandros's forces, had by and large surrendered their provinces, switched their allegiances, and sought to be retained in their posts by Alexandros. Artabazos was one of the very few western satraps who had joined Dareios in Ekbatana.

The eastern satraps, who had yet to confront the prospect of Alexandros's army at their gates, retained their confidence in the ultimate triumph of the Persian Empire over the upstart invaders. They were intimately familiar with the terrain and the inhabitants of their satrapies. They knew better than anyone that these territories had a habit of swallowing invading armies. Even the great Kyros, founder of the Persian dynasty, lost his life trying to enlarge the borders of Sogdiana. Their concern was that, in light of Dareios's recent record of defeats, his army might get swallowed first.

The most vexatious of the satraps was Bessos. As Dareios's fortunes declined, Bessos's self-esteem, backed by his 12,000 cavalrymen, grew ever more strident. At some point, it occurred to Bessos that the odds of saving the empire would increase greatly if he were in command of the entire army, not just the Baktrian hordes. While still in Ekbatana, he approached his fellow satraps, urging a leadership change. Dareios's precipitous and ignominious withdrawal from the Median capital clinched his case.

Once the rump army commenced its mad dash for safety, burning and looting the countryside as it went, the satraps agreed that Dareios had to be deposed. Only two questions remained: Who would take over and what to do with Dareios. Bessos had a ready answer to both questions. Obviously, Bessos would be the new emperor, from which conclusion it necessarily followed that Dareios would have to be killed. The concept of emperor emeritus hadn't been invented in the Persian Empire.

Nabarzanes, the most senior commander among the co-conspirators, was the polar opposite of Bessos. He was educated, cultured, and suave. While he agreed that Dareios was not the man to organize and lead the resistance in the eastern satrapies, the thought of the coarse, brash, and brutal satrap of Baktria becoming emperor of Persia horrified him. Unfortunately, unlike Bessos, he had no troops whose allegiance was primarily personal to him. All he had was his war record, his magnetism, and his wits. The other co-conspirators – Satibarzanes, satrap of Areia; Barsaentes, satrap of Drangiana and Arakhosia; and Astaspes, satrap of Karmania – each thought himself most qualified to don the tiara. However, given a choice between Nabarzanes and Bessos, they secretly preferred Nabarzanes but were too afraid of Bessos and his savages to say so out loud.

Finally, there was Artabazos. He was the only satrap among them who had actually tried, in his youth, to seize the throne. Because of his age, lineage, and experience, he commanded a measure of respect among his fellow satraps. More importantly, he commanded the loyalty of the 8,000 Greek mercenaries in Dareios's army who, although less numerous than the Baktrian horsemen, were better armed and more disciplined. However, years of exile following his unsuccessful putsch had taught him caution. Plus, he was not a traitor at heart. As a result, he refrained from taking an active role in the seditious machinations of his fellow satraps.

Neither Bessos nor Nabarzanes was sufficiently confident of his own strength to hazard a showdown with the other. Eventually, Nabarzanes convinced Bessos that it didn't make sense to kill Dareios. They could use him as an insurance policy. If Alexandros caught up to them and their chance of taking power was lost, they could hand Dareios over to Alexandros, pledge their allegiance to him, and score an important command or a satrapy in return, as so many other satraps had already done. In the meantime, they could defer the decision on who would become the next emperor until they were reasonably certain that the plan to destroy Alexandros and his army would be successful. Bessos reluctantly agreed to keep Dareios alive, which was how the former emperor found himself bouncing along, shackled and bound in the bed of a covered wagon, as the army that used to be his resumed its flight east.

****

Barsine was in the middle of breastfeeding when Artakama joined her. "He looks so peaceful."

Barsine smiled. "He's a good eater. Unfortunately, his teeth are coming in."

Artakama, who'd never been near enough to a man to catch a cold, much less get pregnant, winced. "Doesn't that hurt?"

"Nah, I'm training him not to bite. And don't forget, he's my fifth one, so I'm used to it."

The two sisters sat companionably on Barsine's bed in the semidarkness of the small room. Thick walls and the lack of any windows nearby made this the coolest spot in the entire compound.

"How old is he now?"

"He's almost a year and a half. Can you believe it?"

"How long will you breastfeed him?"

"I'm already giving him other food but I still have my milk and I've got the time."

After a short pause, Artakama abruptly changed the subject. "I wish I had a man."

"No, you don't. First of all, we don't have men; men have us. And second, there is no rush, trust me."

The age gap between the two was small compared to the chasm in their worldly experience. Barsine was still only twenty-six but, in addition to being owned by four men, not counting her father, and giving birth to five children, she'd already been a pampered little princess in Hellespontine Phrygia, a political fugitive in Macedonia, a spoil of war, an inmate in the harems of two emperors, and a self-sufficient woman determined to use the weapons at her disposal to see her son in charge of Persia one day.

Artakama was almost eighteen, well past marriageable age. However, she'd been living in a harem since before reaching puberty and, in all that time, had only really met one intact man.

"Easy for you to talk. You've had all the men anyone could ever want. And from what I could hear, you enjoyed it, too."

"You have no idea what you're talking about, Artakama. All we women have is our looks, our brains, and our ability to produce children. To survive and get ahead we have to use these assets. That's what I've done and that's what you'll have to do as well."

Artakama laughed. "I'm ready, Barsine. I've been ready for years."

"Well, patience is a virtue. Look at this cute little boy. I have to wait until he's a grown man and the emperor of Persia before I can enjoy a little comfort and security."

"I thought you'd enjoy comfort and security when Alexandros married you."

"I've tried every trick I know, Artakama. I've even given him this baby boy. And he certainly seems to enjoy my company but there doesn't seem to be any wedding in the offing."

"Well, if you can't get Alexandros to marry you, how is little Herakles going to become emperor?"

"He'll be emperor because I'll stop at nothing to make it happen. But what about you? Have you given any thought to what you may have to do to make your way in the world?"

"That's all I think about, dear sister."

"I thought all you thought about was bedding your beloved Ptolemaios."

"Same thing, isn't it?"

Barsine burst out laughing. "You're a better student than I thought."

******

Seven days into our mad pursuit, we were all ready to drop dead. It was the height of summer. The elevated altitude didn't do much to diminish the intensity of the sun or moderate the midday heat; all it did was make it harder to breathe. We'd run out of food for the men and fodder for the horses. The retreating enemy burned out every field, village, farmstead, and storage shed; slaughtered every cow, ox, goat, sheep, chicken, and dog; and poisoned every spring, creek, and well. We'd eaten all the food we'd brought with us and finished the last of the wine. Even when we found some brackish water, we were afraid to drink it. The insects were eating us alive. We'd maintained a killer pace and yet, somehow, we were still two or three days behind the enemy.

Fifty miles short of the Caspian Gates, we received word that Dareios had already cleared the last remaining mountain pass. Beyond the Gates awaited the desert, where conditions would be even worse. Reluctantly, Alexandros paused our chase. He dispatched a cavalry force under Koinos with orders to forage as far as necessary to secure sufficient provisions. The rest of us established a camp, conserved our energy, hid from the sun, and cast hopeful glances in the direction from which we expected Koinos and his men to return.

After waiting five long days, we finally saw a cloud of dust rising on the horizon. We gathered hopefully at the gate of our temporary palisade but soon realized that the approaching group of horsemen was far too small to be Koinos's squadrons. Taking up arms, we waited. It proved to be a small contingent of Persians, led by two young men who, judging by their armor, were members of the upper class. When they were within arrowshot, they dismounted and approached, showing us the palms of their hands to indicate their peaceful intentions.

"Hey, I know those guys," Perdikkas called out.

They turned out to be two young noblemen we'd met in Babylon, one of them the son of Mazaios, the Persian satrap Alexandros had left behind in nominal control of the city. They had quite a story to tell. They confirmed that Dareios's army was beyond the Caspian Gates; however, its pace had slowed and it was no longer under Dareios's command.

Listening to the details of the coup d'état, Alexandros could barely contain himself. "That's outrageous! Those men are traitors. When I get my hands on them, I'm going to kill them."

"Begging your pardon, sire," Kleitos interjected, "but how are they different from all those other satraps who switched their allegiance as soon as we appeared on the horizon and surrendered their satrapies to us? You forgave all of them and kept them on as satraps." Then, realizing that the son of one of those satraps was standing in the tent with us, he quickly added, "Present company excepted, of course."

Alexandros, still angry, shook his head. "That's totally different. Those other satraps didn't depose their emperor. They simply transferred their loyalty from the previous emperor to the new one. Same as when my father died and I became king."

"You're right, sire. Exactly the same." Kleitos paused. Then, as Alexandros turned back toward our guests, Kleitos muttered under his nose. "Except Dareios was still emperor at the time."

Alexandros wheeled on him. "What was that?"

"Nothing, sire, nothing."

Alexandros let the matter drop, resuming his interrogation of the two Persian defectors. He wanted exact details on the number of troops being led by Bessos and Nabarzanes, the composition, armament, condition, and morale of each unit, the projected route of their march, the pace of their movement, and their logistical arrangements. He was gratified to hear that old Artabazos, father of his mistress Barsine, had in the end refused to throw in his lot with the rebels and had, instead, stolen away in the middle of the night with his 8,000 mercenaries, heading to the north, in the direction of the Caspian Sea.

After he had squeezed every last drop of intelligence from the two young men, he welcomed them into our ranks. "I wish I could throw a banquet to celebrate your decision to join my army. Unfortunately, we are a little pressed for time." He neglected to mention our lack of food or wine.

Next morning, Alexandros decided he couldn't sit still any longer. He set off with an elite corps comprised of five Companion Cavalry squadrons and two battalions of Silver Shields. He took whatever food and wine were left, telling the remaining troops to follow as soon as Koinos showed up with fresh supplies. In the meantime, they could drink brackish water and eat tree bark, if they had to.

****

Dareios spent his nights gnawing at the knots binding his wrists. After six nights, the rope started to slip. The next morning, when Bessos paid him his customary daily visit, indulging in a few minutes of gloating and torment, he was in for a surprise. After he turned his back, preparing to jump off the wagon, he felt the rope which had formerly bound Dareios's wrists constricting his own windpipe.

A struggle ensued. Dareios was the bigger and stronger man, even at the age of fifty, and he had the advantage of surprise. Bessos, on the other hand, had Tyche, the goddess of luck, on his side – at least for the moment.

Dareios planted the crown of his head between Bessos's shoulder blades, his fists, rope in hand, positioned on either side of the smaller man's neck, and he pulled with all his might. As Bessos was losing consciousness, his arms failing uselessly at his sides, his heels drumming with diminishing force against the slats of the wagon, his face turning shades of purple, his eyes bulging out of his head, one of his men happened to walk by.

Seeing his commander under attack, the man leapt into the wagon, curved sword in hand, and, without a second thought, started slashing at the assailant's arms and back. As soon as Bessos regained his breath, he screamed at his savior. "Don't kill him! We have to keep him alive."

They sent in the camp medic who did what he could. Without bothering to check on Dareios's condition, Bessos and Nabarzanes ordered their ever-diminishing army to set off for their daily march as usual.

That evening, when they stopped for the night, Bessos arranged a little ceremony. To the loud cheers of his savage scrappers and the silent stares of the rest of the troops, he placed the imperial tiara on his own head and declared himself Emperor Artaxerxes Pemptos Bessos. The medic, who tended to Dareios while the ceremony took place, didn't harbor much hope.

Chapter 4 – The Capture

It took us three days to get through the Caspian Gates. We rode and marched eighteen hours a day, through scorching heat, torrential downpours, and ravenous clouds of mosquitoes. Luckily, we had no baggage to worry about and very little food or wine.

At dusk of the third day, we reached what had evidently been the enemy camp. Sitting in the dirt in the middle of the trampled field was a solitary old man. He turned out to be a Greek-speaking interpreter, left behind because he was too old and too sick to keep up with the retreating Baktrians. He told us Bessos, Nabarzanes, and all the rest had left the camp only that morning. He also told us that Dareios was no longer in charge, which we already knew, and that he had been attacked by one of Bessos's men and appeared to be gravely injured, which was news to us.

"When we catch those guys, I will personally execute anyone who had laid a hand on the emperor," Alexandros announced.

"Former emperor," Hephaistion corrected.

"That's right. But still, people can't be permitted to attack emperors, former or otherwise. Well, let's get some rest. Maybe we'll reach them tomorrow."

No one argued, even though it seemed obvious that, at our current rate of gain, we'd be dead of starvation well before we caught up to the enemy.

Trying to be helpful, the old interpreter spoke up. "They probably didn't cover much ground today."

"Why is that?"

"Well, it takes time to destroy everything you see. Plus, they were all hung over this morning from the previous night's celebration."

Alexandros's interest was piqued. "What were they celebrating?"

"Oh, I forgot to mention. Bessos wanted an excuse for his ruffians to get drunk, so he declared himself Emperor Artaxerxes Pemptos Bessos. You should've seen it, your celestial highness. He put Dareios's tiara on his head but it was too big. Good thing his ears stick out so much. Otherwise, it would've fallen all the way to his nose."

The old man was too busy chuckling at the recollection to notice the abrupt change in Alexandros's expression. His merriment was cut short by an earthshaking roar. "He did what?"

All motion in the camp ceased. Even the sentries posted at the farthest reaches of the outer perimeter turned around and stared.

Alexandros drew a deep breath, both to calm himself and to power his next ejaculation. "That man is dead."

"Well, at least we now know where the imperial tiara is," Kleitos, ever helpful, observed.

Alexandros refused to be distracted. "We're catching them tomorrow. And when we do, I'll have the scepter, the tiara, and two dead emperors, the former emperor and the usurper. Now, fan out and find some locals. I need a shortcut to head them off and I need some guides who will lead us there!"

Amazingly enough, it turned out that a shortcut did exist. Some of our scouts dragged in two frightened men. They were barely able to speak, such was their awe and terror at being in the presence of a passing deity. However, the old interpreter proved his worth by getting them to disclose what they knew.

The shortcut, the men told us, led through the desert. No hope of finding water holes or springs along the way. In the winter, intrepid travelers, well-supplied with water and food, riding on camels, occasionally attempted to shave a day or two from their travel time by cutting across the desert. Sometimes they made it and sometimes they didn't. During the summer, it would be sheer lunacy to venture into this blazing inferno. Even desert lizards stayed in their burrows, except perhaps at night. The good news was that the route was easy to follow because of all the bleached skeletons of men and beasts marking the trail. Thus, no need for guides.

Alexandros laughed. "That's perfect. The sun is setting and we're about to leave. Do you think we can get across by dawn tomorrow?"

"Only if you have flying horses, your divine majesty. Otherwise, both you and your horses will break their necks long before dawn."

"Nonsense. We have a full moon and, as you say, the skeletons will show us the way. But can we get to the other side by the time the sun rises?"

The men hesitated. "We don't know about your horses. It takes the camels, if they make it, two days to get across. But they have broad hooves, suitable for walking on sand. It's just not possible for horses to walk on sand."

"Luckily, our horses won't be walking. They'll be galloping most of the way, their hooves barely touching the surface. As you say, we have flying horses."

Alexandros called for five hundred volunteers. Most of the men who stepped forward were young infantrymen who had never been through a desert. Alexandros selected the toughest, fittest, youngest men. A hundred of them were cavalrymen and they got to keep their usual mounts. The four hundred infantrymen were given horses requisitioned from cavalrymen staying behind.

And so, with a bright moon and twinkling stars overhead, we rode into the desert. Sixty of us were still with Alexandros when we emerged from the sand the next morning.

****

At first, I thought I was seeing a mirage. As the sun rose and the ground beneath our horses changed to scrub, I saw a cloud of dust immediately in front of us. And in the dust, gliding like shades in Haides, were silent, spectral, horse-mounted monsters. As we drew nearer, the apparitions resolved into flesh and blood Baktrian barbarians. Turned out, we'd come out of the desert just in time to catch the tail end of the enemy's rearguard.

"Attack!" Alexandros screamed, charging ahead, heedless of whether anyone followed. The sixty of us still with him did our best to keep up, forming a flying wedge.

In front of us was an army of 20,000 or 30,000 men, including Bessos's 12,000 fearsome mounted barbarians. The rearguard alone numbered 3,000 horsemen. They could have annihilated us in a blink of an eye, starting with Alexandros, astride his trusty Boukephalas, his unmistakable white plume matching the white blaze on his charger's forehead.

Well, it was a fun ride, I thought as I drew my sword. But a strange thing happened. There was no one for me to slash. Somehow, the enemy had vanished into their protective dust cloud. The rearguard rode madly forward, panicking the rest of their column as they went. By the time they reached the vanguard, where Bessos and Nabarzanes were riding, the rearguard had their entire army fleeing from what they took to be an all-out assault by Alexandros's forces.

Alexandros, unable to see anything in the dust, finally had the good sense to stop. The rest of us surrounded him and struggled to breathe. We hadn't slept; we'd cantered through a treacherous desert by moonlight; we hadn't eaten in more than a day; we'd barely had anything to drink. We were simply sitting there, waiting to be slaughtered, hoping for the chance at least to catch our breaths before we died.

Bessos, at the moment of decision, chose to emulate the commander whom he had ridiculed and vilified so many times. As Dareios had done before him, he opted to run away. But first, he had the presence of mind to take care of one more task. He rode up to the wagon carrying the badly wounded Dareios and transfixed him with his spear where he lay, pinning the former emperor of Persia to the slats of the wagon like a bug. Then, pushing the hapless teamster out of his seat, he slashed with his sword at the rumps of the yoked oxen, sending the wagon clattering wildly across an adjacent field.

Once the former emperor's wagon had been dispatched, he waved his sword overhead and took off for Baktria, his 12,000 spooked pussycats of the steppes galloping behind him. Nabarzanes, equally unnerved, took off with the remaining cavalrymen, riding north toward Hyrkania. The rest of the soldiers, all infantrymen, literally ran for their lives. Those originally from Drangiana and Arakhosia eventually coalesced around their satrap, Barsaentes, and headed home. Another contingent, led by Astaspes, satrap of Karmania, took off in a southerly direction. The stragglers followed Satibarzanes, satrap of Areia, marching westward.

****

By the time we reached the spot where panic had overtaken the leaders of the opposing army, everyone was gone. There were lots of wagons laden with armor, supplies, and hay, many disoriented beasts of burden, even some tents and court paraphernalia, but nary a human being. We were far too tired to continue and, in any event, had no idea which way to pursue, had we been able to muster one additional ounce of energy. Based on the tracks left behind, the enemy departed in six different directions.

Making a virtue of necessity, Alexandros announced that we would make camp where we stood and give the rest of our comrades a chance to catch up. His order met with universal approval. We fell on the abandoned food like ravenous wolves; our horses did the same with hay wagons; we splintered the empty wagons to make fires; and we used captured canvas to build tents. There was plenty to go around for our meager band of sixty. The only thing still missing was some water, both for us and for our horses.

Alexandros dispatched two-men patrols in every direction with orders to find water. He told the rest of us to search the wagons and sift through the dirt, hoping to find the imperial tiara. Nothing resembling a tiara ever turned up but one of the patrols had better luck in their search for water. They saw the shimmering surface of a water hole in a hollow a few hundred yards ahead. They also saw a team of oxen, still yoked to a wagon, already drinking there. Not knowing who was in the wagon, they approached stealthily; however, finding no teamster about, they simply drove the oxen away and proceeded to quench their own thirst. Their horses did the same, maintaining a discrete separation from their masters.

While the two men were drinking, they heard a soft groan from the wagon bouncing behind the retreating oxen. Not bothering to remount, the men easily caught up to the slow-moving conveyance and peered inside. They glimpsed a shackled man, lying in blood-soaked straw, with a spear sticking out of his belly.

The two soldiers jumped into the wagon, one lurching to the front to halt the oxen while the other knelt in the straw next to the supine figure. He could see the man's lips moving. Leaning in, he heard a couple of whispered Greek words – the man was asking for water. The soldier, using his helmet as a convenient vessel, promptly obliged.

Taking a sip of water, the wounded man whispered his thanks. He told the soldier he was grateful not to die alone. After that, he was silent.

The two soldiers, assessing the wounded man's tattered clothes, which must have been quite opulent once, and his ability to speak Greek, decided that he must be someone important. While one of them stayed in the wagon, the other rode back to the nearby camp to report their find.

By the time Alexandros arrived, the wounded man was dead. Alexandros recognized him instantly, from his clothes, which were identical to the ones he frequently wore, and from the visage, which he had seen on so many coins.

Chapter 5 – Reassessments

Alexandros was of two minds. On the one hand, he was ready to proclaim himself the new emperor of Persia. The previous emperor was dead; he was in possession of the imperial scepter; and a new imperial tiara could be easily improvised. More importantly, he controlled the western half of the empire; he occupied all four capitals; he had repeatedly defeated the armies of the empire; and he'd captured its fabulous treasuries, accumulated over centuries of Achaemenid rule. What more could the Persian nobility, magoi, and hoi polloi expect before acknowledging his legitimacy?

On the other hand, a man who had deposed and killed Dareios, who claimed to control the eastern half of the empire, and who'd proclaimed himself Emperor Artaxerxes Pemptos Bessos was still riding out there somewhere. As long as that man existed, there would always be some people willing to question Alexandros's legitimacy. Plus, that man's continued existence offended his sense of neatness, integrity, and honor.

Something else nagged at the back of his mind: Over their years of struggle, Alexandros had developed a certain respect, even empathy, for his erstwhile enemy. In his imagination, he'd expected Dareios to submit, as so many of the satraps had done, and to abdicate the throne in his favor. Now that Dareios was dead, Alexandros felt an uncontrollable rage welling up within the dark recesses of his mind. How dare Bessos, this savage barbarian, raise a hand against his divinely sanctioned liege and commander and thus deprive Alexandros of his chance to orchestrate a legitimate succession?

Even before most of his army had caught up to us, Alexandros convened a meeting of the available senior commanders to determine our course forward. Many of his most trusted advisors urged him to return to Persepolis, declare victory, and have himself officially installed as the next emperor of Persia. Alexandros listened politely, considered his options, and shook his head. "The regicide must die," he finally declared. There would be no debate, no going back, and no premature declarations of victory. "We will find him and kill him. Then we'll return to Persepolis. Or perhaps Babylon, since there's not much left of Persepolis."

After a moment of silence, while we all assessed the ramifications of this latest detour on the road to Alexandros's destiny, Hephaistion spoke up. "Makes sense, Aniketos. We have to get control of all these provinces sooner or later. And now, we can conquer them as avengers of the death of the previous emperor. Undoubtedly, the locals will welcome us as the executors of divine retribution and agents of their liberation."

Hephaistion's prognostication, while eloquent and pleasing to Alexandros, proved to be less than prophetic.

****

In the Sousa harem, it was the first pleasantly warm day after months of insufferable, stifling heat. All the ladies, as if drawn by a siren song, spilled out of their sumptuous suites, followed by their respective entourages, and rushed to the shady banks of the largest pond on the premises.

Barsine, Artakama, and their two serving women were first to arrive. Barsine was carrying little Herakles, while her three daughters and older son, who were ostensibly the children of the serving women, brought up the rear, skipping along, two by two, holding hands and singing a happy tune.

They had barely settled down on the mossy bank when Antigone appeared. She came, trailed by a single eunuch, who'd drawn the short straw when the day's assignments were meted out by Dilshad that morning. Antigone, while strikingly beautiful and irresistible to most men, was not blessed by a surfeit of intelligence or congeniality. She was the mistress of Alexandros's most daring and accomplished cavalry commander, Philotas. He, while a great soldier, was, like his paramour, imperious, high-handed, and sharp-tongued. When the two of them spent a couple of months sailing on the Nile, the crocodiles dove for cover to escape their screaming tiffs.

"I see you've grabbed the best spot as usual," Antigone said by way of greeting. She meant it as a compliment.

"You're welcome to join us, Antigone. We have enough nuts and mead for all of us to share."

"Thanks, Barsine, but I'm not overly fond of nuts. They get under my teeth." Antigone paused for a moment, then added. "Kind of like little kids who get under foot." She laughed at her own wit.

"Well, there are plenty of other shady places in the garden. Why don't you find a more secluded one?"

"Oh, that's alright. This one is fine." She plopped herself down next to Barsine. "Just tell the serving girls to take the kids away."

Artakama, who lacked her sister's patience and maturity, had had enough. "If anybody gets taken away, you brat, it will be you. Now get out of here!"

Antigone was shocked by the sudden outburst. "What's gotten into you? Your sister and I are just having a pleasant chat."

Artakama sprang to her feet and was about to slap Antigone when Thais, accompanied by her usual retinue of six beautiful, gleaming young eunuchs, appeared on the scene. "Looks like you're having a spirited discussion, ladies. Mind if I join you?"

Artakama's arm stopped in midair and Barsine pulled her back down to the ground. "You're welcome to join us, Thais. Please have a seat."

Thais nodded and one of her eunuchs conjured a small ornate carpet seemingly out of thin air and spread it out a little above the group of women. "No, put it between them," Thais ordered, pointing to a narrow gap between Barsine and Antigone, forcing both of them to move.

"Now, what were you ladies discussing?" she asked after taking her seat. "No, let me guess. You were discussing the merits of your respective lovers. Am I right?"

"We weren't talking about lovers," Antigone snapped. "But, considering your profession, I can understand why you'd think that."

Barsine jumped in. "That's a great discussion topic, Thais. We all know you were the greatest hetaira in Athens. Tells us about some of the men you've known."

"A hetaira never discusses any of her men." She looked straight at Antigone. "It wouldn't be professional, as you put it. But you ladies are amateurs, right? So, tell me, which one of your lovers have you liked best?"

"I've had only one lover," Barsine lied. Her sister smirked but said nothing. The serving girls maintained a straight face. "But he's the greatest lover the world has ever known."

Thais smiled. "Yes, so I've heard."

"Well, my lover is better than Alexandros," Antigone asserted. "I know that for a fact."

"Why, have you tried them both?" Thais sounded surprised.

"No, of course not. I just know it."

Barsine tried to be conciliatory. "At least we can all agree that Alexandros is the greatest warrior the world has ever known."

"Who says?" Antigone asked. She pressed ahead, heedless of the shocked silence. "My Philotas told me more than once that he and his father, Parmenion, were responsible for all of Alexandros's victories."

No one said anything. Finally, Thais got up. "I think I'd better go." The rest of the party broke up soon thereafter.

Unbeknownst to any of the ladies that afternoon, one of the eunuchs gifted to Thais by Alexandros, before she was shipped off from Persepolis to the Sousa harem, was specifically assigned to keep tabs on her and report any inappropriate statements or behavior. That night, having nothing of interest to report about Thais, the eunuch sent a note detailing Antigone's bragging instead.

******

Our soldiers continued to straggle into camp. Of the five hundred who had volunteered to cross the desert with Alexandros, almost four hundred eventually turned up. The rest of the army, including Koinos's squadrons and the provisions they'd managed to scrounge up, showed up in due course as well.

Morale was not exactly high. We finally had some food but it was mostly hulled barley and legumes – hardly adequate for a feast. And to drink, all that Koinos and his men had managed to bring in was some mead, which was barely tolerable, and some fermented mares' milk, which we found disgusting. Wine was apparently not the beverage of choice in this part of the world. Mostly, we, along with our animals, had to drink the local water that quickly became polluted. The troops, exhausted after two months of high-tempo marching in scorching summer heat, started to come down with various intestinal disorders and insect-born illnesses.

Alexandros was, as always, anxious to press on. A couple of factors prevented our immediate departure. Like it or not, he had to give the troops an opportunity to recover. More importantly, he wasn't sure which way to go. Not only were we in the dark as to the plans of the enemy, we didn't even know where we were and what lay ahead. We found ourselves in unknown lands without any maps. Before we could move, we'd have to obtain some intelligence, a few local guides, and perhaps an interpreter or two. And finally, there was the small matter of Dareios's corpse. Alexandros had to decide what to do with the body of his erstwhile nemesis.

That last problem should've been easy to solve. We could've buried the remains, or cremated them, or simply left them for vultures and wild dogs. Alexandros thought otherwise. Somewhat perversely, he developed an attachment to the deceased former emperor that he'd never evinced while the man was alive. We all remembered the time after Issos when Alexandros instructed us to refer to the ruler of the Persian Empire as "the Persian coward." Now, suddenly, the dead Dareios put Alexandros in a morbid state of mind, causing him to forget momentarily that he, unlike Dareios, was meant to be immortal. As a result, Alexandros decided that the corpse had to be returned to Persepolis for entombment alongside his imperial predecessors. There was only one logistical difficulty: We were a long way from Persepolis and the body was beginning to stink.

Luckily, it turned out that a couple of Egyptian soldiers, who'd been with us since we'd conquered their country almost two years earlier, knew something about embalming. They removed all the viscera and as much of the internal fluids and gases as possible, replacing them with some sort of embalming fluid that they'd managed to concoct. Then, Alexandros generously donated one of Dareios's own imperial gowns, so that the decedent would be suitably attired for his final journey. I found it amusing to watch as tailors struggled to restore the garment to its original size before it could be placed on the corpse.

After the dead emperor was properly preserved, dressed, and made up, the entire army spent the better part of a day observing all the usual, as well as invented-by-the-magoi-for-the-occasion, obsequies. Finally, the dearly departed erstwhile enemy leader was on his way to Persepolis and we could turn to more intractable problems.

Our scouts fanned out over the surrounding countryside and spoke to every man they could dig out of his hidey-hole. They returned with precious little useful information. There had been groups of soldiers fleeing in every direction, except west, which was the direction from which we'd come. The escape routes chosen by the various hightailing groups were impossible to determine. Getting a reliable overview of the surrounding topography proved almost as difficult. We found out that directly to our north was a steep but narrow mountain range, with some manageable passes, especially this time of year. Some distance beyond that mountain range lay the Caspian Sea. And in between the two was a fertile strip of land comprising most of the satrapy of Hyrkania. To the east, as far as we could find out, there was nothing but mountains and savages. To the south was a huge, unsurvivable desert.

Alexandros decided that Bessos must have gone north, chiefly because that seemed the easiest direction to go. Plus, the scouts had located a guide who claimed to know the way across the mountains and into Hyrkania. And, most persuasive of all, the description of what awaited us on the far side sounded like paradise compared to where we were just then.

****

Nabarzanes, with a large contingent of Persian knights, was indeed headed north, toward Hyrkania. Bessos, on the other hand, along with his thousands of ruthless ruffians, rode northeast, roughly in the direction of his home satrapy of Baktria. The two leaders had different mindsets and objectives. Nabarzanes, although a proud Persian aristocrat, wanted mainly to survive. If he could preserve the empire in Persian hands and perhaps make himself the next emperor along the way, all the better. The one thing he couldn't countenance was an uneducated, uncouth, uncontrollable upstart from Baktria arrogating the tiara.

Bessos considered himself the new emperor already. Hadn't he just been crowned Emperor Artaxerxes

Pemptos Bessos? Therefore, in his own mind, he was not fleeing before Alexandros's army; he was actually on the offensive, determined to enforce his claim to the imperial tiara against the usurper from Macedonia. All he had to do was execute a tactical retreat to Baktria, collecting reinforcements as he went, and lure Alexandros into a morass from which he would never emerge.

In fact, as he and his band of brutes rode across the wilds of Parthia, volunteers descended from hilltop hamlets and mountain strongholds to join the nascent national resistance movement. By the time he reached Baktria, he had assembled the largest army ever seen in this part of the world, its ranks swollen by ferocious fighters from all over the eastern provinces and the untamed central Asian steppes beyond the borders of the empire.

The rise of his self-esteem kept pace with the increase in his numbers. He was getting used to the trappings of emperorship. He cut his formerly unkempt hair and beard and had them curled and styled every morning. Any time he was off his horse, he donned Persian-style imperial robes. He conducted regular audiences for his commanders, at which he insisted that they approach him on their knees. He did everything in his power to alienate his formerly devoted troops; however, he was unquestionably growing stronger.

****

Nabarzanes was informed by his spies almost immediately after we'd started our march through the Hyrkanian mountains that, of all the directions Alexandros could've chosen, he'd decided to follow in Nabarzanes's footsteps. The renegade commander's first reaction was to redouble the celerity of his retreat. Taking advantage of the fact that his entire force was mounted, he sped north, toward the eastern bank of the Caspian Sea, bypassing the Hyrkanian capital of Zadrakarta in his haste.

Zadrakarta was already occupied by his fellow satrap Artabazos, who had refused to participate in the satraps' conspiracy against Dareios and had gotten a head start going north. The penultimate calamity, as far as Nabarzanes was concerned, would have been getting caught between Artabazos's forces inside Zadrakarta and Alexandros's army catching up from behind. The ultimate calamity, of course, would have been seeing Bessos gain control of the Persian Empire.

Nabarzanes hoped that, while Alexandros spent his time, energy, resources, and manpower besieging Zadrakarta, he could work on recruiting a whole new Persian army and organizing an imperial revanchist campaign, whether against Alexandros or Bessos was not entirely clear. Unfortunately, two factors undermined Nabarzanes's enlistment efforts. First, those Hyrkanian cutthroats most eager to get into a fight had already left to join Bessos's army. Second, the more perspicacious desperados, hearing that the fabled army of Alexandros was on Nabarzanes's tail, decided that perhaps this was not the moment to join a losing cause.

While Nabarzanes persisted in his efforts to augment his army, he also deployed, as a form of insurance, one of the Persian satraps' favorite gambits. He dispatched a delegation to Alexandros with an offer of full, unconditional, and obsequious surrender. He promised to place all his forces at Alexandros's disposal, offered to join with Alexandros in the fight against the regicide Bessos, and threw himself upon Alexandros's legendary mercy. He calculated that, if worse came to worst, Alexandros would name him satrap of some eastern province or other and then, when the time was right, he could always change his mind and stab Alexandros in the back.

****

I was riding with Alexandros and several other bodyguards in the van of our long column when a small squad of Persian knights materialized out of a defile, riding toward us. They were too few to pose a threat but we stopped and assumed a defensive formation anyway. When they reached us, they dismounted and prostrated themselves at Boukephalas's forelegs.

After a moment, Alexandros deployed one of the few phrases of Persian he had mastered: "You may rise."

The knights rose to their feet, searching for the source of the command. Their leader, keeping his gaze resolutely averted, spoke up. "We bring a message from Lord Nabarzanes to his celestial majesty, Emperor Alexandros." He held out a sealed scroll.

Alexandros, managing to grasp the gist of the words, reached down for the missive but the man, still examining details of Boukephalas's right front hoof, failed to notice the gesture. Poked in the ribs by a comrade standing next to him, he looked up, noticed the hand waving impatiently in the air, turned beet-red, and handed over the scroll.

After prying off the seal and scanning the message, Alexandros broke into delighted laughter. "These guys are certainly true to form." He handed the letter to me. "Well, what do you think? Can I trust this guy?"

I shrugged. "I'm sure he swore allegiance to Dareios many times before he clapped him in irons. So, yes, sire, you can trust him as much as all the other satraps who've surrendered to you before."

"That's not saying much, is it? But he has some first-rate cavalrymen, I hear. I'd rather have them with us than against us."

I tried to suppress a smile. "But sire, can you trust them?"

Alexandros winked. "As much as I can trust any cavalryman."

It was a private joke between us. I don't think any of the bodyguards around us, all of whom were cavalry commanders, heard it.

Alexandros raised his voice. "Alright, everybody. Listen up. Nabarzanes has offered to surrender. I'll decide later whether to accept his offer. In the meantime, search this Persian delegation and very politely make sure they're not armed. Treat them nicely; remember, they're ambassadors, in a manner of speaking. When they've been disarmed, we'll turn them around and ask them to lead us to their commander. And, I want somebody to keep an eye on each one of them, day and night. After all, they're known to be honorable men."

We set off in search of Nabarzanes. But before we caught up to his army, we arrived at Zadrakarta. As we approached, the gates flew open and a sizeable group of dignitaries came out to greet us, led by a distinguished old man.

This time, when Alexandros, once again proudly displaying his newfound Persian proficiency, permitted the prostrate men to rise, the old man stood up and responded in Macedonian-inflected Greek. "No need to torture yourself with our barbaric tongue, your highness. We speak your beautiful, mellifluous native language."

Alexandros arched an eyebrow. "Do I know you, sir?"

"We have met, your majesty, years ago, when you were still a child. But I understand you know my daughter much better."

Alexandros, his wit as keen as his sword, brightened. "You must be Barsine's father. Artabazos is the name, isn't it?"

Artabazos bowed almost to the ground. "At your service, your highness."

"Bring this man a horse!" Alexandros ordered. They rode through the city gates side by side.

Artabazos proved to be an adept host. He threw a lavish banquet for the commanders and, outside the mud walls, an acceptable feast for the men.

The banquet was held in the large but dilapidated reception hall of the ramshackle complex that functioned as the Zadrakarta satrapal palace. Alexandros caused a bit of a stir right at the start. When we marched in, our boots reverberating on the stone pavement, Artabazos was already standing at the large head couch. With a flourish, he offered the place of honor to Alexandros. Of course, our leader would have claimed the preeminent spot with or without the invitation but it was a nice gesture. The surprise came when Alexandros, in turn, motioned for Artabazos to join him on the same couch.

"Since when do we offer places of honor to slimy surrenderers?" Philotas whispered, a bit too loudly. Alexandros pretended not to hear.

Much wine was consumed and many toasts exchanged. The only hiccup occurred when Artabazos grandly placed his 8,000 Greek mercenaries at Alexandros's service.

"We do not take Greek traitors captive," Alexandros growled. "We kill them."

Artabazos was left momentarily speechless. Finally, he raised his hands in protest and perplexity. "But they've been loyal soldiers throughout their enlistments and they're the best fighters in the Persian army. They're too valuable to waste."

"Well, we'll keep them prisoners for now. I'll decide what to do with them later."

****

On the shores of the Caspian Sea, Nabarzanes, hearing nothing from his ambassadors, grew impatient. When spies he'd sent to Zadrakarta reported that Alexandros and Artabazos seemed to be getting on quite well, he decided he couldn't wait any longer.

He, along with all his Persian knights, retraced their route back to Zadrakarta. Once the mud walls of the capital became visible, he ordered his army to stay out of sight and then rode on, under a banner of truce, accompanied by a single Greek-speaking aide. When the two lone riders approached the city gate, they were promptly seized by the guards and hauled before Alexandros.

Nabarzanes repeated his offer of unconditional surrender in person, while looking from his knees up to the enthroned Alexandros. The new king of kings listened to the translation without expression.

"I accept your surrender, Nabarzanes," he finally said. "As you know, we always treat those who submit to my authority with mercy. Well, except traitors, of course. Those we kill. But you can understand that, can't you?"

Nabarzanes, still on his knees, blanched but quickly recovered his composure. "Your power, wisdom, and mercy are already legendary, your most merciful majesty."

"So, Nabarzanes, are you a traitor or is your decision to join our campaign genuine?"

"Only a fool would fail to come running to your standard, your celestial invincibility."

Alexandros chuckled. "You're apparently a slow runner, Nabarzanes. How long were you in the previous emperor's service?"

"Six years, your majesty. He chose me as one of his commanders soon after becoming emperor.

"What did you command in Dareios's army?"

"Cavalry, your exalted excellency. Soon after I supported his claim to the emperorship, he named me hazahrapatish of heavy knights, the strongest arm of his army. What you'd call chiliarch. Eventually I became his second in command."

"And yet, you didn't hesitate to shackle your anointed emperor in chains when it suited your ambitions."

Nabarzanes was too stunned to remain on his knees. He fell back on his face while considering his response.

"That's a malicious lie," he finally said, speaking into a crack in the paving stones. "I was always a loyal supporter of the former emperor, merciful majesty. Whoever told you otherwise was lying."

Hearing no response, he continued pleading into the crack, his voice losing some of its resonance. "It was Bessos who placed the emperor in chains. I did my best to oppose him. In fact, I saved the emperor's life when Bessos first deposed him. Unfortunately, Dareios attempted to escape and Bessos killed him as they fought."

Alexandros maintained his silence.

"Kill me right now if you don't believe me, your most wise and merciful divinity."

"It's a tempting suggestion." Alexandros's voice was as dry as the desert. "Take him away."

As he was being lifted off the ground by a couple of guards, Nabarzanes was still pleading. "But I bring you almost 6,000 Persian knights, Emperor Alexandros. The best fighting force in the empire."

"Put him back down!" Alexandros was suddenly furious. "If they are so wonderful, why do they keep losing?"

"Warriors can only be as good as their commander, your invincible majesty. These warriors were poorly led."

"I thought you were their commander."

'I was and I take full responsibility."

"Let me ask you something, Nabarzanes." Alexandros's voice returned to a conversational tone. "Were you in command of the Persian heavy cavalry at the battle we fought near the Gulf of Issos?"

Nabarzanes, growing tired of speaking to the pavement, sat up and faced his interlocutor. "I was, your majesty."

"And you lost, didn't you?"

"Yes, we did lose ... but only because Dareios departed the field of battle prematurely."

"And were you in command of the Persian heavy cavalry at the Battle of Gaugamela?"

"I was, your majesty."

"In fact, it was your job to protect the person of your emperor, wasn't it?"

"Yes, your majesty. That was one of the assignments given to my knights."

"And again, you failed miserably."

"Your majesty was unstoppable that day." For once, Nabarzanes sounded sincere, even awestruck, as he recalled Alexandros slicing through his knights.

"It was your Persian knights who failed to stop me, right?"

"They were ordinary humans, trying to stop a deity."

Alexandros laughed. "Well, that much is true."

Nabarzanes, sensing an opening, rose to his knees and joined his hands in supplication. "That's exactly why I, along with my 6,000 heavy knights, wish to serve your celestial brilliance in any way we can."

"And they are, after all, the best fighting force in the empire ..."

Nabarzanes interrupted, hope straightening his spine once again. "That's exactly right, your majesty."

"... except when poorly commanded." Alexandros's voice was dripping with sarcasm.

Nabarzanes attempted to fight back. "I have never failed them, your majesty. Others, above me, may have."

"Is that so?" Alexandros was beginning to enjoy himself. "Even before the Battle of Issos, didn't Emperor Dareios send you, along with your Persian knights, to Phrygia to intercept my supply and communication lines and to cut off my route of escape to Macedonia after what he assumed would be a Persian victory?"

"Yes, that did happen."

"We, my army and I, were long gone. All I had left in Phrygia was a small holding force of Macedonian veterans, commanded by an old general named Antigonos Monophthalmos. You fought three pitched battles against good old One-Eye's undermanned forces and lost each time, didn't you?"

Nabarzanes slumped, unable to muster a response.

Alexandros pressed home his advantage. "Under your command, Nabarzanes, the best fighting force in the empire keeps losing. It seems to me it's time for a change in command."

The former Persian chiliarch hung his head, resigned to his fate. "Yes, your majesty."

"Alright, take him away." The interrogation was over.

****

We ended up staying in Zadrakarta for almost two months. Alexandros concluded that the troops needed a morale boost and some rest and recuperation before launching our campaign to eradicate Bessos and take full control of the empire. He even encouraged his soldiers to marry local women, if they were so inclined, officiating at the ceremonies and presenting small gifts to the happy couples. Most of the newlywed men ended up staying behind as a permanent garrison.

As satrap, he reappointed a Persian nobleman named Phrataphernes, who had been Dareios's satrap of Hyrkania. Phrataphernes had run away after news of Dareios's fall had reached Zadrakarta but then returned and surrendered, once it was clear that Alexandros was in control. Apparently, Alexandros preferred loyal cowards to brave traitors.

Speaking of traitors, Alexandros eventually made a deal with Nabarzanes. After the former chiliarch agreed to bring in his heavy knights without a fight and to facilitate their integration into our cavalry, Alexandros refrained from executing him. Nabarzanes even received some minor magisterial office but was prohibited from leaving Zadrakarta or engaging in any military activities. Both the satrap, Phrataphernes, and the garrison commander were explicitly instructed to keep an eye on him and ship him under guard to Alexandros if he caused any trouble.

Although Zadrakarta was no Babylon, the troops were happy enough with their holiday. The only thing that bothered them was the integration of the Persian knights into our cavalry. It didn't matter how many times Alexandros tried to explain that difficult fighting lay ahead and these cavalrymen were too valuable to waste. Even after daily drills, our soldiers still thought of them as former enemies who couldn't speak Greek.

Finally, the summer was at an end and the challenge posed by Bessos, the regicide and pretender, could not be postponed any longer. The problem was that we had no idea where he was or how to get there. We assumed that he and his army were in Baktria, which lay somewhere to the east of Hyrkania. But there were no roads, no maps, no landmarks to follow, and no clues as to what obstacles, manmade and natural, we might encounter along the way.

We quickly discovered that informants with reliable knowledge of geography beyond our immediate vicinity were hard to find; that the locals spoke weird languages and interpreters were few and far between; that the farther we marched, the more primitive, nomadic, and savage the inhabitants would become; and that the only constant would be the natives' uniform and unremitting resistance to all outsiders, especially those who showed up as organized armies.

Artabazos, whom Alexandros decided to bring along as his special advisor, did his best to help out. Unfortunately, his knowledge of the Persian Empire, despite his many years of service, was confined mostly to the western half of the vast realm.

And so, on a fine, early-autumn day, the endless column that constituted Alexandros's army left Zadrakarta. Riding among the Companion Cavalry were squadrons of Persian knights, commanded by their own Persian commanders (not including Nabarzanes, who'd been left behind). And bringing up the rear, marching behind the baggage train, were Artabazos's 8,000 Greek mercenaries. Without a word to any of us commanders, Alexandros had evidently decided that they were also too valuable to waste.

Chapter 6 – Into the Morass

Artabazos didn't sound too sure of himself. "I think it's more than a thousand miles to Baktria, your majesty. Maybe two thousand miles."

"Well, which one is it? One thousand or two thousand?"

"It's probably closer to two, your majesty."

"You mean to tell me that it's twice as far from Zadrakarta to Baktra as it was from Persepolis to Zadrakarta?"

"Yes, your majesty. That's what I've heard. And keep in mind there are no royal roads for us to march on. In fact, I doubt there are any roads at all. This is wild, untamed country ahead of us. Plus, there are things between here and there."

"What kinds of things?"

"Well, we have a choice. We can march through unsurvivable deserts or impassable mountains. Chances are we'll have to do some of each. And, don't forget, there are a couple of large satrapies we have to cross to get to Baktria. I'm pretty sure that Parthia and Areia lie between Hyrkania and Baktria."

Alexandros shrugged. "In that case, we'd better get going."

****

One afternoon, soon after we'd set off from Zadrakarta, we spotted a man astride a strange, two-humped camel coming toward us. He wore an ensemble of untanned animal skins, colorful scarves, and a felt cap, all of it accessorized by lots of bracelets and jangly bangles. Despite this profusion of apparel, most of his dark, leathery skin and luxuriant, unkempt hair remained exposed to the elements.

When we approached, he alighted from his beast and stood akimbo, blocking our way. Even in the fading light, his broad, ivory-toothed smile lit up his tattooed face. After the riders in our vanguard stopped, he waved a noisy right hand and shouted something over and over again. Miraculously, someone in our ranks recognized the language and volunteered to interpret.

The fashionably attired Skythian told us his name was Nuraddin. He asked to speak with our chieftain.

Alexandros, intrigued by his appearance, readily identified himself. However, when Nuraddin motioned for him to dismount in order to speak face to face, Alexandros declined. Nuraddin shrugged and remounted his camel. The two set off at a leisurely pace, trailed by the interpreter and a phalanx of senior commanders eager to witness what would happen next.

Nuraddin told Alexandros that he knew the country well and offered to serve as our guide. After our many misadventures with purported guides, our leader was skeptical but found the man's enthusiasm and enterprise hard to resist.

"We don't need a local guide," Alexandros informed him. "We're going a long, long way, to a country called Baktria."

Our would-be guide smiled. "I've been there many times, chief," he assured Alexandros. "In Baktria and many places beyond."

Alexandros looked over his shoulder. "How much harm can he do?" he asked us in Greek. "Hephaistion, give him a couple of coins."

Surprisingly, Nuraddin didn't accept the proffered bounty; he expected to be paid more. After some haggling, he and Hephaistion reached a mutually acceptable arrangement and Nuraddin took his place at the head of our column. He also proved to be largely superfluous.

Soon enough we found out that, although there was no actual road, the path forward was as easy to follow as the Processional Way in Babylon. The mounds of debris left by previous travelers were as regular as mileposts on the Royal Road. Any ground suitable for a camp showed evidence of previous occupation. We could judge the rate of our progress by counting the number of abandoned campsites we passed every day. Nuraddin did prove his worth, however, by pointing out each spring, watering hole, trading post, supply depot, and market town along our route.

A week into our march, we met a large caravan going in the opposite direction. Three hundred camels, each carrying two or three large bundles, were herded along by two dozen heavily-armed men, riding very large horses, almost as big as Boukephalas. To our untrained eyes, they looked to be members of the same tribe as Nuraddin but he took great offense at the suggestion. He called them Massagetai, spitting the name out like someone who'd accidentally bit off his neighbor's ear. "They're robbers, cheaters, and thieves."

"I take it you've done business with them," Alexandros suggested.

"Oh, yes, chief. Many times."

"What are they carrying in those bags?"

"Silk, mostly. But also metal ornaments," Nuraddin shook his bangles to illustrate, "leather goods, jade, spices, ceramics, various luxuries. It's stuff for fancy people like your friend over there." He nodded toward Artabazos. "Not warriors like you, chief."

"You haven't seen him on his throne," Philotas muttered. Nuraddin didn't understand and Alexandros pretended not to hear.

We met, or at least saw in the distance, a couple of other caravans, also headed in the opposite direction. It was apparently the height of the travel season and we were marching along a busy, albeit invisible, highway.

****

Finally, we reached Susia, where we came to a fork in the road. Susia was the largest town in eastern Parthia and the hub of several important routes. In truth, calling it a town might have been an overstatement. What it was, mostly, was a huge open-air market teeming with people, dogs, and flies.

Long, meandering aisles of comestibles, both plants and animals, the latter usually still alive, intersected with lanes dedicated to the sale or barter of fabrics, baskets, pottery, weapons, and other dry goods. An alley of tiny sheds and stalls occupied by purveyors of jewelry, amulets, stamp seals and cylinders, ornamental objects, and votive offerings was squeezed in between various large-animal corrals.

Soothsayers, scribes, and priests tended to have their own booths. Magicians, acrobats, prostitutes, and thieves mingled freely with buyers, sellers, traders, and gawkers. The press of humanity was overwhelming. Men and women, dressed in every imaginable garb, hurried, huckstered, and haggled in languages none of us could understand.

What was missing were actual, permanent streets, large stone buildings, temples, battlements – things that would make the place a city. Instead, warehouses, eating and drinking establishments, brothels, and latrines surrounded the periphery of the market, seemingly scattered at random intervals. There were hardly enough dwelling places to house either the resident or transient populations. They must have found shelter in huge encampments of tents and yurts that stretched out in every direction. If there were any temples, baths, or municipal buildings, I didn't see them.

"Well, this is as far as I go, chief," Nuraddin announced upon our arrival. "You, on the other hand, have a choice to make."

Our guide explained that the route we had been following separated into two principal branches. Going northeast, we'd be marching mostly through flat steppes on our way to Baktria, although we would have to cross a couple of major rivers. It was the easier and faster route, except for one major drawback. It led through the lands of the Massagetai, who were not known for their hospitality toward invading armies.

Going south, we would be staying within the boundaries of the Persian Empire. The route would be longer and more mountainous and would take us to Artakoana, the capital of Areia province, before we could turn once again toward Baktria.

Alexandros chose the southern route. "We have to assert our authority over all our satrapies sooner or later. We might as well pay a visit to Areia along the way."

****

We reached Artakoana three weeks after leaving Susia. Although it felt as if mountains were closing in on us from every direction, the route turned out to be fairly easy. We followed the course of the Hareios River most of the way. As a result, even though we were steadily gaining altitude, we were able to maintain a good tempo.

Provisions also turned out to be plentiful for once. The valley was fertile and the harvest had just been brought in. Best of all, we noticed that many of the slopes rising from the floor of the valley were covered with grapevines heavy with ripe fruit. The locals, used to dealing with Persian overlords, didn't cause any problems. As soon as they realized we were willing to pay for whatever we took, their main interest was in extracting as many gold darics from our quartermasters as possible.

When we came within sight of Artakoana, the holdover satrap, Satibarzanes, rode out to meet us. He greeted Alexandros with the slithering obsequiousness which we had observed from so many other Dareios appointees. Needless to say, Satibarzanes surrendered both the city and the province and pledged his eternal loyalty to Alexandros.

Artabazos, who was in a position to know, tried to warn Alexandros that Satibarzanes was one of the co-conspirators who had participated in the overthrow of Dareios. "He was right there, your celestial highness, kissing Dareios's feet until the moment he jumped up and cut his throat."

"I thought it was Bessos who murdered the previous emperor."

"As far as I know, your highness, it was Bessos who administered the final blow. I was speaking figuratively when I said Satibarzanes cut Dareios's throat. You'll recall I left before they killed the former emperor. All I know for sure is that this man was among the satraps who pulled Dareios down. When you arrived on the scene, he hightailed it back to his satrapy and now he's pretending to be your loyal servant."

"I hear what you're saying, Artabazos, but right now we've got to catch up to Bessos and destroy his army. I'll leave some men behind to make sure that, this time, Satibarzanes keeps his promises."

******

Artakoana was slightly more deserving of the city appellation than Susia but not much. It was also mostly a caravan hub with a large marketplace. Still, it boasted actual streets lined with mudbrick dwellings, a modest satrapal palace, a wooden but rugged fort, and some places of worship. A middling mud wall, topped by a wooden palisade, surrounded the entire town, except for the marketplace.

Per expected custom, Satibarzanes invited Alexandros and the senior commanders to a lavish feast at the palace. Included among the invited commanders were our newly acquired Persian colleagues who had, until recently, served under Dareios and Nabarzanes. Alexandros took the time to change into full imperial regalia before making his appearance, a gesture not calculated to delight his Macedonian commanders. These rugged fighters, who had served Alexandros and, in many cases, his father before him for years, had already been displeased by the sight of Alexandros sharing the place of honor at the Zadrakarta banquet with Artabazos. In an apparent effort to mollify them, Alexandros invited Hephaistion to share the place of honor this time. On the other hand, when our new Persian colleagues prostrated themselves upon his entrance, Alexandros was clearly pleased. He obviously expected that the humiliation of the Persians would appeal to the Macedonians. He was only partly right. The veteran commanders enjoyed the spectacle of groveling Persian noblemen but, at the same time, they profoundly disapproved of the Persian airs being put on by a young man who, until relatively recently, used to treat them as brothers in arms.

The troops, who were bivouacked outside the city walls, were invited to their own generous repast, staged in the marketplace, which had been cleared of merchants, hawkers, hucksters, and assorted riffraff for the occasion. Their meal featured many spicy, exotic dishes whose ingredients were impossible to discern. Wine flowed freely at both venues and no one asked to see the recipes.

The banquet at the palace lasted well past dawn. It might have continued much longer had a dust-covered soldier not barged in. He hesitated in the doorway, not sure what to do next. Alexandros, who seemed on the verge of passing out minutes earlier, was suddenly alert. He beckoned the soldier over and listened attentively to his whispered report.

The two walked out of the hall, immersed in a sotto voce conversation. When Alexandros returned a few minutes later, he was all business. "Gentlemen, the party is over. I have just learned that, while we're lolling about here in Artakoana, Bessos's army in Baktria is growing in strength every day. We have no time to waste. We march at dawn tomorrow."

The Macedonians in the room, having heard that last sentence so many times before, couldn't help but smile. The Persians' faces betrayed various degrees of consternation.

While we were getting our units ready to march, Alexandros was busy making the necessary administrative arrangements. In keeping with his usual custom and against the advice of Artabazos, he reappointed Satibarzanes satrap of Areia after receiving fulsome assurances and solemn oaths from the oleaginous opportunist. Not being completely naïve, he also left behind a small garrison, consisting mostly of elderly and sick veterans. He appointed an experienced company captain named Anaxippos, who was both elderly and sick at that moment, as commander of the garrison, with instructions to keep a close eye on Satibarzanes.

****

We were hardly out of Artakoana when soldiers started to complain of intestinal distress. In camp that night, the latrines were busier than a whorehouse after payday. By next morning, a significant number of men were too ill to continue marching. They were put on horses or placed in wagons and carried along. Many more were sick by the end of that day. The next morning, a few of the men were dead. The number of seriously ill men made it impractical to transport them any farther.

Alexandros was raging. He was convinced the men had been poisoned during the feast in Artakoana, although this seemed unlikely given the lapse of time and the gradual spread of the disease. If he could've done it, Alexandros would've split himself in two. Half of him wanted to go back and kill every man in Artakoana, starting with Satibarzanes. But the other half wanted to catch and defeat Bessos more.

Muttering darkly about the lack of loyalty and honor in the world, he decided to press ahead, toward Baktria, with all possible speed. The ill and the dead would have to be left behind. Those who recovered could catch up later.

"You can't just leave them here," protested Philotas, whose brother Nikanoros was among the ill. "They need people to protect them, feed and care for them and, if necessary, see to it that they are buried with full military honors."

"Of course. I didn't mean to imply we'd abandon them by themselves. We'll leave food, drink, a couple of medics, and a squadron of cavalry to protect them and to escort them to us, once they recover. I just need a volunteer to command the operation."

Philotas, who wanted to remain with his gravely ill brother, immediately raised his hand.

Alexandros nodded. "You've got the job, my friend." And with that, we were off to Baktria.

****

Three days later, a soldier on a lathered horse caught up to us. "Sire," he yelled, without bothering to dismount, "Satibarzanes has revolted and massacred our entire garrison."

"I should've killed that snake when I had the chance." It took Alexandros ten minutes to put together an elite cavalry force of 1,000 men and set off on the return trip to Artakoana. He left Krateros in command of the rest of the army, with orders to follow with all deliberate speed. We covered the 100-mile distance back to Artakoana in less than two days. The main-force army took five full days. Both groups made sure to give wide berth to the encampment of our sick and dying soldiers.

Satibarzanes started running as soon as he saw the dust of our hooves. When we barged into the city, there were only a couple thousand rebels left and they fled as fast as their horses, camels, mules, asses, or feet would carry them. Our job was to ride them down and kill them as they ran. After what they did to our garrison, there would be no quarter given.

Those rebels lacking horses took refuge in a primeval stand of trees, choked with decaying logs, thorny bushes, and impassable undergrowth.

Alexandros threw a cordon around the grove. "Torch it," he ordered, once we were in position. "And kill anyone who comes out."

Only a handful of men ran out of the inferno, some with their clothes ablaze. They were massacred before they took too many steps beyond the flames. We could hear, and smell, the rest of them perish.

We searched the grove after the embers cooled. We couldn't tell much by looking at the incinerated bodies but we were pretty sure Satibarzanes, along with his mounted rebels, was not among the dead. Alexandros's fury knew no bounds.

We returned to Artakoana to await the arrival of the rest of our army. Alexandros spent his time drinking and ranting. For the self-proclaimed darling of destiny, he was decidedly dissatisfied with his recent run of luck. He felt the reins of power over the entire Persian Empire as well as mainland Greece and all the islands of the Aegean tantalizingly tickling the palms of his hands. And yet, he was unable to tame this unruly, three-headed beast. Obviously, someone out there had to be responsible. But who? The most obvious candidate was Bessos and he certainly received his fair share of invective. But Bessos had plenty of company. All the perfidious satraps, starting with

Satibarzanes and Nabarzanes, featured prominently in Alexandros's diatribes. After a few more cups of wine, his focus shifted to the two traitors in Pella, Antipatros and Kassandros. And, as night turned to dawn, he tried a few tirades against his own commanders on for size. The absent Philotas starred in one particularly caustic screed. Finally, to everyone's relief, Alexandros passed out and went to sleep.

Soon after Krateros arrived with the bulk of the army, our spies collected incontrovertible evidence that Satibarzanes, along with his cavalry, escaped to the south and joined forces with Barsaentes, the satrap of Drangiana and Arakhosia. Apparently, their aim was to raise rebellions in as many of the eastern provinces as they could. Alexandros, to his immense frustration, was forced, once again, to defer his pursuit of Bessos in order to deal with this new, more immediately pressing problem.

The one bright spot amidst all the insurrections was the arrival of additional reinforcements from Thrake, sent by Antipatros, and from Lydia and its environs, sent by Antigonos Monophthalmos. Evidently, there was no shortage of men in other parts of Alexandros's empire eager to float their fortunes on the irresistible tide of his conquests. And the newcomers were more than welcome in light of the ongoing attrition of our numbers to sickness, fighting, and loss of morale.

Before leaving Artakoana, Alexandros made new, sturdier administrative arrangements in an effort to prevent additional rebellious outbreaks in Areia as soon as we marched off to Drangiana. Instead of simply leaving a garrison in Artakoana, he founded a new, fortified capital for the province, called Alexandria-in-Areia, a few miles to the south of the existing capital. This new, strategically situated city would be permanently settled by older, fading veterans, by troublemakers, and by men who'd found wives and sired children and were eager to settle down. The inhabitants might have come from diverse parts of the Greek-speaking world but they shared a common bond forged in the crucible of Philippos's and Alexandros's campaigns. Their job was to serve as an outpost of Greek civilization and culture in a primitive land and as a bulwark against unremitting waves of rebellions, reprisals, reversionary impulses, and reactionary movements, constantly lapping against, and eroding, imperial authority.

Alexandria-in-Areia became the home base of the garrison, the administrative center of the province, and the satrapal seat of Areia. It also became the template for Alexandros's new approach to unifying and maintaining control of his growing empire. Unfortunately, there weren't enough Macedonian and Greek commanders or administrators in his army to serve as satraps in all the Persian provinces. Besides, Alexandros needed those men for the upcoming campaigns and battles. As a result, for better or worse, he was forced once again to select a Persian nobleman, Arsakes, as the new satrap of Areia. He hoped, despite all his experience to the contrary, that this one might prove to be loyal.

****

As soon as the administrative arrangements for Areia were in place, we were once again on the march, heading south toward Drangiana, in pursuit of Satibarzanes and Barsaentes. It was an easy march, through plains and low mountain passes, with plenty of food and drink and nary a hostile bandit or rebel in sight. And yet, nobody was happy. Alexandros was frustrated by his inability to confront Bessos, defeat his army, stamp out all remaining pockets of resistance, and consolidate his control of the former Persian Empire. His Macedonian and Greek commanders were distressed by the presence of Persian and other barbarian troops in our ranks, by the rising influence of former Persian commanders, nobles, and courtiers in Alexandros's upper echelons, and by the increasing Persianization of Alexandros himself in his dress, manner, and attitudes. And the ordinary soldiers, especially the veterans, became ever more vocal in expressing their desire to start marching back home, where they could once again enjoy their wives, children, and the fruits of their victories, instead of wading even deeper into an unremitting quagmire.

Fortunately, our enemies had no idea of the army's sinking morale. They still lived in dread of our fearsome reputation. In fact, as we approached Phrada, the capital of Drangiana, both Satibarzanes and Barsaentes took off once again, leaving the city – such as it was – undefended. Satibarzanes and his small band of rebels disappeared into the mountainous wilderness somewhere between Areia, Drangiana, and Arakhosia. Barsaentes and his gang of supporters fled to a mountainous region to the south of Drangiana ruled by an Indian raja named Sambos. The two had served side by side at the Battle of Gaugamela and had apparently developed a friendship. Sambos was not interested in joining an uprising against Alexandros but he did afford refuge to Barsaentes and his men.

Alexandros was at his wits' end. Brushfires of insurrection kept flaring up all around us, while the wildfire of Bessos's rebellion continued to grow ever larger. Plagued by atypical indecision, he concluded that we all needed some rest. After occupying Phrada, which was actually a more prosperous city than Artakoana, and taking possession of all the municipal buildings and their contents, he gave the soldiers a couple of weeks off. They were told to set up camp between Phrada and the nearby Seistan Lake and given liberty to hunt, fish, or loot what little the local populace might own.

The commanders were told to scout the vicinity of Phrada for a suitable location to build another fortified garrison town. It turned out that remnants of a previous fort still existed atop a nearby hill. When the men grew tired of hunting, fishing, and looting, they were put to work renovating and enlarging the outer walls of this new upper town, which was to become another link in the chain of strongholds intended to maintain control of these turbulent eastern provinces. For reasons best known to Alexandros, he named this outpost Prophthasia, meaning anticipation.

Chapter 7 – Philotas

Philotas finally caught up to us while we were relaxing on the shores of Seistan Lake. He brought only bad news. His brother Nikanoros had succumbed to the illness which had swept through the army after our stay at Artakoana, as had more than half the soldiers left behind in the improvised hospital camp. The soldiers who'd managed to survive buried the dead and then, under Philotas's command, made the long, slow march to rejoin the rest of the army. They were alive but far from fully recovered. Physically, they were pale, hunched, and emaciated. Their mental state was even worse than their physical appearance and they did little to lift the morale of their comrades when they rejoined our encampment.

Alexandros, growing more impatient with each passing day, supervised construction of the dwellings and fortress walls of Prophthasia and mingled with the troops in an attempt to enthuse them for the coming campaigns into unknown deserts, mountains, and wilderness at the edge of the world. His efforts met with limited success.

Alexandros designated the troops showing the most recalcitrance for garrison duty in the newly-founded stronghold, under the command of an old Macedonian warhorse. He named Arsames, one of Artabazos's many sons, as the new satrap of Drangiana and spent the rest of his time seeing to administrative arrangements for the satrapy, making preparations for the upcoming campaign against Bessos, and brooding.

He was sitting in his tent, watching the leaves fall, on a gloomy, late autumn morning when one of his guards alerted him to the arrival of a messenger from Sousa. "Get whatever messages he brought. I don't need to see him."

Handed a number of scrolls, tubes, tablets, and scraps, he methodically read all the reports, letters, and messages until coming to a wooden tablet sewn tight in a leather pouch. The short note painted on the polished tablet struck him like a blow to the head.

Sometimes, when a boulder sits perched on the verge of a chasm, all it takes is a slight nudge from a twig blown by the wind to push it over the edge. Such was the effect of the tablet on Alexandros's febrile mind.

The note seemed innocuous enough. It simply quoted Antigone's ill-advised statement that: "My Philotas told me more than once that he and his father, Parmenion, were responsible for all of Alexandros's victories." During happier times, Alexandros would've laughed it off, perhaps with a dose of good-natured ribbing directed at the father-and-son team. Not this time.

Ever since leaving Persepolis, Alexandros had been agonizing over the rising discontent among his soldiers, especially the Macedonian veterans. However, it had never crossed his mind – until that very moment – that they could actually mutiny against his leadership. Among other things, who else could they possibly follow? Now, suddenly, the obvious answer popped into his head. They could follow the most experienced, battle-tested, respected commander in the army, the man who'd been a senior commander since before any of them enlisted, the man who'd successfully seen them through battle after battle. Admittedly, he didn't have the youth, élan, charisma, and favor of the gods that Alexandros enjoyed but he was certainly competent enough to lead them out of Asia and back home, which is what most of them wanted.

Alexandros shook his head. It was a ridiculous idea. Parmenion had been the most loyal servant of both Philippos and Alexandros his entire adult life. It was inconceivable that he would lead a revolt against Alexandros. Plus, Parmenion's one remaining son, who was finally back in camp, was in effect a hostage for his father's good behavior, although Alexandros had never thought of Philotas that way before. "Still," Alexandros muttered, "I shouldn't have humiliated the old man by leaving him in Ekbatana." Pleased with his new insight, Alexandros almost smiled.

Then a new thought struck him. *Parmenion would never lead a mutiny but Philotas certainly might.* He was a terrific cavalry commander, universally admired by his troops. He had been, ever since the start of the invasion, the commander of the first squadron of the Companion Cavalry, and thus hipparchos or the overall commander of the entire division. He was also an arrogant prick who liked to question orders. *He probably thinks he's a better leader than I am.*

"This is insane," Alexandros said out loud to his empty tent. "All these pressures are starting to get to me. I will not let such thoughts cross my mind again." But they did.

****

After a late-afternoon meal, Philotas was rushing into Alexandros's command tent for a senior staff meeting when he was intercepted by a dandified albeit disheveled young man. "Sir," the painted youth exhaled, enveloping Philotas in a cloud of cheap wine vapor, "I must speak with you."

"I'm late for a staff meeting, rentboy. Surely, this can wait 'til tomorrow."

"No, no. I must speak to you now."

"Well, what is it?"

"May we step into that tent over there, sir? For privacy."

"Listen ... And what's your name, by the way?"

"Kebalinos, sir."

"Listen, Kebalinos, I have no problem with the way you earn your living but personally I prefer women. So, will you please go away?"

"I'm not here to proposition you, sir. I have important information."

The man's voice was fairly quiet but he leaned in for extra emphasis. Philotas could just imagine the commentary their encounter would elicit from his fellow commanders if this discussion continued outside Alexandros's tent. "Alright, let's go in there but make it quick. And keep your voice down!"

"Thank you, sir," the painted man said once inside the tent. "I come to you because you're the commander of the Companion Cavalry. It's about one of your men – Dimnos is his name."

"The name rings a bell but I can't quite put a face to it right now. What about him?"

"He's my little brother Nikomachos's lover."

"You mean regular customer?"

"Well, you could put it that way. But I think they had genuine feelings for each other."

"I don't judge my men based on their sexual preferences. Especially on the march, when we have so few women around. Anyway, you say, '*had* feelings for each other.' I take it they've had a falling out. I'm sorry to hear that but I really have to get to my meeting. So, can we *please* talk about this tomorrow?"

"No, no, sir. It's not that at all. In fact, they were together earlier this evening. While they went about their business, Dimnos let slip a terrible secret. My little brother got scared and, as soon as he could, ran to tell me. I didn't want to be the one keeping the secret either, so I decided to let you know right away. Because you're the man's commander."

"Well, he's not in my squadron, so he has his own squadron commander, but indirectly I guess I'm his commander. Anyway, what's this big secret?"

"Dimnos let slip that he's planning to assassinate our king three nights from now."

Suddenly, it all became clear in Philotas's mind. The cavalryman and the male prostitute had a fight, probably about an unpaid fee. To get back at his deadbeat customer, the prostitute made up this inherently implausible accusation, which he tested out on his brother. Of course, both of them were intoxicated at the time. Next thing you know, here is this guy keeping me from my meeting.

"Listen, Kebalinos – or whatever your name is – why are you bothering me with this? Why didn't you go directly to Alexandros and tell him your story? Or better yet, send your little brother to tell his story directly to Alexandros. But wait 'til the morning. Now, good night."

"But sir, men like me and my brother could never get close enough to our king to say anything to him. That's why I'm here. I'm asking you to tell our king."

"Alright, alright. I'll be sure to do that. Now get out!"

And with that, Philotas shoved Kebalinos out of the tent and went to his meeting. He didn't give the matter a second thought.

****

Kebalinos was lying in wait for him when he returned to the command tent the next evening. "Have you told the king, sir?"

Philotas was not in a good mood. "Have some patience, man. Maybe I'll get a chance to tell him tonight."

Kebalinos hung around in the shadows, waiting to be summoned into the king's presence. The next day, he gave up on Philotas and approached one of Alexandros's pages as the youngster was about to enter the command tent. The young lad, who was used to fetching water and polishing armor, had no idea what he was supposed to do under these circumstances. One thing he did know was that pages were not expected to exercise discretion. So, he shrugged, continued walking into the tent, and told Alexandros what Kebalinos had just told him.

Alexandros was instantly interested. He had Kebalinos brought in, listened to his story, and asked a few questions. As soon as the interview ended, he sent a squad of his personal guards to find Dimnos and bring him back for questioning.

Unfortunately, something went awry with the service of the summons and Dimnos didn't survive his arrest. He was still breathing when dragged into Alexandros's tent but bleeding heavily from a couple of wounds in his torso and no longer conscious. He expired a few minutes later.

Deprived of an opportunity to interrogate the alleged would-be assassin, Alexandros exploded into one of his increasingly frequent rages. The aides and guards in the tent, having experienced these outbursts before, did their best to remove themselves from his presence.

Alexandros's mind flashed back to another assassination attempt six years earlier. Of course, in that case the assassin actually succeeded in murdering

Alexandros's father. It was the same story all over again. Some soldier reported to Philippos that he had been sexually abused by other soldiers; Philippos ignored the complaint; the aggrieved soldier snuck up on him during a parade and killed him. The soldier was then chased down and killed in turn, before he could be questioned.

Needless to say, Alexandros had never forgotten his father's assassination. More importantly, he never got over his conviction, which may have been based on inside knowledge, that the assassin had not acted alone. [15] The difficulty lay in identifying the co-conspirators. Rather disingenuously, Alexandros steered suspicions in the direction of a cousin named Amyntas who, coincidentally, had a colorable claim to the royal diadem.

The day Philippos was murdered, Amyntas was out of town, which, according to Alexandros, pointed to his guilt. He was allegedly hunting in the deep forests of Lynkestis with two brothers named Heromenes and Arrhabaios, who were scions of that region's leading family. Their youngest brother, Alexandros, was a member of the Companion Cavalry and had not gone on the hunt. (To differentiate between the two Alexandroi, the younger brother of Heromenes and Arrhabaios was referred to as

---

[15] There was widespread suspicion at the time that Alexandros, and especially his mother Olympias, had played a role in inspiring Philippos's assassination. If so, Alexandros had managed, by this point, to banish that aspect of the conspiracy from his memory.

Alexandros of Lynkestis, or simply as Lynkestis, whenever there was a risk of confusion.)

Alexandros, the newly-minted king, ordered Amyntas's arrest but the young man couldn't be found. The two brothers, however, were located and brought in for questioning. Alexandros of Lynkestis, in addition to being a member of the Companion Cavalry, also happened to be Antipatros's son-in-law. Based on his father-in-law's advice, he was the first officer to rush up to the new king to pledge his allegiance, thus managing to deflect the king's suspicions. His two older brothers were not as fortunate. When they proved unable to name their co-conspirators during questioning, they were subjected to remorseless torture. On the point of death, they signed the confessions prepared for them. They were then dragged before the army. Alexandros recited the charges against them and read out their confessions. The army, functioning as the jury, voted to convict them by voice vote. The brothers were summarily executed. Amyntas was eventually located and murdered as well, without benefit of a mock trial.

All that history flashed through Alexandros's mind as he convinced himself that not only had he been fortunate to escape assassination but that his would-be assassin couldn't have been plotting against his life all alone. There had to be some co-conspirators.

Kebalinos and his younger brother Nichomachos were brought in for questioning. Neither one was able to identify any conspirators, other than the dead Dimnos. An increasingly exasperated Alexandros rounded on the brothers. "If you're not involved in this conspiracy, why did it take you two days to get this information to me?"

"We tried, sire, to inform you immediately," Kebalinos blurted out. "I went to see one of your senior commanders and told him the whole story. He promised to get the information to you. When he hadn't done it in two days, I tried to get it to you using a different route."

A skeptical Alexandros raised an eyebrow. "Who did you talk to two days ago?"

"I spoke to Philotas, sire," a trembling Kebalinos responded.

It proved to be the magic incantation. Alexandros dismissed the brothers with a wave of his hand and ordered his guards to bring in Philotas.

****

Philotas sauntered in, suspecting nothing. Alexandros dispensed with pleasantries. "Why didn't you inform me?"

"Inform of you of what? A third-hand report of some drunken tiff between a rentboy and his customer? If we reported to you every stupid thing said in this army, you'd have no time to take a shit, much less conduct a war."

"This particular stupid thing was a threat against my life."

"First of all, it was not a credible threat. I didn't believe for one second what one drunken fop came to tell me about what a second drunken puff allegedly may have heard. Besides, how is some ordinary cavalryman going to get close enough to you to make an attempt against your life and why would he bother discussing his plans with his piece of ass?"

"An ordinary soldier, who also happened to be a puff, as you called him, managed to get close enough to kill my father."

"That was completely different. And, to tell you the truth, I actually considered for a minute coming to tell you what that drunkard had said."

"So, why didn't you?"

"Because then I considered what your likely reaction would've been. Not for a second would you have believed the story. You would've been sure I was simply trying to create dissension in the ranks. We both know there's been plenty of that already and we both know how you've reacted. Forgive me for saying so, but you haven't been in the best of moods lately."

"I don't forgive you and you're completely wrong. Had you come to me in a timely manner, I could've had this soldier brought in and I could've questioned him."

"What? You would've asked him, 'Soldier, are you planning to kill me?' And he would've said, 'Yes, sire, that's what I was planning to do.' Is that what would've happened?"

"In fact, I did have the soldier brought in. Unfortunately, he was dead by the time he got here. What does that tell you?"

"That you should've sent more competent guards to bring him in?"

"No, it tells me that he was conspiring to kill me and, when he realized the jig was up, he chose the only escape route left to him. And I'll tell you what else I think. I think he was not acting alone and he didn't want to be forced to divulge his co-conspirators."

"That's ridiculous, sire. You have no basis for saying that."

"Oh, really? Well, let me share another thought. I think you were one of the co-conspirators."

Philotas was left momentarily speechless. Then he burst out laughing. "Now you've really lost your mind."

"Here, read this." Alexandros handed Philotas a polished tablet with some writing on it. "It's from your harlot."

Philotas grew red in the face. "She's no more a harlot than your Barsine. And it's not from her. It's a malicious libel, written by some Persian eunuch, intended to drive a wedge between you and me. Are you really going to believe this nonsense? You used to be better than that."

Now it was Alexandros's turn to fly off the handle. "You still have the gall to lecture me? You've been insolent and insubordinate since the day I became king. And now you and your father are busy plotting to get rid of me."

"You, sire, are letting your military successes go to your head. You're a fine soldier but so am I. The difference is, I don't put on Persian airs nor do I suffer from delusions of divinity. You, sire, … ."

Alexandros cut him off. "That's enough! You can explain your part in this treasonous plot to the army."

******

The army convened the next morning. Alexandros, confident of his ability to sway the troops, presented the prosecution case. He trotted out Kebalinos and Nichomachos, to many catcalls and little effect. He read the statement, attributed to Philotas, that he and his father, Parmenion, were responsible for all of the army's victories.

"Can you believe that? This man wants to steal from you all your glory. And he tried to steal from you your leader, leaving you stranded in this miserable land, with no way to get home."

He wrapped up by playing his trump card. "You all know Philotas. He's not one of you. He has always thought himself to be better than you. And, by the way, he has always thought himself as superior to me, too. We appreciate what he's done but now he's like a festering wound. If we don't cut him off, he'll kill us all."

Philotas spoke next. He easily swatted away the flimsy and evidence-free accusation against him. He spent most of his speech recalling the long list of victories by squadrons and, later, by brigades under his command. "Am I right?" he yelled. He received a positive response from the troops after each item on his list.

He managed to allude to his personal skill and bravery in combat and to the many soldiers' lives he'd personally saved. "Am I right?" The troops clapped and yelled.

He reminded the assembled jury that there was a reason why Alexandros himself had named him commander of the entire Companion Cavalry and, in effect, the second most important commander in the army. "Am I right?" This time the troops were ready and started to roar while the question still hung in the air.

As he prepared to launch into his peroration, Alexandros stepped in. "The hour is late," he announced. "We'll resume tomorrow."

****

Philotas was taken to an isolated tent beyond the camp palisade. Alexandros assembled a torture team composed of his most senior and most loyal commanders, including Hephaistion, Krateros, Perdikkas, Koinos, and Leonnatos. He left clear instructions. "I want a full and complete confession, including the names of all the co-conspirators. And make sure he names his father as one of them."

The team got to work. After a while, a fading Philotas turned to Hephaistion. "Why don't you just tell me what you want me to say."

In the end, he confessed to plotting the assassination of Alexandros but refused to name any co-conspirators or to implicate his father in any wrongdoing.

He was carried out before the army the next morning, no longer able to walk and barely conscious. Alexandros read out his confession. He asked Philotas whether he had anything to add. There was only a gurgling groan in response.

Alexandros's call for a vote was greeted by sullen silence. He professed to hear a majority vote in favor of conviction and nodded to the executioners. Three men standing by buried their spears in Philotas's torso, pinning him to the ground.

****

Alexandros was not quite ready to dismiss the assembled army. It was still early in the day and his blood was up. "The time has come to deal with another traitor," he told the assembled troops. "Go fetch Alexandros of Lynkestis."

After his brothers were executed in the wake of Philippos's assassination, Lynkestis continued to serve in the Companion Cavalry and was part of the main-force invasion of the Persian Empire. Following the successful campaign through Ionia, he was even appointed commander of the allied cavalry and assigned to assist Parmenion in consolidating the army's gains in western Anatolia. At that point, Lynkestis's fortunes turned once more. He fell under suspicion for a second time and was placed under arrest. For the past three and a half years, he had been part of the baggage train, hauled around behind the army, shackled in his own wagon-borne cage.

Ironically, the charge against Lynkestis was based on an uncorroborated report that he was plotting with Dareios to assassinate Alexandros. In those heady early days of triumph, Alexandros refused to condemn a man based on an unsubstantiated rumor. Much had changed in the intervening years and by now Alexandros had become a different person.

The treason trial of Alexandros of Lynkestis didn't take long. The accused was brought in, looking old and broken, notwithstanding the fact that he was still in his thirties and had been a vital, vigorous warrior. The charge was presented, the incriminating note read out loud, Lynkestis given an opportunity to defend himself. He tried to say something but was unable to find the words. After a couple of false starts, he gave up, shrugged his shoulders and hung his head. The army wanted to get to its midday meal. Lynkestis was condemned, run through, and left to die next to Philotas's corpse.

And with that, Alexandros retired to his tent. But he wasn't done yet.

******

Parmenion had been a loyal Macedonian soldier for more than forty years. He had risen in the ranks to become Alexandros's second-in-command. In staff meetings, he had been the voice of reason, balancing the youthful and impetuous enthusiasm of the commander-in-chief. He had played a pivotal role in each of Alexandros's victories. He was beloved by his troops. And he had been tossed aside in Ekbatana.

If anyone was in a position to overthrow Alexandros, it was Parmenion. He commanded a large, strategically positioned garrison. He controlled, or had access to, most of the treasure seized in the course of the Persian conquest. He stood astride Alexandros's logistical and communication lines. And most importantly, he could count on the loyalty and confidence of almost every soldier in Alexandros's army, most of whom just wanted to go home.

Nevertheless, the notion that Parmenion was plotting to overthrow Alexandros was completely fictitious. On the other hand, in the wake of Philotas's execution, it did become rational for Alexandros to consider what the old general's reaction might be to the news of the death of his last remaining son.

Alexandros, who was a meticulous planner, decided to leave nothing to chance. He dispatched Polydamas, a Thessalian cavalry officer, along with two native guides, to ride on racing camels across plains and deserts to Ekbatana. He wanted to make sure they got to Parmenion before any news of his son's fate could reach him. They made the journey, which normally would have taken at least four weeks, in eleven days.

When the trio arrived on the evening of the eleventh day, they did not seek out Parmenion. Instead, they hid in a nearby grove until nightfall. Once darkness fell, Polydamas quietly slipped into the tent of Parmenion's deputy, Kleandros, and handed him detailed written orders from Alexandros.

The next morning, Kleandros informed Parmenion of a messenger's arrival and the two, accompanied by Sitalkes, Herakon, and Agathon, sought out Polydamas. Parmenion, eager to read whatever messages Polydamas may have brought, didn't stop to ask why the messenger hadn't come to his headquarters instead.

At the edge of the grove, they saw Polydamas, standing alone in a clearing, waving to them. Neither his racing camels nor his two guides were anywhere in sight. When Parmenion reached him, Polydamas handed over two letters, one evidently from Alexandros, the other from Philotas. Parmenion, his face beaming with anticipation, chose to read his son's letter first. As he was breaking open the seal, Kleandros stabbed him from behind. Parmenion, who was an old man, tried to fight back. He was quickly overpowered. Kleandros, Sitalkes, Herakon, and Agathon kept stabbing, slashing, and piercing him long after he was dead.

The commotion attracted the attention of a sentry standing outside the grove, who quickly raised the alarm. Soldiers, hearing that Parmenion was being attacked, poured in from every direction. Discovering that their beloved commander was dead, they turned on the five men standing around the body. Even though Kleandros was frantically waving Alexandros's letter ordering the assassination of Parmenion above his head, how he and his accomplices escaped being lynched remains a mystery.

Immortal Alexandros

****

When the news arrived in Pella, Antipatros read the dispatch with a mix of outrage and horror. He and Parmenion were almost the same age. They had both served King Philippos and then his son Alexandros for decades. Other than the king, they were the two leading statesmen and military leaders of Macedonia. The idea that Alexandros would arrange Parmenion's murder without so much as a hint of an accusation meant that no one was safe.

The fates of Antipatros's son-in-law Lynkestis and his son's good friend and contemporary Philotas simply proved the case. Antipatros had no reason to doubt that they were both innocent of the charges against them. Yet, they were subjected to sham trials and executed. And now he had to go tell his daughter that her husband and the father of her children was dead. Then he would go tell his son to stay away from Alexandros.

There was only one person who approved of Alexandros's actions – his mother Olympias. As she told her daughter Kleopatra, "To be a king, you must do what it takes."

Chapter 8 – Hindu Kush

Alexandros split Philotas's position as hipparchos of the Companion Cavalry between Hephaistion and Kleitos, having resolved never again to vest command of this elite division in one man. And with that, he was ready, at long last, to get on with the business of catching Bessos, the self-proclaimed Emperor Artaxerxes Pemptos, and crushing all remaining resistance to becoming the universally recognized, legitimate successor to Emperor Dareios Tritos. And, while he was at it, reaching the end of the world and conquering all that lay between here and there.

Unfortunately, reality intruded once again. Satibarzanes emerged from whatever hole he'd crawled into and ignited another rebellion in Areia. Barsaentes, while hiding out in the kingdom of Raja Sambos, worked assiduously and successfully to create pockets of guerrilla resistance in his former satrapies of Drangiana and Arakhosia. Even Nabarzanes, feeling safe from Alexandros's influence back in Hyrkania, changed sides once again and attempted to start an insurrection in that satrapy.

Alexandros sent a couple of squadrons of cavalry, commanded by Erigyios, back to Areia to deal with Satibarzanes. He sent agents laden with gold to Zadrakarta to neutralize Nabarzanes. With the rest of the army, he set off for the mountainous wilderness of Drangiana and Arakhosia. To add to his difficulties, winter was now in the air.

Erigyios succeeded in cornering Satibarzanes in Areia. Trapped, along with his band of rebels, in a narrow defile with no way out, the perfidious scoundrel contrived his most audacious stratagem yet. He challenged Erigyios to resolve their dispute by single combat, hoping to galvanize his ragtag band of desperados by this show of bravado. To his horror, the Macedonian commander accepted the challenge. The contest between the middle-aged sybarite, who'd spent his life as a professional conniver and sycophant, and the young man, who'd been a professional warrior his entire adult life, lasted less than a minute. Demonstrating exemplary efficiency, Erigyios dispensed with trying to spear or stab his opponent. Instead, he simply separated Satibarzanes's head from his body with a single stroke of his sword. He left the body for disposal by the local fauna but took the head along as proof of the assignment's completion. The remaining rebels, having witnessed the demise of their leader, attempted to surrender. Their attempt was rebuffed.

When Erigyios and his squadrons caught up to us, Alexandros was pleased to see the bloody head but truly delighted to hear the tale. "I wish I'd been there!" he exclaimed. "What a glorious way to end a rebellion. I'd love to get a chance to do the same with Bessos." Erigyios enjoyed the laurels of his victory for the rest of his life.

Meanwhile, the agents sent to Zadrakarta accomplished their mission with less panache but just as effectively. It turned out that Phrataphernes, the newly appointed satrap of Hyrkania, his loyalty reinforced by bags of gold coins, was happy to be rid of a dangerous rival. His spy network located cultured, urbane, and suave Nabarzanes, his palace guard clapped him in chains, and the next merchant caravan headed east delivered him to Alexandros. He was executed upon receipt.

Extinguishing the guerilla brushfires in Drangiana and Arakhosia proved to be a tougher task. The terrain was impossible. Mountain chain followed mountain chain, each carved up by steep, narrow river valleys, all at altitude and getting very cold with the approach of winter. Our numerical superiority was of no use against the enemy's hit and run tactics. We were losing men by the dozen, without ever being able to come to grips with the rebels. At the same time, the casualties we suffered during these sporadic, indecisive clashes were dwarfed by the number of men we continued to lose to disease, accident, and loss of morale. Still, given Alexandros's determination to press ahead, we had little choice but to keep on hacking, putting out one brushfire after another.

During our pacification efforts, we ventured too close for Raja Sambos's comfort. He decided to emulate Phrataphernes and deliver Barsaentes to us in chains. Barsaentes soon joined Satibarzanes and Nabarzanes in Haides or wherever dead Persian renegades congregate.

Finally, after months of effort, we gained a semblance of control over the satrapies of Hyrkania, Areia, Drangiana, and Arakhosia. Near the capital of Arakhosia – and once again the term 'capital' is a generous appellation for a jumble of open-air markets, stalls, tents, yurts, huts, and some actual houses – Alexandros implemented what was becoming a regular feature of his administrative arrangements: He founded another fortified garrison town, imaginatively named Alexandria-in-Arakhosia.

This time he dispensed with the appointment of either a native or a Persian satrap. Instead, he plucked out a veteran Macedonian soldier and made him both satrap and garrison commander. We were in the depths of winter by this point and unable to move. The soldiers kept warm by building the new garrison town, including its fortifications, drinking wine, and huddling near campfires. Alexandros was heated by his frustration at not having achieved, as yet, uncontested recognition as the new Persian emperor and by his irritation at having to cool his heels, waiting for the weather to loosen its grip.

****

Barsine was tending to her private garden in the courtyard of her apartment, enjoying the balmy climate of Sousa in winter, when a panicked call rent the air. "Where is Herakles?"

Larrisa, one of Barsine's two serving women, ran into the courtyard. "Has anyone seen Herakles?"

The other children playing in and around the small pool in the middle of the courtyard shook their heads and shrugged. Barsine dropped her trowel, sprang to her feet, and rounded on Larrisa. "I thought you had him. Where is Iolanthe?" Iolanthe, the other serving woman, was at the brook, doing laundry.

"Well, don't just stand there," Barsine yelled, a note of panic creeping into her voice, "start looking!" Noticing Artakama in one of the doorways, she turned to her. "Run to all the women and ask for help."

Within minutes, the entire harem was in an uproar. It was a small, enclosed, self-contained world, in which it was difficult to disappear, even for a rambunctious toddler. After a quick, fruitless search of the immediate vicinity of her apartment, Barsine stationed herself at the front entrance and tried to organize a more systematic search.

Thais walked up to her. "Go ahead and start searching, Barsine. I'll stand here a direct the traffic."

Barsine, who was having trouble thinking clearly, gratefully accepted the hetaira's offer. "Thank you, Thais. You're a lifesaver."

"I hope so. Now go and join the search."

Even Dilshad turned up, offering to help. Thais told him to send a few eunuchs to search beyond the harem walls. "He might have snuck past the gate somehow. And have them check around the postern gate as well."

For once, Dilshad forgot to put on his domineering airs. He nodded. "I'll send them right now." As he turned to leave, he murmured, mostly to himself, "I didn't think anybody even knew about the postern." But Thais was already busy organizing the next group of women.

Soon, Barsine's oldest daughter, Amastrine, came running, waving something in her hand.

"What is it?" Thais asked.

"It belongs to my little brother. His father gave it to him when he was just a baby."

Thais couldn't help but take a moment to examine the toy. It was a tiny, exquisitely carved ebony horse, with a white dot painted on its forehead. "You'd better show your mother." She pointed out the direction where Barsine's group was painstakingly searching through the thick underbrush.

After Amastrine ran off, Thais turned to the Sisygambis, who happened to be standing in front of her, awaiting her orders. "That's the kind of toy an emperor gives to his heir."

It was simply a matter-of-fact observation but, for some reason, it caused the old dowager to flare up. "The little brat must've stolen it from my Ochos."

"I doubt it, my lady, unless Dareios had owned a black charger called Boukephalas prior to his demise. Now, why don't you take your grandchildren and start looking through that stand of trees over there."

Sisygambis hesitated, rummaged her memory for a suitable riposte, and, coming up empty, turned around and did as she was told.

Amastrine held out the toy horse to her mother. Barsine took one look and collapsed to her knees. "Where did you find it?" The twelve-year-old pointed. "Take me to the spot!" her mother ordered.

Even before they reached to location of the find, Barsine had grasped the implication. "He went to the pond," she screamed. "Look in the pond!"

They all ran and squinted at the gently rippling surface. The toddler's soaked tunic was almost invisible amidst the dazzling facets of reflected sunshine. Shielding her eyes, Artakama thought she saw something. "There he is," she yelled.

The assembled women peered into the glare and then, as one, waded into the pond. For an adult, the water wasn't very deep but the slippery bottom and the resistance of the water slowed their progress. Artakama dove in and swam. Barsine, fighting toward the bobbing, greenish-gray tunic, distractedly wondered how her sister had ever learned to do such a thing.

When Artakama reached the submerged little body, she lifted the boy's head out of the water and, grabbing him by the armpits, started to drag him toward the shore. Reaching her sister, she handed Herakles over. Barsine cradled the limp little bundle and carried it the rest of the way.

The boy's eyes were wide open, as if he'd been surprised by the turn of events. His lips were blue and he wasn't breathing. Barsine placed him face down on the grass and pounded his back, imploring one god after another to bring him back to life.

The women, their clothes dripping, hovered above mother and child in a tight circle. Thais broke through and ordered them to step back. "Give them some air!" she demanded. Then she knelt down next to Barsine and gently arrested her arm before the next downstroke. "Let me try."

She turned the boy on his back and stuck a long finger into his mouth to make sure the tongue was out of the way and there was nothing blocking the throat. She placed her ear close to the boy's face. After a moment, she shook her head to indicate that she'd heard nothing. Then she placed her own mouth over the boy's mouth and nose and blew a long, forceful breath into the little chest.

Nothing happened. Barsine started to keen. Thais hushed her and once again placed her ear close to the boy's face. "I think I heard something. Everybody, keep quiet!" Then she forced another lungful of air into the boy.

This time, there was an audible gurgle, followed by a jet of water. There was a small cough and Herakles's eyelids fluttered. Barsine picked up her son, placed him over her shoulder, and gently patted his back, as if burping him after a feeding. A slow, steady stream of water soaked the back of her chiton as a smile spread across her face. Then the little boy started to cough convulsively and everybody cheered.

Barsine stood up, handed her son to Artakama, and gave a long, tight hug to Thais. "Thank you," she whispered into the hetaira's ear. Then, one by one, each of the women stepped up, gave Barsine a squeeze, and said a few words.

Sisygambis was the last to step forward. She embraced her archrival. "I'm glad," she said.

Barsine pressed the old woman against her bosom. "I'm sorry you lost your son."

The two mothers remained locked together and wept, one with relief, the other in sorrow.

****

By early February, Alexandros could stand it no longer. The time to attack Bessos and his army was long overdue. The only problem now was finding him. As he and Dareios had demonstrated during the run-up to the Battle of Issos, large armies can miss each other, like two ships passing in the night, even when the geography of the area is accurately mapped, the location and intentions of the opposing armies reasonably well known, and the desire for a decisive showdown mutually shared. The current situation was markedly different. Far from having any maps, Alexandros didn't have the slightest idea of the overall geography of this part of the world. His information about Bessos's location and intentions was based on vague rumors and unfounded guesses. And while he was certainly eager for a decisive showdown, Bessos didn't necessarily share his enthusiasm.

Alexandros was, as usual, meticulous in his planning for the upcoming campaign. He worried about the physical and mental preparedness of his troops, especially in light of the travails they had endured over the previous few months. He worked hard to finalize the administrative and defensive details for Arakhosia and the logistical arrangements for our march forward. He consulted the scientists and geographers who were part of our baggage train, as well as local officials, merchants, and wise men, for any insights they might provide about the best route to Baktra, the capital of Baktria, and the obstacles we might encounter. He recruited guides allegedly familiar with the local topography. Unfortunately, despite his best efforts, all he managed to gather was a collection of confused, contradictory, and far-fetched yarns, tall tales, and ghost stories. His inability to obtain reliable intelligence was driving him mad.

People kept telling Alexandros that Baktra lay more or less directly to the north of our current location. They also told him that the best way to get to Baktra was to march northwest, all the way back to Susia in Parthia, and then resume going east. This advice didn't make a lot of sense to Alexandros. It seemed like ages since we'd left Susia, followed by months of hard marching and many unfortunate delays in Areia, Drangiana, and Arakhosia, to get to where we were. He wanted to forge ahead, not retrace our steps. Every meeting of senior commanders started and ended with the same refrain. "Why can't we just go straight north?" I, alone among his staff, could've told him why. But, given the strictures of the Prime Directive, I was not at liberty to disclose what I knew.

As soon as the latest garrison town of Alexandria-in-Arakhosia was ready for occupancy, Alexandros, headstrong as always, ordered the army to march north, even though winter had yet to loosen its grip. It was a tough climb. We started out at high altitude and clambered higher. Our guides tried to lead us up through river valleys but sometimes the cliffs closed in, leaving barely enough room for our wagons to pass. We found ourselves slipping and sliding on frozen streams. Sometimes the ice gave way, which was worse. Eventually, every stream would turn into a creek, then a brook, a rivulet, and finally a moss-covered wall of granite. If we were lucky, we found burbling springs of sweet, ice-cold water at the source of these streams. But then, we would have to clamber over the next ridgeline, on trails that would have challenged the agility of a mountain goat. Theoretically, our beasts of burden were supposed to haul our supplies, gear, and equipment, including our disassembled wagons, on their backs. Unfortunately, when the trails became too challenging for the animals, we became the beasts of burden, leaving our horses, mules, and oxen unencumbered, in the hope that they would make it past the treacherous stretches in one piece.

We caught glimpses of natives living in these mountains but they stayed out of our way. Perhaps our numbers intimidated them or perhaps they believed that nature would take care of us soon enough. And we, for our part, made no effort to engage with them, busy as we were simply moving ahead and trying not to freeze or plunge to our deaths.

And then, when we surmounted yet another ridgeline, we caught sight of an apparition that froze us in

191

our tracks much more effectively than the cold temperature. Ahead of us, up in the sky, above the clouds, floated the snowcapped peaks of a majestic mountain range. Alexandros was ecstatic. "We're almost there, boys," he kept repeating. Our guides said nothing.

After another few days of marching, clambering, climbing, and portaging, we were no closer to the peaks than when we first spotted them. We did, however, descend into a relatively flat plateau. The land was mostly barren, trackless, and carved up by numerous gullies and ravines. By some miracle this large plateau was occupied by hamlet after hamlet of people who evidently managed to scratch out a living in this hostile environment.

At first it was difficult to tell how far ahead the chimerical mountain peaks actually were. Ever so slowly, after days of marching, those distant snow-capped summits started to materialize into the uppermost pinnacles of the most imposing mountain range we'd ever seen. It gradually dawned on every soldier in Alexandros's army why everyone told us to return to Susia and proceed from there, rather than attempting to march straight north to Baktra.

Alexandros, on the other hand, was undeterred. He asked our guides whether any passes existed through this mountain range. He was assured that there were several such passes. Of course, they couldn't be traversed in winter, which in these parts lasted until at least May. However, in the summertime, when most of the snow and ice had melted, it was difficult but not impossible for able-bodied, determined men to negotiate these mountain passes. Whether an army could get across, with all its gear, animals, and camp followers, was another question. The guides, fully aware of the answer Alexandros wanted to hear, assured him that they could lead us to the other side, provided we waited until warm weather arrived and understanding that it would take at least a couple of months to get the job done.

As proof, the guides pointed out that the large plateau where we were currently encamped supported a fiercely independent tribe of warriors who managed to lead comfortable lives by trading with, and despoiling if necessary, the tribes who lived on the other side of the formidable mountain range ahead of us. When Alexandros expressed some skepticism at this story, the guides offered to take him to the largest of the communities occupied by these fierce brigands. They cautioned him, however, to arrive heavily armed and surrounded by a large contingent of troops.

Alexandros set off, accompanied by two squadrons of Companion Cavalry, the next morning. The guides took us to a sprawling, hilltop, fortified village of perhaps two thousand people. In response to an invitation to parley, conveyed from a safe distance by our guides, the locals launched a cloud of deadly arrows. "I guess they don't wish to talk," Alexandros observed.

We returned the next day with ten squadrons of cavalry and destroyed the village. Most of the inhabitants, who couldn't have been surprised by our attack, managed to disappear into the surrounding mountains. We did capture a couple of men whom Alexandros promptly added to our corps of guides, promising generous rewards if they got us across the mountain range safely. The new guides echoed the advice of the old guides: Wait until summer; proceed with caution; leave the heavy gear behind.

The end of winter was still far away. Alexandros had no choice but to wait for a few more weeks. He decided that this plateau, which controlled the highlands of Arakhosia and the mountain passes into Baktria, was of sufficient strategic importance to warrant another fortified garrison town. He put his men, who had nothing better to do, to work building the new town. He called it Alexandria-in-the-Caucasus. The name, when I heard it for the first time, hit me like a thunderbolt.

****

We were in the foothills of the Hindu Kush. The Caucasus Mountains lay between the Black and Caspian Seas. They formed the northern border of the satrapy of Lesser Armenia and thus the northern border of the Persian Empire in that region. The closest we ever came to the Caucasus foothills was during our visit to Zadrakarta in Hyrkania, at which point we were still a couple of hundred miles away. Having marched almost 2,000 miles from

Zadrakarta, we were now half a continent removed from that mountain range. The fact that Alexandros couldn't tell the difference between the Caucasus and the Hindu Kush was a major problem.

He has no idea where we are. I'd suspected as much for some time but willfully chose to suppress in my own mind the inescapable ramifications of Alexandros's ignorance. It really made little difference what name he gave to his latest settlement or how confused he was geographically, for that matter. The critical issue was his lack of appreciation of the challenges that lay ahead.

The nearest pass over the Hindu Kush, which is the one Alexandros intended to traverse, also happened to be the highest. The elevation of the pass, as opposed to the peaks hemming it in, which were much taller, was more than sixteen thousand feet. Not one of his soldiers had ever been at such an altitude. The distance from one side of the pass to the other was more than a hundred treacherous, mountainous, trackless, windswept miles. There were hidden crevasses, unstable rock fields, permanent glaciers, and unexpected storms. Getting an army through the pass would inevitably entail a substantial loss of life, even during the short summer months. Attempting the crossing without adequate information and during winter conditions was suicidal.

The danger was shared by all of us in Alexandros's army. But my personal situation was different. Unlike my companions, I had a fairly good grasp of Central Asian geography. I could see what was coming. How could I, in good conscience, simply stand by and not reveal what I knew? Alexandros's telling mistake in calling his latest garrison town Alexandria-in-the-Caucasus forced me to confront the quandary that had been tormenting me for the better part of my sojourn in this ancient era. I had done my best to keep this inexorable dilemma below the level of conscious thought but, with Alexandros's blunder, it had suddenly burst into my mind with the force of an avalanche.

****

Through ignorance and arrogance, Alexandros was about to lead us, during winter conditions, across one of the tallest and most treacherous mountain ranges in the world. Along with the adjacent Himalayan, Karakoram, and Pamir Mountains, the Hindu Kush was part of the complex of mountain ranges that the locals justly called the Roof of the World. As one of Alexandros's trusted advisors and the only person in his army who had at least a rudimentary knowledge of the overall geography in this part of the world, surely I had it in my power to save hundreds, possibly thousands, of lives. All I had to do is persuade Alexandros to delay the crossing by a couple of months and, perhaps choose a different, easier pass.

And then, the Prime Directive reared its ugly head once again. "Don't fuck with the future!" our instructors repeated at least ten times a day. Much as I hated to admit it, saving hundreds, possibly thousands, of lives amounted to interference with the natural flow of events. And yet ...

We had been taught that most minor violations of the Prime Directive would dampen out over time, thanks to the inertial tendencies of the temporal stream, so they would not cause any real harm. Of course, there was no way to tell in advance whether a violation would prove to be minor or major. Who could've imagined that saving the life of a single, fourteen-year-old shepherd in the highlands of Macedonia would end up changing the history of the world? But there it was.

Oh, to hell with it, I told myself. *What difference will one more transgression make?* But I continued to vacillate. It was one thing to commit an inadvertent violation and something else altogether to flout it deliberately. *Only nine more years to go. Why are you jeopardizing your chance to return home?*

That last thought set off another earthquake in my mind. Was my refusal to intervene really more about my desire to go home than a concern for those proverbial generations yet unborn? I had already violated the Prime Directive, perhaps more than once, that much was obvious. And my violation had changed the course of history. That, too, seemed self-evident by now. Yet I still believed implicitly that it would all go back to normal before my own native era and, as a result, I could still return home as if nothing had changed. *Isn't that the real reason I continue to abide by the strictures of the Prime Directive?*

There were three weak links in that deductive chain. First, what reason did I have to believe that my own native era had remained unchanged notwithstanding my blunders twenty-six centuries earlier? None. In fact, the failure of the artificial time portal to materialize as scheduled and the failure of any rescue to team to arrive thereafter was suggestive evidence to the contrary.

Second, even if the reverberations of my interference dampened out and the river of time returned to its previous course well before reaching my native era, what about the folks pursuing their lives on the banks of this metaphorical river just a short interval downstream from the moment of my meddling? Wouldn't they get caught in the flood of change and drown no matter how quickly the elastic resilience of history returned the torrent of time back to its original course?

And third, there was something truly perverse about my letting hundreds of friends and comrades die based on some quasi-religious article of faith that might turn out to be impossible to carry out at best and complete hogwash at worst.

After much hesitation, I came to a final resolution. I would warn Alexandros and if that meant that I couldn't go home again, so be it.

****

I caught him alone in his tent after our midday meal. "Do you have a moment, Aniketos?"

"For you, Ptolemaios, always."

"Sire, I believe you should delay the crossing and perhaps take a different pass."

"And why should I do that?"

"The pass you've chosen is more difficult than you realize. These are some of the tallest mountains in the world. Neither you, nor I, nor any of our soldiers have ever marched at such heights. Many of our men will die unnecessarily."

"Well, my friend, we constantly march over terrain we've never experienced before, through mountains, deserts, marshes, and forests. There's nothing nature can throw at us that we can't get through; it's people I worry about, but not too much. No army has been able to stop us yet. And I'm told by the locals that we won't be encountering any people during our transit of this pass."

"There is a reason for that, sire. Humans cannot survive for long in that environment. Because the pass is so high, the air is thinner. It is more difficult to breathe. It is also much colder than you'd expect this late in winter.

There's snow, ice, harsh winds. At least postpone the march by a couple of months. It will save men's lives."

"How do you know all this?" Alexandros interrupted. "Have you been through here before?"

"No, sire, but I've seen maps of this region."

"That's great. Let's have them."

"I don't have them with me, sire. I saw those maps as a youngster, before I left my home."

"That reminds me: Where is your home?"

Not you, too. "My home is far away, sire, and I left it long ago. You wouldn't have heard of it."

"Try me."

I told him the name of my hometown.

"Where is that?"

"It's beyond the Caucasus," I lied.

"Wonderful; so is Baktria. When we get through the pass, maybe we can stop by your house and you can show me all those maps."

Alexandros showed me out the tent. "The crossing will proceed as scheduled."

Immortal Alexandros

Saved, in the nick of time, from my own stupidity, by the inertial tendencies of the temporal stream, I told myself as I left. Didn't find much consolation in the thought.

****

We set off on a brilliantly clear, incredibly cold morning in the middle of March, 257 Z.E. Our troopers, most of whom grew up within spitting distance of the Aegean Sea, looked in vain for the first shoots of spring pushing up through the snow. Days were growing longer and rays of sunshine stronger, to the point of creating small puddles amidst the immense snowdrifts, but the puddles didn't last; they'd turns into treacherous crusts of ice within minutes of falling in shade. And the only shoots we saw were made of granite. Winter clung tenaciously to its dominion in this part of the world.

Per Alexandros's instructions, the entire army, except for the garrison left behind at Alexandria-in-the-Caucasus, assembled for one last inspection, to be followed by an orderly departure. We still had close to 55,000 fighting men, plus the usual contingent of courtiers, pages, grooms, guides, servants, savants, priests, seers, craftsmen, artisans, and assorted camp followers. There were many thousands of horses, both fighting steeds and working nags, mules, donkeys, camels, and a large herd of strange, hairy bovines the locals called yaks. The animals were meant to carry provisions, fodder, and gear, not people. As a last resort, they could be butchered for their meat. Some of our gear was also loaded onto light, two-wheeled carts, which could be carried around obstacles in case of need. Alexandros had decided to leave the oxen and heavy wagons behind. The marchers were arranged in order of speed, with the cavalry and elite infantry units in the front and the camp followers bringing up the rear. We all started on the same day but, by the time we reached Baktria on the other side of the Hindu Kush, the column would inevitably stretch over many days.

Alexandros, as always, wanted to move fast, in order to surprise the enemy and outrun the elements. We didn't get very far before starting to discover the flaws in that plan. The first problem was the altitude. It's difficult to maintain pace when you can't breathe. Apparently, living at high altitude for a few weeks, as we had in the foothills of the mountain range, was not enough to get acclimated to the lack of oxygen. Besides, the goat trail we were following into a cleft in the mountains continued to rise. Men became winded, then tired, then exhausted, then dizzy and headachy, and finally disoriented. We were forced to stop early for the night.

A gentle snowfall greeted us as we climbed out of our tents the next morning, groggy, thirsty, and chilled to the bone. We still had ample supplies and, after some porridge, washed down with copious amounts of freshly melted snow, we were ready to resume our dash to the other side. The snowfall stopped, the clouds evaporated and were replaced by brilliant sunshine. We admired the stark scenery. Vertical cliffs rose on either side of us, sculpted over the eons by the patient, tireless forces of nature into walls, columns, ledges, and crevices, decorated with delicate white ribbons of water, frozen in midfall. The bottoms of these cliffs were lost amidst giant rockfalls and snowdrifts. It was a beautiful, awesome cathedral of a cold, sterile, scary, inanimate god.

There was no vegetation in evidence. We were thousands of feet above the tree line. If any lichens, mosses, or plants existed at this elevation, they were all covered by a thick blanket of snow. Any animals managing to survive in this harsh environment must have been hibernating out of sight. All we saw were rocks, snow, ice, and dazzlingly sunshine. And then, out of nowhere, a pair of vultures appeared in the sky and lazily soared above the van of our column for many distressing minutes. Vultures are supposed to be a bad omen but we were thrilled to see that some life could survive in this environment.

For a bunch of our men, the vultures proved to be the last thing they saw, at least temporarily. All of a sudden, many of the men began to come down with snow blindness. It started as a painful, burning sensation in the eyes, accompanied by sensitivity to light, and swollen, red eyelids. The men kept rubbing their eyes, in a futile effort to get some nonexistent irritant out. Pretty soon, they were complaining of headaches and blurred vision. Some claimed to see strange colors and others lost sight altogether.

By trial and error, our medics discovered that the most effective treatment was simply to keep all light out of the eyes by covering them with linen strips. After a day or two, the malady went away. In the meantime, however, the afflicted men couldn't see and had to be led by hand over the treacherous terrain. This didn't do much for our tempo.

And then the blizzard came and we all went blind. This time the snowflakes weren't soft, fluffy, wet, or beautiful; they were tiny, hard, and sharp as needles. Whipped by gale-force winds, they scoured any exposed skin, insinuated themselves into seams in our clothes and gaps in our boots, and made it impossible to see beyond the tips of our frozen noses. All attempts to erect tents or start fires proved futile. The best we could do was huddle in large piles of human and animal flesh, sharing what little warmth we collectively possessed, and hope for the storm to end.

It did vanish as suddenly as it had come but some of our men disappeared with it. Whether they froze and were buried in a snowdrift, or fell into a hidden crevasse, or were blown away like tumbleweed, we never found out. We were too busy ministering to the survivors. Men were suffering from windburns, frostbite, and hypothermia. Alexandros had a simple remedy: "We have to redouble our pace. The faster we go, the warmer we'll feel and the sooner we'll be back down into the warm, level valley on the other side."

Immortal Alexandros

The men were too tired, too frozen, too scared to complain. They scrambled across rockfalls and icefields as quickly as they could, they climbed up steep slopes and skidded down twisty chutes. We abandoned carts, food, animals – anything that could slow us down. We lost men every day to injury, sickness, accidents, and despair. But the army got across the highest pass in the Hindu Kush in winter conditions, something that, I was fairly certain, no other army had ever done before.

The lead elements of our column negotiated the one hundred plus miles of treacherous terrain in an unbelievable seventeen days. Other units took much longer. And some three hundred men never made it out at all.

When we reached a valley on the far side of the pass, we were still at altitude and it was still cold but, as promised by Alexandros, it felt like paradise. The handful of surprised inhabitants scattered at our approach, leaving warm yurts, burning fires, half-eaten yak meat, and fermented mares' milk behind. We ate, drank, and slept, without pausing for a moment to consider what Bessos might be up to.

When we awoke and sent out scouts, it turned out that there was nary an enemy soldier to be found.

Chapter 9 – Baktria

In Baktra, the capital of Baktria, Bessos was not sitting idly by. In his own mind, he was the rightful emperor of Persia. What's more, he aspired to revive and reinvigorate the Persian Empire that had become, as far as he was concerned, old, smug, feeble, and in danger of being overrun by some barbarian upstart. His call to arms to resist the foreign invaders resonated with a lot of people.

The self-proclaimed Emperor Artaxerxes Pemptos, uncouth, uneducated, and unconventional though he might've been, was also ruthless, effective, and shrewd. He was loved by his Baktrian horsemen, admired by aspiring cutthroats, brigands, and pillagers everywhere, and feared by most everyone else. And he invented a concept that had not previously occurred to any Persian leader – nationalism.

The word 'nationalism' didn't exist, of course. The Persian Empire was not a nation. It was a huge amalgam of former kingdoms, tribes, and clans cobbled together by brute force over a span of centuries. It comprised peoples of different races, ethnicities, religions, language groups, and cultural norms, ranging from feral savages to sophisticated sybarites. And yet, somehow, Bessos managed to persuade many of these disparate folks to join his ragtag army to fight a war of national liberation.

Even though he emulated, as much as his current circumstances permitted, the high-handed ways of previous Persian emperors, he succeeded, at least for the moment, in getting his followers to overlook his own despotic pretensions and, lest we forget, his murderous ways, by defining himself as the leader of the opposition to the foreign invader. To fulfill his mission of national liberation, he immersed himself in energetic preparations for the inevitable confrontation with Alexandros and his army.

Would-be warriors continued to pour into Baktria. They arrived by ones and twos, in small bands, and large hordes. They all brought horses, sometimes more horses than men. Some brought their women, cattle, and yurts. The only thing they lacked was armor, weapons of war, and discipline.

Bessos tried to mold them into a cohesive fighting force. Of the original 12,000-man Baktrian cavalry that he had led at Gaugamela, perhaps 7,000 fighters remained. To these fierce and battle-tested soldiers he added the survivors of the rebellions mounted by Satibarzanes, Barsaentes, and Nabarzanes. Plus, there were the unaffiliated young men looking for adventure, mayhem, and loot. Finally, his army got a big boost with the arrival of two prominent warlords from neighboring Sogdiana, Spitamenes and Oxyartes, who brought sizeable contingents of their own followers.

In total, Bessos's army numbered perhaps 30,000 men. They were no match for Alexandros's army, which was more numerous, better armed, and honed to a fine fighting edge by constant training and, at least for the veteran core of the army, by years of actual organized warfare. Bessos had no illusions about the ability of his men to take on this irresistible juggernaut in a pitched battle. His plan was to deprive the enemy of provisions, pick them off in hit-and-run sorties, demoralize them, and let the climate, terrain, disease, and desertion finish the job.

The men arriving in Baktria also brought valuable intelligence. As a result, Bessos was aware of the revolts in Areia, Drangiana, and Arakhosia. He also knew that those revolts were eventually suppressed by Alexandros but only after substantial expenditures of money, lives, and time. As far as Bessos was concerned, his former rivals Satibarzanes, Barsaentes, and Nabarzanes had done valuable work igniting insurrections throughout the eastern satrapies; learning, through trial and error, the most effective ways to fight the enemy; and, most important of all, buying time for Bessos to get organized. The fact that all three of these rival claimants to the imperial tiara ended up dead was simply a nice bonus.

Immortal Alexandros

Bessos was also able to follow the movements of Alexandros's army. Within a matter of weeks, Bessos knew that Artakoana and Phrada had fallen and that Alexandros had established several garrison towns, the last of which was located in the southern foothills of the Hindu Kush. He even learned that Alexandros intended to cross the formidable mountain range, rather than take the more sensible route around it.

Bessos made two miscalculations, however, in evaluating the situation. First, he failed to appreciate the fact that his understanding of local geography was far better than Alexandros's. Second, he underestimated Alexandros's lack of patience. As a result, he mistakenly assumed that Alexandros knew enough about the Hindu Kush to take the easiest pass across and that he had enough sense not to attempt a wintertime crossing.

As soon as Bessos found out that Alexandros intended to invade Baktria by going over the Hindu Kush, he moved his army to the point where he expected Alexandros to emerge from the mountains. His scouts scoured the area until Bessos knew the local topography better than the ubiquitous eagles and vultures soaring high overhead. He found bluffs where companies of ruffians could lie in wait and then rain arrows, rocks, boulders, fire, death, and destruction on any army units passing below. He identified groves to conceal battalions of mounted soldiers, adjacent to flat ground suitable for lightning strikes and befuddling disappearances. He clambered up rock-strewn and forested mountainsides and scampered back down through thickets, looking for high ground that neutralized the organizational prowess of the enemy and maximized the effectiveness of undisciplined but scary savages. Then he laid out detailed plans, assigned commanders to various units, and saw to it that they practiced getting into position quickly and executing their assaults effectively.

When not engaged in drills, the troops were sent out to evict the civilian population from the immediate area of anticipated conflict, to confiscate all provisions they could find, to kill all livestock and burn anything of value they couldn't carry away. Admittedly, the soldiers who called this part of Baktria home were not pleased. They deserted and worked to save their own families, homesteads, and property, but those soldiers were a small minority of the overall force.

Progress in executing the scorched-earth policy was slow but Bessos preferred to be methodical, rather than fast. After all, it would be another two or three months at the earliest before Alexandros and his army could emerge from the mountains.

Except Alexandros hadn't waited until the end of winter to start his crossing. And the lead elements of his army, including my own squadron of the Companion Cavalry, had fought our way through more than a hundred miles of some of the most inhospitable terrain in the world in seventeen days. And we debouched from the Hindu

Kush mountains eighty miles east of where Bessos awaited our arrival. Even worse for the satrap of Baktria and would-be emperor of Persia, Alexandros and his army had outflanked his carefully selected conflict zone and were now closer to Baktra than Bessos and his desperados.

When the first sighting of Alexandros's army in Baktria was reported to Bessos, he did the only thing he could. He rounded up his ragtag army and hightailed it out of Baktria, across the Oxos River, and into the adjacent satrapy of Sogdiana, in hopes of living to fight another day.

****

Alexandros was eager to get on with it. The elite soldiers in the lead elements of his army, having survived the harrowing crossing of the Hindu Kush, wanted to stop and wait for the trailing units, arguing that we should reassemble the entire army before proceeding farther. Left unsaid was the soldiers' desire for a pause to catch their breaths, to recover from their injuries, to regain some of the weight they'd lost, and to bask in the relative warmth and bounty of the valley in which we found ourselves. Alexandros, however, would brook no delay. He was impatient to catch up to Bessos who, he believed, was still holed up in Baktra. After two days' rest, we started our march across Bessos's satrapy.

Baktria was an ancient land situated on an elevated plateau perhaps two thousand feet above sea level. In the south and east, it was hemmed in by the Hindu Kush mountains, in the west by the great Karmanian desert, and in the north by the Oxos River. Its climate was dictated, to a large extent, by its proximity to some of the tallest mountains in the world. The monsoon rains that reliably watered much of the Indian subcontinent below never reached Baktria. Usually, the spring months saw some showers but there was precious little precipitation during the rest of the year. Because it was a landlocked country, far from the moderating effects of oceans or seas, it experienced bone-chilling winters and sizzling summers, with hardly any spring or autumn in between.

Surprisingly enough, however, a wide strip of land, running east and west and stretching from the foothills of the Hindu Kush in the south to the capital of Baktra in the north, was fertile and prosperous. A number of rivers and creeks, fed by springs and melting snows in the mountains, crossed this strip, flowing northward. For countless eons, these streams carried sediment from the mountains and covered the plain below in a deep layer of rich, fecund soil.

Once upon a time, these rivers and creeks flowed all the way to the mighty Oxos. But that was a very long time ago, before farmers arrived and dug a dense network of irrigation ditches crisscrossing the fertile strip and diverting all the water before it could reach the northern border of Baktria. As a result, the upper half of the country, from Baktra to the Oxos, was covered by arid steppes, prickly brush, and barren desert.

The people who occupied Baktria since time out of mind were proud, autonomous, and affluent. Although technically subjects of the Persian Empire, they were not Persians, they resented their Persian overlords, and they labored unceasingly to throw off the Persian imperial yoke. About a quarter of the Baktrians were farmers who lived in the fertile zone and worked hard to bring forth a crop of wheat, barley, and assorted legumes year after year. Tribes of nomads, who constituted more than half of the population, lived in the arid zone, drove huge herds of horses and other domesticated animals across the endless steppes, and engaged in occasional brigandage along the way to supplement their diets and increase their treasure hoards. Urban dwellers, living in Baktra and a few other, smaller cities, made up the rest of the population.

The farmers were sufficiently industrious and the land sufficiently fertile to feed not only the farmers but also the rulers, priests, artisans, and merchants who lived in the cities, with enough surplus left over to supplement the diets of the mounted nomads. These itinerant herders, who learned to ride before they knew how to walk, protected the farmers and the city dwellers, for a price, of course. They also launched massive raids against other nomadic tribes living across Central Asia and supplied the manpower for the fearsome light cavalry units of Persian emperors. In between official military engagements, they were available for hire by local warlords and, when lacking paid work, maintained their martial prowess by freelance attacks against the numerous caravans travelling on both sides of the Oxos River on their protracted journeys between East and West.

As we crossed the fertile zone on our march to Baktra, the farmers stopped running away. Unlike Bessos's army, we didn't destroy all we saw. On the contrary, Alexandros issued explicit orders that we were to pay for any provisions we took. The farmers, who were born hagglers, discovered that they could bamboozle these foreigners, who had plenty of coin but little food, into paying exorbitant prices. Pretty soon, groups of farmers came to meet us, bringing foodstuffs, wine and mead, horses, camels, goats, sheep, and poultry. The only items that were strangely missing were olives, olive oil, and cattle. We discovered that, although they were familiar with almost all the plants grown in the Greek-speaking world, for some reason they didn't cultivate olive trees. And, being Zoroastrians, they considered cattle sacred.

Baktra turned out to be a real city, as compared to the capitals of Areia, Drangiana, and Arakhosia. First, it was protected by impressive city walls. Although built of unfired mud brick, straw, and earth, the walls were thick, tall, and capable of withstanding an assault by marauding horsemen firing arrows. When we arrived, the city gates were wide open. While there was no welcome committee to greet us, there was no opposition to our entry either.

Second, Baktra was big. Based on information we collected later, it boasted approximately 20,000 permanent residents. In addition, on any given day, several caravans passed through or near the city with their complements of merchants, drovers, guards, servants, and slaves. On market days, additional thousands poured in to sell, buy, or gawk. During our stay, however, the population was substantially reduced by the absence of so many men of fighting age.

Third, Baktra looked like a proper satrapal capital. It was packed, gate to gate and wall to wall, with streets, temples, government buildings, inns, taverns, bakeries, brothels, shops, dwellings, military barracks, and an ostentatious satrapal palace. The barracks and the palace were vacant at the moment.

A large area within the city walls was reserved for market stalls and perhaps military drills. The day we arrived was not a market day but the area was still teeming with people and animals. The sheer variety of races, ethnicities, pursuits, attire, and languages was overwhelming at first. It didn't help that people were shouting to be heard above the din and competing for space with horses, beasts of burden, stray dogs, sacred cows, and that day's edible meats, still on the hoof and hock.

Alexandros took possession of the palace, along with his senior commanders, Persian courtiers, personal bodyguard, and assorted servants. The rest of the troops moved into the vacant barracks, although there was barely enough room. As additional units, which had fallen behind during our crossing of the Hindu Kush, caught up to us, they would have to bivouac in their usual encampment outside the city walls.

"Don't get too comfortable," Alexandros kept repeating. "We're only staying here long enough for the entire army to assemble and for me to make the necessary administrative arrangements. As soon as that's done, we're off in pursuit of the regicide."

He spent a couple of days interviewing a nonstop parade of local dignitaries, suppliants, informants, savants, and busybodies. His appetite for information was as insatiable as ever. His foremost concern, of course, was to glean as much intelligence as possible about the likely whereabouts of Bessos and the strength and composition of his army. Once he discovered that Bessos had fled to Sogdiana, he wanted to know about the alternative routes to reach the Oxos, how best to get across it, and the myriad logistical details necessary to sustain an army on the march.

He still found time, however, to satisfy his curiosity about the people, sites, and history of Baktria. Based on the reputation of the savage scrappers of the steppes, he expected to meet a steady stream of impecunious, uncultured, and unkempt primitives. It turned out that the inhabitants of Baktra were just the opposite. The people who came, or were dragged into, the palace were a hodgepodge of ethnicities, backgrounds, and attainments, defying easy categorization. On the whole, they were quite prosperous. And, most important to Alexandros, they tended to be fascinating.

One elderly gentleman showed up decked out in colorful silk garments, adorned with gold, jade, precious stones, and carved ivory. "I supply provisions to caravans," he said by way of explanation.

Another wizened oldster claimed to be a Greek, or at least a descendant of Greek people. He spoke not one word of his putative ancestral tongue but he did bring scrolls written in Greek, Attic-style pottery, and small votive offerings to Asklepios. After further investigation we discovered that some one hundred and fifty years earlier the first Emperor Dareios, upon conquering the Greek colony of Kyreinaike in North Africa, deported its inhabitants to the farthest place he knew, which happened to be Baktria. The old man standing in front of us was apparently one of the descendants of these deportees.

And then, on the third morning after our arrival, a tall, dignified man, swathed from head to toe in sparkling white sheets, showed up. He claimed to be a Zoroastrian priest. Alexandros, who was not only interested in religions of all kinds but also inclined to sacrifice to local deities, on the ground that it couldn't hurt, gave the man a respectful hearing.

The audience was supposed to last five minutes. The priest was still going strong three hours later. He told us that Zoroastrians acknowledged Ahura Mazda as the principal god or Wise Lord, as the priest called him. "However, Ahura Mazda is not in charge of our conduct," he quickly added.

Alexandros raised an eyebrow. "He isn't? Then who is?"

"We are."

This response elicited puzzled looks from several of the senior commanders who had gathered to listen to the sage. Hephaistion voiced what most of us were thinking. "If you believe that Ahura Mazda is the ruler of the universe, doesn't it follow that he also controls the actions of us ordinary mortals and dictates our fates?"

"Well, it turns out that the universe is more complicated than that," the old man replied. "The great revelation received by our prophet Zoroaster was his realization that, in addition to Ahura Mazda and all the lesser spirits and demons, there are also two primeval forces in the universe. One is called Asha and it strives to increase order, justice, goodness, and light in the world. Its adversary is called Druj and is a force for deceit, error, evil, and darkness. These two forces are engaged in a constant, never-ending, bitter struggle for supremacy. Each tries to recruit, seduce, and take us in its thrall. The tension between these two forces gives us the freedom to choose to become followers of one or the other. Our free will is the result of the equipoise between these forces. So, you see,

Ahura Mazda doesn't control our actions nor determine our fate – we do."

Hephaistion pounced on what he saw as a fatal flaw in this worldview. "If Asha and Druj are in balance, as you say, why should we try to be good, just, or pure? We might as well be evil, dishonest, and sneaky and get ahead of the pure, naive, law-abiding fools."

"That's where you would be wrong, sire. The great Zoroaster taught us that, while Asha and Druj may be in balance, choosing to become an adherent of one as opposed to the other will have very different consequences for their respective followers."

"Such as?"

"Eventually, the struggle will end. Asha will overcome and extinguish Druj. The universe will be rehabilitated and Asha's followers will have their bodies and souls reunited. They will ascend to Heaven. The souls of Druj's lackeys will remain separated from their bodies forever and they will be condemned to spend eternity in Hell."

Hephaistion smiled. "That's all well and good, assuming it's actually true, but what benefit is there to choosing to follow Asha in the meantime?"

"In the meantime, sire, by thinking good thoughts, saying kind words, carrying out the correct rituals, helping the poor and the unfortunate, doing good deeds, and generally leading a virtuous life, we strengthen Asha, delight ourselves, bring light into the world, celebrate the divine order of the universe, and come a step closer to joining Ahura Mazda and the other deities in Heaven."

"My mother used to say the same thing," Kleitos laughed, "except she put it more succinctly. She used to say, 'Virtue is its own reward.' And I don't think she ever heard of Zoroaster. He sounds like a windbag to me."

"No, no, you're wrong, Kleitos," Alexandros interjected. "This man's philosophy sounds very interesting." He turned back to the priest. "Tell me more about this prophet of yours, holy man."

"Oh no, sire. I'm a long way from becoming a holy man; I'm just an old priest. But I can certainly tell you about the life of our prophet and author of our sacred writings. To begin with, did you know that Zoroaster was born right here in Baktria?"

"At this point, the entire circle of Alexandros's aides erupted in laughter. "Of course he was," Hephaistion cried out. "And Dionysos was his uncle."

"I have no idea who this Dionysos was, sire. But I can prove that Zoroaster came from here. I can even show you the house in which he was born."

That was all Alexandros needed to hear. "Alright men, time to get back to work. You each have your assignments. See to it that they're carried out promptly. Ptolemaios and I will go and check out Zoroaster's birthplace in the meantime."

Alexandros was an inveterate sightseer. Wherever his conquests led him, he sought out all things famous, historical, unusual, or plain fun. He was also an easy mark for any local purveyor of relics, mementos, souvenirs, and hoary tales. And, for some reason, I was his preferred sightseeing companion.

We hadn't run across any notable curiosities since leaving Persepolis. As a result, Alexandros was primed to play the role of the gullible tourist and the old priest was happy to serve as his enabler. He took us to a large, well-maintained wattle and daub abode not far out of town. A well-to-do family must have lived there once upon a time but now it was inhabited only by ghosts.

Another, younger priest met us at the entrance and, without saying a word, stuck out his hand. Alexandros nodded. "Pay the man." I handed over a gold daric, likely doubling the annual revenues of the establishment.

We were led through a series of windowless chambers, lit by oil lamps, each dustier than the last. One room was furnished with tables and shelves covered by heaps of votive objects and amulets. Another contained a statue of Zoroaster, surrounded by soft rugs, suitable for kneeling. A third room was made to look like a stable, complete with stinking straw. "That's where he kept his ass," the older priest intoned reverently.

Finally, we reached a little room, bare but for a straw-filled mattress lying under a small window opening. It was evident from the priests' ardent expressions that this was the culmination of our tour. They sank to their knees and fervently prayed to a large brown stain in the middle of the mattress. Finally, the older priest rose to his feet and pointed. "This is where he was born."

"How long ago was that?" I asked.

"Two hundred fifty-seven years ago, sire."

Both Alexandros and I were amazed. "How do you know the exact number?" he wanted to know.

"Our calendar runs from the date of his birth, sire. This is year two hundred fifty-seven."

Alexandros nodded. "I understand."

"So," I hemmed and then, with some trepidation, spit out my next question. "Are you telling us that this mattress is two hundred and fifty-seven years old?"

"Exactly, sire. It lies here under the personal protection of Ahura Mazda."

I kept a straight face. "I guess not even Ahura Mazda can keep the straw from stinking after all these years."

The three other men in the small room didn't appreciate my humor. "Get out!" Alexandros barked. "We'll catch up to you later."

I stood outside the house, enjoying the fresh spring air, when Alexandros called me back inside. He was beaming with joy. "Look what they gave me." He waved a walking stick in his hand. "It belonged to Zoroaster himself. He used it to walk the entire width and breadth of the Persian Empire. Look, you can see the scuff marks."

I dutifully examined the walking stick.

"Beautiful, isn't?"

It was only a stick, but I nodded my agreement.

"Pay the man!"

I handed over another daric.

"No, no. That's not enough. Give him a couple."

Luckily, I had accompanied Alexandros on these excursions before, so my money pouch was quite full, at least to start.

"There are many other sights we can visit, sire," the older priest said.

We spent two weeks traipsing in and around Baktra. Word had evidently preceded our arrival because at each place we stopped, Alexandros was handed precious, ancient curiosities for which I was then obliged to pay. The need to march out immediately in pursuit of Bessos was momentarily forgotten.

****

Finally, the old priest and his accomplices ran out of sights to show and relics to sell. Alexandros finalized his administrative arrangements for Baktria. For garrison duty, he selected a relatively small contingent of Macedonian veterans, who were either too old, too ill, too tired, or too discontented to continue. This seemed an adequate force, since Baktria had been stripped of its fighting men. Finding a reliable new satrap presented a tougher challenge. The Macedonian commanders who had been with us since the start of the invasion were too valuable to waste on garrison duty in such a backwater. The new commanders, whether Persian turncoats or recently arrived Greek mercenaries, had demonstrated their flexible understanding of loyalty. The dilemma was solved when old Artabazos stopped in for a visit one morning. He confided in Alexandros that he was feeling his age and the recent crossing of the Hindu Kush had taken a toll on his health. He was the only

Persian nobleman whom Alexandros had grown to trust. He was appointed the new satrap of Baktria on the spot.

We were now ready to resume our pursuit of Bessos. It was the beginning of summer. Less than an hour out of Baktra, as we started our march toward Sogdiana, the terrain began to change. The irrigation canals stopped, as did any sign of cultivation. Fields of barley were replaced by unending seas of tall, yellowing grass. The temperature rose faster than the sun. By noon, it was unbearably hot. Alexandros called a halt and we hid from the sun as best we could, beneath canopies jerry-rigged from our tents, in the shade of wagons, horses, and camels, and under scraggly, stunted trees and bushes. We ate, drank, and slept. Alexandros announced that, for the remainder of our trek to the Oxos, we'd march at night and rest during the day.

We resumed at dusk. As we progressed, the grasslands were gradually replaced by scrub, which eventually gave way to parched earth, drifting dust, sharp rocks, and giant boulders. The terrain was flat but riven by ravines, ditches, crevasses, cracks, and sink holes. The night was bright, illuminated by a gibbous moon, with no clouds in sight. Still, given all the hidden hazards, it was impossible to ride on horseback. We had enough trouble negotiating the innumerable pitfalls on foot. As for our animals, all we could do was hope they possessed some instinct that would keep them from breaking their necks. On the plus side, our incessant shivering kept us from falling asleep. Considering how unbearably hot the previous day had been, it was shocking how cold it got as soon as the sun sank below the horizon.

When we collapsed, exhausted and sleep-deprived, into our tents, lean-tos, and canopies the next morning, we had little inkling that the previous night's adventures would prove to be just a mild foretaste of what was to come. We still had food and drink, our exposed skin had not yet turned an angry shade of red, and some blessed spots remained beneath our clothes that hadn't yet been infested by insects.

The next night the wind picked up. Our guides informed us that these were mild breezes for the arid zone of Baktria and we could expect much worse. It was just as well we didn't ask what they meant. Instead, we gritted our teeth, which was easy to do since they were full of sand, and pressed ahead. We tied lengths of cloth around our mouths and noses, which made it harder to breathe but didn't appreciably reduce the amount of sand we inhaled and swallowed. The only thing we could do to protect our eyes was to keep them shut, which was a suboptimal solution, considering the treacherous terrain.

The men wanted to stop for the night. The guides convinced Alexandros to keep going. They pointed out that we were carrying limited supplies of water, there would be no water holes along the way, and the weather would only get worse. So, we leaned into the wind and put one foot in front of the other.

The next night, we had to stop. The roar of the wind made it impossible to communicate. It was strong enough to peel layers of soil from the ground and transform them into stinging whips of dust that lashed us mercilessly. Men and beasts were knocked off their feet and rolled along the rough terrain like so many bits of tumbleweed. Not many of us expected to see the coming dawn.

In the morning, the wind subsided to a moderate gale. The sun rose, dim and red because of the dust suspended in the air, turning the landscape into an eerie, desolate, flaming hell. Men staggered about, collecting their possessions and checking to see which of our animals had survived the night. The dust kept the temperature down but we didn't march that day. When twilight arrived, we ate a nourishing meal, drank the last of our water, and set off for the elusive Oxos River. We had four more nights of marching left.

The next morning, Alexandros decided we would keep going till noon before taking a break and then resume again before dusk. "Lack of water will kill us faster than exhaustion," he said over and over again to groups of men as they trudged by.

We lost a few men and some animals on that march but surprisingly many of us made it to the river. When it appeared on the horizon, more a shimmer in the air than a hint of blue incised into the brownish gray ground, the men picked up speed. Once they could actually see a ribbon of water and smell moisture in the air, they abandoned their packs, possessions, and animals and started to run. The animals took the hint and started to run as well. Many horses reached the river before the men did.

This is insanity, I thought. *Drinking that water will kill them for sure.*

I'd never studied medicine and knew nothing more about pathogens and the etiology of diseases than any average person living in my native era. However, I knew enough to realize that drinking untreated river water was dangerous under the best of circumstances. In this case, with tens of thousands of men and thousands of animals polluting the water as they drank, an outbreak of waterborne illnesses was inevitable.

This time I didn't dither or vacillate. I'd fought my own internal war over the strictures of the Prime Directive and was not inclined to relitigate the issue each time lives of people in the here and now were at stake. I'd resolved to save lives, if I could, and hope that my interference fell within an attenuation loophole in the inexorable, remorseless logic of time travel. I mounted my steed and tried to get ahead of the men.

I did beat most of the men running on foot to the riverbank. "Stop!" I hollered, windmilling my arms. "We've got to boil the water first."

Nobody paid the slightest attention. As soon as the men reached the river, they flopped on their bellies, rolled down to the water's edge, and drank the brackish liquid as if it were life-giving nectar. Many had distended bellies by the time they were willing to rise and let others take their places.

I recognized one sodden fellow staggering about as our regimental cook. I grabbed him by the shoulders. "Where is your gear?"

He was in a good mood, a loony smile lighting his face. "We'll cook later, sir. Right now, the men just wanna drink."

"We have to boil great big vats of water. Find your cooking equipment. I'll try to gather some flammable stuff in the meantime. Meet me back here as soon as you can."

Eventually, I'd organized an entire row of pots, kettles, and vats and set soldiers to work gathering sticks, dried grass and dung. We also chopped up carts for firewood. Unfortunately, by the time the water was boiling, everybody had slaked his thirst. No one was interested in hot, tasteless water.

A few of the men who'd grown up in this part of the world collected leaves from some bushes they recognized and threw them into the boiling vessels. The leaves gave the water some taste and a pleasant aroma.

We ate what food we had left and drank the flavored water. But it was too late. The next day, men started to vomit, shiver, and defecate uncontrollably. In two or three days, most lay prostrate, feverish, and delirious amidst their own bloody emissions. In a week or so, the illness passed but several hundred men didn't live long enough to see it go. So much for my efforts to save lives in defiance of the Prime Directive. Evidently, the inertial tendency of time had more than one trick up its sleeve.

Ten days after we'd reached the river, Alexandros called a general assembly. In full armor, sitting astride Boukephalas, he made an imposing figure. "Men, the time for recuperation is over. There is a bounty of food, drink, women, and loot on the far side of this river. Let's go get it."

The men were not impressed. "More like an army of savages, led by Bessos, waiting for us on the other side," somebody called out.

"Yes, that's the best part. It's been a while since we've had a good scrap and I for one can't wait."

If Alexandros expected approval, applause, and acclamation, he was disappointed. Most of the discontent seemed to originate in the ranks of our Thessalian allies, who'd been riding with us since the start of the invasion. For most of that time, they had served under Parmenion's command and, even though he was Macedonian, they'd grown to love him. Far from forgiving his murder and forgetting their resentment, they let it burble and seethe in their guts and now it came pouring out.

Had Alexandros not been surrounded by his Companion Cavalry, the Thessalians might have killed him on the spot. As it was, they made it clear that their days of following Alexandros's orders, crossing mountains, deserts, and rivers at his command, and engaging in brutal "scraps" with savage fighters on his behalf were over. Alexandros, always good at sensing the mood of his troops, didn't press the issue.

"I'll detach a couple of guides to lead you back to Ekbatana without having to cross too many deserts and mountain ranges. There, you will be paid a bounty equal to four years' pay and provided with provisions to make your way back to Thessaly. You'll spend the rest of your lives enjoying the comforts of victory and the admiration of your fellow citizens. I thank you for your service."

Hephaistion drew himself up in his seat. "Thessalian cavalry, dismissed!" he bellowed. The Thessalians didn't wait to be asked twice. Surprisingly, a number of Macedonian veterans decided to join them on the long march home.

"To hell with them all," Alexandros said loudly enough for the men around him to hear. "We can recruit plenty more, and better, horsemen from around here." It was not a sentiment designed to endear him to his remaining troops.

Chapter 10 – Bessos

How we would get across the Oxos was not at all obvious. In the vicinity of our camp, it was a wide, swift, and turbulent river. Neither our guides nor the scouts we'd sent out were able to come up with a more easily fordable location.

Alexandros was undaunted. "We can do this, men; the Danube was worse. Remember how we got across that one and surprised the Getai? We'll do the same to Bessos."

Crossing the Danube had been one of Alexandros's early triumphs. Shortly after acceding to the Macedonian throne, Alexandros mounted an expedition into Thrake designed to pacify and control various obstreperous local tribes before launching his invasion of Asia. During that campaign, he decided to enlarge the reach of his kingdom beyond the Danube, something no Greek or Macedonian army had ever done. This impulsive notion presented several challenges, including the difficulty of crossing a

232

swift, wide river and dealing with a fierce group of warriors waiting on the far side.

Alexandros, still short of his twenty-first birthday at the time, overcame the challenges with the brio and panache that came to characterize all his subsequent campaigns. He got his army across the Danube during a daring nighttime crossing, at a location left unguarded by the Getai, snuck up on their formidable forces from behind, and destroyed them. Now, he was proposing to pull off a similar operation against Bessos's army.

There were, however, several significant differences between the Danube crossing six years earlier and what Alexandros was proposing to do now. First, the army he commanded at the Danube was young, fresh, healthy, and eager, a description that fit almost none of the troops encamped on the southern bank of the Oxos. Second, on the Danube Alexandros actually had some ships at his disposal; not enough to build a pontoon bridge and not enough to ferry the bulk of his troops, but sufficient to get the advance units of cavalry across quietly, stealthily, and with relatively little risk. We had no boats on the Oxos. In fact, we didn't have so much as a tree trunk to build a raft. Trees didn't grow in the arid region of Baktria. And finally, we had no idea where Bessos's troops might be waiting for us. Presumably, they'd noticed our arrival at the Oxos ten days earlier and were busy making preparations to oppose any crossing we might attempt but, no matter how hard our scouts tried, they couldn't locate them.

None of these considerations deterred or even slowed Alexandros down. "We'll do exactly as we did on the Danube. The men will sew up their tents, stuff them with straw, and use them to float across. The baggage train, camp followers, and all the rest can wait for us here until we dispose of Bessos and return with sufficient wood to build some boats."

Nobody said anything. We'd learned that it was useless to argue with our commander once he'd seized upon a notion. Finally, Kleitos raised his hand. "When do we start the crossing, sire, and where? And how will the first men to get across stay alive long enough to be reinforced by later arrivals? Even if we use all our tents and none of our men drown in the attempt, we can only get a small fraction of the infantry over to the other side at any one time. And we certainly can't get any of our cavalry over at all."

"The horses will swim, with their riders floating nearby on tent rafts and holding their reins. And if the horses drown, those men will join the infantry. But have no fear, Kleitos, we'll establish a beachhead on the other side and we'll hold it and, in due course, we'll destroy Bessos and his band of ruffians."

It took us several days to ferry the men and their equipment across the river. Surprisingly, we lost relatively few men and little equipment in the effort. Even most of the horses made it across. Of course, we were aided in achieving this outcome by the absence of any enemy soldiers throughout the operation.

****

Bessos could have thwarted our crossing, just as the Persians repulsed our attempted attack across the much narrower Granikos River. But Bessos was not present at the battle on the Granikos and evidently hadn't been briefed about that encounter. Beyond that, he was committed to his strategy for defeating Alexandros. He continued to devastate Sogdian territory as part of his scorched-earth policy, biding his time, waiting to lure Alexandros deeper into the morass, hoping to destroy his army, little by little, using guerrilla tactics.

It was a strategy that might have worked, except for one fatal flaw. The savage Sogdian scrappers, who by this point outnumbered Bessos's original Baktrian core, hated to see their countryside devastated and failed to appreciate the subtle brilliance of Bessos's guerrilla tactics. They liked commanders who were aggressive, fearless, and victorious. At the moment, Bessos was none of those things. He had failed to stop Alexandros's army from crossing the Hindu Kush, stood by while we occupied his capital of Baktra, and permitted us to cross the Oxos unopposed. As far as his troops were concerned, all that Bessos had managed to accomplish was to ravage his own satrapy of Baktria and the adjoining satrapy of Sogdiana. Bessos's arrogant personality and imperial pretensions didn't help his cause.

Eventually, egged on by Spitamenes, the new Sogdian recruits had had enough. They mutinied, seized Bessos, and prepared to execute him on the spot. His original Baktrian troops, who had witnessed the destruction of their own farmsteads, agreed with the rebels and did nothing to defend their former commander.

At the last minute, Spitamenes saved Bessos's life. He convinced the mutineers that Bessos was worth more alive than dead. "All Alexandros wants is Bessos," he explained. "Once he has him, he and his army will withdraw to Babylon and leave us alone. In fact, he's likely to reward us for doing his work for him. He's got plenty of loot, which he doesn't need and certainly doesn't want to haul back across the Hindu Kush. He'll be glad to let us take it off his hands. It's too bad he doesn't know there's an easier way back to Babylon."

The soldiers laughed at Alexandros's stupidity. They tied up the hapless would-be Emperor Artaxerxes Pemptos and dispatched a delegation to meet with Alexandros and negotiate the terms of the handover. As head of the delegation, Spitamenes appointed a low-ranking member of the Persian nobility who had thrown in his lot with the rebels. The new leader of the rebellion reasoned that this man was no different from the lesser aristocrats who had chosen to side with Alexandros and who were welcomed into his army with open arms.

Spitamenes misread Alexandros on several counts. When his delegation reached our camp, Alexandros ordered that they be disarmed and held under close guard. "Can you believe they sent a Persian turncoat as their chief negotiator? Every Persian I've appointed to a responsible position has betrayed me as soon as I turned my back. Why would I trust this guy?"

"Same reason you trust all these other Persians you keep at your court." Kleitos's face betrayed nothing but innocence and naivete. Alexandros ignored him.

"This is undoubtedly a trap," Hephaistion agreed. "They want us to send a high-ranking delegation ostensibly to take possession of Bessos but, once we get there, their entire army, probably led by Bessos himself, will pounce and destroy our delegation, thus getting rid of most of our top commanders in one fell swoop."

"Still, it might be worth a try," Perdikkas opined. "We should at least find out if the offer is genuine."

The low-ranking Persian nobleman was brought in and promptly fell to the ground. Alexandros motioned impatiently to get him back up. "So, where is this Bessos? When can you bring him in?"

"Your celestial highness, thank you for agreeing to hear me out. We're happy to turn the traitor over as soon as we can work out some minor details."

"Such as?"

"First, we need to agree on a rendezvous point where we can hand him over without exposing either your men or ours to any danger."

It took a moment for Alexandros to digest the import of this statement. "Are you trying to imply that, if you had brought the murderer with you, I would've somehow harmed your delegation?" Alexandros's voice started to rise. "Who do you think I am? Unlike you savages, we hold ambassadors sacrosanct."

"Of course, your imperial majesty. No such thought had ever entered our minds. It's simply that, when arranging an exchange, it's customary in our country to select an open, neutral ground. Each side then places the items to be exchanged near each other but far enough apart to avoid any danger of an accidental clash. Once both sides are satisfied that the other side's offerings are in accord with the agreement, the exchange is completed and the parties go their way."

"What are you talking about? What exchange?" Alexandros was screaming by now. "You're giving us Bessos and we're giving you nothing. If you're lucky, we'll let you return to your gang alive and unharmed. Isn't that the deal?"

"That's the crux of it, your brilliance. However, another custom in our country is to provide a small gratuity in return for services rendered. I have been sent to negotiate the size of the gratuity with your majesty."

"What did you have in mind? We can feed you and your delegation before we send you back."

"That would be much appreciated, your highness. However, my commander asks that you leave behind the loot you have accumulated since leaving Ekbatana. There can't be much because you've been traversing poor lands. And the loot would only burden you as you made your way back, across the Hindu Kush and toward Ekbatana. It's as a token of friendship that my commander offers to relieve you of this burden."

Alexandros reached for the nearest javelin. Only the quick intervention of Hephaistion and Perdikkas saved the emissary from being transfixed on the spot. He was quickly hustled out of the command tent, while Hephaistion got to work trying to get his leader and friend to calm down.

The remaining negotiations were carried out between Hephaistion and Spitamenes's emissary. They agreed that the exchange would take place in the market square of a nearby village. They agreed that we would send a delegation to pick up Bessos at the appointed time and we would give nothing in return. "That will save you the trouble of having to wait around and exposing yourselves to danger. You can leave Bessos tied up in the middle of the square. We will promise not to launch an attack against your army for at least one day after the exchange."

The emissary left, promising to return in three days' time with Spitamenes's reply. It took five days but the emissary did come back. Surprisingly, Spitamenes had agreed to our proposal.

This response made Alexandros more suspicious than ever. He was convinced that Hephaistion's original reaction was correct, that this was simply a trap. On the other hand, several commanders argued that it was worth assuming some risk if it might yield the bloodless capture of the enemy commander.

Alexandros was eventually swayed by this latter faction. "Alright, we'll go and find out. Who wants to lead our delegation?"

No one stepped forward. Finally, Perdikkas, standing at the back of the group, spoke up. "Send Ptolemaios, sire. He seems smarter than the rest of us and always lands on his feet."

I was too stunned to speak. Perdikkas had a habit of volunteering me for suicide missions but this was too much. Alexandros didn't wait while I gathered my objections. "Well, that's settled then. Ptolemaios, you'll set off in the morning."

"But sire, it's a trap. You said so yourself."

"Maybe it is, maybe it isn't. We don't know. But don't worry, Metoikos, we will take good care of you."

His use of my old nickname got me more worried than ever. It was not exactly a term of endearment and Alexandros didn't normally use it as a compliment. "I'll need to take a few squadrons of Companion Cavalry with me," I said, playing for time.

"Naturally. How many were you thinking of taking?"

I decided to name an absurd figure, hoping that the magnitude of the number would illustrate more eloquently than mere words the peril of the proposed mission. "Twenty squadrons, sire," I said.

"That, my friend, is not 'a few squadrons of Companion Cavalry.' That is the entire corps. We can't risk our entire Companion Cavalry on this silly mission."

"I realize that, sire. But if all of Bessos's horsemen are lying in wait for us, we will still be outnumbered three to one, perhaps four to one."

"Tell you what we're going to do, Ptolemaios. I'll lend you eight squadrons; that's 1,600 of the finest cavalrymen in the world. Plus, you'll have 4,000 Macedonian infantrymen; that's four brigades. Surely, that's a big enough force to defeat the entire undisciplined, sordid crew led by Bessos or this other guy, Spitamenes, if Bessos has really been deposed. In fact, if they did attack you, they'd be doing us a tremendous favor. I'm sure you'd wipe them out and put a quick end to this entire execrable rebellion."

I realized he was serious and there was nothing I could do to change his mind. "Yes, sire!" I said crisply. "We will carry out your orders."

I started to walk out when he called after me. "And take one of our new Persian commanders with you. You may need someone who speaks their language." I nodded and continued to walk. *Is it a good sign or a bad sign that he thinks I may need an interpreter?*

****

As we approached the village, I ordered the cavalry to fan out and form a tight perimeter. "Nobody gets out," I told my squadron commanders. "More importantly, keep most of your men facing out. If anybody detects any movement coming toward us or sees anything suspicious at all, raise the alarm."

Once the cavalry was in place, I gingerly led the infantry into the village. In reality, calling it a village was an overstatement. If it comprised forty huts, I would've been surprised. That meant I had a hundred men for each hut. And still, I was nervous.

I ordered the men to spread out and search each hut. "I don't want any violence or property damage. On the other hand, I don't want any of you hurt, either. So, proceed with caution!"

It turned out that the village was deserted and stripped bare, except for a dozen old women hiding in some of the huts. Apparently, their assignment was to keep the man sitting tightly bound in the middle of the small central clearing from either fleeing or starving to death.

My men kept an eye on the women as I approached the prisoner. He was surprising young, unkempt, and dirty, but doing his best to sit straight and look uncowed, which was not easy, given his current undignified circumstances. He had a tall, unfurrowed forehead and piercing, determined eyes.

"Ask him his name," I told my interpreter.

"I don't need to, sir. I recognize the man. He's Bessos, the rebel leader and former satrap of Baktria."

Well, that was it, then. I had completed my assignment. The only problem was, I had no idea what to do next. When Alexandros dispatched me on this mission, all of us in the tent considered several possible outcomes. Taking Bessos prisoner alive and without a fight was not among them. As a result, I had no pertinent instructions.

My first order of business, with the village and the prisoner secured, was to send a patrol back to Alexandros to report on the outcome of the mission and request further instructions. By then, the sun had set and it was getting dark. I decided we'd spend the night in the village. I set the men to work digging a defensive ditch and erecting a palisade, using materials from the huts. Unfortunately, this meant that the huts had to be torn down in the process. *Unavoidable collateral damage*, I thought.

After the night watch assignments were made, sentries posted, and bonfires lit, we settled down to our evening meal. While we ate, I had Bessos brought to me. When his hands and arms were unbound, I offered him some food, which he consumed avidly.

After he finished eating, I plied him with wine and commenced my interrogation. Although I mixed in a few irrelevant inquiries to keep him off balance, there was really only one thing I wanted to know: Where was his army and who was in charge of it?

Bessos was surprisingly forthcoming. He made clear his unhappiness with his erstwhile supporters and repeatedly expressed his desire to join Alexandros's army and serve him in any way he could. Knowing how Alexandros felt about him, I doubted that Bessos's overtures would be well-received but I kept those doubts to myself. Instead, I used his eagerness to cooperate to extract as much intelligence as possible.

Of course, he might've been lying. In fact, given his milieu, that was likely his default mode of communication. However, as I listened to him, I concluded that he was our prisoner against his will and genuinely outraged at his captivity. If his function was to serve as bait in an elaborate trap, it was not a role he'd chosen voluntarily. I consider myself a good judge of veracity. I probed his answers for internal coherence, plausibility, and consistency with known facts. Given his current position, his evident agitation, and his state of inebriation, it seemed unlikely that he could've sustained an elaborate hoax for hour after hour. By the time the first glimmers of dawn arrived, I'd concluded that most, if not all, of what he'd told me was fairly reliable.

I had him tied up again, assigned three men to watch him, and decided to catch up on my sleep while I awaited word from Alexandros on what I was supposed to do next.

****

The patrol didn't return until midmorning the following day. They handed me a sealed tablet with Alexandros's orders. He obviously wanted to make sure that I followed his instructions to the letter.

I started to read. "Greetings, Commander Ptolemaios." *Pretty formal*, I thought. "Congratulations on capturing the regicide. Keep him in close custody and maintain maximum defensive security. The army and I are on our way toward you. By the time you read this, we should be within shouting distance of your current position.

"As soon as you have finished reading, make the following arrangements: I want the prisoner stripped naked, bound hand and foot, and tied to a post in a ditch by the side of the road leading into your village. I'll take over once I arrive.

"So orders Emperor Alexandros, king of kings, lord of many, Ahura Mazda's representative on Earth, and keeper of his flame."

I did as I was told and, true to his word, Alexandros and his army arrived well before sunset that day. As troop after troop rode or marched by, they were vastly entertained by the sight of the naked man hanging from a post, knee-deep in muck. They directed derision and invective at the captive but refrained from launching any missiles in his direction.

Alexandros came abreast of Bessos, riding the impressive Boukephalas and looking magnificent as usual in full parade armor. He dismounted and walked up to the edge of the ditch, accompanied by his retinue of bodyguards and courtiers. "Why did you kill Dareios?" he asked.

When the question was translated for Bessos, he gave exactly the wrong answer. "We wanted to make a present of him to you, your majesty, so that you could take over the throne of Persia."

Alexandros flew into a rage. "The Persian throne is not yours to give to me, you worm. And to whom were you going to present my body when you got tired of me as your emperor?"

He didn't wait to hear Bessos's response. "Tie him up and take him to Baktra," he ordered. "We'll try him for the murder of Emperor Dareios when I get back there. In the meantime, I've got a satrapy to take in hand and a rebel army to destroy."

****

It would take close to a year before Alexandros had a chance to conduct Bessos's trial. Since the crime had been committed on Persian soil, against a Persian emperor, Alexandros decided that Persian rules should apply. On the appointed day, he showed up dressed from head to toe in Persian regalia, surrounded by his newly acquired Persian commanders and courtiers. Full prostration protocols were in effect.

The ultimate outcome was a formality, of course. Bessos was convicted of regicide. In accordance with Persian custom, his ears and nose were cut off. He was not killed immediately, however. To maximize the pedagogic and deterrent value of his execution, he was transported to Ekbatana and impaled before a large audience of Persian nobles, priests, dignitaries, and ordinary people. But all that was still in the future. Right now, we were stuck in the wilds of Sogdiana, trying to suppress a raging insurgency.

Chapter 11 – Quagmire

Alexandros was in a buoyant mood. "Mark my words, Spitamenes will be crawling into our camp soon enough, begging for forgiveness and offering to bring his ragtag band over to our side. That's what these Persian rebels do, time and time again, don't they?"

"You've got that right, Aniketos." Hephaistion's fawning assent was as predictable as diarrhea after fermented mare's milk.

We were sitting around a meager campfire, which generated more stench than heat. Wood continued to be an elusive commodity, even on the Sogdiana side of the Oxos, so we had to make do with dried dung as fuel. But Alexandros remained cozy, warmed by the afterglow of Bessos's capture.

"The fact that he handed over the regicide without preconditions or recompense proves he's ready to surrender. Don't you think so, Ptolemaios?"

Reluctant to burst his balloon, I tried evasion. "It's hard to know what's in the minds of these renegades, sire."

"You seem pretty good at reading other people's minds. And in this case, you even had a chance to interrogate one of these renegades. So, what did you find out about Spitamenes during your questioning of Bessos?"

"Sire," I laughed, "you can hardly expect Bessos to give an objective account of the man who led a mutiny against him, trussed him up, and handed him over to us."

"C'mon, Ptolemaios. Tell us what you found out."

I shrugged. "I found out, sire, that Spitamenes is an experienced and wily warlord. He's about forty years old. He has good connections to various Massagetan tribal leaders. He's even married to a Massagetan princess. He now commands an army of more than 30,000 men, including many Massagetan fighters. They're wild, undisciplined, and poorly armed, but they've fought many a battle, they're deadly archers, able to shoot with equal effectiveness from the ground or from horseback, and they're desperate to destroy us. They've been convinced by their chieftains, shamans, and seers that they're engaged in a war to defend their tribes, their lands, their women and children, and their way of life. They mutinied against Bessos because they didn't think he was sufficiently aggressive in opposing us. So, no, I don't think Spitamenes is coming to surrender. And his men are certainly not surrendering any time soon."

"Well, we'll wait here for a week to see whether you're right. If he doesn't turn up, we'll just have to go get him. In the meantime, I'll send out some foraging parties to bring in provisions and procure a bunch of those big, spirited horses they breed around here to replace the ones we've lost."

****

The foraging parties brought back mostly dead and wounded comrades. The countryside had been scoured clean of people, beasts, and provender. It seemed that the only inhabitants left were guerrilla fighters who struck stealthily, from a distance, usually under cover of darkness, and with lethal results.

After a week, Alexandros had had enough. "Spitamenes must be holed up in Marakanda," he declared, without benefit of any supporting intelligence. "We'll march over, surround the place, and accept his surrender."

The march proved relatively uneventful. The steppe was slightly less arid than in Baktria but provisions were still difficult to find. The terrain continued to be riven by unexpected pitfalls; however, we were getting better at avoiding the various dips, cracks, and holes hidden beneath the swaying grass. Ghostly men, barely visible against the horizon, shadowed our movements day after day. Every night, we hunkered down in our encampments, hiding behind ditches and palisades, hoping the occasional incoming arrows would fall to the ground without doing any harm. Most of the time they did.

We reached Marakanda, the capital of Sogdiana, after ten days' march. As predicted by Alexandros, the city surrendered without a fight. However, neither Spitamenes nor any of his troops were anywhere to be found. Most men of fighting age had chosen to enlist with the guerrillas or simply fled to parts unknown. Per Alexandros's instructions, we occupied the city but refrained from inflicting any casualties or causing too much property damage. "Now that we own it, men, let's not break it," is how he put it.

Marakanda was similar to Baktra, except larger and more impressive. The city walls were taller, sturdier, and more ancient. The population of some 40,000 comprised an eclectic mixture of Sogdians, Baktrians, and Persians, with smaller populations of other ethnic and racial groups from all corners of the Persian Empire and beyond.

The streets were lined with dry goods and food stalls, taverns and inns, and many dwellings, ranging from palatial to impoverished. Temples, each with its own sacred precinct, adjoined many of the major crossroads. The central market square teemed with merchants, farmers, shoppers, beggars, and stray dogs, even with most men gone. The city was clearly not suffering from a shortage of food or drink. Establishments displaying an astonishing abundance of gold and silver goods, embroidered textiles, little bells, statuettes, amulets, votive figurines, ornamental objects, pottery, ceramics, and an assortment of carved, engraved, and painted items made of copper, bronze, ivory, and wood occupied two sides of the square. Governmental buildings and temples delineated the remaining two sides.

The Polytimetos River, known to the locals as the Zeravshan, meandered through the lower city. The upper city was dominated by a huge, ancient castle, which was showing its age but still served as the seat of government for the Sogdiana satrapy. An entire sprawling metropolis was nestled in a fertile river valley between the foothills of adjacent mountains that rose gradually to towering heights to the south and east of the city.

****

After a quick tour, Alexandros chose the castle as his headquarters, with troops moving into the more desirable dwellings throughout the city. This usually required pushing the current occupants aside but they were in no position to object. Instead, they were persuaded, sometimes by money and sometimes by the threat of force, to host a series of lavish feasts for their new overlords. The biggest banquet, of course, took place in the old castle. It continued, in the usual Persian fashion, for several days and nights.

Even as he gradually sank into an inebriated stupor, Alexandros used the occasion to acquire as much information as possible about local history and lore. An impressive succession of scholarly-looking old men was dragged in, placed at the foot of Alexandros's improvised throne, and minutely questioned, while the rest of the guests ate, drank, talked, ogled the entertainers, snoozed, and drank some more.

A few of us senior commanders gathered around Alexandros and listened in on his interrogations. We learned precious little about the intentions or whereabouts of the enemy but a great deal about Marakanda's origins, current inhabitants, municipal organizations, religious beliefs, and sources of its evident prosperity. None of Alexandros's informants could tell him when the city was founded. Its protected and bountiful location, with ample water supply and easy access, had attracted human habitation long beyond the reach of records, ruins, or legend.

On the other hand, the hoary sages, shamans, and charlatans were happy to provide Alexandros with a long list of tribes, peoples, kings, conquerors, rulers, holy men, religions, and deities that had found their way to this spot in the middle of the boundless steppes of central Asia. Some left, or were pushed out, or died out, but the descendants of the rest continued to mix freely in this blessed city.

To account for the sources of the city's wealth, they pointed to Marakanda's ideal location astride numerous trade routes. It was the first city reached by caravan traffic coming from beyond the Tien Shan mountain range.

Because of insurmountable mountains to the south and the lethal, savage-infested steppes and deserts to the north, the only practicable routes between East and West led through the Zeravshan valley. As a result, all merchandise coming from the East, including ceramics, silks, jewelry, carvings, coins, and ornamental objects, and all raw materials going in the other direction, including gold, silver, copper, tin, ivory, jade, furs, hides, and textiles were duly taxed in Marakanda. In addition, there was the lively traffic sailing up and down the Zeravshan River and the caravans heading south to Baktria and beyond.

The city's inhabitants did more than tax, however. They engaged in active trading, provided supplies and hospitality to travelers, and became expert craftsmen renowned far and wide for the quality of their embroidery, gold- and silversmithing, copper engraving, and textile weaving. And for a long time, they fielded an army capable of protecting their freedom and independence.

Had Alexandros listened more attentively or, perhaps, had he consumed a little less alcohol, he might have noticed that many of the luxury goods described by our informants came from points far to the east of our current location, implying that there had to exist some civilization beyond the borders of Sogdiana. However, he was too spellbound by the stories about a long-dead Persian emperor, the original Kyros, to absorb information that might have pierced his preconceptions about the outer bounds of the world or, at the very least, the farthest reaches of civilization.

Alexandros was already familiar with the Kyros story from his reading of Herodotos during his school days in Mieza. In fact, in his boyhood pantheon of heroes, Kyros occupied a prominent place. He was, after all, beloved of the gods, invincible in battle, the founder of a great empire, and an inspiration to a youngster dreaming of glory. Back then, Alexandros still thought of immortality figuratively and, by all objective measures, Kyros had achieved it. After all, two hundred years after his death, his fame continued to endure in the memory of men. In a literal sense, however, Kyros died in battle, defeated not far from Marakanda by a horde of Massagetai led by, of all things, a woman.

The fatal battle took place just beyond the Jaxartes River, which marked the northeastern boundary of Sogdiana, the farthest border of the Persian Empire, the outer limit of civilization, and the end of the line for the great Kyros. Alexandros found the mixture of lore, legend, history, and myth being retailed by the local sages as intoxicating as the uncut wine he was imbibing. They filled in the gaps in Herodotos's story that had always intrigued Alexandros.

It occurred to him that Kyros, on his way to expand the borders of the Persian Empire ever outward, must have spent some time in that very castle. No one knew exactly how old the castle was but it was already ancient when Kyros visited and possibly enlarged it, almost exactly two hundred years earlier. "What was Kyros thinking as he prepared to attack the Massagetai?" Alexandros wondered out loud.

The sages had no idea, of course, but that didn't stop them from spinning their yarns. They positioned the story as a morality tale of conflict between an insatiable conqueror, seeking to master the entire world, and an indomitable queen, determined to defend her people and the endless steppes they occupied. Her name was Tomyris. She was, in their telling, as beautiful as he was handsome. They were both shrewd, successful, and beloved by their people. They both enjoyed the favor of the gods until, at least for a crucial moment, the gods' attention wandered.

They were also, in many ways, polar opposites. He was the avatar of a new, progressive, sophisticated, avaricious civilization, while she was the defender of an ancient, nomadic, pastoral, idyllic way of life. He was boundlessly ambitious, willing to stoop to any trickery or deceit to achieve victory. She, on the other hand, placed honor and honesty at the top of her cherished values. She was, as her people liked to say, a straight shooter.

Their interaction started with correspondence. Kyros, wishing to conquer her lands without a struggle, sent a flattering letter offering to marry her and thus combine their two lands. He didn't need to spell out who would be in control of the united empire. Tomyris declined the offer.

Instead, she offered Kyros some advice. She told him that he was far from home, in over his head, and doomed unless he stopped before it was too late. Kyros rejected the advice and prepared to cross the Jaxartes River.

Seeing his preparations, Tomyris, certain of the military superiority of her fierce mounted fighters, offered to save him some trouble. She suggested that, instead of attempting a messy and difficult crossing that would only result in polluting the pristine waters of the Jaxartes with the bodies of his dead soldiers, she would withdraw her fighters to a three days' marching distance from the river and permit his army to reach the far bank without opposition. Once safely back on dry land, the two armies could then meet at a mutually agreed time and place and settle the issue once and for all. Or, in the alternative, if Kyros preferred to fight on his own side of the river, he could withdraw and she would come across with her army.

Kyros decided to resort to deception. He sent a letter accepting her offer to let his army into Massagetai territory without opposition and then engage in a set piece battle. Tomyris duly withdrew her troops and Kyros, along with his entire army, took up positions on the far bank of the Jaxartes. At that point, Kyros sent out a small contingent of his soldiers with most of the food and wine they possessed to a forward position, where they cooked the fare, set up tables, and indulged in a great feast. Long before they finished their comestibles and potables, they staggered off to relieve themselves and pretended to fall asleep.

A contingent of Massagetai, led by Tomyris's son, then ventured onto the feasting ground, drove off Kyros's contingent, and finished all the food and wine left behind. The Massagetai, not accustomed to drinking wine, were soon drunk and asleep. At that point, Kyros and the rest of his army swooped in, killed most of the sleeping Massagetai, and captured Tomyris's son.

Tomyris sent one more letter. She asked Kyros to release her son and to go home in peace to rule over lands he already controlled. If his bloodlust drove him to persist in his war against the Massagetai, she would annihilate him and all his men and quench his bloodthirst once and for all.

Kyros did release Tomyris's son but the young man's sense of honor caused him to commit suicide as soon as his shackles were removed. This unfortunate incident served as the signal for all-out hostilities to commence. The Massagetai, true to Tomyris's word, wiped out the entire Persian army, Kyros included. Afterward, the queen walked the battlefield searching for the great emperor's corpse. When she found it, she cut off his head and threw it into a wineskin filled with blood. "This should slake your thirst for good."

For two hundred years, no Persian emperor attacked the Massagetai.

Of the many morals that Alexandros could have drawn from this story, he fixated on two: One, the Persian Empire, which was now his by right of conquest, ended at the Jaxartes River, as did the civilized world, for that matter – there was no reason to venture beyond; and two, the great Kyros was not immortal after all.

And then he received reliable reports that Spitamenes and his rebel troops had withdrawn to the far side of the Jaxartes and formed an alliance with the Massagetai. Alexandros promptly forgot the lessons of Kyros, quickly implemented his usual administrative arrangements in Marakanda, and set off in pursuit of Spitamenes.

****

On the banks of the Jaxartes, we discovered a chain of abandoned and dilapidated forts, allegedly built by the great Kyros himself. After a cursory inspection, Alexandros decided to reoccupy these seven forts with his own "unreliable" veterans and mercenaries and set them to work on cleaning, refurbishing, and modernizing the old forts. In addition, he decided to establish one more garrison town, to be called Alexandria Eschate – Alexandria the Farthest – to which he consigned the rest of his "unreliables."

With the constant turnover of personnel and the ever-lengthening campaigns to the ends of the Earth, the implicit trust between Alexandros and his troops had begun to fray. And then, the Philotas "conspiracy" tipped

Alexandros over into outright paranoia. He recruited an elaborate network of informants to spy on his own soldiers; he deployed a multilingual company of literate recruits to open and read every piece of incoming and outgoing correspondence; and he asked his principal scribe Kallisthenes to maintain a list of unfit, disaffected, and troublesome soldiers. This was the list he used when making assignments for garrison duty.

Alexandros was still finalizing his arrangements for Alexandria Eschate and making preparations for crossing the Jaxartes when Spitamenes counterattacked. He used the threat of an invasion by Alexandros's army into their territory to rouse the fiery Massagetai into action. Additional volunteers streamed in by the thousands.

Practically overnight, Spitamenes had created seven new volunteer units, organized by tribes and led by their own tribal leaders. He then used these units to launch simultaneous attacks on the forts recently garrisoned by Alexandros's "unreliables." He personally led his main force straight at Marakanda, neatly bypassing Alexandros and his army in the process.

Before Alexandros could move out of his newly-founded Alexandria Eschate, the Massagetai surrounded the forts. The three largest forts resisted but were easily overwhelmed and their defenders slaughtered to a man. The four smaller forts then surrendered without a fight.

Their capitulators were promptly slaughtered to a man as well.

Marakanda fared a little better, thanks to its stout walls and larger garrison. They locked the gates and hunkered down, waiting for Alexandros to return and rescue them.

Somewhat surprisingly, Alexandros considered the Massagetai holding the forts a bigger threat than Spitamenes and his rebel army besieging Marakanda. He continued to believe that Spitamenes was simply "negotiating by other means" his change of allegiance and acceptance into Alexandros's service.

"What I need to deal with Spitamenes is a diplomat who can command our forces but, more importantly, can speak his language. Do we have such a man?"

A newly-arrived commander whom none of us really knew stepped forward. "I'm your man, your highness," he said in accented Greek.

I turned to Seleukos. "Who is he?" Seleukos tended to know these things before the rest of us.

Seleukos motioned with his hand to keep my voice down. "He's …"

Before Seleukos could answer, Alexandros beckoned the volunteer forward. "Yes, yes, I remember you. You brought us a battalion of Lykian volunteers recently, didn't you? Remind me, what's your name?"

"Pharnouches, sire."

"He's a mongrel," Seleukos whispered under his breath. "His father was an Ionian Greek who enlisted with the Persian Immortals. While on duty here in Sogdiana, he was awarded a captive Massagetan woman as his share of booty after some battle or other. Our Pharnouches over there is the product of that union."

Alexandros nodded. "That's right, Pharnouches. Now I remember. How did you happen to be in Lykia before deciding to join us?"

"My father was Lykian, sire. When I found out that your highness had become our new emperor, I knew it was my duty to join your army and support you in any way I could."

I winked at Seleukos. "The typical Persian bootlick, spinning like a weathervane."

"Shush," Seleukos hissed. "We'll talk about this later."

In the meantime, Alexandros's job interview of Pharnouches continued. "What did you do before you heard the news of my accession?"

"I was an interpreter and diplomat, your highness."

"Serving whom?"

"I was in Persian service, sire. Because my mother is Massagetan, I speak all the local languages around here. At first, I was simply an interpreter accompanying government officials as they traveled throughout these satrapies. After a while, I was sent out on my own as a representative of the emperor. Eventually, we had so many changes of emperors that they lost track of me. So, I went back home to Lykia and did various jobs for my father.

"But once we heard about your arrival, your highness, and all your great victories, I immediately set about organizing a group of volunteers intent on joining your great campaign. Almost a thousand ethnic Ionian Greek warriors signed up and here we are, ready to serve you."

"That's great, Pharnouches, just great. Let me tell you what we're going to do. In addition to your volunteers, I'm going to assign to you three squadrons of cavalry. They have their own commanders, of course, but you will be in overall command."

"I understand, your highness."

"You will march back to Marakanda, which is currently under siege by Spitamenes and his gang. You will engage Spitamenes and, with the help of our soldiers inside the city, you will lift the siege."

"Yes, your highness, thank you. In all fairness, sire, I should mention that my military experience ..."

"Don't worry, my man. When I said 'engage,' I didn't necessarily mean 'engage militarily.' I want you to use your diplomatic and linguistic skills to meet with Spitamenes, find out what he wants, and negotiate his surrender to our forces. Got that?"

"Yes, sire."

"Good." The job interview was at an end. Alexandros identified the three squadrons he was assigning to Pharnouches, told him to contact the three commanders, and ordered him to march out the next day.

Once Pharnouches was out of the tent, Alexandros turned to the main item on the agenda, which was our response to the Massagetai's attack on our forts.

****

We marched out that night. We arrived at the walls of the first fort in less than a day from the moment we received word of the massacre of our garrisons. It then took us three more days to retake four of the seven forts. No Massagetai survived our attacks. Alexandros was not in a clement mood. His disposition was not improved by an enemy arrow that pierced his thigh during one of our assaults.

The next fort we reached was the largest. It appeared to be impregnable. We settled in for a siege. Alexandros, impatient as always, sent men to look for weaknesses in the fortifications. This was an unenviable assignment because it had to be carried out under a hail of arrows and other projectiles. Most of the scouts managed to return uninjured but reported finding no vulnerabilities. One man, however, took the initiative to investigate a drainage ditch flowing out through an opening in the wall. He reported that the grate that barred the opening reached below the level of the effluent but not all the way to the bottom. He thought that it might be possible for a man to slither under it and into the fort, provided he could hold his breath and tolerate the stench.

That night an entire infantry company did just that. Wearing full armor and carrying their swords and daggers, they crawled under the grate, one by one, silently and unobserved. Once inside, they fought their way to the gate and threw it open. The rest of our forces, waiting right outside, rushed in. Alexandros, notwithstanding his recent thigh wound, limped in with the first wave of his troops. Eddies of fierce, hand-to-hand combat ensued but our men outnumbered the defenders by at least ten to one. Very quickly, there were no defenders left. We suffered relatively few casualties; however, among the injured was Alexandros. At some point in the melee he was hit on the head by a rock that left a large dent in his helmet and an ugly contusion beneath it. He lay unconscious for quite a few minutes. When he came to, he was dazed, unable to see, and unable to speak. His worried men rushed him out to his tent, where he lay, drifting in and out of consciousness. Philippos the Physician could do very little for him, other than making sure he didn't become dehydrated. Neither he nor anyone else could predict whether Alexandros would live or die.

Two days after being hit in the head, Alexandros woke up, his sight and speech restored, ate a hearty breakfast, and pronounced himself good as new. That seemed a bit of an overstatement. He was still limping from the recent arrow wound, he was rubbing and shaking his head a lot, he drank a lot of poppy-infused wine to dull his headache, and he was in an even worse mood than he had been prior to our assault on the fort.

In the meantime, the Massagetan occupiers of the remaining two forts, seeing the handwriting on the wall, surrendered without a fight. Alexandros ordered his troops to line them up on a flat, grass-covered plain between the two forts and strip them of all weapons, armor, and valuables. Once this was done, he ordered his troops to slaughter the Massagetai. The troops hesitated. At least the oldtimers flatly refused to kill unarmed captives. The newbies eventually shook their heads, grumbled under their breaths, and carried out the order.

******

Back in Marakanda, Pharnouches was not faring nearly as well. When his forces approached the city,

Spitamenes's besiegers melted away, letting Pharnouches enter without hindrance. However, as soon the detachment was inside, Spitamenes's men returned and resumed the siege. Pharnouches sent two men under a truce banner to negotiate the terms of Spitamenes's surrender. The men were returned with their heads cut off.

Having concluded that negotiations were unlikely to yield a positive outcome at that moment, Pharnouches sallied forth from the city, accompanied by his entire detachment. Once again, rather than put up any resistance, Spitamenes's men galloped away in the direction of the Jaxartes. Pharnouches ordered a vigorous pursuit, which proved to be unsuccessful.

Having lost sight of the retreating enemy, and with daylight fading, Pharnouches directed his men to make camp, consume their rations, fetter their horses, and settle in for the night. Believing that Spitamenes must have fled to the far side of the river by then, he neglected to post sentries or take other defensive precautions.

Spitamenes and his army returned before dawn and showered the unsuspecting Pharnouches battalion with salvo after salvo of arrows. It was a clear night but the clouds of incoming missiles blotted out the moonlight. Except for a couple of men who pretended to be dead, neither Pharnouches, nor his soldiers, nor their horses, ever got to see the light of day. Spitamenes, leaving the corpses and carcasses of the enemy for disposal by wild animals, birds, and forces of nature, then rode back and resumed his siege of Marakanda.

****

When one of the survivors of the Pharnouches battalion was brought into Alexandros's tent, shortly after the massacre of the Massagetan prisoners of war, he reverted to his default mood of late – outrage. He quickly completed arrangements for Alexandria Eschate and the seven forts and marched back to Marakanda with the rest of the army.

At our approach, Spitamenes once again lifted the siege and withdrew. Alexandros, backed by the entire Companion Cavalry, gave chase. In the course of our pursuit, we noticed a large kettle of vultures soaring on thermals up ahead. We also saw a black murder of crows circling below. Then the wind shifted and we were hit by the stench. And finally, we reached the site of Pharnouches's last stand. As far as the eye could see, the steppe was littered by human and animal remains. The corpses and carcasses had been torn apart and scattered by wild beasts. They bit off more than they could chew and, in an attempt to save the rest for later, scattered the skeletons, covered with lots of flesh and bits of clothing, for miles around. The vultures and crows tried valiantly to clean up the mess but the volume of putrefying carrion exceeded even their prodigious gluttony. In due course, rodents, worms, bacteria, and the sun would have completed the job and left nothing but a gleaming carpet of white bones and vivid green grass, accented by bits of cloth and rusting iron. As yet, however, insufficient time had elapsed to let nature finish its sanitation work.

Alexandros stopped the chase and ordered all the human bodies collected and buried in a mass grave. The horses were interred in their own pit. When we were finished, Alexandros had had enough. "We'll catch them another day," he said. We returned to Marakanda and worked on healing our wounds and repairing our morale. Alexandros spent his time conducting audiences in the old castle, hosting banquets, and attempting to run an empire from its farthest periphery. By the time we had all recovered, the campaigning season was over. Alexandros decided we would spend the winter in Baktra, which was slightly more centrally located, but not much. He'd squandered a year accomplishing more or less nothing, except perhaps getting a lot of people killed, many of them his own men.

****

The first order of business, once we arrived in Baktra, was Bessos's trial. That took one day. For Alexandros, it was mostly downhill from there. He was inundated by a relentless flood of administrative headaches. He tried to delegate as much of the work of running the empire as he could but finding reliable Persian collaborators to fill various bureaucratic posts proved impossible.

His old Mieza gang, which formed the core of his senior command staff, was busy trying to welcome, train, and integrate reinforcements who arrived almost weekly. They were a dispiriting crew of mercenaries, fortune seekers, and desperados, some Greek, some Persian, some speaking languages none of us recognized.

Keeping everyone fed, housed, and equipped was the responsibility of Artabazos, the Alexandros-appointed satrap of Baktria. The old man was finding the job too challenging, even with the help of numerous officious functionaries. Alexandros, who found Artabazos to be the only member of Persian nobility whom he was willing to trust, wanted to add the satrapy of Sogdiana to Artabazos's portfolio. And the veteran courtier was tempted, if only for the sake of his daughter Barsine, whom he hoped to see married to Alexandros very soon. The idea of their son, and Artabazos's grandson, Herakles, inheriting the throne of Persia one day was a heady thought indeed. But in the end, Artabazos was honest enough to admit that he was hard-pressed to deal with the satrapy of Baktria and couldn't possibly take on responsibility for the wild and possibly ungovernable satrapy of Sogdiana. As a result, that post remained vacant.

****

At about the same time in Sousa, Barsine glanced out into the courtyard of her apartment and did a double take. Sisygambis, who normally shuffled along at the stately pace of a tortoise, was running, her arms failing furiously.

She stepped through the doorway to intercept the intruder. "What is it, my lady?"

Sisygambis skidded to a halt, collapsed to her knees, and enfolded Barsine's legs in her arms. She tried to speak but couldn't find sufficient breath to spare. Finally, she managed a deep inhalation and blurted out: "They're taking Ochos away."

"Who's taking him away? Where are they taking him? Why?"

"The eunuchs. They caught him spying on Parysatis in the bathing pool. They claim his manhood was sticking straight out."

"Oh, they're just jealous," Barsine laughed.

"This is no laughing matter, your grace. He's the son of the previous emperor. No new emperor can allow a claimant to the imperial tiara to grow up." Sisygambis broke into sobs, unable to continue.

Barsine picked up the old woman by the armpits. "Let's see what we can find out."

She escorted Sisygambis back to her apartment, accompanied by Barsine's entire household. As they approached, a curious tug-of-war greeted their eyes. On one side, a strong young eunuch was holding the thirteen-year-old Ochos by the arm and tunic, trying to haul him away. On the other side, Stateira and Drypetis were desperately clinging to their brother, pulling him back. Everyone was screaming. As Barsine watched, Ochos's tunic gave way and the youngster was left wearing nothing but his loinwrap. It seemed like one of his arms might come loose next.

Barsine broke into a run, calling to Artakama over her shoulder. "Go get all the other women! Hurry!"

When she reached the eunuch, she shoved him with all her strength, which was considerable. The large eunuch didn't budge but, surprised by the unexpected assault, released the boy. Stateira and Drypetis stumbled backward and fell to the ground. Ochos landed on top of them.

The eunuch rounded on Barsine. "You'll pay for this, you tart!"

Barsine held her ground. "On the contrary, you fat turd, you're a dead man." Then she laughed. "Oh, I forgot. You're not a man at all, are you?"

The eunuch drew back his fist. Barsine didn't flinch. "Go ahead! Strike the mother of the next emperor!" The eunuch's arm dropped to his side.

Other women came running in ones and twos. The eunuch withdrew in the direction of the guards' barracks.

"They'll be back," Thais said loudly. "Let's arm ourselves and put up a barricade at the entrance of this apartment."

As the women looked at her uncomprehendingly, she amplified her orders. "Break into the communal kitchen and bring whatever knives, spits, pots, and pans you can find. Or go to your own quarters and return with your chamber pots – no need to empty them first. And grab anything you can throw; the heavier the better. The rest of you, start dragging furniture out here to build the barricade."

By the time Dilshad arrived on the scene, trailed by every single eunuch employed in the harem, the barricade and adjoining rooftops bristled with armed women. Thais, Barsine, and Artakama stood side-by-side on the nearest roof, hefting adobe shingles and stone building blocks.

Dilshad surveyed the scene, a look of amazement on his face. "Ladies, what's the problem?"

Thais responded for the rebels. "You can't have Ochos. He stays with us."

"Be reasonable, my lady," Dilshad pleaded. "He's a man. We can't have men living in the harem."

"He's not a man; he's a boy."

"He's old enough to impregnate one of you ladies. Maybe a few of you. How would that look to your lords and masters?"

"Don't be crazy. He's thirteen."

Dilshad shook his head. "I'm surprised at you, Thais. You, of all people, should know that thirteen is old enough."

Barsine stepped in before Thais could rise to the bait. "This has nothing to do with impregnating anybody and you know it. We're not letting you take little Ochos away."

They reached an impasse. Dilshad was pretty sure his eunuchs could prevail in a physical confrontation. Even without testes, they were bigger and far stronger than the women. And there were more of them. As a last resort, he could call in actual soldiers, with weapons and intact scrotums. The problem was that some of the women were bound to be injured or even killed in any fight. Dilshad's job was to assure that all the women remained unblemished and untouched when their owners showed up to claim them. An unexpected scar could easily turn into a death sentence for Dilshad.

"Alright, alright, ladies, have it your way," he called out. "But don't expect to see any food until you turn Ochos over. In fact, don't expect any of the services we usually provide."

Thais jumped up. "Does that mean you won't be guarding the gate? So, we can just walk out?"

Dilshad, who was already walking away, turned back. "No, my lady, it doesn't mean that. But nice try."

The next morning, the eunuchs prepared a nice, aromatic, communal breakfast, taking over a job usually performed by female slaves. Only a few women availed themselves of the feast. By the next morning, they'd worked out a new system. Half showed up for breakfast and, after eating their fill, brought back an equal amount of food and drink for the other half, laughing at the stupidity of the eunuchs as they carried their loot.

When they reached Sisygambis's apartment, they were in for a surprise. The dowager, her grandchildren, and their servants were among the women who had chosen to remain behind, afraid of being ambushed as they walked to the communal dining hall. Unfortunately, while the other women were eating, a group of eunuchs quietly surrounded Sisygambis's apartment, bound and gagged all the residents as they encountered them, and carried young Ochos away, also bound and gagged.

After the women were untied, they rushed to the barracks and confronted Dilshad. The principal eunuch was his usual smooth, unctuous, reassuring self. "Don't worry, ladies. He's been taken to the palace to live with the other courtiers. He'll be trained as one of the satrap's pages. I'm sure we'll able to arrange a chaperoned visit by him soon enough."

For once, Sisygambis, Barsine, Thais, and all the rest were left speechless. Ochos was never seen again.

****

In the spring of 258 Z.E., Alexandros resumed his chase of Spitamenes. He left Krateros behind, with 4,000 troops, to make sure the inhabitants of Baktra didn't rebel while we were in the field. Artabazos was still the satrap of Baktria and Alexandros trusted him implicitly, but not enough to leave him in command of any actual troops. In fairness, Artabazos was also old and ailing.

Alexandros came up with a novel strategy to combat Spitamenes's favorite tactic of hitting us with a quick strike and then disappearing into the wilderness. Contrary to orthodox military doctrine, Alexandros split his forces into five columns, which would proceed across Baktria and Sogdiana in parallel lines, like the tines of a rake, sweeping up all opposing forces as so many fallen leaves of autumn. The five columns were commanded by Alexandros, Hephaistion, Perdikkas, Koinos, and me. While proceeding on tracks a few miles apart, we were in frequent communication with the other columns to make sure that our clearing operations were coordinated, leaving no armed resistance behind. In addition, Alexandros established small, fortified camps in our wake to prevent any resurgence of resistance once we'd swept through an area.

Spitamenes, in the meantime, was hiding out among the Massagetai on the far side of the Jaxartes, recruiting still more mounted fighters for a return engagement. By the middle of the summer, we'd cleaned out Baktria and most of Sogdiana. Unfortunately, the pernicious climate, brutally cold in the winter and scorching hot in the summer, was starting to take its toll on our soldiers. Alexandros had no choice but to order a pause in our campaign. The five columns met at Marakanda for a couple of weeks of rest and recuperation.

Spitamenes, having replenished his losses, chose that very moment to resume his guerilla war. He re-crossed the Jaxartes and started to pick off small detachments of our men once again. Although Alexandros had lots of scouts roaming the steppes, Spitamenes easily eluded detection until he was ready to strike. He captured a couple of our small, fortified camps, leaving their defenders' unburied corpses behind like so many putrefying pin cushions. Unexpectedly, he showed up in the vicinity of Baktra, causing havoc and doing his best to destroy Artabazos's and Krateros's ability to keep the city calm and fed.

Finally, Krateros ventured out of Baktra and managed to catch some of Spitamenes's forces in the field. A pitched battle ensued, which Krateros's men easily won, killing about 150 enemy fighters in the process. But Spitamenes and the rest of his forces vanished once again into the wilderness.

Chapter 12 – Kleitos

The two-week hiatus in Marakanda stretched to four. For the first time in his life, Alexandros was undecided on how to proceed. The notion of chasing after ghosts in the scorching heat of the dry steppes of Sogdiana didn't have much appeal to the troops. On the other hand, the lack of progress in pacifying the eastern satrapies and getting on with the campaign didn't thrill them either. The allegiance of the new recruits to their leader varied in proportion to his success. In the last two years, there had been much toil, disease, fighting, and death, but precious little plunder.

Alexandros spent his time in the old castle drinking, ranting, and raging. Even the incessant feasts failed to raise his spirits. The veteran Macedonian commanders, just as unhappy as Alexandros, blamed all that had gone wrong on their new Persian "allies." The Persian courtiers, used to the fickleness of their leaders, worked assiduously to cultivate Alexandros's favor. All three – Alexandros, the

Macedonians, and the Persians – drank themselves into stupor every night, drinking sour, undiluted wine.

Gone were the civilized banquets of old, featuring good food, lively conversation, titillating entertainment, and watered but savory wine. Despite Alexandros's efforts to foster an esprit de corps among all his commanders, regardless of their origin or ethnicity, the parties tended to break up into segregated affairs. This was probably just as well, given the proclivity of the attendees to get into fights along ethnic lines.

Two developments, one good, one bad, finally broke through the enervating miasma. On the positive front, Nearchos the Kretan showed up. He was one of Alexandros's oldest friends and advisors. When the then-eighteen-year-old Alexandros got into a nasty argument with his father and was expelled from Pella for his troubles, Nearchos was one of only four friends who joined him in exile. (Erigyios, Harpalos, and I were the other three.) After Alexandros became king and was ready to launch the main-force invasion of Asia, he had put Nearchos in charge of assembling the flotilla that would take us across the Hellespont, because all Kretans were presumed to be naval experts. Then, after the successful conclusion of our campaign in Ionia, Alexandros named him satrap of Lykia. Now, finding himself short of reliable commanders, he'd recalled him to join the old gang. Nearchos arrived bearing gifts: 4,000 infantrymen and 500 cavalry. Alexandros was pleased to see his old friend and even more pleased with the reinforcements.

Less auspicious was a message received from Artabazos in Baktra. Pleading ill health, he asked to be relieved of his position as satrap of Baktria and to be allowed to return to his ancestral home in Hellespontine Phrygia. Having little choice in the matter, Alexandros granted the request and Artabazos departed. Eventually we found out that he'd died before reaching home.

Alexandros, short of reliable administrators, now faced the need to find someone else to put in charge. After considering, and rejecting, a number of candidates, he picked Kleitos Melas as the new satrap of Baktria. Kleitos was none too pleased, viewing the appointment as a demotion. However, a good soldier as always, he bowed to the wishes of his commander.

Naturally, a banquet was incumbent to celebrate the new appointment. As luck would have it, a new shipment of somewhat better wine had arrived earlier that day. Everyone in the castle was looking forward to another boisterous, besotted party. As usual, all the important people were invited, including veteran Macedonian commanders and newly-minted Persian courtiers.

Alexandros, as had become his custom on these occasions, was resplendent in Dareios's old imperial, suitably altered vestments. Persian courtiers, upon arriving in the great hall, prostrated themselves as a matter of course. Then, depending on their rank, they would rise to their knees and bow deeply once or twice, touching their foreheads to the ground. The more senior and noble commanders would rise directly to their feet and bow standing up. The most favored Persians, after being acknowledged by the emperor, would blow a kiss in his direction. At Dareios's court, it had been the custom for the most senior courtiers to approach the emperor and kiss him on the cheeks. Alexandros enjoyed the ceremonial entrance of the Persians into his presence but thought himself far too exalted for anyone to touch his skin or, for that matter, any other part of his person. The Macedonian commanders, in the meantime, simply walked in and, if they were not distracted talking to each other, waved to their king and perhaps called out a greeting. They reserved their acts of proskynesis for their gods. Alexandros, although highly irritated by their obstinate refusal to accord him the respect to which he believed himself entitled, pretended not to notice.

Notwithstanding their divergent views of court protocol, all the guests appreciated the quality of the newly-arrived wine. Well before midnight, everyone in the room was roaring drunk. Any semblance of civilized conversation had long since been drowned in a sea of loud singing, lewd heckling, and bellicose bickering. Inebriated Persians, wishing to make sure the emperor heard their ingratiating and servile comments above the general uproar, abandoned their assigned seats and swarmed around Alexandros's couch. Some, either as a sign of reverence or vertigo, approached on their hands and knees, others by scooting on their butts like tired toddlers.

The Persian courtiers competed in the eloquence of their exaltations. They compared Alexandros favorably to his ancestor Herakles, commented on his resemblance to his heavenly father Ammon-Zeus, and generally fanned his delusions of divinity. They praised his military victories, starting with Chaironeia, while denigrating the contributions of his earthly father Philippos, of his Macedonian military commanders, and of his veteran fighting men.

Everything about this performance irritated the oldtimers in the room, who'd been with Alexandros since before he'd become king of Macedonia. They resented his imperial airs and Persian attire. They considered his efforts to mandate proskynesis blasphemous and they found the newcomers' willingness to comply contemptible. But what they hated most was Alexandros's failure to acknowledge that he had not achieved his military victories by himself.

A loud, rowdy, belligerent debate, fueled by alcohol, erupted between the Macedonians and the Persians. Alexandros mostly kept his own counsel but managed to convey the impression that he agreed with the Persians' view of things and resented the Macedonians' failure to acknowledge either his divinity or his personal credit for all their victories.

Before the debate could degenerate into an all-out melee, Alexandros called for the start of the evening's entertainment. New rounds of wine were poured and the entertainer stepped forward. Unfortunately, it was not a comely lass but a middle-aged comedian. This particular jester didn't simply recite his humorous monologue; he delivered it as a grating, nasal, singsong chant. He also chose an unfortunate topic for his comedy routine: Feigning sympathy for the newly-appointed satrap, his theme was that Kleitos had his work cut out for him. Then, encouraged by the laughter and applause of the Persians in the room, the comedian segued to poking fun at the ineptitude of the forces trying to hunt down poor, lonesome Spitamenes, culminating in a gleeful recounting of the recent annihilation of the detachment led by Pharnouches.

The Macedonians in the room had had enough. They leapt from their couches and attempted to strangle the "comedian," who was in fact a paid Persian provocateur. In response, the Persian noblemen sprang to their feet to protect the man. Many punches flew but few landed. Eventually, a bemused Alexandros intervened, stepping into the middle of the brawl and telling the combatants to calm down and return to their seats. Reluctantly and with much muttering, the men complied and the "comedian" was hustled out of the room. But the bickering continued unabated.

Somehow, despite the deafening noise, an off-hand comment by Alexandros cut through the din. "Pharnouches wasn't much of a commander, was he?"

Kleitos, occupying a couch near Alexandros as the guest of honor at the banquet, came to Pharnouches's defense. "He died for you, Alexandros. How can you say such a thing?"

Kleitos's words brought the emperor to an instant and blinding fury. It was not so much the rebuke that incensed him as the mode of address. It had been a long time since anyone had called him just plain, unembellished Alexandros. He rounded on his commander, his eyes blazing. "You guys are constantly finding excuses for your failures. I'm sick of your ineptitude."

Kleitos climbed off his couch. "Yeah, ineptitude – a big word from a little man swaddled in big robes. We heard no complaints from you at Granikos, where you would've had your head sliced in two but for my ineptitude. In fact, if it hadn't been for the ineptitude of your Macedonian brothers in arms, you would've been dead eight times over by now."

Alexandros jumped off his couch, sword drawn, and rushed toward Kleitos. Luckily, Hephaistion and Perdikkas intervened and took away his sword before he could do any harm. Seleukos and I, in the meantime, hustled Kleitos out of the room.

We were all still gasping for breath and counting our lucky stars when Kleitos reentered the hall through another door. He resumed his spouting. "Alexandros of Epiros was right. While he fought against men in Italy, you spent your time trying to defeat mice in Asia."

This time, before anyone else could react, Alexandros ripped a spear from the hands of a surprised bodyguard and buried the tip in Kleitos's chest. My friend sank to the floor, his hands grasping the quivering shaft. He died without uttering a sound, his lightless eyes wide open, whether in surprise or anger it was impossible to tell.

****

Alexandros's reaction revealed thespian gifts none of us had suspected. In the immediate aftermath of the murder, a stunned silence seized the great hall of the ancient castle. Alexandros, his head whipping from side to side, looked from corpse to Macedonian veterans to Persian courtiers and back again, gauging their reactions. All he could see was disbelief. Then, very gradually, the expressions started to change. A rising tide of anger flooded the Macedonian faces, while the Persians blanched with fear. Before anyone could actually move, Alexandros sank to his knees, prostrated himself next to Kleitos's cooling body, careful not to let the pooling blood stain his robe, and emitted an anguished, inarticulate howl.

He beat the stone floor with his fists, grabbed his luxuriant blond hair and feebly tried to tear some of it out.

Then, noticing a pillow lying nearby, he moved his body ever so slightly and, still holding his hair, started beating his head against the pillow.

When Hephaistion and Perdikkas gently raised him back to his feet, his cheeks were streaked with tears, his eyes pinched in agony. "What have I done?" he wailed. "I've killed Kleitos, my friend and one of my best soldiers. Zeus, my father, I beg you, kill me now!"

Casting a sidelong glance at his veterans, he saw several rise unsteadily to their feet and reach for their swords, whether to kill him or their fellow Persian commanders was not entirely clear. Perceiving the threat, he let himself be dragged out of the room, barely able to move his feet, continuing to keen. The veterans, immobilized by confusion, anger, and sorrow, milled about aimlessly. The Persians quietly but quickly vacated the premises.

****

When I was little and misbehaved, one of my mother's favorite sayings used to be: "Remember, I brought you into this world and I can always take you out." She meant it in a loving way, of course. As I tried to cope with the death of my friend, similar thoughts coursed through my mind, except there was no love involved. Rage, for sure; grief, undoubtedly; and a great big dollop of confusion.

Maybe I should've killed him while he was bent over the corpse, putting on his act. That wouldn't have brought Kleitos back to life but perhaps it would've balanced the moral calculus of the universe. It was a silly, impractical thought, I knew. I would've been killed on the spot and then many, many more people would've died.

I searched desperately for a rational, principled, ethical compass to guide me through this morass. The only religious principle I'd ever followed was the Prime Directive but, at some point, I'd lost my faith. The one notion I couldn't escape was my belief that human beings possessed free will. Perhaps, unbeknownst to me, I'd been a Zoroastrian all along. I shook my head with a bitter laugh.

I had tried at least three times to alter the flow of time. First, I'd saved Kleitos's life and now Kleitos was dead. Then, I'd intentionally violated the Prime Directive by trying to talk Alexandros out of a suicidal effort to cross the Hindu Kush before the end of winter. Alexandros had simply ignored my entreaties and men meant to die had died. Finally, I'd tried to keep my fellow soldiers from drinking the contaminated water of the Oxos. They drank it anyway and many of them died. So, what did that say about the contest between people's free will and the inertial tendencies of the temporal stream? More importantly, what did it say about my determination to avenge my friend and kill Alexandros? I had no answers.

Immortal Alexandros

I retired to my tent and stayed up all night trying to reason out the right thing to do. Alexandros, in the meantime, remained in his tent, refusing to eat or drink and lamenting loudly whenever he sensed anyone nearby. He vowed to starve himself to death as penance. No one dared to enter his tent.

In the end, I didn't make an attempt on Alexandros's life. Instead, I saw to it that Kleitos received a respectful funeral, attended by most of his comrades in Marakanda. I said a few words before the body was set ablaze, followed by perhaps a dozen more eulogies. We found a dozen ways to say the same thing: He was a great soldier and a better human being; he was funny, beloved by all; he would be terribly missed; he was honest and was murdered for it. Then, before we could get into more trouble, we quietly poured his still-warm ashes into a silver urn, buried it in a pit, covered it with freshly dug soil, and placed a temporary wooden stele to mark the place.

His comrades scattered to nearby taverns to drink to his memory and drown their sorrows. I walked back to my quarters alone, lost in thought. An unwelcome idea lurked in the recesses of my mind. Try as I might, I couldn't chase it away. After Granikos, I'd lost my ability to know what the future held. Now, I'd lost my ability know the righteous path to get there. *Oh, well,* I thought, *now I'm just like everybody else.*

******

Two days after the murder, Hephaistion snuck into Alexandros's tent, smuggling in some food and drink. "How are you holding up, Aniketos?"

A haggard Alexandros was contrite. "I've killed one of my best commanders, Hephaistion. And the man who saved my life. All my aspirations are ruined."

"Nonsense. A commander always knows, when he sends men into battle, that some of them won't come back. That's one of the burdens of command."

"Yes, but Kleitos didn't die in battle. He died at a banquet."

"There are many different battlefields, Aniketos. Right now, you're fighting to create an army capable of conquering the world. And those who get in the way have to be eliminated. It's always been a mark of your greatness that you do the really dirty work with your own hands."

Alexandros nodded. "Makes sense, what you say, but it doesn't make me feel any better."

"Poppycock, my friend. You're just hungry. Luckily for you, I've managed to snag some choice treats. And the wine's not too bad either."

Alexandros eagerly availed himself of the small feast that Hephaistion spread out in front of him. "That is tasty," he murmured between bites and gulps. "Tell me, how did the ordinary soldiers take the news? Kleitos was a popular fellow, wasn't he?"

"They were understandably upset at first but they're calming down now. They're beginning to worry that if you starve yourself to death, they may never get out of this godforsaken hole."

"Well, that's good to hear. But if I emerge from this tent looking hale and hearty, they may forget their fears and go back to hating me for killing Kleitos."

"You're right, Aniketos," Hephaistion laughed. "So maybe you should slow down with the gorging."

Alexandros stopped eating. "Good point. I guess I screwed up again."

"Not to worry. You keep starving in here for two more days. By then, the soldiers should be beside themselves with worry and you should be looking nice and emaciated. And I'll have a suitable ceremony organized by the time you come out."

****

When Alexandros finally emerged from his tent, after four days of penance, he was barely able to walk. As the soldiers, massed ten-deep around the entrance to the tent, looked on, with tears and pity in their eyes, he staggered. He would have undoubtedly fallen but for the timely intervention of Hephaistion and Perdikkas, who grabbed him under each arm and kept him upright. Soldiers rushed toward him, offering food and wine. Alexandros, enfeebled though he was, waved them away. "I must attend to my ritual obligations first."

He was half dragged, half carried to a nearby improvised altar, where he fell to his knees and started to pray. Before he had gotten very far, Kleomenes of Lakedaimon, who was Alexandros's new soothsayer-in-chief, rushed up and threw himself on the ground between Alexandros and the altar. "Forgive me, sire, for all the pain and suffering I've caused you. Please forgive me."

Alexandros let him lament and beg for a while, before bidding him to rise. "Tell me what you've done, Kleomenes. I promise to forgive you, if I can."

"Sire, on the night of your friend's death, I had just slaughtered a chicken, as I do every night, to read the entrails. This time, the omens were unusual and left me confused. The liver was unusually large and discolored. At the same time, the intestines were tangled and hard to read. After a while I realized that I was seeing repeated curls of deltas, knotted into a whorl of kappas."

Alexandros nodded, as if this nonsense meant something to him. The charlatan continued.

"Don't you see, sire? It suddenly dawned on me. Dionysos was in an ugly mood with some mortal, but who?"

The crowd of soldiers surrounding the two drew nearer as they listened in fascinated silence.

"It should've been obvious but it took me a while. I had to examine the lungs and especially the heart to be sure. Then it hit me: The god was angry at Kleitos Melas. I tried to find out why but the auguries were silent. Too late, I remembered that Kleitos was to be the guest of honor at that night's banquet.

"I ran to the castle as fast as I could. I wanted to warn Kleitos, who was, as we all know, occasionally flippant in his worship of the gods, to be especially reverent and punctilious in performing the rituals and libations at the banquet if he was to have any chance of propitiating the enraged deity. Had I arrived in time I might have saved his life.

"Alas, I arrived too late. By the time I got to the great hall Kleitos was already dead. And then I heard that Dionysos had chosen you, the great and divine Alexandros, as the instrument of his vengeance. I was absolutely shattered and I panicked. I quickly left and hid in my tent and prayed to the gods for salvation.

"I knew I'd caused you agonizing anguish and suffering by being too slow to apprehend the signs and warn you. And then I compounded my mistake by praying to the gods for salvation instead of coming immediately to you, exalted highness, and praying to you for clemency, thus prolonging your pain. Can you ever forgive me, oh, merciful Alexandros?"

When he had finished his carefully prepared speech, Kleomenes once again threw himself on the ground, wailing and sobbing uncontrollably.

Alexandros ignored the histrionic diviner at his feet. Instead, with fresh tears coursing down his cheeks, he addressed the assembled troops. "My fellow soldiers, you all know that Kleitos had saved my life once, so, in a sense, all I've become since, I owe to him. More importantly, though, he was my very good friend, as I'm sure he was a very good friend to many of you. He had a knack for making friends with everyone he met. We all miss him terribly, I most of all. But none of us, not even I, can either understand the ways of the gods or their reasons. Only the Moirai, weaving the tapestry of our fates, know whither the strands of our lives may lead and when they will end.

"Because of a callous whim of a capricious god, we have lost our beloved comrade. I promise you here and now that, when we return home, I will see to it that a stone likeness of Kleitos is erected at the foot of Mt. Olympos, which will remind all passersby of this great warrior's achievements long after we're all gone.

"We're all subject to the will of gods and none of us can oppose what the gods have decreed, even when we can't understand why they've done it. We will conduct a banquet tonight to perform all the libations and rituals due to Dionysos in the hope of appeasing him and in celebration of Kleitos's life."

There was no applause or acclamation. The soldiers simply dispersed in silence. Not many of them bought the carefully staged theatrical performances by Kleomenes and Alexandros. At the same time, they all understood that their survival depended on Alexandros's staying alive. And Alexandros realized that there was no limit to what he could get away with.

Chapter 13 – Tying Up Loose Ends

Summer slowly turned to fall, which soon gave way to winter, and still no progress. Spitamenes kept harassing us and we kept chasing him, in a desultory fashion. We'd managed to establish a measure of control over parts of Sogdiana but Spitamenes had slipped into the wilderness across the Jaxartes River. He was avidly recruiting reinforcements among the Massagetai, promising them the opportunity not only to preserve their independence but also to snatch lots of loot to boot.

Once reports came in that Spitamenes was on the far side of the Jaxartes, Alexandros dispatched Koinos, with a substantial force, in the direction of Farthest Alexandria. His assignment was to reinforce the seven forts on the riverine border and to fill in the gaps between the forts to prevent Spitamenes from crossing the river for his troublesome hit-and-run attacks. After securing the southern bank, Koinos was to get across the river himself, find Spitamenes, and destroy him.

Koinos did secure the southern bank but delayed crossing over. Although the water level was at its seasonal low, the continuing lack of suitable boats or rafts and the threat posed by the Massagetan archers, if they caught his forces midstream, persuaded Koinos that tactical delay was his best policy. He viewed the entire undertaking to capture or kill Spitamenes as a wild goose chase, given his lack of intelligence as to the enemy's whereabouts amidst the horizonless seas of waving grass. On the other hand, he didn't dare openly to disregard Alexandros's orders, so he temporized. Back in Marakanda, Alexandros continued to seethe and fulminate.

****

Unbeknown to us, Spitamenes was beginning to have problems of his own. A split developed between the original elements of his band, mostly Baktrian and Sogdian fighters left over from Bessos's army, and his new recruits from among the Massagetai. All of these raiders and brigands were used to living in rough conditions but the Baktrians and Sogdians, having lived in the Persian Empire and having fought in the Persian army, represented the height of civilization compared to the truly primitive Massagetai. One point of contention was the available diet. The Massagetai ate mostly horseflesh, supplemented by fish caught in the Jaxartes and its tributaries. They avoided drinking water, which they rightly considered unhealthy. Instead, they drank fermented mares' milk, augmented occasionally with horse blood. Even the savage Baktrians and Sogdians found this diet revolting.

What the Massagetai lacked in the trappings of civilization, they more than made up in pride, dignity, and self-sufficiency. They were also ferocious fighters, with a long history of tribal independence and self-government. They resented these pretentious interlopers, Spitamenes foremost among them, who presumed to lecture them about acceptable mores and preferred military tactics. And they grew impatient waiting for the promised treasure troves of loot.

As winter approached and conditions deteriorated, there was talk of mutiny. In desperation, Spitamenes decided to launch an all-out guerrilla strike. On a moonless night, he and his men crossed the Jaxartes, intending to seize one of the forts. Koinos's sentries detected the crossing as soon as it was launched and, by dawn, when Spitamenes's forces had finished their crossing, Koinos's army was waiting for them. It was an unequal contest. The Baktrian and Sogdian fighters and their Massagetan allies may have been the savage scrappers of the steppes but, in a pitched battle, they were no match for the disciplined, professional army of Alexandros. In short order, the Baktrian and Sogdian soldiers, who had once fought in the Persian army, surrendered and offered to join Alexandros's forces. The Massagetai stood and fought and were mostly killed. Spitamenes, along with the surviving Massagetai, fled back across the river.

When Spitamenes finally reached his tent that night, his wife, the Massagetan princess, was none too pleased to see him. She refused to clean him up or feed him, ordering him to get out. Instead, he raped her. When he fell asleep, she cut his throat.

In the morning, upon hearing what had happened, her fellow tribesmen finished the job by cutting off Spitamenes's head and sending it as a peace offering to Alexandros. To sweeten the deal, they also sent Spitamenes's twelve-year-old daughter Apame along. The final item was perhaps the most important piece in the entire package: the imperial tiara, which had somehow found its way into Spitamenes's possession. It meant nothing to the Massagetai but proved deeply satisfying to Alexandros.

Without ever talking to each other directly, both Alexandros and the Massagetai concluded that they'd had enough. The Massagetai agreed to stay on their side of the river. They were not seen riding the steppes of Sogdiana for at least a generation. And Alexandros never again thought of marching to the north of the Jaxartes.

Spitamenes's head adorned the main gate of Marakanda, serving as bird feed, until a cheeky macaque absconded with it in the dead of night. Apame was sent off to join the ladies of the harem in Sousa. And the tiara was expected to feature prominently when Alexandros's long-delayed coronation finally took place.

****

It was now the dead of winter. Outside the old castle walls a blizzard was raging. Its fury, however, was tame compared to Alexandros's continuing conniptions. It was getting close to two years since he and his army had crossed, at great peril and cost, the Hindu Kush. And what had all that sacrifice, expenditure, and lost time brought them? Tenuous control of two former Persian satrapies that contained almost nothing worth possessing. With other lands out there waiting to be conquered, he was bogged down in these interminable steppes and deserts. Specifically, India beckoned.

Alexandros had known about the Persian satrapy of India[16] since reading Herodotos as a schoolboy in Mieza. Unfortunately, Herodotos had never been to India and, most likely, had never met anyone who'd been there. His stories of this exotic land were more akin to adult fairytales than reliable travelogues. Among other things, he described ants bigger than foxes that dug for gold. Alexandros wanted to capture some of these ants and send them to Aristoteles for study, while keeping the gold for himself. More importantly, at one time the satrapy of India constituted the farthest southeastern corner of the Persian Empire. The

---

[16] The Persian satrapy of India should not be confused with the subcontinent of India. The satrapy, although variable in size during its existence, comprised a relatively small area in the northwest corner of the subcontinent even at its maximum extent. See Map 12 at AlexanderGeiger.com.

Achaemenid emperors had lost control of this satrapy a long time ago but, to Alexandros, it represented a piece of the empire that should now, by all rights, be his. And, as far as he knew, once his army crossed the Indos River and ventured beyond India, they would quickly reach the shore of the world-encircling Okeanos River. Then, having conquered the eastern end of the world, they could finally turn around, return to Babylon, and start thinking about fighting their way down the Mediterranean Sea, all the way to the Atlas Mountains and the western end of the world. His dream was to conquer Earth's entire habitable zone, from top to bottom and from end to end. Unfortunately, for the time being, even India was beyond his reach.

First, there was the deadly weather outside. No sane person would march out into the treacherous terrain of the eastern satrapies during the winter months. Second, he had to make sure that Baktria and Sogdiana didn't slip from his grasp the moment he left for India. Controlling these satrapies was like trying to nail down quicksilver, except quicksilver didn't kill you, unless you ate it. Third, India was almost a thousand miles away, on the other side of the Hindu Kush. Not even Alexandros could talk his army into another wintertime or early spring transit.

Of these issues, the most pressing was the continued existence of local warlords in the mountainous foothills reaching out like fingers into the steppes and deserts of Baktria and Sogdiana. They held these lands in their iron grip, notwithstanding the illusions of successive

Persian emperors who believed that they controlled these satrapies. After the elimination of Spitamenes, there were still four more warlords left in the field. Each of them possessed an impenetrable mountain fastness, from which he could terrorize, tax, and despoil the population and the land within his local sphere of control, from which he could launch devastating raids against the other warlords and against the central authority, and into which he and his people could retreat when finding themselves under attack. Alexandros was quite sure that, as soon as he and his army were on the other side of the Hindu Kush, these warlords would rise up as one, slaughter his garrisons, and reassert their autonomy. He couldn't really leave until he had subdued them all.

As soon as the blizzards subsided, Alexandros and his men set off for the nearest of the four strongholds, which was called the Sogdian Rock and belonged to Oxyartes, the erstwhile colleague of Spitamenes. It also happened to be the largest and most imposing of these lairs. An unassailable fortress, sitting atop a tall butte and swathed in clouds most of the time, it could shelter, in case of need, more than ten thousand souls. Sheer rock faces, hundreds of feet tall, comprised three sides of the chimneylike outcropping atop which the fortress sat. On the fourth side, a narrow, precipitous path clung vertiginously to the granite wall. This lone approach, which could only be traversed single file by physically fit folks not afflicted with acrophobia, was guarded by three thousand ferocious fighters. Their commander was named

Ariamazes. The defenders had ample supplies, including cool, clean, fresh water from an abundant, reliable spring spurting from a niche within the fortress.

Considering the time of year, Oxyartes didn't anticipate trouble any time soon but, having seen Alexandros in action and being a shrewd judge of men, he knew trouble would come eventually. To be on the safe side, he sent his wives and children to shelter in the fortress until the danger passed.

Led to the base of the butte by a local guide, Alexandros had to take the man's word that a fortress crowned the top of the mountain. When the fog and clouds finally lifted, two days later, even our invincible leader had to consider the possibility that he had come across an impregnable stronghold. After a careful survey of the butte from all sides, he decided that the best strategy would be to convince the defenders to surrender. He rode to the bottom of the approach path, accompanied by only a half-dozen cavalrymen as his bodyguard, and informed the sentries that he wished to speak with their commander.

Ariamazes, a jovial fellow, promptly showed up, trailed by a handful of fighters, and invited Alexandros and his men to an impromptu feast, right there at the foot of the path, intended mostly to illustrate how bountiful his supplies were. After sharing a friendly meal, Alexandros suggested that he surrender "to avoid unnecessary bloodshed." Ariamazes laughed at him good-naturedly.

"Sire, your prowess as a commander is legendary. You've defeated the great armies of the Persian Empire. I would never presume to oppose you on the battlefield. Legions of dead men, all better fighters than I, can attest to the foolishness of such an endeavor. But sire, look up there, into the clouds. We're not talking about a field of battle. We're talking about a fortress in the sky. Unless you have soldiers who can fly, there is no way you can get to us."

Alexandros, his eyes harder than the granite supporting Ariamazes's fort, said nothing. So, the smiling commander forged ahead. "Sire, if you have need of any supplies or any other assistance, we will gladly provide you with anything you request. But please pass us by and be on your way. The lives you'll save will be those of your soldiers, not ours."

Alexandros didn't like to be laughed at. As the clouds rolled in, he rode back to our camp, calm, confident, and undaunted. He called for volunteers to scale the sheer rockface of the butte, promising a reward for each man who reached the fortress sufficient to make him a king in his own land. For those who didn't make it, he promised to send the reward to their families, enabling their sons to be kings. Three hundred mountaineers in our ranks stepped forward. Two hundred and seventy made it to the top. When they appeared above the fort's walls, emerging like celestial apparitions from the clouds, the stunned defenders were too stupefied to move. The surviving mountaineers sauntered to the sole gate leading into the fort and kept it open while Alexandros's men, who had been plodding up the path, poured in. The defenders of the Sogdian Rock surrendered without a fight. Alexandros spared the lives of all the defenders but one. In fact, he offered to enlist them in his army. The one exception was Ariamazes, who was quietly executed.

****

Alexandros released all the women and children captured in the fortress as well, including Oxyartes's family. He was persuaded by Hephaistion to hold back his fifteen-year-old daughter, however. "She's the most beautiful woman in Asia, Aniketos. You've got to see her."

Alexandros laughed. "How many times have I heard that? There must be hundreds of these most beautiful women of Asia. But if you really think so, let's hang on to her for now. After all, it's been a long time since I've seen Barsine."

"You'll have to judge which of them is more beautiful but this one is young and fresh, and she's here now."

Before Alexandros had a chance to visit his newest captive, her father showed up. Upon arrival, Oxyartes prostrated himself in the usual Persian fashion, handed over large crates of treasure, flattered his new overlord to the skies, and thanked him for his generous treatment of his fighters and his family. Alexandros, attired in Dareios's best vestments, nodded slightly, lest his newly-acquired tiara slip, and bid the visiting supplicant to rise.

The emboldened warlord stood up, bowed deeply, and blew a kiss toward Alexandros. "Your exalted, divine majesty! Thank you again. If I may be so bold as to request one more indulgence: Could you please also release my eldest daughter?"

Alexandros smiled. "I haven't released you yet, you old bandit. Why don't we start there, before worrying about your daughter?"

"There's no need to release me, your celestial highness. I'm your servant for life. You may do with me as you please. But it would give me comfort to have my entire family with me."

Alexandros winked toward Hephaistion and whispered sotto voce." I like this guy. He may be of use to us." Then he turned back to the man standing below him. "We'll have a victory feast tonight. I'll have you seated near me. We can discuss it then."

In the end, they struck a bargain. Oxyartes agreed to surrender all his remaining troops, swore eternal allegiance to Alexandros, and promised to assist him in a campaign to conquer the remaining mountain fastnesses. Alexandros, in turn, agreed to release Oxyartes's daughter, although the timeframe for her liberation was not entirely clear. With the negotiations completed, the men drank themselves to the edge of stupor to seal the deal.

As the banquet broke up, with men either staggering off to their tents or simply falling asleep where they lay, an inebriated Alexandros decided to have one look at this fabled daughter before turning her over to her father. Accompanied only by an equally drunk Hephaistion, they snuck into the young woman's tent and gazed at her peaceful visage by the light of a single oil lamp. Alexandros was smitten, in addition to being besotted. He sent Hephaistion on his way and awakened the sleeping beauty. "What's your name?" he asked, once she'd stopped blinking.

She stared at him uncomprehendingly.

Alexandros patted his chest. "Alexandros."

She smiled. "Roxane."

****

The next morning, Oxyartes, full of newfound confidence, merely knelt and touched his forehead to the ground upon being ushered into the emperor's presence. Alexandros didn't bother to motion him to his feet. "I've decided to keep your daughter," he declared, without preamble or explanation. "You may leave."

Oxyartes, once the words were translated, didn't wait to be told twice. He stormed out of the command tent and left the camp in a fury, taking his troops with him. Alexandros made no effort to stop him or his fighters. Seeing the questioning faces of his commanders, he shrugged. "I broke our bargain first."

****

The next stronghold on Alexandros's itinerary was held by a warlord named Chorienes. Although not as imposing at first glance as the Sogdian Rock, it turned out to be an even tougher nut to crack. A broad-shouldered, glacier-covered mountainside served as the back wall of the fort, while its front was protected by a narrow but extremely deep ravine. Presumably, a rope bridge provided access to the fort during more tranquil times but no means of ingress was evident when we arrived. Nor would there be any mountain-climbing heroics this time. Aside from the fact that word of Alexandros's ruse in seizing the Sogdian Rock had undoubtedly reached Chorienes before we appeared on the other side of the ravine, there was simply no way to surprise the vigilant defenders of the fort this time. Any soldiers who managed to rappel to the bottom of the ravine without getting killed would then have to climb up the other side under the watchful, and undoubtedly amused, eyes of the defenders, who could easily pick them off at their leisure with arrows, bolts, rocks, or boiling water. Summiting the huge mountains in the back of the fort and then descending unobserved was equally impractical.

However, Alexandros was not a man easily deterred. "Nothing to it," he told us cheerfully. "We'll build a bridge across the ravine by filling it with boulders and soil and then putting a wooden roadway on top of this base. Ptolemaios here knows all about it, don't you?"

Everyone looked at me expectantly. Most had no idea what our leader was talking about. I knew he was referring to a causeway to New Tyros, the construction of which I had supervised. We did eventually build that mole but it took six months and cost thousands of lives. I couldn't believe Alexandros wanted to dredge up that particular memory but I guess we did in the end reach New Tyros, which had been a great and impregnable city, and razed it to the ground.

I snapped to attention. "Yes, sire. I remember it clearly. This should be an easier job."

"Well, there you have it. The army and all its resources are at your command. Shouldn't take you more than a week, should it?"

I nodded and got to work. Obviously, it was going to take a lot longer than a week and men would die, but Alexandros would get his wish. I did have tens of thousands of men at my disposal and abundant building materials lay at our feet. We started by hauling all the large boulders we could find to the edge of the ravine and tipping them over. Then we tossed lots of rocks. Finally, we poured in dirt by the wagonload.

As long as we worked on our side of the ravine, we were safely out of range of enemy missiles. The defenders had to content themselves with jeering and throwing stones that only added to the pile at the bottom of the ravine. No matter how hard they tried, they couldn't reach us. But it was not possible to finish the mound, much less build a wooden roadway on top of it, without sending men closer to the other side. To the accumulation of boulders, rocks, and dirt, we started adding bodies of soldiers who either fell to their deaths or were killed by enemy arrows.

We built some temporary wooden awnings to shelter the men as they worked. It helped, but our progress continued to be excruciatingly slow. As one week turned into two and then three, and as our casualties grew, so did Alexandros's impatience. "You're wasting lives, Ptolemaios," he remarked one day as he stood next to me, watching the ongoing operations. "And I know how much you hate to do that. Now, if you would just get the damn causeway built, we could stop losing men."

I was about to tell him that I wasn't the one wasting men's lives. Fortunately, before I could get myself into deeper trouble, a commotion broke out in the camp behind us. Both Alexandros and I ran toward the noise to discover the cause of the clamor. It turned out that Oxyartes had chosen that moment to return, accompanied by a sizable escort, and was refusing the sentries' orders to disarm.

Alexandros stepped in before any blood was drawn. He gently tapped the former warlord on the shoulder with his sword and pointed to the ground. Oxyartes got the message and promptly flopped on his belly. Alexandros looked at his entourage and raised an eyebrow. They all followed suit like a synchronized diving team.

After everyone was disarmed and adequately humiliated, Alexandros invited Oxyartes into his tent. "What brings you back, my friend? Did you run out of little boys to molest?"

"Your celestial highness, I heard about the difficulties you've encountered with that scoundrel Chorienes. I came immediately to see how I could help. He used to be my subject, you know. I think I can talk him into coming over to our side."

"*Our* side? Since when are you on my side?"

"It's always been my highest desire to serve your divine greatness, sire, if only you'll give me a chance."

"I gave you a chance last time."

"Sire, my personal god came to me in a dream and told me that I must retrieve my daughter before proceeding on any other venture. That's what I asked for before and that's what I'm here to ask you again."

I expected Alexandros to fly off the handle but, unexpectedly, he found the effrontery of the smarmy turncoat disarming. "You're too late, old man. I think I'm in love with your daughter, so I can't give her back."

Before Oxyartes could reply, Hephaistion intervened. "Why don't you marry her instead, Aniketos? That should make all three of you happy."

Three years earlier, Alexandros had refused to marry Barsine, another beautiful woman who had enthralled him, even after she gave him a son. She wasn't royal enough in his eyes and a spoil of war to boot. But Alexandros had changed since then. "A splendid idea," he agreed, his tenting robe providing a small exclamation point. Oxyartes found the idea of becoming the emperor's father-in-law similarly alluring. Roxane's views were not solicited; it was presumed that she would be enchanted with the news.

Alexandros organized a great feast, right there by the ravine, with sufficient wine to get everyone drunk. Then, with the entire army serving as witnesses, he took the beautiful Roxane as his wife. Despite his intoxication, he carried her into his tent, accompanied by a chorus of catcalls from his men offering suggestions on how he should sack the citadel.

Immortal Alexandros

****

When the bridge over the ravine was finished, Alexandros sent Oxyartes as his envoy to Chorienes. The erstwhile warlord proved to be a persuasive negotiator. The sight of the finished causeway undoubtedly enhanced his eloquence. He brought back not only word of Chorienes's surrender but also the man himself.

Another banquet was mandatory, of course, at which both Oxyartes and Chorienes pledged eternal allegiance to Alexandros in the usual Persian fashion. Setting eternity aside, the alliance did last long enough to persuade the remaining fortresses to surrender. Alexandros then used his marriage to Roxane and the support of all the former warlords to finally exert some semblance of control over Sogdiana and Baktria.

To make sure that they remained quiescent, Alexandros reinforced the chain of forts on the Jaxartes River by turning them into military settlements, garrisoned by substantial forces. He also founded a few more Alexandrias throughout both provinces. These moves served the dual purposes of not only securing his control but also enabling him to streamline his army by leaving the old, injured, disloyal, and disaffected behind. At the same time, he continued to add new mercenaries from the militias formerly employed by the local warlords and from the bands of eager young desperados streaming in from Macedonia, from Greek cities on both sides of the Aegean, and from various subject nations of the Persian Empire, all attracted by tales of Alexandros's invincibility, generosity, and unimaginable wealth.

One loss we suffered during this time, which we all felt keenly, was the death of Kallisthenes. He had served Alexandros as campaign historian and personal scribe since the start of the invasion. His place was taken by a smooth-talking, sticky-fingered Greek named Eumenes but no one would ever replace the sweet, cheerful, bright young man who, instead of martial prowess, had a talent for thinking clearly, writing legibly, and making lifelong friends.

The final concern that Alexandros wanted to address before invading India was his officer corps. The ranks of his trusted veteran commanders, who had been with him since leaving Macedonia, were slowly shrinking to the vanishing point through death and disability, assignments to garrison commands and administrative duties, retirements back to Macedonia, and, most distressing of all, incipient disloyalty, as Alexandros saw it. With respect to his new commanders, drawn from enemy officers who'd changed sides, there was nothing incipient about their disloyalty; their unreliability was a given.

Alexandros, although he liked to cultivate the impression of being an impulsive and rash leader, was in fact a farsighted, strategic thinker and a meticulous planner. To replenish his officer corps, he conceived an audacious scheme: He had fond memories of the training school set up by his father in Mieza for him and the sons of Macedonian nobility, which served as the incubator for Alexandros's original officer corps. He decided to do something similar but, typically, on a much bigger scale. Before leaving Sogdiana, he dispatched dozens of agents with orders to fan out across the Persian Empire and recruit suitable officer candidates. They were to be fourteen-year-old boys, intelligent, strong, graceful, and preferably upper class. Once selected, they were given no choice in the matter. An invitation to become a page to the emperor was understood to be not only a singular honor but also a command that couldn't be refused. They were to attend a School of Pages near Babylon, where they would be taught natural philosophy, introduced to the classics of Greek literature, and trained in the martial arts. The tactics to be taught were Macedonian; the language of instruction Greek. They were expected to be ready to join the ranks as junior officers in three years' time. Until then, they'd make useful hostages for the good behavior of their fathers.

The current Macedonian commanders were not thrilled by this School of Pages but Alexandros didn't seek, or need, their approval. His plans for the school were detailed and thoroughgoing, which was not surprising. What was extraordinary was the number of boys to be enrolled in this school. Alexandros wanted, and he got, 30,000 boys from every corner of the empire. And with that detail out of the way, he was ready to invade India.

Chapter 14 – On to India

By the time all the loose ends had been tied up, the season had advanced into spring, which was just as well, because another crossing of the Hindu Kush awaited. In the two years since the last crossing, Alexandros had lost a lot of men, time, and good will but perhaps he'd acquired a better understanding of local geography. And he'd certainly increased the size of his army.

Despite all the casualties, defections, and garrisons that had to be left behind, the force which set off for India was the largest army Alexandros had ever commanded. We had 92,000 men, of whom 12,000 were cavalry and 80,000 infantry. It was also his least Macedonian army.

Of the 12,000 mounted warriors, only 2,000 were Macedonian. The rest were local horsemen, now furnished with some Macedonian weapons and training, but deep down still the barbarian fighters they'd always been. The cavalry was divided into eight brigades of 1,500 horsemen and the brigades were further subdivided into squadrons of between 180 and 200 mounts. Every brigade was led by a Macedonian commander but many of the squadrons were made up exclusively of local fighters, commanded by Persian and former tribal leaders.

The infantry was composed of 15,000 Macedonians and 65,000 mercenaries drawn from all corners of the Greek and Persian world. We now had "oldtimers," who were Macedonian veterans who'd been in the army since before the invasion, "new veterans," who'd been with us for a few years, "old newbies," "fresh meat," and "mercenaries." (Needless to say, these were not formal designations, but everybody used them.) Again, top infantry commands were held by oldtimers but most of the lesser posts were occupied by new veterans and old newbies and by non-Macedonian mercenaries, some Greek, some Persian, and some drawn from barbarian tribes.

We had also collected, once again, a substantial baggage train of camp followers, who seemed to stick to us like barnacles to the hull of a ship. By the time we set off, perhaps as many as 40,000 grooms, tradesmen, servants, and assorted riff-raff came along. However, wives, mistresses, and unattached women of general availability were not allowed to accompany us. Alexandros considered a transit of the Hindu Kush, even in the summertime, too strenuous for the "gentler gender." All the women were to be escorted to Babylon, along with the newly-recruited pages, using the traditional caravan routes that skirted the highest mountains and deadliest deserts. Roxane, Apame, and a couple of other high-value hostages would then continue on to the harem in Sousa.

****

We re-crossed the Hindu Kush without any major mishaps. This time around, led by local Baktrian guides, we followed an easier route, through the lowest, rather than highest, pass. We'd also waited until the winter blizzards had blown over and at least some of the snow and ice had melted. And then, on the other side, we found ourselves in another land – nominally a part of the Persian Empire but, in reality, ruled by a colorful coterie of local warlords. Except here they were called rajas.

Our first stop, before entering the satrapy of India itself, was the erroneously named Alexandria-in-the-Caucasus. In the two-and-a-half years since its founding, the small garrison fort had grown into a bustling commercial and trading center. Alexandros always had a good eye for strategic locations.

The cavalry made it through the pass much faster than the infantry, which in turn was much faster than the baggage train. Those of us attached to the cavalry ended up drinking, gambling, and waiting for almost two months. It took much less time for word of Alexandros's presence in this corner of Arakhosia to spread far beyond the borders of the satrapy. As a result, he was treated to a daily stream of well-wishers, worshippers, and supplicants.

Immortal Alexandros

Among the early arrivals seeking an audience was a minor raja named Sisikottos. He ruled over a nearby small principality, which he ostensibly held as a vassal of the Persian emperor. With the imperial change of control, Sisikottos considered it advisable to rush over, bring offerings as generous as he could afford, abase himself in the best Persian fashion, and seek to be confirmed in his position by the new man in charge.

The presents he brought were trifling compared to those brought by other satraps and warlords on previous occasions. However, he had one incomparable asset in his gift that Alexandros was quick to discern and exploit: He had spent a lifetime engaged in military and political adventures throughout the India satrapy, scheming to obtain and retain power, intriguing with and against his fellow rajas in an ever-shifting kaleidoscope of alliances and feuds. Anything he didn't know about his fellow rajas, and about the India satrapy in general, wasn't worth knowing. To a man thirsting for reliable intelligence about the country he was about to invade, Sisikottos was a gusher of cool, sweet water.

Among other things, Sisikottos identified by name and location the rulers of various domains within the India satrapy and even a few beyond its borders. With his aid, Alexandros dispatched emissaries, along with interpreters and heavily armed "advisers," to each of the rajas. They carried letters informing the rajas of the arrival of the new maharaja in their neighborhood and inviting them to come to Alexandria-in-the-Caucasus at their earliest convenience. There was no need to mention that the rulers were to arrive without their armies but heavily laden with glittering gifts. The rajas had been through this exercise before and many of them promptly responded to the summons.

Not all rajas had been created equal, however. Some were simply tribal leaders who controlled little more than a fortified hilltop. Others ruled large, walled cities, as well as much adjoining territory. Atop the pyramid sat three great rajas who, among them, asserted authority over the entire India satrapy, plus swaths of adjacent fiefdoms, and who considered the lesser rajas their vassals. The lesser rajas, for their part, were constantly jockeying for better terms, changing their fealties and enmities in a wriggling tapestry of alliances and antagonisms.

The three great rajas were Omphis, Abisares, and Poros. They devoted their lives to stirring the pot of intrigues, pledges, oaths, and betrayals, as had their predecessors since time immemorial. For a while, Persian emperors had kept a lid on this seething cauldron of machinations, skirmishes, and all-out wars, but their hold had loosened over the decades. Alexandros was now proposing to reassert imperial control.

The great rajas took three different approaches to dealing with their new, putative overlord. Omphis came in person. Tipped off by Alexandros's emissaries, he brought magnificent offerings, including Alexandros's favorite gift –

elephants. He brought twenty-five of them, immediately endearing himself to the new man in charge. He also offered to surrender his capital and promised to aid Alexandros in his campaigns, especially against the other two great rajas. Abisares sent a son, who explained that his father was indisposed but he also brought gifts and made promises of assistance that his father had no intention of keeping. Poros simply ignored Alexandros's summons.

By the time all these diplomatic overtures were completed, the monsoon rains had arrived. We ended up staying in the highlands of Arakhosia, which were said to be less pestilential than the lands farther south, until the rains abated. The troops had sufficient food, drink, and access to baggage train amenities, which mitigated their restlessness. It was late fall when we finally moved out.

****

"The India satrapy was shaped by its rivers," Sisikottos had told Alexandros. "The largest river, which flows the entire length of the satrapy, from the mountains in the north to the Indian Sea in the southwest, is called the Indos River. It's the biggest river in the world."

Alexandros was skeptical. "Bigger than the Nile? Or the Euphrates? Or the Tigris?"

"Your exalted highness, I've never heard of any of those rivers you name. But the Indos is the biggest river

I've ever seen and it's the lifeblood of this area of the world."

"And where, in relation to this river, is Omphis's kingdom? Taxila, is it?"

"Yes, sire. Both the kingdom and its capital are called Taxila. They are on the east side, or the far side from here, of the Indos River. Omphis controls most of the land between the Indos and a large tributary farther east called the Hydaspes."

"Well, since Omphis was kind enough to visit us here and to invite us to visit Taxila, I guess it's only fair if we pay him a return visit. What's the shortest way to get there?"

"Depends on what you mean by shortest, sire. If you mean the shortest time, then it's the route through the Khyber Pass; if you mean the shortest distance, then it's up the Euas River valley, across a narrow mountain range, and then down along the Soastos River, all the way to the Indos. The Khyber Pass takes you a little out of your way and it leads through rugged mountains but it's safer for that precise reason. No hostile tribes make their homes along that route. The path itself is mountainous but negotiable by wagons and animals and has been used by travelers for thousands of years. It's wider, lower, and easier than the Hindu Kush passes. And the bandits who prey on the travelers along the Khyber Pass route should be no threat to an army. Beyond the pass, all the rajas of the intervening territories, between the Khyber and the Indos have already appeared here in Alexandria and tendered their submissions."

"Well, that sounds fine. But why do you say that the Euas and Soastos route would take us longer if it's a shorter distance than the Khyber Pass route?"

"The Euas and Soastos route, sire, takes you across lands occupied by several belligerent tribes, led by chieftains who command large bands of fierce fighters and hold strong, fortified towns and unassailable mountaintop fastnesses. The Khyber Pass route, even though it's longer in distance and physically more challenging, is easier because you'd be opposed only by disinterested nature, rather than bellicose humans."

****

In the end, Alexandros decided to take both routes. Having learned that it was less dangerous to divide his forces than to bypass hostile warlords, he sent half the army, along with the camp followers, elephants, and baggage train, to the town of Ohind, located on the west bank of the Indos River, using the Khyber Pass. Hephaistion, who was a terrific manager, was nominally in charge of this force. However, Hephaistion was not a great military leader and Alexandros was objective enough to recognize this fact. Therefore, Perdikkas was named joint commander of the force. In the event any of the minor rajas along the way forgot their pledges to surrender their cities and territories, Perdikkas was there to refresh their recollections. As it turned out, Sisikottos's forecast proved accurate and no military force was required. The appearance of even half the army was quite sufficient. Each of the cities and territories en route from Alexandria-in-the-Caucasus to Ohind was occupied in turn. As soon as the force arrived at the Indos, Hephaistion got busy preparing a base of operations in the city and assembling the necessary materials to build a pontoon bridge across the river.

****

Once Hephaistion and Perdikkas were on their way, Alexandros set off with the other half of the army up through the mountainous terrain to the north of the Khyber Pass to clean out any packets of backward brutes not sufficiently sophisticated to surrender without a fight. The inhabitants of these regions proved to be tough adversaries.

When we entered the Euas valley, we were confronted by a fortified hilltop village called Aspasia, forcing us to lay a siege. To make matters worse, Alexandros sustained an arrow wound to the shoulder in the course of the operation. As usual, the wound darkened his mood. When the army finally took the hilltop, they were instructed to slaughter every man, woman, and child, which they did.

Next, after some additional mountaineering, we entered the broad, beautiful, fertile valley of the Soastos

River, home of the powerful Assakenia nation. They had a big army of 2,000 cavalry, 30,000 infantry, including 7,000 Indian mercenaries, and thirty elephants. Their cities were protected by strong walls, topped by elaborate battlements. Their capital, and most strongly fortified city, was Massaga. They chose to put their faith in their strong walls and big army. We settled in for a series of sieges. While Alexandros directed operations at Massaga, he sent Koinos with a smaller force to besiege the second largest city, named Barikot, and he sent Polyperchon with yet another detachment to besiege a small, pesky city named Ora.

Massaga was the first to fall, betrayed from within. This time, Alexandros confined his massacre to the 7,000 mercenaries, letting their fates serve as a warning to the remaining inhabitants. He then hurried to Ora, which was putting up quite a fight. He also ordered Koinos to come to Ora, leaving only a token force to maintain the siege of Barikot. Ora fell in short order, with all inhabitants slaughtered. While the killing continued, the residents of Barikot took the opportunity to steal away in the dead of night, leaving their city deserted.

The last Assakenian stronghold left standing was a fortress called Aornos, built on a bluff overlooking a bend in the Indos River. This was, to all appearances, another unassailable fastness, protected by unscalable cliffs plunging, on three sides, all the way to the river. Of course, Alexandros had previously proven that every fortress could be taken but we didn't know whether the defenders were aware of this detail. In the meantime, Ohind was tantalizing close, less than a hundred miles downriver, but Alexandros was determined not to leave any unconquered positions in our rear. It turned out that news of Alexandros's prowess did indeed fly on eagles' wings because, one moonless night, the defenders of Aornos simply vanished. We found out later that they swam across the river and made their way north to the kingdom ruled by the ambivalent Raja Abisares.

Having spent more time than he had intended reaching the Indos River, Alexandros was not inclined to chase after the escapees from Aornos or to get into a fight with Abisares. Instead, anxious to rendezvous with the Hephaistion and Perdikkas forces, he directed us to make our way to Ohind as quickly as we could. A few lucky soldiers, as well as the elephants we had captured from the Assakenoi, accompanied by their mahouts, were able to float downstream on improvised rafts. The rest of us marched on the riverbank. Fortunately, we encountered no further obstacles and reached Ohind five days later.

****

While we had fought our way across the lands of the Assakenoi, Hephaistion and Perdikkas had been busy making preparations for the army's excursion into Taxila. Perdikkas kept the troops sharp with incessant close-quarter drills and strenuous forced marches. At the same time, Hephaistion's engineers built from scratch a pontoon bridge spanning the mile-wide river. As soon as the bridge was completed, Omphis used it to send additional presents, including a 700-man-strong squadron of his best cavalry, thus demonstrating that the bridge was indeed sound, that he continued to be a loyal vassal, and that he was keeping a wary eye on developments across the river from his kingdom.

Alexandros was ready to march into Taxila the day after we had arrived in Ohind. His troops had other ideas. It had taken us many months to fight our way up the Euas and down the Soastos valleys; spring was in full bloom; and the soldiers wanted a break. Reluctantly, Alexandros acceded to their wishes. Hephaistion, having completed his previous assignments, threw himself into organizing the most spectacular festivities that the hundred-thousand-plus soldiers and camp followers had ever seen. They were treated to a month of feasts, athletic and artistic competitions, and wine-drenched bacchanals. For a big finish, Hephaistion organized a three-day service of thanksgiving, with lots of non-bovine sacrificial animals, a score of soothsayers strutting their prophetic stuff, and phalanxes of clergymen alternately imploring and thanking their respective deities. And then, finally, we were ready to cross the Indos.

****

The crossing, notwithstanding the width of the river and the massive quantities of people, animals, wagons, and matériel involved, was uneventful. Once the entire army was assembled inside the kingdom of Taxila, we set off for its eponymous capital. When Raja Omphis learned of our approach, he came out to greet us, riding aboard his largest elephant. He was accompanied by his entire army and by what seemed to be most of the population of the city. Included with his army, of course, were his cavalry and his elephant force.

Alexandros, riding in the vanguard as usual, was among the first to note the approach of the welcoming committee. Seeing the huge hordes of armed men emerging from the dust, he assumed we were under attack. He promptly ordered us into battle formation. Had he looked a little longer, he might have noticed that many of the approaching groups were dancing, rather than running, and were decked out in festive, rather than martial, attire. But, by this stage of the campaign, eight years after crossing the Hellespont, Alexandros's reason tended to be overborne by his delusions and paranoia.

Omphis, looking toward Alexandros's army, watched in amazement as tens of thousands of soldiers fell into precise, tight formations in a matter of minutes, without any evident sound, confusion, or panic. It dawned on him that a one-sided clash, and a likely massacre, were in the offing. He quickly tapped his mahout on the shoulder; the mahout whispered urgently in the elephant's ear; and the animal started to pick up speed. It wasn't running exactly, because elephants don't run, but it was certainly moving faster and faster. Omphis's ceremonial guard of two dozen horsemen eventually had to break into a gallop to keep up.

By the time his small group reached our vanguard, the celebratory mob was left far behind. The elephant screeched to a halt amazingly quickly, considering how much momentum its legs had to dissipate, but not quickly enough to avoid spooking our horses. Several of our riders found themselves seated in the dust. Boukephalas was more disciplined than most war horses, and also considerably older, so he reared only a little. And Alexandros was as good an equestrian as anybody in the army, so he didn't get thrown off.

When order was finally restored, with the elephant standing still and our guys back on their horses, Omphis gracefully dismounted, jumping from his howdah to the elephant's right front thigh, obligingly held out for him by the well-trained animal, and then to the ground. Before he could prostrate himself at Boukephalas's feet, Alexandros surprised us all by leaping from his charger and grasping Omphis by the shoulders, allowing the raja to kiss him on the cheeks. We couldn't decide which was more surprising, that Alexandros extended this courtesy, practiced only between the Persian emperor and his highest-ranking noblemen, to a mere Indian raja, or that Omphis was aware of this custom and proceeded with the kissing ceremony without a blink.

While all this was going on, the celebratory hordes of Taxilans reached our front ranks. Trunks of treasure were placed at Alexandros's feet while young women and children handed out yellow marigolds, pink dahlias, and fragrant jasmine blossoms to our soldiers, still standing in their orderly formations. Soon, happy chaos reigned everywhere.

Omphis invited Alexandros to join him atop his elephant for the ride back to Taxila. Alexandros demurred and had a splendid white stallion brought up for Omphis's use instead. The two men, separated by an interpreter running between them, paraded at a slow walk back to the capital, with Omphis chattering and pointing incessantly and the interpreter, fighting to catch his breath, failing to convey most of it. Alexandros didn't seem to mind. Before we reached the city walls, he had already confirmed Omphis as the raja of Taxila. Presumably, this was one pronouncement that the interpreter managed to communicate to his employer.

******

Taxila was a wealthy and exotic city. It had been a provincial capital long before the Achaemenid emperors chose it as the administrative center of their India satrapy and it continued to prosper after Persian rule gradually receded into the realm of tacit fiction and native rajas resumed actual control. The city's prosperity flowed from its location between the Indos and Hydaspes Rivers and at the junction of three great trade routes leading to the Indian Sea in the west, the Gulf of the Ganges in the east, and the fabled trans-Asian caravan routes in the north. It also benefited from a benign and competent government, which fostered commerce, culture, institutions of higher learning, and religious shrines, temples, and stupas.

Thanks to a history of endemic warfare among the Indian principalities, Taxila had acquired imposing fortifications and a powerful army. However, Omphis had correctly surmised that neither the fortifications nor the army were likely to withstand a determined siege by Alexandros. Accordingly, he opted for diplomacy, discretion, and bribery. Immediately upon our arrival in the city, he staged three days of feasts for the population and ordinary soldiers and three days of banquets for Alexandros, his senior officers, and the city's dignitaries.

Each night was more festive than the last and each featured lavish gifts for Alexandros. Finally, our leader couldn't take it any longer. He grew concerned that the Taxilan raja might appear richer or at least more generous than he, the Persian emperor. So, at the next banquet, Alexandros gave all the presents back to Omphis, except for the elephants, and added spectacular gifts of his own, including fancy Persian royal outfits, thirty Sogdian horses, some golden goblets, and one thousand gold darics. Of course, all of this treasure had been recently looted from the Persians but still, Alexandros's excessive generosity didn't sit well with his veteran Macedonian officers. One of them, named Meleager, observed in a stage whisper: "I guess the reason we had to fight our way across thousands of miles of Asia and lose thousands of our comrades was to finally find a man worthy of such largess."

This time, Alexandros didn't run him through with a spear. But if looks could kill, Meleager would've been a dead man. As it was, his career with Alexandros's army was finished.

****

There were two additional items on Omphis's wish list, now that he had been confirmed as raja of Taxila. He wanted Alexandros's army out of his kingdom and he wanted it to leave in a specific direction; to wit, across the Hydaspes River. Omphis took a shrewd tack in making his case. Night after night, he regaled us with tales of a fabulous land beyond the Hydaspes ruled by a great warrior named Raja Poros. The story was intrinsically interesting to Alexandros because he had been told that the India satrapy, and hence the Persian Empire, ended at the river's edge. As far as he, and any Greek for that matter, knew, the world ended just a few miles beyond the Hydaspes. Now he was hearing for the first time that yet another prosperous kingdom, called Paurava, existed in this narrow strip of land between the river and the world-encompassing realm of Okeanos. Naturally, he would have to conquer this land before he could fairly consider his mission to the East completed and thus be able to turn around and go home.

Omphis's stories about Poros's martial prowess and invincibility only added to Alexandros's zest to take him on. After all, there could only be one invincible military leader in the world. He quickly fell into detailed discussions with Omphis about the strength of Poros's army, about the logistical challenges of crossing another wide river, and about the best tactics to employ against an army deploying a great many specimens of the most fearsome military weapon known to man, a trained elephant controlled by a skilled mahout.

And then there was still the kingdom ruled by the third great raja Abisares, nestled to the north of Paurava, above the kingdoms of Omphis and Poros and below the Himalayas. If Abisares were to join his forces with Poros's army, then even a combined effort by Alexandros's army and Omphis's forces might run into trouble. And that was assuming Omphis could be counted on in a pinch.

Alexandros decided to try diplomacy first. Maybe, based on his reputation, all three of the great rajas could be persuaded to submit peacefully, as Omphis had already done and as Abisares had promised, through his son, to do. Even if Abisares simply joined the coalition, it would still make the conquest of Paurava, led by the legendary Poros, more manageable. So, Alexandros sent emissaries to Abisares and Poros, asking them to meet him on the banks of the Hydaspes and tender their submissions.

We spent two months in Taxila waiting for an answer. Abisares, calculating that his best strategy was to temporize until it was clear whether Alexandros or Poros had prevailed in their conflict, at which point he could join the winning side, sent a delegation to Alexandros announcing that he would be honored to become his vassal. However, he didn't show up in person and his delegates were unable to provide a date for his putative submission. At the same time, he also sent a message to Poros, warning him of the coming invasion by Alexandros and promising to come to his aid if and when the attack materialized.

Poros, on the other hand, took a more direct approach. He sent a message telling Alexandros that he'd be happy to meet him on the banks of the Hydaspes, but for the purpose of battling to preserve the freedom and independence of his kingdom, rather than submitting to any man. Alexandros, who did not consider himself "any man," set in motion preparations for the great showdown.

Chapter 15 – Hydaspes

Barsine's first reaction was to laugh. "He did what?"

Thais, who was somehow always the first to hear every rumor, repeated what she'd just found out. "Alexandros has married some wild savage. She and a couple of her companions were quietly smuggled in through the postern gate last night."

"Let me get this straight. I'm not good enough to be his wife, even though I bore him his only son and even though I am the great granddaughter of a Persian emperor, but he takes some hussy from the steppes for a wife?"

It was now Thais's turn to be amused. "How do you know she's a hussy?"

"Just a guess. Why else would he marry her? He probably hadn't seen a woman for years and she must have thrown herself at him."

"Barsine, Barsine – I'm surprised at you. You, of all people, should know better. He needn't have married her just to have his way with her."

"Well, that's true. Which makes it all the more puzzling."

Artakama chimed in with a more pertinent question. "What does she look like?"

Thais shrugged. "Nobody has seen her. The eunuchs snuck her and her companions into the visitors' compound near the back wall under cover of darkness and now they're standing guard outside, making sure no one goes in or out."

"That doesn't make any sense either. When you joined us, your entrance was quite a show."

"Well, that's why I'm Thais and they're not."

Artakama nodded. "That's true. There is only one of you. Plus, I bet they showed up dirty, smelly, and wearing skins. The eunuchs are probably trying to clean them up and get them properly dressed."

Barsine grew serious. "Somehow I doubt that. Let's get some treats together and pay these ladies a visit to welcome them to our community."

"The eunuchs will never let us in."

Thais snorted. "They can be bribed with a smile. But why waste a smile on those wretches? Let's just give them a couple of pastries and a jug of wine."

****

As always, Thais got her way and the little delegation marched into the courtyard of the visitors' compound. They were met by a belligerent hound. The dog didn't attack, exactly, but it didn't retreat either. It ran up as close as it dared and barked vigorously.

They were rescued by a young girl who appeared in a doorway and yelled a couple of words in a language only the dog understood. It stopped barking, trotted back to her, and lowered its head. The young girl scratched it behind the ears and approached the group of women, with the beast ambling by her side. She looked to be about fourteen, with a ruddy complexion, reddish blond hair, high forehead, inquisitive eyes, and a ready smile. She was properly dressed in the latest Persian fashion.

"Are you our new servants?" she asked in accented Persian.

"No, we are your new neighbors. We are here to welcome you. My name is Barsine; this is my sister Artakama; and that is my friend Thais. What is your name?" Barsine's Persian was aristocratic, elegant, and impeccable.

The young girl blushed. "I'm terribly sorry, your highness. I didn't know. Please forgive me."

"Nothing to forgive. But you haven't told me your name."

"Oh, I'm sorry. They call me Apame, your highness."

"It's a nice name. Are you the emperor's new wife?"

Apame giggled. "No, your highness. That's the other one. I'll go get her. In the meantime, please come in and make yourselves comfortable."

Barsine, Artakama, and Thais were seated on plush carpets and soft pillows in the compound's main reception room when Apame returned, accompanied by a slightly older girl. "This is Roxane, your highnesses, the emperor's new wife."

Roxane seemed unsure whether she should stand, sit, or prostrate herself at the feet of the other women. She settled on crouching on her haunches.

Barsine patted a pillow. "Come and sit next to me, Roxane," she said in Greek. "And welcome to the Sousa harem."

Roxane smiled but clearly had no idea what had been said to her. Barsine repeated herself in Persian.

Roxane still failed to understand. This time, Apame stepped in and interpreted.

Roxane said a few words that only Apame understood and sat down facing the three visitors. Apame sat down next to her.

For a moment, Barsine stared at her rival. Roxane was young, exotic, and beautiful. Her jet-black hair, parted in the middle and plaited into two long, thick braids, framed a broad, golden, unlined face. On this canvas, nature sculpted prominent cheekbones, generous lips, an emphatic nose, deep blue eyes, and creaseless eyelids. Her skin was perfect, unmarred by blemish, wrinkle, or life's toll. Her gaze was open and fearless.

Barsine broke the lengthening silence. She called out in Greek and the serving women came in from the courtyard, carrying silver platters and clay pitchers. They uncovered the platters and placed them on the floor between the women.

"Please take some," Barsine said.

The two girls didn't move. Barsine laughed. "Don't worry, they won't kill you." She picked up a pastry and started to eat. Thais and Artakama followed suit. Seeing their evident enjoyment, Apame and Roxane also took a cautious bite. Then they quickly ate the rest and smacked their lips. Roxane whispered something to Apame, who interpreted for the rest of the group. "She wants to know what this is."

"It's a pastry we call gastrin. It's good, isn't it?"

Apame nodded. "She wants to know the recipe."

"It's very easy," Barsine said, still speaking Persian. "You knead and pound the dough until it's nice and thin. Then you make the filling using various nuts, fruits, and honey. Whatever is available. We like to add some sesame and poppy seeds. Then you bake it until it's golden brown. After it cools off, you cut it into squares and drizzle some more honey over it. I'll send one of my serving women to show you how it's done."

Apame interpreted and the two girls engaged in an animated conversation. Finally, Apame turned back to Barsine. "We accept, your highness."

After some additional chitchat, Barsine grew impatient with the cumbersome interpretation routine. "Do you speak Aramaic?" she asked Roxane in Aramaic and received a blank stare in response. "How about Phrygian?" Still nothing. She turned to Apame and reverted to Persian. "What language does Roxane speak?"

"She speaks Sogdian, Baktrian, and Massagetan, your highness. She's very good with languages, except the ones you've tried."

"And yet, she evidently didn't learn any Greek or Macedonian from the soldiers who escorted you here. You must have spent months on the road with them. For that matter, how did she communicate with her new husband?"

"I don't think they did much speaking, your highness."

"Well, never mind. Do you girls have some cups for the wine? We'll need some clean water too, to dilute it."

Apame giggled. "Where we come from, women seldom drink wine. But we're certainly happy to try it."

Just as they started to get comfortable, their amiable conversation was cut short by a shriek. "What was that?" Artakama asked.

The three of them ran out of the reception room, looking for the sources of the sound, leaving Apame and Roxane sitting on the floor. The women in the courtyard could only shrug. The eunuchs guarding the entrance pointed vaguely toward one of the residences. Then they heard a new sound, a long, low wail that gradually built in volume. The keening led them to Antigone's quarters.

They found Antigone sitting on the ground in her courtyard, her face buried in her hands, her body racked by sobs. A Macedonian veteran knelt on one knee next to her, trying to comfort her. Dilshad crouched on the other side, making sure no untoward contact occurred. Other soldiers, eunuchs, and women stood in silent vigil around the trio. Antigone tried to say something but the words were swamped by fresh torrents of tears.

"What happened?" Artakama asked one of the women standing next to the entrance.

The woman put a finger to her mouth. "Not so loud. The soldiers just told her that Philotas is dead."

Despite the woman's quiet voice, Antigone heard her lover's name, which triggered new paroxysms of grief. Someone offered her a cup of wine. She knocked it aside and watched with sightless eyes as the red liquid seeped into the dirt. Another woman knelt down in front of her to offer condolences but Antigone simply turned away and threw herself to the ground, face down, her tears turning the parched earth near her cheeks a darker shade of brown.

Thais turned to Barsine and Artakama. "Let's come back later," she whispered.

They walked toward their suites, lost in thought. Antigone was not a particularly likeable person but her grief had touched all three of them. They could easily imagine themselves in a similar situation.

Suddenly, Artakama stopped. "Shouldn't we go back to those two barbarian girls?"

Barsine shook her head. "Nah, we'll visit them again some other time. And they're not barbarians, by the way. They are royal princesses. Well, at least one of them is."

Thais's ears pricked up. "Do you really think so? Do you think Alexandros still remembers he married her? I think you were right the first time. He just wanted to screw her and, being drunk as usual, blurted out something that other people misunderstood."

"I wish you were right, Thais, but I don't think so. If you were right, why would he send her to the harem?"

"Maybe she's a good lay?"

"Better than you, Aunt Thais?" Artakama asked mischievously.

The three women dissolved into laughter, Antigone momentarily forgotten.

"Well, one thing is for sure," Barsine observed. "She may be beautiful but she's not very smart."

Thais shook her head. "That's irrelevant, my dear Barsine. What's much more important is that she's not pregnant."

Barsine walked into her suite with renewed spring in her step.

****

Alexandros made the usual arrangements. Although Omphis had pledged his army's support in the coming campaign against Poros, and possibly against Abisares, Alexandros considered it prudent to leave behind a large garrison in Taxila, commanded by a veteran Macedonian officer. He also collected as much intelligence as possible about the strengths and weaknesses of Poros's army, about his usual tactics and logistical arrangements, and about the best locations for crossing the Hydaspes. Finally, we started our march toward the Paurava frontier.

As always, Alexandros was a man in a hurry. This time, he was anxious to engage Poros before Abisares, whom he suspected of treachery, could bring his army to Poros's assistance. And we were making good progress, too, until the rains came. We thought we had experienced the monsoon season in Arakhosia but here, on the fertile plains of Taxila, the torrential downpours were an order of magnitude worse. There were occasional pauses but basically it rained day and night. During the day, sheets of water made it difficult to see two steps ahead; at night, frequent lightning made sleep difficult. There were no roads, paths, or trails, only boundless, churning, sucking, voracious fields of mud. Small streams became raging rivers. Our weapons started to rust in a matter of hours. Anything containing organic material, including not only food but also leather, canvas, linen, and wool, became moldy overnight. Clouds of insects buzzed, dived, and penetrated every opening in our clothes, no matter how small, and every orifice of our bodies. Everyone in the line of march became sick, suffering from prickly heat, foot rot, chills and fever, diarrhea and vomiting.

And still, we marched ahead, driven by the hope that the new day would bring some surcease. In a sense it did because, after a few days, we reached the Hydaspes. Of course, the rains continued but our native guides assured us that this was a "light" monsoon season and we would soon get used to it. That sounded vaguely menacing. "Exactly how long is this 'light' monsoon supposed to last?" we asked. "Usually, it's over in three or four months," was the cheerful answer.

We made camp near the alleged shallows that, Alexandros had been told, was the best place to ford the Hydaspes. Thanks to the monsoon rains, the river was more than a mile wide, swift, and deep at this location. Nobody was going to cross without a bridge or some watercraft any time soon. A short way downstream from the putative shallows was a small town, whose name I never learned. Apparently, it prospered by catering to the many travelers using this crossing point. The town was under water and there were no travelers or inhabitants to be seen. By contrast, the other bank was bristling with troops. Poros had beaten us to the punch.

It soon became clear that Poros had no intention of crossing into Taxila. Evidently, he had received some briefings about the proclivities of our leader as well. He was content to occupy the far side of the ford and await the inevitable, audacious, reckless crossing attempt by Alexandros. When it came, he was prepared to repulse it, as many times as necessary, exacting a heavy price in lives and matériel with each attempt.

Poros had three further allies on his side: The river, the climate, and time. The rains had made the river unfordable; the monsoon season meant that the rain would not end for months; and the insufferable conditions, lack of supplies, and stretched logistical lines placed an outside limit on how long we could keep trying before being forced to retreat.

Needless to say, Alexandros was undaunted. He dispatched Koinos with four squadrons of cavalry to return to the Indos, to dismantle the pontoon bridge we had left behind, to break down the boats we had built, and to bring all the pieces by oxcart to us as quickly as possible. Koinos accomplished the mission, under miserable conditions, in four weeks.

While we waited, Alexandros and Poros engaged in a game of feints and counterfeints. Our cavalry would charge down the bank toward the river's edge, simulating the launch of a cross-water attack, even though this was clearly impossible. Poros would respond by deploying his elephants and his archers on the other bank. The sight of the elephants, and especially their trumpeting, scared the living daylights out of our horses. The sight of the archers, and especially the roar of the rushing, muddy water, kept us riders on edge. Even Alexandros recognized that any attempted crossing would be suicidal.

We settled down to a routine. During the day, especially when the rains eased off, we made a big show of receiving a steady stream of fake supplies, delivered by wagons and oxcarts, sufficient to keep us in the field indefinitely. At night, Poros made sure that his soldiers kept us awake with their loud dancing and singing, while the elephants kept our horses jittery with their trumpeting. The next day, we would respond by galloping a few squadrons of cavalry up and down our bank of the river, forcing Poros to follow our movements with his own troops. Of course, all this merriment was taking place in knee-deep, sticky mud and pouring, relentless, unending rain. We were all getting sick and tired of the endless quagmire, both literally and figuratively. At the same time, we could tell that Poros's soldiers, his horses, and especially his elephants were not enjoying all this traipsing in the mud and rain either.

After a while, Poros stopped shadowing our every move. He simply stationed small detachments of cavalry at every plausible crossing point and let them serve as pickets, instructed to raise the alarm in the event we tried something, and then hold us off until reinforcements arrived. We, on the other bank, enjoyed no such luxury. Our job was to ride around, crazily and noisily, day after day, to desensitize the enemy and cause them to decrease their vigilance.

In the meantime, Poros kept sending messages to Abisares, urging him to unite their forces against Alexandros. He argued that jointly they were invincible and, after victory was achieved, they could go back to living in an uneasy equilibrium, as they had heretofore. Abisares continued to stall, calculating that the best strategy for him was to let Poros and Alexandros destroy each other, after which he could ride in and pick up the pieces. Even if one of the armies managed to limp away after destroying the other, Abisares would still have an easier time dispatching the ostensible victor.

And while we were riding every day, loudly and mindlessly along the bank, Alexandros's scouts were carefully scouring the river for miles in either direction, hoping to find a more suitable crossing point than our current shallows. Finally, they found what Alexandros wanted seventeen miles upstream from our camp.

At this spot, there was a large, uninhabited, wooded island in the middle of the river, which the locals called Admana. The channel on our side of the island was relatively narrow and the trees on the island screened any movement on our side from observers on the far side. After a personal, surreptitious inspection of the site, Alexandros pronounced this location "perfect." All we needed now were some boats.

Finally, our sentries spotted the first of Koinos's oxcarts returning. Per Alexandros's instructions, they were not permitted to reach our camp. Instead, they were directed to stay several miles inland from the Hydaspes and veer upstream, until they came abreast of the Admana crossing site. At that point, they were to turn toward the river, screened by the wooded island. In addition, all the oxcarts were to arrive in the middle of the night, preferably during a thunderstorm. Since thunderstorms were a nightly occurrence, that instruction was easy to achieve. Once the oxcarts were unloaded, the oxen, along with the empty oxcarts, were quietly dispatched back inland and then downstream to join the daily charade of supply trains laden with provisions arriving at our camp. In the meantime, crews of carpenters got busy silently reassembling our flotilla in the lee of Admana Island.

As the carpenters were finishing their work, Alexandros asked various soothsayers, priests, and shamans for the most propitious day to launch our attack. While the seers equivocated, our spies provided the answer. They reported that Abisares and his army were finally on the march. Whether they were coming to Poros's aid or simply approaching to pick up the pieces after the battle was impossible to tell but Alexandros was not about to take a chance on the two rajas combining forces against us. He ordered an attack for that night.

****

On the face of it, our attack was doomed to failure. It's always easier to defend than to attack but in this case Poros had several other factors working in his favor. First, there was the river. Its level was swollen by the melting snows of the Himalayas and the monsoon rains, its current swift and turbulent. We lacked suitable watercraft. Getting our men across promised to be a daunting undertaking. Getting our horses to the other side, riding on rickety rafts, was well-nigh impossible. If the roar of the river, the bucking and tossing of the rafts, and the thunderclaps overhead were not enough to spook them, a couple of trumpet blasts from Poros's elephants waiting on the opposite shore would probably get most of them to leap into the raging river in a blind panic. As for our elephants, of which Alexandros had acquired a few, there was no chance we could get them across. We didn't have enough rafts for the horses, much less elephants. Alexandros also lacked experienced mahouts who were both capable of controlling the animals and whose loyalty he could trust. And besides, he had no idea how to utilize elephants in a battle in any event.

Second, Poros was the leader of a large, well-trained, efficient, and battle-tested army, comprising 4,000 cavalry, 50,000 infantry, 6,000 archers, 300 chariots, and 200 elephants. They also benefited from familiarity with the terrain, short supply lines, and brilliant, experienced commanders, starting with Poros himself. It also helped that their men, unlike ours, were used to the monsoon season. They also knew how to maintain fast, reliable communications utilizing a system of shouting relays capable of operating day and night, regardless of weather and ground conditions. And, finally, they were fighting to defend their homes and families.

We had some advantages of our own, however. Our army was larger than Poros's. Of the 92,000 fighting men who'd crossed the Hindu Kush, we had lost a few thousand to death, disease, and garrison duty but those losses were more than offset by the addition of several thousand Indian troops supplied by Omphis. Plus, the veteran core of this army – the Macedonian commanders, cavalry, and infantrymen, who'd been with Alexandros since he'd become king – were the best warriors in the world. They were already superior as a result of the improved equipment and tactical innovations introduced by Alexandros's father but they'd become, through years of fighting and survival of the fittest, the best soldiers the world had ever seen. Unfortunately, by this point, the Macedonian oldtimers made up no more than ten percent of the army and they were getting mentally tired and physically old and scarred. The rest of the army was uneven, although some of the training, attitude, and determination of the Macedonian oldtimers had rubbed off on all of them. We also benefited from first-rate equipment, adequate supplies, battle-tested commanders, and a track record of victories. But most importantly, we had Alexandros on our side.

****

The attack on Poros was the most intricate and brilliant operation planned by Alexandros to date. Even the weather gods cooperated. During phase one, he made sure that, as viewed from across the river, everything in our camp appeared as chaotic as usual. At dusk, a myriad campfires blazed into life, illuminating a beehive of activity. The nightly, noisy, sham sorties up and down the riverbank galloped off as before, although Poros's forces had long since given up shadowing our feints.

Hard by the river, the bulk of our army commenced their theatrical preparations for the long-awaited crossing. There was an inordinate amount of traffic in and out of the command tent, with officers rushing about in the heavy rain. Orders were barked and soldiers assembled in their respective formations. A figure wearing a simulacrum of Alexandros's armor, up to and including his helmet with its distinctive while plume, emerged from the command tent, looking very much like our commander-in-chief. Accompanied by his normal entourage, he supervised the preparations and inspected the troops. Evidently dissatisfied with something, he was yelling and waving his arms, ordering groups of soldiers hither and yon. In fact, this man was an ordinary soldier whose main qualification for the job was that, from a distance, he looked a lot like Alexandros. The man actually in charge of the forces left behind at the ford was Krateros. Also left behind were the five thousand Indian soldiers commanded by Omphis.

Farther away from the river and lost among the general hubbub, other troops disappeared from view, silently and stealthily taking advantage of the moonless night and the absence of bonfires on the far side of our camp. Squadron by invisible squadron, five thousand horsemen stole into the night. Ten thousand crack Macedonian infantrymen and various auxiliary forces vanished into the darkness as well. This ghost army, led by the real Alexandros aboard his trusty steed Boukephalas, reappeared, undetected, at the Admana crossing, well after midnight.

At about the same time, a second, smaller, spectral army, comprised of our mercenary cavalry and infantry, took up their positions, again without alerting the enemy sentinels and spies, at one of the main fords halfway between the camp and the Admana crossing. They took advantage of what was left of the night to get some rest and contemplate their odds of surviving the coming day.

Those of us at the Admana crossing, by contrast, still had much work to do in the three hours left before the first tendrils of dawn rent the night's protective cloak. Seventeen thousand men and five thousand horses had to be transported to the other side of a raging river.

The mounted forces included not only the entire Companion Cavalry but also selected squadrons of the newly-integrated Baktrian and Sogdian light cavalry and Massagetan mounted archers. Hephaistion, Perdikkas,

Koinos, Demetrios, and I were among the cavalry commanders.

The foot soldiers included elite battalions of the Silver Shields brigade, veteran Macedonians of the Guards brigade, the Agrianian light infantry, and archers, slingers, and chuckers of various nationalities. Seleukos was in overall command of the infantry units, with Lysimachos as his second-in-command.

Loading all these men and horses onto various vessels quickly and efficiently would have been a challenging task under the best of circumstances. In this case, the entire operation had to be accomplished in the dark, in torrential rain, and undetected by Poros's sentinels on the other side of the river. It helped that this section of the riverbank was hidden from sight by the wooded island in the middle of the stream. In addition, as the first squadrons of cavalry started boarding the galleys and rafts, a providential thunderstorm broke out. The more or less continuous lightning flashes created a strobing effect that made it easier to see where we were going, in an eerie, jerky, slow-motion way. The thunderclaps covered the noise of our embarkation. Unfortunately, the celestial show also had two negative side effects: It made the horses difficult to control and it killed two men who happened to be standing near a tree when it was struck by lightning.

At daybreak, Poros's startled sentinels rubbed their eyes, surprised to see hundreds of boats and rafts, carrying thousands of men and horses, floating into sight from beyond the downstream tip of Admana Island. But they didn't gawk for long. Utilizing their unparalleled system of relay criers, they sent word of our impending incursion to Poros's command post. And then, they prepared to resist our disembarkation on their side of the river.

Of course, the few dozen Poros soldiers stationed on the east bank across from Admana Island never had a chance against our massed forces. We took the bank and our men, horses, and weapons continued to pour ashore unopposed.

Poros, in the meantime, was caught on the horns of a dilemma. Although now aware of our landing some seventeen miles upriver from his main camp, he had no way of knowing the size of our force. At the same time, he had just received word of another detachment preparing to cross at the major crossing point some eight miles upriver. And, most confusing of all, he could see with his own eyes what appeared to be the main prong of the enemy trident preparing to ford the shallows from the enemy camp to his current position. It seemed to him, from the swarming phalanxes of infantry on the other bank, from all the bristling weapons and armor visible across the river, and most importantly, from the sight of the officer in charge, who certainly looked just like Alexandros, that this had to be the main-force invasion.

Poros marshaled his forces and – fatefully – hesitated. He was reluctant to start marching toward Admana Island, afraid that, as soon as he left his camp, the main-force invasion from across the camp, led by Alexandros, would gain the ground behind him and take him in the back. At the same time, he was reluctant to stay where he was, afraid that the Admana force and the middle force, once established on his side of the river, would prove too difficult to dislodge. And he was reluctant to divide his forces, afraid that Alexandros would find a way to defeat each diminished portion of his army, one by one.

After his moment of indecision, he picked the best available course of action. He divided his forces to oppose Alexandros's divided forces. Unfortunately for Poros, this short delay was enough to enable Alexandros to get his entire Admana assault force across and organized on Poros's side of the Hydaspes. The cavalry lined up on the right, hard by the river; the infantry fell in on the left, away from the water; with the auxiliaries salted throughout. Once organized, this expeditionary corps started marching, in battle formation, toward Poros's original position.

The detachment dispatched by Poros to oppose this corps was assembled in haste, selected for maximum speed, and too small to accomplish its mission. It numbered 2,000 cavalry, plus 120 chariots, which were the jewels of Poros's army and were meant to spread terror among the enemy. The detachment was commanded by one of Poros's sons. Their primary assignment was to disrupt the landing efforts of the amphibious enemy corps. Failing that, they were to take on the enemy and, at a minimum, fight them to a standstill until reinforcements arrived.

This turned out to be a hopeless charge. Badly outnumbered by the best troops Alexandros had at his disposal, and their chariots rendered totally useless by the veteran Macedonian and Agrianian soldiers who had much experience in neutralizing and destroying these outdated fighting platforms, the detachment was quickly defeated. Four hundred men were killed outright, including Poros's son, while the rest fled in panic and disorder toward Poros's main force. The most serious casualty on Alexandros's side was a wound sustained by Boukephalas, which would subsequently prove fatal.

As soon as Poros's detachment was routed, Alexandros led the cavalry at full speed ahead, instructing the infantry and the auxiliaries to follow as fast as possible. When the cavalry came abreast of the middle ford, they scattered Poros's forces stationed there without a fight. Once the bank was secured, our assault force stationed on the opposite side struggled across the ford, using sewn-up tents, stuffed with straw, as improvised flotation devices. During this operation, our infantry caught up. Then the combined, reinforced corps continued its dash toward Poros.

At this point, Poros, reacting to the rapidly evolving situation, concluded that the force across the shallows, scurrying around, making much noise, and putting on a show of preparing to cross the river, was nothing more than a diversion. He left behind a small detachment, including some elephants, to resist any attempted crossing, should it ever materialize, and marched the bulk of his army, including all the surviving cavalrymen, 50,000 infantry, 6,000 archers, the remaining chariots, and close to 200 elephants, toward Alexandros's oncoming combined force.

After slogging through some heavy mud, Poros found a wide, sandy field that was drier and offered better footing for his elephants and chariots. He halted his troops and arranged them for the coming set piece battle. He deployed his elephants in a single line, spaced at regular intervals, all across the battlefield. He himself sat in a spectacular howdah placed atop the largest elephant of all. This magnificent beast stood at the center of the line.

Immediately behind the elephants, Poros arrayed his infantry in a single, dense, deep line, covering the entire width from one end of the line of elephants to the other. Beyond each end of the infantry line, he placed his longbow archers, and then, beyond the archers, he stationed his cavalry, 2,000 horsemen anchoring each end. In front of the cavalry, he parked his chariots, about eight on each side. It was an absolutely beautiful sight. Even the weather gods paused the rains to get a better look.

From the vantage point of an oncoming army, Poros's battleline looked like a four-mile-wide, solid, impenetrable, unassailable fortress. The serried, uninterrupted line of infantry, with the elephants standing just in front, looked from a distance very much like a long, crenellated castle wall, with massive shooting towers placed at regular, one-hundred-foot intervals. The only difference was that this castle wall was flamboyantly colorful. Unlike the Macedonian soldiers, whose attire and accoutrements consisted of dull, worn, brownish leather skirts, woolen tunics, and dented, muddy, rusting armor, and even whose horses ranged mostly from bay to black, the Indian infantry soldiers wore gleaming white linen outfits, highlighted by vivid splashes of red, yellow, green, and purple. Miraculously, in the middle of the monsoon season and after marching through mud and elephant muck, the outfits had remained spotlessly clean. The howdahs atop the elephants, housing archers, were jewel boxes of exotic woods, shining fabrics, and glittering precious stones and metals. And the chariots flanking this colorful fortress wall were masterpieces of martial art, far more beautiful on parade than useful in battle.

When Alexandros, accompanied by his cavalry, came close enough to get a good look at the enemy, he halted his riders in order to give the men and the horses a moment to rest, to allow the infantry and the auxiliaries time to catch up, and to take the opportunity to carefully scout the opposing forces and formulate a plan of attack. The fact that Poros's army greatly outnumbered his expeditionary corps didn't disturb him in the least. His men had faced much greater odds than this and had emerged victorious each time. Plus, he had huge reserves, commanded by Krateros, waiting just beyond the shallows. His best arm, the cavalry, actually outnumbered the enemy's cavalry. Even if Poros commanded ten times as many horsemen, they would have been no match for the Companion Cavalry or, for that matter, even for the Baktrian mounted fighters. Alexandros knew instantly that his cavalry would play the key role in the upcoming battle, as they had in so many engagements before. But he worried about the elephants.

Alexandros didn't believe that his horsemen, battle-tested, formidable, and fearsome as they were, could successfully attack elephants. The horses, which had never before come up against elephants in battle, were simply too scared of them. His foot-soldiers were plenty scared as well but they were tough warriors and their courage would grow as they saw the tactics devised by their commander succeeding in action. He just had to protect them from the enemy infantry, cavalry, archers, and chariots, so they could do their work against the elephants.

The chariots were not a problem. His soldiers had long since learned how to cope with them. All they had to do was open lanes to let the horses charge through and kill or injure the animals as they ran by. Once the horses were disabled, the charioteers were easily dispatched. Really, by this point the chariots had become something of a joke among his veterans. The infantry's main job was to keep the Indian infantry in check until Krateros arrived with his reinforcements, at which point the combined infantry forces could methodically dispose of their Indian counterparts. The enemy cavalry would be our cavalry's assignment, led by Alexandros in person. As for the enemy archers, our men would just have to use their shields and hope for the best until the archers could be killed or disabled.

The men rested, ate, and drank diluted wine. Alexandros walked among them, greeting many by name, cracking jokes, and projecting a cool confidence. He conferred with his commanders, making sure each one understood not only his unit's specific role but also alternative assignments, if necessitated by battlefield developments. When the preparations were complete, he made sure the troops addressed their prayers to whichever gods they worshipped and then sang a couple of paeans together. All this time, Poros's soldiers stood in their formations, wondering what awaited them, getting more tense and tired by the minute.

Finally, Alexandros was ready to attack. Leading about two thirds of the cavalry, he galloped at the tip of our usual wedge formation directly toward the left end of Poros's line, where half of the Indian cavalry was stationed. En route, without slowing their gallop, our Massagetan mounted archers disposed of the chariot screen in front of the Indian cavalry by a few accurate flights of arrows, quickly disabling the chariot drivers. The Indian archers, standing next to their cavalry, proved as ineffectual as the charioteers. Although their long bows had a greater range and their arrows more killing power than our archers', the Indian archers, in order to shoot, had to prop one end of their bows on the ground. Luckily for us, in the trampled, wet, and muddy soil, the bow ends tended to slip just before the moment of release, causing the arrows to fly astray.

Once Alexandros's horsemen reached their Indian counterparts, they went to work with gusto. In this sector, our horsemen outnumbered theirs three to two and our guys were by far the better fighters. In short order, the Indian horsemen started to retreat.

In the meantime, the one third of our cavalry that had been unobtrusively left behind, stood and watched the battlefield situation evolve. These squadrons were commanded by Koinos and Demetrios. Their specific orders were to wait and see what Poros did with the other half of his cavalry, stationed on the right end of his line. If they remained standing in place, then Koinos and Demetrios were to launch an attack against them. But not too soon. If it turned out that Poros moved the right half of his cavalry across the field to the left end of his line in order to relieve the pressure on their beleaguered colleagues, then Koinos and Demetrios were instructed to let the Indian horsemen ride by unmolested, leaving them to the tender mercies of our cavalry squadrons led by Alexandros, which were already engaged in the fight. As Alexandros expected, Poros couldn't bear to watch the left half of his cavalry get hacked to pieces without doing something. Soon enough, he did in fact send the other half of his cavalry across the field to aid their comrades.

The moment the right half of Poros's cavalry moved, the Koinos and Demetrios squadrons galloped to the position those horsemen had just vacated, outflanked the right end of Poros's line, and then dashed across behind Poros's army to the left end of their line. Alexandros's horsemen, in the meantime, were doing just fine, even facing the combined forces of the Indian cavalry. Their fighting spirits were kept high by their knowledge of what would come next.

When the Koinos and Demetrios squadrons reached the left end of Poros's line, they attacked the surprised Indian horsemen from the back. In truth, the only chance the Indian cavalry ever had against our more numerous and superior cavalry was by taking advantage of the fact that the Indians' horses were used to war elephants and able to operate among them. But by the time Poros realized that his cavalry was on the verge of extinction, caught in the pincer movement of Alexandros's cavalry, it was too late. His elephants were, by that point, otherwise occupied.

As soon as Seleukos saw the Koinos and Demetrios squadrons round the right end of Poros's line, he launched an all-out assault by the infantry and auxiliary forces under his command. The men ran across the gap toward Poros's forces, yelling, screaming, and singing. Once again, neither the remaining chariots nor the Indian archers were able to do much to slow them down. The Indian infantry, funneling through the gaps between the elephants, came out to meet our onrushing infantry but, despite their great numerical superiority, they were no match against the heavily armed, experienced, and well-trained men, who also had momentum at their backs. The Indian infantry line found itself steadily pushed back.

When our infantrymen forced their way within shooting range of the elephants, the auxiliaries scattered among them launched whatever missiles they possessed. The archers shot arrows, the slingers slung stones, and the javelin men hurled spears, all in an effort to kill the mahouts sitting just behind the heads of their giant, armored, terrestrial destroyers. It didn't take long to kill all the mahouts. And, once the elephants lost their helmsmen, they became indecisive and confused. At that point, Seleukos's infantrymen and auxiliaries shifted their lethal efforts to the elephants.

In the meantime, Alexandros's cavalry, having disposed of the Indian horsemen, rode to the back of the Indian line and attacked the Indian infantrymen from behind, causing some of them to turn around and fight, others to retreat toward the elephants, and the remainder to flee the battlefield. Krateros, watching from the other side of the shallows, decided that this was the moment to enter the fray. His men struggled across the strong current and treacherous footing as best they could. Those fortunate enough to get to the other side immediately got busy pursuing the fleeing Indian infantrymen, as well as joining the attack on the ones still attempting to resist. Among the men fording the river were Omphis and his 5,000 Indians, who were anxious to inflict as much damage on their brethren as possible.

Caught between Seleukos's forces pushing them from the front and the combination of Alexandros's cavalry and Krateros's infantry attacking from the rear, Poros's infantry found itself getting squeezed into a narrower and narrower space next to and in between the rudderless elephants. Seleukos's men, in addition to fighting against the Indian infantry, did their best to wound the elephants by aiming their missiles and weapons against the few vulnerable spots on their bodies, such as their eyes, the ends of their trucks, and their genitalia. Some of the men chopped furiously at the elephants' feet and legs, even if their blows had little effect.

Gradually but inexorably, the niggling injuries started to add up and take a toll. The confused, frightened, and hurting animals started to panic and grow increasingly more aggressive. They grabbed men with their trunks and dashed them into the ground. They transfixed men with their tusks. They mashed men into a bloody pulp under their feet as they charged and whirled this way and that.

They didn't discriminate between friend and foe. Eventually, they lumbered away from the fighting, leaving a carpet of mangled bodies in their wake. Even Poros's elephant, with the wounded, barely conscious raja still aboard, ambled away.

All that was left on the battlefield was a small, sad remnant of Poros's once great army, surrounded and getting chewed up piecemeal. Alexandros, who bore the Indians no ill will, stopped the slaughter and took the survivors captive. He was particularly anxious to accept the surrender of Poros whom, in some mysterious fashion, he had come to admire in the course of the battle.

He sent Omphis as his emissary to negotiate terms with Poros, figuring that the two rajas, speaking the same language, would be best able to communicate. This turned out to be a miscalculation. The two rivals, who had spent a lifetime fighting against each other, were not equipped to engage in a civil conversation. As soon as Poros saw his chief antagonist and tormentor approaching, he mustered enough strength to slip off his elephant and, notwithstanding the javelin sticking out of his left shoulder and his numerous other wounds, lunged at Omphis with his sword. The raja of Taxila, who was supposed to bring Poros to Alexandros and not kill him, chose to abandon his diplomatic mission.

Soon after Omphis's departure, Poros sank to the ground. Alexandros dispatched a litter and his personal physician to extract the javelin, stanch the bleeding, and bring the great commander back. After a long and hazardous operation, the physician succeeded in his assigned task.

When the litter bearing him approached Alexandros, Poros insisted on getting off and standing on his own two feet. Even in defeat, and dressed in blood-soaked bandages, the raja had an imposing presence. He stood a towering six-and-a-half feet, his well-proportioned body exuding strength, his face handsome and composed, his posture lofty, and his countenance self-assured.

Alexandros dismounted and approached the defeated foe. Speaking through an interpreter, he asked Poros how he would like to be treated.

"As a king," came the blunt reply.

"Yes, of course. But what specifically can I do for you?"

"Everything," said Poros, "is contained in that one request."

Alexandros liked that answer.

******

It was a virtuoso victory but it came at a cost. All told, Alexandros lost 4,000 men, mostly infantry. However, the death that hit him hardest was that of Boukephalas, who succumbed to his wounds and old age. Hephaistion organized funeral rites that were simultaneously solemn and spectacular. The bodies of the dead men were cremated on huge pyres; their ashes carefully collected, poured into amphorae, and buried in group graves, sorted by nationality and military unit. Alexandros intended to place permanent stone stelai on the graves, listing the names of the dead. Boukephalas received his own huge pyre and his own grave. His stele was actually erected before Alexandros left the area.

The usual rituals for the dead, funeral games, and feasts followed. For once, there was no shortage of supplies, thanks to Poros's captured baggage train. It turned out that the raja had brought ample provisions for a months-long standoff. He himself was recovering from his injuries and treated as an honored guest at several banquets. Alexandros made sure that Poros and Omphis were never invited to the same event.

At one of the last banquets, Alexandros gave Poros generous gifts and confirmed him as raja of Paurava, while incorporating that kingdom into his empire. This was more a notional absorption, since no taxes were imposed and no duties required. However, Poros did pledge his eternal allegiance.

Raja Abisares, who had been hoping to swoop in and scavenge the spoils after his rivals had killed each other off, never made an appearance. He did send his brother, with treasure and elephants, but claimed that his royal duties prevented him from showing up in person. Alexandros was outraged and threatened to come after him but, on further thought, decided that his mountainous kingdom was not worth the effort. In the end, Alexandros confirmed Abisares as raja as well, hoping that the three rajas would keep one another in check, rather than uniting against him the moment he'd turned his back. Omphis and Abisares did just that. Poros remained loyal until the day Alexandros died.

Other than food and drink, there was not much loot to distribute among the troops. The best Alexandros could do was give the men thirty days of rest and recreation before resuming the campaign. Unfortunately, women were scarce. Poros, unlike Alexandros, was fighting near home and therefore had seen no need to include the normal complement of camp followers in his baggage train. However, the usual athletic and theatrical contests were conducted. Their festive atmosphere was somewhat dampened by the ongoing monsoon rains, the clouds of insects, the ubiquitous rust, rot, and mold, the food-, water-, and insect-borne illnesses, and the homesickness of the troops.

Before leaving, Alexandros founded two garrison towns in the area to maintain control of the region and keep an eye on the rajas. He located one of these fortified positions on the site of our camp near the shallows. He named it Boukephala. He put the other incipient town at the Admana crossing. This one he called Nikaia.

When the thirty days ended, Alexandros was ready to resume his march southeast to the Okeanos River, also known as Land's End. Once there, he planned to sail west, following the coast of India, until he reached the Persian Gulf. To facilitate this ambitious undertaking, he left behind a sizeable force, under Krateros's command, with instructions to collect and salvage the watercraft used to cross the Hydaspes, chop down all the trees they could find, and get busy building an even bigger and better fleet for the voyage home. Once Alexandros had reached the end of the world and had a better handle on the geography of the area, he would send word to Krateros, telling him to bring the fleet around.

Alexandros was excited to see what came next; the troops not so much. They worried that the campaign would never end, that they would run into more elephants along the way, and that they would never get home. And the monsoon rains were still coming down in sheets.

Chapter 16 – Heading to the Sea

By the time the army moved out, Alexandros had a much better idea of what lay beyond the Hydaspes River. He'd interviewed captured soldiers, spoken with Poros, consulted local guides and sages. He knew that the Paurava kingdom, which started at the Hydaspes, ended on the banks of another great river called, confusingly enough, the Hyphasis. Therefore, his immediate objective was to reach, and cross, the Hyphasis. He still believed that the Okeanos River was not too far beyond the Hyphasis.[17]

The march across Paurava was uneventful. The trouble started when the army reached the Hyphasis. This was another dangerous, rain-swollen river, with nothing too inviting on the other side. The soldiers didn't have the benefit of briefings from rajas, sages, and seers. They had their own local experts, drawn from among the traders, hustlers, and whores of the baggage train. And what they heard were stories of many more rivers to come, some

---

[17] To better visualize these confusingly named rivers, see Maps 14 and 15 at AlexanderGeiger.com.

larger than either the Hydaspes or the Hyphasis; tales of impenetrable forests, treacherous marshes, and parched deserts; and tales of lands inhabited by savage cannibals, man-eating tigers, vicious monkeys, and vengeful gods. It was now the height of summer, the heat was suffocating, the insects voracious, the climate pestilential, their prospects unpromising, and the relentless rain continued to pour.

The soldiers had had enough. They had understood the objective of taking control of every square mile of the Persian Empire and, with any luck, reaping a harvest of riches in the process, but they had now marched beyond the borders of the farthest satrapy in pursuit of some nebulous goal of reaching the end of the world. That wasn't what they'd signed up for. And the bonds of loyalty, trust, and camaraderie between them and their commander had become frayed over the years of marches, combat, and suffering. All the soldiers in the army felt this way but the Macedonian oldtimers considered themselves more aggrieved than the rest.

When Alexandros assembled the army on the banks of the Hyphasis to tell them his plans, the soldiers just stood there. There was no open rebellion or mutiny. They didn't heckle or argue, possibly because by now they realized that an angry Alexandros could be a murderous Alexandros. Instead, they simply, silently, sullenly dug in their heels.

Immortal Alexandros

Alexandros tried every method of persuasion in his repertory. He gave his soldiers permission to ravage and plunder the land. He staged feasts. He pleaded, cajoled, and threatened. He even visited the baggage train and sought to enlist the women in his cause, promising them money, rations, and freedom. Nothing worked. At the next assembly, the army, led by the Macedonian oldtimers and veterans, proved immovable.

In a fury, Alexandros dismissed the soldiers and called his Macedonian commanders to his tent. He gave an impassioned speech, arguing that they didn't have much farther to go, that the going wouldn't be as hard as rumored, that the natives were not as numerous, bellicose, or savage as reported. Beyond that, he told them that he was destiny's darling, that his destiny was to march to the ends of the Earth, and that, in any event, their life's work was to keep marching. "It's the journey, not the destination."

The commanders, who understood the situation better than the common soldiers, and who knew their Alexandros better, too, just stood in defiant silence. Finally, after an interminable moment, during which Alexandros stared, wild-eyed, from face to face, fingering the hilt of his sword, Koinos stepped forward. He was tired, prematurely gray, sick, and, as Parmenion's son-in-law, the last surviving relative of the old man in the army.

"Sire," he said quietly, "we have no choice but to turn back. The men are not able to go farther, whether they want to or not. They're not as young as they once were. So many of them have died. The ones who've survived this long have aged beyond their years. They don't have the physical or mental stamina to go on. All they want is to go home." The assembled commanders nodded. A couple of them clapped Koinos on the back.

Alexandros leaned in, thrust his chin out, and roared. "Get out! All of you!" He unsheathed his sword and physically chased them out.

He called them back the next day. "I've decided to go on, with or without you," he told them. "Some of the men will follow me and, in any event, I won't stop until I've fulfilled my destiny, even if I have to go on alone. And you, you can go home to your old wives and dogs and plows and tell everyone you meet that you decided to leave your leader in the lurch."

The commanders said nothing. After a long, embarrassed pause, without saying a word, they began to filter out of the tent, backing out by twos and threes, until Alexandros was left standing alone.

When the servants brought food and wine, Alexandros chased them away, telling them he intended to starve to death.

This time, the commanders called his bluff. They figured their chances of extricating themselves from this mess and getting home alive were at least as good on their own as with a raving Alexandros in charge.

After two days of seclusion, Alexandros emerged from his tent. He announced that he was getting ready to proceed across the Hyphasis but needed to check the auguries first. He ordered Kleomenes of Lakedaimon, his chief soothsayer, to conduct various rituals and prognostications. All the omens proved unfavorable. Alexandros bitterly admitted that, in light of the portents, they couldn't go on. The soldiers and their officers were overjoyed. Alexandros never forgave them.

****

Alexandros was forced to retreat to Nikaia, where Krateros's men were still busy building the big new fleet. The soldiers assumed that the shipbuilding would stop and that, after a brief rest at the Hydaspes, they would retrace their route over the Hindu Kush, across Baktria, and then west on the well-traveled caravan routes all the way back to Ekbatana. Nobody was under any illusions that this would be an easy march but at least it had the benefit of familiarity. Alexandros had other ideas.

Having reluctantly taken a small step back, he was still intent on forging ahead to the world-encircling Okeanos River. All he had to do was convince his troops that this new route would get them where they wanted to go faster and more easily. Alexandros told them that they could sail down the Hydaspes, which would eventually merge with the Indos, which would in turn flow into the ocean. Once they reached the ocean, they could sail north and west, along the shores of the Indian Sea, until they hit the Persian Gulf, which would take them to Sousa, Babylon, and back to Macedonia. "As easy as falling off your seat at a drinking party."

This time, Alexandros was able to persuade the troops. His credibility was enhanced by the fact that, unlike at the Hyphasis, his geography was sound, as confirmed by the soldiers' usual sources. There were, however, a few things Alexandros neglected to mention during his sales pitch. Foremost among these omissions was the disparity between the capacity of the ships being built and the size of the army. Not all the ships in India could have carried Alexandros's huge army, as well as all the camp followers, horses, elephants, oxen, mules, donkeys, and dogs, all the provisions, armor, equipment, treasure, and accumulated dross. After all, this multitude, had they settled down, would have instantly become the second or third most populous city in the Persian Empire. Many of these folks would soon discover that there would be no sailing, only marching.

The odds of securing a coveted place on one of the boats got longer with the arrival of massive reinforcements of mercenaries from Greece, Thrake, and Babylon. Perhaps as many as 20,000 infantrymen and 4,000 horsemen came, each hoping to find his fortune. The veterans might be jaded, tired, and disillusioned but rapacious replacements could always be found among the landless hordes eager to draw the winning lots from the cauldron of war. Whether these mercenaries could come anywhere close to matching the fighting qualities of the veterans remained to be seen but, in sheer numbers, they were more than enough to make up for all the losses we had suffered since leaving Baktria.

The reinforcements, however, were incidental to the primary purpose of this huge relief expedition, which had been assembled and organized by Harpalos, the man Alexandros had left behind in Ekbatana as his tax collector and treasurer. After the murder of Parmenion, Alexandros had relocated Harpalos to Babylon and put him in charge of the financial affairs of the entire empire. The man we had known as a prankster, whose main claim to fame was his lifelong friendship with Alexandros, had gradually grown into his important new position. As the custodian of the imperial treasures seized by Alexandros during his conquest of Persia, Harpalos was arguably the richest man in the world. Of course, the money wasn't his but he did exercise day-to-day control over it. Inevitably, Harpalos's standard of living began to creep upward. He was a lame, ugly, thirty-five-year-old former court jester who suddenly found himself the toast of the most sybaritic, libertine, and decadent city in the empire. He was invited to many banquets and felt obliged to repay the favor by hosting even more symposia himself, each outdoing in opulence and debauchery the previous one. He imported alluring hetairai and spent lavishly on them. His one quirk was that he was monogamous with his mistresses, sticking to one paramour at a time. Perhaps he was a romantic or maybe he simply had a healthy appreciation of his physical limitations.

In order to import the most desirable female companions, Harpalos felt the need to establish good trading relations with Athens, home to the most seductive and sophisticated hetairai in the Greek world. At that time, Athens was suffering from a severe grain shortage, brought about by several consecutive poor harvests in Attika and by the fact that Alexandros was soaking up all the grain supplies from Mesopotamia and from around the Mediterranean and the Black Seas for his army and the many garrisons he had established. Harpalos decided to play the role of the great humanitarian and, using Alexandros's money, he sent large shipments of grain to Athens. The Athenians were understandably grateful. They made Harpalos an honorary citizen and kept him well supplied with the most enchanting and complaisant of their maidens.

Alexandros had heard rumors of Harpalos's profligacy, decadence, and generosity toward Athens but, remembering Harpalos as a good friend and a charming buffoon, laughed them off as the compensatory efforts of a man trying to make up for his lack of natural endowments. And besides, with all that wealth in the treasury, what difference did a little petty thievery make? His thinking started to change at some point during the protracted campaigns in Baktria and Sogdiana. The costs of keeping the army in the field were great and the spoils of war far too meager to cover them. Before leaving Baktria for India, Alexandros sent an urgent message to Harpalos, asking for reinforcements, suits of armor, and – most importantly – lots of coin.

It had taken a very long time for Harpalos to respond to Alexandros's order, which was bad enough but understandable, given the distances involved. What was far worse was the quality and quantity of the men, armor, and money that finally arrived. The number of mercenaries was adequate, although Alexandros could never have enough men. But these were far from the finest fighters the world had ever seen. By the same token, the quality of armor sent by Harpalos was fine but he had only managed to procure 25,000 complete sets. Harpalos had mobilized all the armorers of Babylonia, Mesopotamia, and Assyria, and had exhausted the supplies of iron and other necessary materials from all the adjoining satrapies but this was far short of what Alexandros was hoping to receive. After much fighting, two crossings of the Hindu Kush, and two monsoon seasons, all of his soldiers needed new armor and Harpalos's shipment was barely enough to supply a quarter of them. But what irked Alexandros the most was the lack of coinage. By the time Harpalos's expedition arrived, Alexandros was literally out of money. And the sum Harpalos had sent, which approximated the annual revenue of all the Greek states combined and required hundreds of wagons to transport, was only enough to keep Alexandros's enormous and newly enlarged army in the field for three or four months.

Given Alexandros's gradual descent into paranoia and delusion, it was unsurprising that he started to suspect treachery. And, as always, some people in his circle were happy to stoke his worst instincts. They whispered in Alexandros's ear that Harpalos was taking advantage of his strategic position in Babylon and his control of the imperial treasury to recruit a private army, with the eventual aim of taking over the empire, in the event Alexandros never made it back to Babylon. To his credit, Alexandros, displeased as he was with his treasurer, refused to believe the whisperers. Of course, it's possible that Alexandros would've been inclined to believe the worst but, at that moment, he had a simmering rebellion by his veterans on his hands, he was stranded in the wilds of India, and he was not really in a position to do much about checking Harpalos's excesses, no matter what he might have thought about his former childhood buddy.

******

The season was turning to autumn and the monsoon rains were finally ending by the time Krateros's men finished their work. They had built an amazing flotilla of some 1,800 ships, ranging in size and sophistication from large triremes and galleys to medium-sized barges and horse transports to small, primitive rafts and rowboats, many of the latter bought or commandeered from the nearby riverine communities.

On a fine sunny morning, the first one in many months, Alexandros announced his dispositions: Nearchos the Kretan was put in charge of the fleet. The Companion Cavalry, along with our horses, would get to sail. So did the Silver Shields and the Guards Brigade. Everybody else, including the ever-growing throngs of camp followers, would have to march. The endless baggage train would bring up the rear. Krateros would march on the right bank, with all remaining cavalry and infantry. Hephaistion would march on the left bank, with all the rest of the soldiers and our 200 elephants. Another commander by the name of Philippos would trail behind Krateros on the right bank, with the sick and the lame, the camp followers, and the baggage train.

One commander who would not be marching with us was Koinos. He never recovered from his lingering illness and eventually succumbed before our departure from Nikaia. His veterans were allowed to stage a funeral for him, with all the requisite military honors. Alexandros made an appearance but his funeral oration was ambiguous at best. By this stage in his career, he neither forgot or forgave officers who had the effrontery to bring up inconvenient truths.

Before we could proceed, Alexandros made sure that all the requisite rituals were performed. Sacrifices were carried out; entrails examined; libations poured; deities propitiated. The ceremonies lasted all day, after which we feasted on those portions of the sacrificed animals not consigned to the flames for the gods' benefit. Finally, at dawn, we were off.

****

Our first rendezvous point was just beyond the confluence of the Hydaspes and Akesines rivers. The trip started out fine. Some natives, curious to witness the once-in-a-lifetime spectacle, came out and cheered. Most of the inhabitants, being more cautious, simply stayed out of our way and hid. Krateros and his column, marching on the right bank of the Hydaspes, marched much faster than our flotilla could sail. Even without pressing too hard, they reached the rendezvous point in a few days, without incident. They set up camp and waited for the rest of us.

The flotilla was doing fine as well, until we reached the confluence. It turned out that the merger of these two great rivers was anything but peaceful. Squeezed into a twisting, rocky channel, chiseled over the eons through a shallow mountain range, the two powerful rivers fought for primacy like two armies racing to occupy a strategic mountain pass. Tremendous volumes of water rushed over cataracts, picking up speed and turbulence as they went. Unexpected eddies and whirlpools snatched at anything attempting to float through, sucking it all beneath the waves and smashing it to bits against the rocks. How our quickly built and fairly fragile vessels got through I'll never know. We certainly had quite a few narrow escapes, including the near sinking of Alexandros's own command ship, but somehow we survived, with nary a vessel, man, or beast lost in the process. It was with great relief that we spotted Krateros's camp after surviving our passage.

In the meantime, Hephaistion and his group, including the 200 elephants, marching on the left bank, found themselves trapped on a narrow triangle of land where the two rivers met. It was impossible for anyone to get across to the right bank of the Hydaspes at that point. The long column of people and animals was forced to retrace its steps to the first reasonable crossing point and wait. Alexandros, when he grasped their predicament, had some of our ships disassembled and carried back upstream to where Hephaistion was waiting. Then, in an operation lasting more than a week, the entire Hephaistion group was ferried across the river and was then able to march down and join us in camp. It took such a long time to ferry the Hephaistion group to the right bank that even Philippos's group, baggage train and all, which was on the right bank all along, was able to beat them to our rendezvous point.

Once everyone was assembled, Alexandros gave us a few days of rest while scouts ventured downriver to gather intelligence. The news they brough back was alarming. Tribes ahead of us, farther down the Hydaspes, were hostile. News of our mighty victories had evidently not reached them. Instead, their priestly caste was busy inciting them to resist. Specifically, we were told that there were two powerful, vicious tribes ahead, the Malli and the Oxydrakai, which, between them, could field as many as 100,000 fighting men and which were getting ready to confront us. The accuracy of these reports was impossible to confirm but when sketchy summaries filtered down the ranks, they aroused a certain amount of consternation among the men.

The oldtimers and veterans who had mutinied on the Hyphasis were particularly unhappy. "It sounds a lot tougher than falling off our seats at a drinking party," they muttered. But what could they do? Having mutinied once, and having decided they were better off letting Alexandros lead them home than trying to follow someone else, they found themselves committed for the duration of the ride.

****

Two days out of camp we ran into the first resistance. A handful of villagers came out of their huts, armed with spears and making an awful racket, hoping to persuade us to bypass their village on our way downriver. The veterans were in a bad mood. They slaughtered the handful of armed men and then they slaughtered every other inhabitant of the village and then they slaughtered all animals, trampled all the crops, and vandalized the irrigation canals. Finally, they moved on, taking no loot, because there was no loot to take. Throughout all this, Alexandros said nothing.

And so it continued, day after day. We would roust some unfortunate villagers, who would run for the hills or the marshes. We would take whatever provisions we could find and continue on our way.

Eventually, we reached a fortified Mallian town. We never learned its name. Alexandros ordered the bulk of the army to continue ahead and set up camp farther downriver, while he kept a couple of battalions of Macedonian veterans and three squadrons of the Companion Cavalry with him, presumably enough force to overawe the defenders of the town. The defenders refused to surrender and Alexandros ordered the town sacked. The veterans were reluctant.

While Alexandros was busy urging them to deploy and commence the attack, an incredible thing occurred. Some obscure soothsayer, whom I'd never seen before, stepped forward and informed Alexandros that the omens were bad. He suggested it might be better to bypass the town.

Alexandros rounded on him. "Can't you see I'm busy right now, trying to sack this city? Do I interrupt you when you're reading the auguries?" The soothsayer shrank back under the vehemence of the attack, encouraging our commander to deliver the coup de grace. "Do you think I'm interested in hearing what some superstitious charlatan has to say?" The man slunk away. The soldiers stared in amazement. I just shook my head. *Who would've thought that I would hear those words pass Alexandros's lips?*

Alexandros ordered the troops to bring the ladders and scale the wall. Nobody moved. In an effort to shame his own soldiers into action, Alexandros grabbed the nearest ladder and put it in place. Still, nobody moved. At that point, in a typical display of bravado, Alexandros mounted the ladder himself and clambered onto the wall. To the surprise of the Mallian defenders massed on the other side and to the consternation of his own troops, Alexandros reared up on the wall, turned toward the Mallians, raised his arms in triumph, and shouted abuse at them.

It took only a split second for the first of the arrows to whiz by Alexandros's shoulder. In a moment, a cloud of arrows darkened the sky, all headed toward his head. His soldiers were finally jolted into action. They lifted the remaining two or three ladders and started to make their way up toward the top of the wall. Alexandros, in the meantime, jumped off the wall, before the arrows could hit him. But he didn't jump back to the safety of our side of the wall. No, he went the other way, landing amidst a clutch of shocked Mallian fighters.

He unsheathed his sword, stepped toward a large tree growing just inside the wall, and, using the shelter of the wall behind his back and the tree to his left as a shield, awaited the assault of the dozens of incensed fighters facing him. He didn't have long to wait.

Recovering from their stupefaction, the defenders descended on him like a murder of crows, screaming, thrusting spears, slashing with their daggers, launching arrows, and hurling any missiles that came to hand.

By the time the first three veteran commanders – Leonnatos, Peukestas, and Abreas – reached the top of the wall, they were greeted by the sight of Alexandros, standing on a small carpet of bodies, surrounded by a semicircle of enraged fighters. The three men jumped down and joined the fray. The rest of the Macedonians, stunned by what they imagined to be happening on the other side of the wall, finally sprang into action and ran as one toward the ladders. Unfortunately, as they all tried to scramble up simultaneously, all they managed to accomplish was collapse all the ladders, without a single additional man making it to the top of the wall.

Men attempted to scale the wall without benefit of ladders. Mostly, they kept falling back down. Other men, grabbing battering rams and axes, worked frantically to break down the gate into the city, located less than a hundred feet away. It was a stout gate and interminable minutes went by before the gate gave way.

Finally, a few soldiers managed to scale the wall, just as other soldiers started to pour in through the shattered gate. What they saw froze the blood in their veins.

The ground where Alexandros had jumped down was covered by dozens of bodies. Some of the bodies were still moving but most were still. The pile of bodies was surrounded by enraged Mallian fighters, poking and thrusting, shooting and throwing. A warrior in Macedonian armor, shot through the face, lay motionless toward the front of the pile. His comrades recognized him as Abreas. Another warrior, instantly identifiable as Alexandros, lay farther back on the pile, an arrow protruding from his chest. He wasn't moving either. Peukestas crouched in front of him, shield in hand, trying to protect him against the unremitting, merciless shower of arrows and missiles arriving from all sides. Leonnatos was still on his feet, screaming, his sword whistling through the air.

The men jumping from the wall and pouring in through the gate made quick work of all fighters in their way. Upon reaching the pile, they confirmed that Abreas was dead. Alexandros was unconscious but still breathing. They placed him on a shield and raced back to the other side of the wall. All who saw their cargo assumed that their leader was dying or perhaps dead already. Except for those of us engaged in carrying or caring for Alexandros, the rest of the soldiers went back to work, sacking the town in a matter of minutes and killing every living thing within its walls.

******

We hesitated briefly, trying to decide what to do. The bulk of our army had already moved on before the action started. None of the physicians had stayed behind and we had no tent or shelter nearby. A pallet was hastily improvised for Alexandros in the bed of a wagon. He was pale, not moving, barely conscious, unable to speak.

Horses were hitched and a teamster tried to ease the wagon into motion without jarring the injured man. This proved impossible, of course. Runners sprinted ahead toward the main body of the army, seeking Philippos the Physician. For whatever reason, Philippos couldn't be found.

Several other medics, already on hand, leapt into the wagon bed, took a quick look, and ran the other way. No one was willing to take any action for fear of reprisal once the inevitable denouement came to pass. Finally, Perdikkas, Seleukos, and I jumped up and took a look. It was clear that the arrow had pierced Alexandros's cuirass, his tunic, and his flesh. Beyond that, it was impossible to assess the severity of the wound.

We carefully cut the arrow shaft, trying to keep it as still as possible. Once the fletching end was severed, we lifted off the cuirass, cut off his tunic, and wiped away the blood. The arrowhead had lodged in his sternum. On the one hand, this was a "lucky" break. But for the resistance of the bone, the arrowhead would've continued farther into his torso, likely severing a major artery, if not hitting his heart or lungs. Either way, he would've been dead by now.

On the other hand, there was no way to extract the arrowhead. These deadly tips were made to go in and not to come out. They were wedge-shaped and barbed. The normal method for removing arrowheads that had fully penetrated inside the body was to push them through and pull them out on the other side, hoping that no vital organs were pierced in the process. The success rate of such operations was low but the alternative was certain death.[18] In this case, it was not possible to push the arrow through.

The three of us stood there, looking at each other. We tried to pour some wine into his mouth but it simply dribbled back out the sides. We asked for Philippos once again. Daylight was beginning to fade. We watched helplessly as life oozed out of our leader.

"We have to do something," Perdikkas finally said.

Seleukos arched his brows. "What?"

---

[18] Elite Persian horsemen wore silk tunics strong enough to wrap themselves around arrowheads without tearing, making it possible – sometimes – to pull out a buried arrowhead. Although Alexandros affected Persian dress at times, he disdained such effeminate accoutrements on the battlefield. Besides, if he couldn't provide his men with such protection, he certainly wouldn't consider wearing it himself.

Perdikkas fingered his dagger. "Maybe we can cut it out?"

Seleukos shook his head. "That'll kill him for sure."

"It's worth a shot," I finally decided. I saw a torch lying nearby and asked a soldier to light it and hand it to me. Holding the lit torch, I turned to Perdikkas. "Give me your dagger." I let the flame play over the blade until the hilt became almost too hot to hold. Then I handed the dagger back to Perdikkas. "Go ahead. Give it a try. Enlarge the wound just enough so we can pry it out."

"Isn't he suffering enough already?" Seleukos asked.

Perdikkas, who'd survived a few serious war wounds himself, didn't seem too concerned. "After a moment, he won't feel a thing."

He was right, of course. As soon as we set to work, Alexandros lost consciousness. Perdikkas prodded and pushed, trying to lever the point out. Seleukos held the end of what remained of the shaft, pulling on it as hard as he could. And I stood across from them, a huge pitcher poised in my hands, doing my best to keep the wound clear with torrents of uncut wine.

After a short moment that felt like an eternity the arrow came loose, causing Seleukos to lurch backward and almost fall over the side of the wagon. The arrowhead was followed by a fountain of bright red blood spurting from the newly liberated wound. Handing the pitcher to Perdikkas, I grabbed Alexandros's blood-saturated tunic, soaked it in wine, balled it up, and pressed it against the wound, hoping to stanch the flow of blood. I don't know how long I crouched there, pressing and hoping, when Philippos finally showed up. He took over and I staggered off the wagon. I stood with a small group of other commanders and some common soldiers. None of us thought there was any hope.

Somehow, Alexandros lived through the night.

****

The priests, shamans, soothsayers, and charlatans had a field day. They maintained a continuous relay of rituals day and night. The common soldiers wept and importuned the gods. Alexandros drifted in and out of consciousness for a week.

Rumors that Alexandros was either dead already or about to die quickly engulfed the main camp erected a few miles downriver. Despair gripped every soldier. Despite all their grumbling and their rebellion on the Hyphasis, the thought had never crossed these soldiers' minds that Alexandros might die. He was, as he had often told them, destiny's darling. Some even believed he was immortal. All of them had hitched their fortunes to his star. Yes, they wanted to go home but they also assumed he would lead them there. They realized that their journey back would be perilous, whichever route they took, but they had faith in his leadership and his luck. Now, they feared, he was out of both.

The soldiers respected, and even liked, most of their officers. Alexandros had assembled, or possibly had lucked into, an unparalleled cadre of outstanding military commanders. All of us might have been sought-after luminaries in any other army. (I include myself in that description because humility was never one of my vices.) But in Alexandros's army our lights shone as brightly as any of the heavenly stars at high noon; i.e., not at all. To the soldiers, the army was unimaginable without Alexandros.

After a week of hovering at the edge of death, Alexandros reached the point where he could reliably remain conscious while not sleeping, which was about six hours per day. His wound was still oozing and was nowhere near scarred over. He was unable to lift his head or do much more than wiggle his fingers. It took him long minutes to recover from a single whispered sentence. His only nourishment was broth gently spooned into his mouth.

Philippos was crystal clear that, at least for the next couple of weeks, his life still hung in the balance. Under the circumstances, he couldn't be moved until his condition stabilized and he regained at least a modicum of strength. In the meantime, while he lay on a pallet in a makeshift tent, the troops grew more and more restive. With nothing better to do, the soldiers spent their time debating the consequences of getting stranded in this faraway, exotic, hostile land inhabited by fierce savages, ferocious beasts, and insects the size of dogs. They competed with one another to see who could imagine the scariest scenario for their inevitable demise. By the time they finished their nightly drinking bouts, they could hardly keep from soiling themselves.

Finally, Alexandros could wait no longer. He had two boats lashed together and an elevated platform built in the middle of this catamaran. He wanted us to place his pallet atop this stage, thus making him visible from the shore. Philippos warned that this proposed stunt could be the death of him but Alexandros insisted. We carried him aboard as if he were a giant egg poised in the middle of a polished mirror.

After Alexandros was secured atop the platform, Philippos ordered that the catamaran be allowed to free-float down the river without the use of any oars. All other river traffic was banished for a half mile in either direction to avoid creating any waves. An honor guard of four soldiers held an awning aloft to protect Alexandros from the beating sun as we pushed off.

When the catamaran came abreast of a group of Macedonian soldiers standing on the riverbank, they simply stared, unsure whether they were looking at a corpse or a mannequin. With a supreme effort, Alexandros lifted his right hand and fluttered his fingers, ever so slightly. This barely perceptible gesture set off a paroxysm of wild jubilation that spread at the speed of sound along the Hydaspes River all the way to the main camp.

Several hours later, we pulled up at a dock next to the camp. The embankment on both sides of the dock was teeming with wildly cheering soldiers. As we lifted Alexandros on his pallet, he lifted his hand to stop us. The riverine excursion and, more importantly, the rejoicing of his soldiers had apparently worked miracles. He sat up on the pallet, swung his legs over the edge, and stood up. We were all too stunned to say anything. How he accomplished this feat of defiance, I'll never know.

After making sure that he was able to maintain his balance, he walked onto the dock and then proceeded to his command tent. As he walked, soldiers called out greetings, uttered prayers of thanksgiving, attempted to touch him or his clothes. We made sure there was no physical contact and Alexandros kept walking, slowly but steadily, a rigid smile fixed on his face.

The tent was not far away but he barely made it. As soon as the flap unfurled behind his back, he collapsed in a dead faint. We could not revive him until the next morning. A distraught Philippos kept repeating that his recovery had been set back by several weeks. In fact, he would never fully recover from this wound. But his soldiers went to sleep reassured.

****

Two months later, with spring around the corner, Alexandros finally ordered the army to move out. The division between those lucky enough to sail and those forced to march remained essentially unchanged, as did the order of the march, except now all the units remained on the right bank. In a little more than three weeks, we reached the confluence of the Hydaspes and Indos rivers. We paused long enough to build another garrison city and then resumed our progress along the Indos River.

En route, we encountered fierce, fervent resistance, inspired by the priestly Brahmin caste. The native clans fought desperately, fanatically, suicidally. Alexandros's soldiers, who had long since run out of patience, responded cynically, efficiently, and brutally. The casualties among the native population were appalling. The army scourged the land like a cyclone, causing devasting damage but leaving no lasting impact. Alexandros founded a number of garrison cities along the Indos but there were no Alexandrias left on that stretch of the river within a couple of years of the army's departure.

****

As we sailed on, and marched next to, the great waterway, Alexandros continued assiduously to seek out intelligence about the local geography. Reassuringly, the farther we went, the more accurate and consistent the reports became. He now knew for sure that the Indos River emptied into the Indian Sea, whose waters formed the southern border of the Gedrosia satrapy. Although that satrapy was mostly desert and mountains, it was at least somewhat known to the Persian bureaucrats and mapmakers. To the west of Gedrosia lay the satrapy of Karmania, which included the straits leading into the Persian Gulf, at the other end of which Sousa awaited. Therefore, if they hugged the coast, whether sailing on water or marching on land, they would eventually get past the desert and reach familiar territory. Alexandros, wishing to improve the morale of his soldiers, made sure everyone in the army was aware that the great turn toward home was near.

The last city on the Indos River, sitting at the apex of the delta formed by the branches of the river as its waters rushed toward Okeanos's vast realm, was called Pattala. The army reached it, in a state of great excitement and anticipation, in June of 261 Z.E., a month after the start of another monsoon season. The excitement was short-lived because we found the city abandoned. It was clear, however, that the residents had fled shortly before our arrival. Presumably, reports of the army's atrocities, as we traveled down the Indos, had preceded us.

Alexandros, who realized that the city would have to serve as the staging area for the next great leg of our campaign, immediately dispatched agents to chase down the escaping Pattala residents and persuade them to return to their homes. The agents were supposed to convince the residents that they had nothing to fear. On the contrary, the fact that Alexandros's huge army had chosen to visit their city was the greatest stroke of good luck ever to befall them, because Alexandros was a powerful and wealthy emperor and Pattala's residents would reap great economic benefits from hosting his army for a short time. Amazingly, the agents succeeded in their mission and the residents reappeared in short order.

Some of what the agents told the Pattalans was actually true. Alexandros had no intention of sacking the city or harming its residents, as long as they cooperated with his requirements. In fact, he desperately needed to obtain provisions, for which he intended to pay. He also wanted to employ a majority of its able-bodied men in various construction projects necessitated by his plans. It was also true that he was a powerful and wealthy emperor. However, at that particular moment he didn't have an obol to his name. The money sent by Harpalos had long since run out. Fortunately, many of the men in Alexandros's entourage had managed to accumulate substantial fortunes of their own in the course of Alexandros's never-ending campaigns. At this moment of temporary financial embarrassment, he was able to prevail on them to lend him some of the funds they had accumulated. "I'm the richest man in the world," he told them. "I'm good for the money and I'll pay you back with interest as soon as we reach Babylon." Whether they believed him was beside the point. It was the kind of request they were in no position to refuse.

A great many preparations needed to be made before we could proceed. Among other things, we had no idea how large the delta was. If it was anything like the Nile delta, we had a ways to go before we ever reached salt water. It would also be helpful to know which branches were navigable and whether it was possible to get to the ocean shore by land.

Alexandros planned to lead the exploration of the delta in person but, before leaving the city, he put Hephaistion in charge of the many projects he had in mind. First, he wanted to strengthen the existing fortifications in Pattala, which he intended to leave behind as the last of his garrisoned outposts. He also wanted several large, seaworthy vessels built; new docks to facilitate embarkation constructed; the harbor dredged; and lots of supplies and provisions collected. True to his word, he enriched Pattala and its residents by buying goods at exorbitant prices, by paying generous wages for services rendered, and by leaving behind a new fortress, manned by capable troops, new docks, and a better harbor.

While all this activity was taking place in the city, Alexandros kept busy exploring the delta. First, using one of the existing triremes, he sailed down the right-hand arm of the Indos. It proved navigable enough but, just as they reached the sea, a storm blew in and threatened to sink their ship. After a mighty struggle the crew managed to fight its way to shallower and safer waters and they all breathed a sigh of relief. At which point, a new disaster befell them. Unexpectedly, the water level began to drop and, before they could do anything about it, they found themselves beached on land, stranded. The water receded so rapidly that soon they were hundreds of feet from the sea. They despaired of ever being able to get away from this desolate, rocky, wet stretch of sand. With no better ideas for escape, they sank to their knees amid the seaweed and implored the gods for deliverance. After a despondent few hours, a miracle occurred, the water returned and lifted their boat, and they were free to sail once again. They gave thanks to whichever god had rescued them. In a couple of days, they realized that this phenomenon recurred twice a day with celestial regularity. They had learned that, unlike the Mediterranean, there were actual tides in the Indian Sea.

Screwing up their courage, they sailed farther into Okeanos's realm and found an island not far from the entrance to the delta. Alexandros insisted that they disembark and perform a full-fledged service of thanksgiving, offering prayers not only to Okeanos but also to Poseidon and all the other gods with arguable jurisdiction. They wound up the rituals by drowning two gaurs, which they had captured on the island, as a tangible sacrifice to the gods. Then they carved their names into some trees and sailed back to Pattala.

In the meantime, Hephaistion was making good progress on the various projects assigned to him but the shipwrights, masons, and construction workers had quite a bit of work yet to do. The acquisition of provisions and supplies was also proceeding apace but another few weeks would be required. Alexandros, restless as always, chose to use the time to explore the left-hand branch of the delta. He discovered that, while this branch was longer than the right-hand branch, it was more sheltered and calmer. Therefore, he decided that the fleet would use the left-hand branch when the time came to sail off to the sea. The portion of the army that would march across the Gedrosian desert, on the other hand, would march partway along the right-hand branch and then proceed westward, roughly paralleling the coast and rendezvousing periodically with the fleet, which would be sailing near the coast in the same direction.

Chapter 17 – From Pattala to Salmous

When the ships were finished, provisions assembled, and local arrangements settled, Alexandros called a meeting of his command staff. He surprised us all by unrolling a large map in front of our feet. "Pay attention, men. This is our route ahead to Sousa." Holding a stick in his hand, he made a sweeping gesture from the right side of the irregularly shaped hide to the left.

In the spare light of the tent, it took a moment for our eyes to adjust. We saw brown areas adjacent to blue ones, with some winding blue lines and a few black dots. *All that blue pigment must have cost a fortune*, I thought.

Using his stick, Alexandros tapped on a dot near the lower, righthand corner of the map.[19] "We're currently here, in Pattala. The blue line is the Indos River. As you can see, on its way to the sea, the Indos splits into two

---

[19] For the location of some of the places mentioned by Alexandros in his briefing, see Map 15 at AlexanderGeiger.com.

branches, right here at Pattala. Well, actually, it splits into many more branches but these are the two main ones. As you know, I've personally explored both branches, as well as the sea beyond. The big blue sea at the bottom here is part of the great Okeanos River. The brown area above the sea is the Gedrosia satrapy. Are you with me so far?"

Everybody nodded.

"Good. Let's proceed. The first portion of our march will take us from Pattala to Pura, the capital of the Gedrosia." He tapped another dot a fair distance to the left of the Indos delta.

"How far is that, Aniketos?" Hephaistion asked.

"We should be able to march there in less than a month, easily."

We all knew the word 'easily' had a suspect meaning when used by our fearless leader but no one had the temerity to question Alexandros's estimate too closely. Instead, someone at the back of the tent spoke up. "Doesn't that route take us through a desert, sire?"

"Yes, yes, of course. But, as I'll explain in a minute, I've made provisions for that. In the meantime, let me continue. After Pura, we'll march to Salmous, which is located right here, on the border between the Gedrosia and Karmania." He tapped another dot. "It sits on a navigable river called Anamis that flows into the Persian Gulf right next to the Harmozia straits. This blue area is the Persian Gulf; the narrow entrance got its name from this small town here, called Harmozia." Another tap.

"We'll probably take a couple of weeks to rest up once we get to Salmous. I'm sure the men would appreciate that."

"Yes, they would, sire!" a couple of the more sycophantic commanders called out.

"And after that, it's a straight shoot along the coast of the Persian Gulf all the way to Sousa." He tapped a dot near the top of the Persian Gulf. "We'll be there before you know it."

Another anonymous voice in the back asked the question many of the men in the tent wanted to ask: "How do you know all this, sire?"

Alexandros patiently listed all the newly arrived mercenaries in our ranks who hailed from the various areas shown on the map and who were consulted in its preparation. "As for the desert, not only did I speak with a dozen local men who'd been there but I've hired a few of them to be our guides across it."

None of us thought to ask whether any of those men had ever actually crossed the desert. Later on, once we were in the desert, the answer would become painfully obvious.

"Now, as far as the division of our forces goes, I've decided on a slightly different approach. Most of us will march with me on the route I've indicated. I'm sending a small fleet to sail parallel to our route of march. The idea is that they'll support us by carrying a lot of our gear and our food supplies while we'll make sure they have access to fresh water during their voyage. We'll get together every few days; they'll hand over the provisions we need and we'll give them water from the wells we have dug."

At this point, Seleukos interrupted. "How do we know that it's even possible to dig wells in this desert that will yield potable water?"

Alexandros laughed. "I've thought of that, Seleukos. You and I've been through a few deserts together. But the guides assure me that, near the shore, you can dig wells that will fill up with fresh, sweet water. And, in fact, I've sent an expedition of our men down to the shore to make sure the guides know what they're talking about. Our men have confirmed the guides' information."

What Alexandros failed to mention was that the exploration team only ventured three days out from the Indos delta before returning, convinced that the well-digging scheme was feasible. Instead, he forged ahead with his plans.

"The fleet will be smaller because you can't send little dinghies out onto the sea. You need big ships able to cope with Okeanos's, Poseidon's, and Aiolos's tantrums.

I've selected Nearchos as hyparchos of the fleet. He's a Kretan, as you know, and all Kretans know how to sail. And I've tried to give him men who're used to ships. It's going to be a pretty small group, as I've said.

"All our prime units will be marching with me. I've also made alternative arrangements for anyone who might find the march across the Gedrosian desert too challenging. All our sick and injured men, all the men past their prime, most of the camp followers and most of the baggage train will take a longer but easier route. I've selected Krateros as the commander of this group, with Polyperchon as his second-in-command. I'm also giving Krateros 2,000 prime infantrymen, in case they run into trouble along the way."

Alexandros had no need to mention that all the disgruntled oldtimers and many of the other veterans were being assigned to Krateros's group of misfits. Everybody in the tent understood that getting rid of those soldiers and their incessant complaints was one of the motivations behind Alexandros's division of forces.

"And, by the way, I'm sending our 200 elephants with Krateros. I don't want to take any chances on jeopardizing their well-being. Krateros's group will go back to Alexandria-in-Arakhosia. I understand an easy pass through the mountains exists that will get them there. From Alexandria-in-Arakhosia, they'll travel west, across the upper, fertile regions of Gedrosia, to Lake Seistan, and then south, across Karmania, to Salmous. Hopefully, we'll still be in Salmous by the time they catch up. It shouldn't take them too long; it's a pretty easy route."

If it's so easy, why aren't we all taking it? It was a question that had probably occurred to others in the tent but nobody was willing to ask it out loud.

"Any questions? Well, in that case, get your people ready. We're moving out in three days."

It seemed like a good plan at the time.

****

Summer was ending and the monsoon season was expected to end in a week or two. It would've made sense to wait but that wasn't Alexandros's way. "We're used to marching in monsoon rains and winds by now," he told us.

We set off along the northern bank of the right-hand arm of the delta, as planned. By the evening of our third day on the march, we could smell the salty air of the sea nearby. At this point, we turned right and marched into the "desert," not wishing to get too close to the brackish, intertidal zone, where we had gotten stranded during our previous exploratory sail. This "desert" proved to be less challenging than expected. Although the soil was sandy, somewhat salty, and relatively dry, it was covered with vegetation. In fact, the profusion of thorny bushes and trees became a nuisance. Many of the men originally from the Levant remarked on the number and size of myrrh-producing trees. "The amount of myrrh we could collect here would make us rich men back home," they kept saying. As it was, they simply forced their way through, wounding and trampling the plants in the process. One unexpected benefit of their stomping was the pleasant-smelling, perfumed air we inhaled with every breath. We also saw lots of birds and animals, although they mostly scattered at our approach. In the distance, we saw some desert gazelles, wild cats, and what might've been jackals or foxes.

And then we ran into people who lived in this region. In all our travels, we'd never seen such primitive, ill-kempt, foul-smelling wretches. They lived in hovels; their diet consisted mostly of fish and other sea creatures; they wore the barest of rags and had practically no material possessions. They certainly posed no threat to us and, luckily for them, they had nothing that we might've wanted. They hid in their holes and we ignored them.

After another few days of marching, the narrow strip of pseudo-desert petered out and we could see nothing but sand ahead. Alexandros decided this would be a good spot to set up camp and await the arrival of our navy. We dug wells, which promptly filled with tolerably drinkable water, especially when mixed with wine. After a few days, our food supplies began to run low, so Alexandros dispatched a couple of squadrons of light cavalry to see whether they could obtain some food from the indigents we had just passed. He sent other soldiers, who had experience with the sea, to catch fish and other edible sea creatures. Idleness being bad for morale, he set the remaining soldiers to work building another garrison town, figuring this place, at the start of the desert proper, was as good a place as any to control any traffic or commerce between the Indos delta behind us and the entrance to the Persian Gulf, which was, we hoped, not too far ahead of us. He named the new town Rhambakia for reasons which at this point elude me. He appointed a prominent but not very martial-minded Macedonian named Apollophanes as satrap of Gedrosia, with Rhambakia serving as his new seat of government. As usual, he also appointed a military man to keep an eye on the new satrap. What was surprising was the identity of the man he selected. Leonnatos was one of his oldest comrades and one of three men who'd saved his life after his foolish leap into the Mallian town. Making him garrison commander of what had to be the most godforsaken outpost in the entire empire was apparently Leonnatos's reward for saving Alexandros's life.

Rhambakia was all finished, our food stocks continued to shrink, the foragers and fishermen returned with very little to show for their efforts, and everybody was antsy to get the desert behind us. And still, no sign of the fleet.

Finally, Alexandros ordered a resumption of the march. He told Leonnatos to urge Nearchos, if he ever turned up, to redouble his speed and keep his eyes on the coast. We took what little food was left, telling Apollophanes to fend for himself until Nearchos arrived. We left our wagons behind, because they were unwieldy in the desert and because our horses and mules were more than sufficient to carry the meager provisions we had left, and we stepped off into the sand dunes.

****

In the meantime, the fleet had barely managed to clear the delta by the time we left Rhambakia. Nearchos had decided to wait in Pattala until the monsoon season ended and the weather cleared before sailing out, thus losing two weeks. He then utilized the left-hand arm of the delta as ordered and reached salt water in less than a week. But then he waited another two weeks before the trade winds finally became favorable and the fleet was able to venture out into the open sea, turning north toward the Persian Gulf. They reached Rhambakia eight days after we'd left. Leonnatos urged Nearchos to hurry after us because we were sure to run out of food soon.

****

At first, the desert trek seemed manageable, although we were clearly entering a real wasteland. We saw a few inhabitants the first day but they made the wretches we'd encountered earlier look civilized by comparison and they certainly had no food. Vegetation grew more and more sparse. The wells we dug started to come up dry, no matter how deeply we dug. And the heat became unbearable.

Once again, we were forced to march only at night, spending our days hiding from the sun and looking longingly to the sea, hoping to see some sign of our fleet.

And then we ran out of food. A couple of days later, we hit a mountain range, running perpendicular to the shore. The cliffs extended well into the waves, making it impossible to squeeze through between the precipitous bluffs and the roaring surf. With no obvious way to climb over the ridgeline, we had no choice but to turn away from the sea and march along the mountain range until we found a pass through it.

After marching for two more nights – and by now "marching" might've been an overstatement – we reached a defile in the sheer rockface that, upon further exploration, yielded a treacherous but negotiable trail to the other side. We clambered over the pass, with hope in our hearts. Alas, what we saw when we descended from the mountain was simply more unremitting desert.

We were out of food and out of water. Rather than struggling back to the coast, we decided to proceed straight ahead, hoping that, by cutting across the desert, we'd shorten our route and save our lives. We started killing our pack animals. They didn't have much left to carry and were likely to die soon of their own accord. The men reasoned that we might as well eat their flesh and drink their blood while they had some left. It only took a few days for us to run out of pack animals to kill. At that point, we started killing our war horses, which gave us another couple of days. Every few days, there was a brief shower. We caught as much of the precious rainwater as possible but you can't catch much rainwater in five or ten minutes.

Willingly or otherwise, the commanders, including Alexandros, shared the common soldiers' hardships. We all walked, including those of us who used to be cavalry, through the night and sometimes well into the day, in order to reach a suitable resting place. We hoped to find some large boulders or towering dunes that might afford a bit of shade for our tents and lean-tos. Alexandros, notwithstanding his recent, near-fatal injury, always walked at the head of the column. And everyone, including officers, ate only when the rest of the soldiers ate and, of course, drank only the water we could catch in our helmets or the fabric of our tents.

Every day, conditions grew worse. We trudged mindlessly ahead, trying to keep various patches of sunburnt skin from getting worse. We squinted through the shimmering air for any sign of life, vegetation, or water. Our guides had long since ceased to be of any use. It was clear they'd never ventured this far into the desert and had no idea which way to go. What was less clear was whether any humans had ever made it across this desert.

While we rested during the midday heat, Seleukos would entertain us with fairytales. Two of his stories featured people who'd allegedly survived. The first, according to him, was a legendary Assyrian queen named Semiramis who, many centuries earlier, had led an army down the Indos River, much as we'd done. Her army was defeated and she had to flee for her life across this desert. The story didn't include mention of others who may have attempted the crossing with her and their ultimate fate. Alexandros was skeptical. "I've heard stories about Queen Semiramis while we were in Babylon. Half the temples in Babylonia and Mesopotamia were allegedly built by her. I suspect that local guides, when they have no information, attribute everything to this mythical woman. I doubt she ever existed." I tried to suppress a smile as an irreverent thought flashed through my mind. *And here I was, sure that Alexandros swallowed whole any hoary tale retailed by local guides.*

Seleukos's second story starred the legendary Emperor Kyros. According to this tale, the great conqueror attempted to invade India by crossing this desert with his entire army, going in the opposite direction. It didn't go well. He was eventually forced to turn around and get out of the desert the way he'd come. By the time he emerged, only seven men were still with him out of his entire army.

Alexandros found this story amusing. "Yes, I've heard that story as well and I think this one is true. The good news is that it shows there's an end to this desert."

Hephaistion joined in the laughter. "The bad news is that almost nobody marching with Kyros survived." The rest of us in the tent found the exchange incredibly amusing as well. I guess it was either gallows humor or sunstroke.

When Alexandros finally caught his breath, he delivered his ultimate rejoinder: "Ah, but those men were not marching with Alexandros." Somehow, we all found the hubris of our leader comforting, the way a drowning man finds the presence of a straw floating nearby comforting.

I've often wondered why Alexandros had chosen this particularly hazardous route back when the entire army could've simply taken the much easier route that Krateros was ordered to follow. I've considered and rejected many theories: Maybe he wanted to explore the ocean coast and the sea route back to the Persian Gulf. But to do that, all he needed was the fleet and the sailors it could carry. There was no need for an overland march through the desert. Or perhaps he wanted to punish his men for forcing him to turn around at the Hyphasis and for causing his grievous injury at the Mallian city. Or maybe, he just didn't like going back the way he'd come. He liked to explore new places. Most likely, in my mind, he wanted to test himself and prove, once again, that he was the greatest leader who'd ever lived, even greater than the legendary Kyros.

Soon, the sun was setting and we had to resume walking once again. And people started to die.

******

Immortal Alexandros

While we staggered, lost in the desert, Nearchos's fleet, oblivious to our presence far inland, blithely sailed by.

****

The first people to perish were the camp followers who'd chosen to stay with our elite corps, rather than taking the longer route with Krateros. These were men, women, and children used to tagging along as part of the baggage train, hoping to catch a ride every once in a while, falling steadily behind but eventually catching up when the army paused for a rest. These were not trained young men, in peak condition, used to marching more than twenty miles a day, day after day. They couldn't possibly keep up with the soldiers, even at their slackened, desert pace. And they were doomed by the cruel, merciless, iron law of the desert: Anyone who falls behind dies.

Eventually, they all fell behind. Of the two thousand camp followers who'd started out with us in Pattala, not one – not a single man, woman, or child – survived our trek through the Gedrosian wilderness.

The trained soldiers didn't fare much better. The first mass cull of Alexandros's desert corps arrived, shortly after we emerged from the mountain pass, courtesy of a sudden sandstorm. It was not as bad as the sandstorm some of us had survived on our way to the Oasis of Ammon in Africa. But most of our soldiers had never experienced anything like it.

At dusk one day, right after we'd started shambling along, the wind picked up. In the dying light, we saw an ominous, dun-colored, sky-high cloud racing atop the dunes toward us. And then, in minutes, it swallowed us. I tried, without success, to find shelter behind a rock or in a crevice. Unable to see, I fell to the ground, covering my head with my arms. Soon, it became difficult to breathe. Every orifice filled with sand. Eventually, the roaring, scouring wind gave way to a sepulchral calm as I found myself buried under a thick layer of sand.

Slowly, tentatively at first, and then frantically, I dug for air. When I was finally able to sit up, I took a deep breath, shook the sand out of my hair, and opened my eyes. The nightmarish day had turned into a limpid, moonlit night. All around me, looking very much like a giant ghostly colony of Himalayan marmots, I saw thousands of men poking their heads out, struggling to their feet, glancing around timorously, trying to figure out whether they were shades staggering in the underworld or living men trapped in hell.

After a while, the soldiers started to accrete into small clumps of survivors. They attempted to find and, if necessary, dig out their friends and comrades. Hundreds of our men – no one ever determined the exact number – were never unearthed.

We left our dead behind in the desolate, moonlit, eerily quiet landscape and resumed lumbering along. Every few minutes, a man would stumble and sink to the ground. At first, his comrades on either side would pick him up and even carry him a few steps but soon no one had any strength left. After a few words urging the dropouts to rise and keep going, they were left where they lay with no one except other doomed men left to hear their cries and lamentations. At first, we would lose a dozen men during a night's march, then a score, then a hundred, until finally we were losing an unknown number every night.

One evening, just as we were setting out again, we heard a shout from one of our soldiers. He had stumbled onto a fissure in a large rock that contained a bit of water. With the help of his mates, the soldier managed to drain the water into his helmet and came running to Alexandros. With the last of his strength, he offered the life-saving draft to our leader.

Alexandros took the helmet, thanked the soldier, and then, with a smile, he tipped the makeshift vessel and spilled its contents into the sand. "Not enough for all of us," he explained.

Inexplicably, all the soldiers cheered.

****

Eventually, we managed to get back to the coast, where we were able to capture some sea creatures and where we finally dug a well that produced an appreciable quantity of potable water. By then, we'd lost more than half the men who'd started out from Rhambakia. We rested on the shore for a couple of days, hoping to sight Nearchos and his fleet but of course by that point they were long gone.

We resumed our march along the coast. Even though we had a bit of food now and an occasional sip of water, we continued to lose men every day. On the sixtieth day after we first entered the desert, we stumbled upon a semblance of a road. Although we had no idea where it led, we were desperate men. Any destination had to be better than where we were now. With renewed hope and what might have been spring in our feet, had we had any strength left in our legs, we followed the road even as the sun grew hotter. In a couple of hours, we saw the edge of the desert and, beyond it, what looked like a city. This time, it wasn't a mirage.

It turned out to be Pura, the old capital of Gedrosia. Of the 40,000 soldiers and 2,000 camp followers who'd started the march out of Rhambakia, fewer than 10,000 soldiers made it to Pura. While we rested and recovered, Alexandros, who was among the survivors, was fuming. It couldn't have been the gods who did this to us, so it had to be the fault of some human beings, but which ones?

None of the survivors emerged unchanged, least of all Alexandros. The damage to our leader was both physical and psychological. As word of his survival filtered out, troubling reports began coming back. Alexandros's decision to march through the Gedrosian desert had not been kept a secret, of course. The people most interested in this latest turn in the new emperor's campaigns – the Persian satraps he'd appointed or confirmed in their positions and the Persian nobility he'd displaced – were also the people with some knowledge of Persian geography in general and the impassability of the Gedrosian desert in particular. They didn't expect Alexandros to emerge alive. Their belief was reinforced when no one heard from his expedition in two months and they'd begun planning for a post-Alexandros Persian Empire. Ironically, while there was no doubt that Alexandros's paranoia became worse as a result of the harrowing experiences he had endured, it was also true that more men with conspiratorial thoughts roamed the land by the time he came out of the desert than there had been when he went in.

******

After a short rest period in Pura, Alexandros and his survivors headed to Salmous for the rendezvous with Krateros and his formerly superfluous forces. The remnants of the army marched through the fertile upper portion of Gedrosia and Alexandros permitted his soldiers to indulge all their appetites, letting them celebrate their survival and rejoice in life while they could.

It took us less than a week to reach the borderlands between Gedrosia and Karmania but it was more than enough time for Alexandros to conceive, nurture, and internalize an irrational but irrefutable conviction that two men in particular were responsible for the travails of his troops: Apollophanes, the newly-appointed satrap of Gedrosia, and a Persian noble named Astaspes, whom he had recently confirmed as satrap of Karmania. He grew convinced that these two officials had conspired with each other, and with other satraps, to kill him and his army in the Gedrosian desert. In Alexandros's mind, both Apollophanes and Astaspes were supposed to keep his army provisioned during the desert crossing and had inexplicably failed.

On the road to the Gedrosia/Karmania border, Alexandros dispatched a message to Leonnatos to have Apollophanes executed. Conveniently, the hapless Apollophanes was killed in a skirmish before Alexandros's order reached Leonnatos. At the same time, Alexandros also ordered the unsuspecting Astaspes to meet his army at the border with provisions. Astaspes duly arrived with the requested supplies, as well as additional gifts, and was promptly placed under arrest. By the time we reached Salmous, Astaspes was dead.

Alexandros named new satraps for Gedrosia and Karmania. He also summoned the heads of the surrounding satrapies to report to Salmous with horses, armor, and other goods. In addition, he commanded four Macedonian officers in Ekbatana to appear: Kleandros, who had been second-in-command to Parmenion in Media and had found himself in charge of the satrapy after he participated in his commander's murder, along with his three accomplices, Sitalkes, Herakon, and Agathon. Since the four were Macedonian officers, Alexandros afforded them the courtesy of a trial by the army. The soldiers despised the four because they'd murdered their beloved commander Parmenion. Alexandros despised them because he was sure they were conspiring to take over the empire and because they were living witnesses to his leading role in Parmenion's murder. Needless to say, the four were convicted and executed on the spot. Similarly, those satraps who showed up in Salmous didn't leave alive.

Finally, Alexandros summoned the one man he'd decided was the ringleader of the entire, empire-wide conspiracy, his treasurer in Babylon, Harpalos. The former court jester, being smarter than he let on and having learned from the fate of the others, wisely ran away. He took his current mistress, plus 6,000 mercenaries and 5,000 talents of silver, marched to the coast, and sailed for Athens. No one could ever explain why he took "only" 5,000 talents when he could've taken twenty times as much. Perhaps he was an honorable thief who took only what he believed was his due. Or maybe that was all the treasure he could assemble and transport on short notice. As it was, 5,000 talents of silver was enough to make him the richest man in Greece.

Having killed all the perceived enemies he could get his hands on, Alexandros ordered the remaining satraps to disband their private armies, pay their mercenaries in full, and send them home. He'd read Xenophon's Anabasis, which recounted the story of a rebellious satrap who had assembled a strong private army, composed of Greek mercenaries, and then marched against the rightful emperor in Babylon (who happened to be his brother). That uprising failed but Alexandros wanted to make sure there would be no repeat performance while he was emperor.

****

Alexandros was just getting started with his purge when Krateros and Polyperchon arrived in Salmous, with their veterans, misfits, camp followers, baggage train, and elephants. Even though they had taken the longer route, it only took them a week longer to make the trip from Pattala to Salmous than it had taken us, and they'd managed to arrive with practically no loss of people or possessions. They hadn't even lost a single elephant.

Alexandros was thrilled to see the new arrivals. Krateros, unlike many other leaders in Alexandros's orbit, continued to rise in his leader's esteem with each successfully completed assignment. Even more important at that moment, however, were the troops Krateros had brought along. With the ranks of the army depleted by the disastrous crossing of the desert, Alexandros desperately needed reinforcements. His grievances forgotten, Alexandros warmly welcomed the oldtimers, veterans, and misfits he had been anxious to unload only a couple of months earlier. The rapprochement wouldn't last for long.

Nearchos showed up in Salmous soon after Krateros's arrival. His fleet had been lying at anchor at the mouth of the Anamis River, near the small town of Harmozia, for almost a month. It was there that he'd received word of Alexandros's arrival in Pura, as well as an account of the horrendous losses suffered by Alexandros's army in the desert. There is no record of Nearchos's reaction to the news. Perhaps he was surprised. Having failed utterly in his mission of keeping the marching army provisioned, he had every reason to assume they'd perished to a man in the desert. Hard to know whether he was pleased to receive word of Alexandros's survival or worried about the vengeance his leader was sure to exact for the deaths of tens of thousands of soldiers Nearchos had caused.

While sitting on his flagship pondering his next move, Nearchos began hearing rumors about the purge taking place in Salmous. These stories didn't elevate his eagerness to report to his commander. He considered his alternatives. He had a fleet at his disposal and a decent complement of capable mariners but few other resources. Worse yet, having spent his entire adult life in Alexandros's service, he had no place he could call home, no safe harbor in which to hide, and no realistic chance of outrunning Alexandros's ire. It took him a month to decide what to do.

Finally, Nearchos sailed up the Anamis from Harmozia to Salmous in a decrepit little ship, dressed in rags, and accompanied only by five of his most trusted sailors, all of them as dirty, disheveled, and emaciated as he could make them. They were met at the dock by Alexandros, who looked distinctly unhappy at the sight of them. Nearchos threw himself on the ground in the best Persian fashion and, upon being lifted to his feet by Alexandros, tearfully launched into his apologia for his utter dereliction of duty. "Sire, we tried. I swear upon all the gods that we did everything possible to find you and deliver the provisions."

Alexandros was noncommittal. "So, what happened?"

"We couldn't find you. We sailed as close to the shore as we dared and I had half a dozen lookouts posted on my ships at all times.

"Yes, yes. Continue."

"We never saw you, sire. Neither you nor any of your men. After we arrived in Rhambakia and were told by Leonnatos that you had already left, we weighed anchor immediately and hurried after you. But at no point before reaching Harmozia did we ever catch sight of the army."

"Wait a minute!" Alexandros interrupted. "You reached Harmozia?"

"Yes, of course."

"How many ships made it?"

"All of them, sire."

"How many of your men survived?"

Nearchos hesitated a moment, sure that instant doom would arrive with his next response. "They all survived, sire. We didn't lose a single man." He lowered his eyes, not wishing to see the fatal blow that he knew was headed his way.

Instead, he heard the sound of rushing feet, then felt arms tightening around his back. It was a powerful embrace but not fatal. He looked up and was surprised to see Alexandros's smiling face, tears coursing down his cheeks. "I was so upset, Nearchos. I thought you and the five sailors with you were the only survivors of the fleet." Alexandros kissed him on both cheeks. "I'm so happy to see you."

****

There was a great, celebratory feast that evening, Nearchos was assigned the seat of honor next to Alexandros, who wanted to hear all about the voyage on Okeanos's hazardous domain. Nearchos obliged him with a barrelful of tall tales about the treacherous obstacles and death-defying adventures that had caused the fleet to miss all their appointments. Somehow, Alexandros never asked why it had taken Nearchos more than four weeks to actually hit the sea and Nearchos chose not to dwell on that detail.

Chapter 18 – From Salmous to Sousa

Somewhat surprisingly, Alexandros employed a similar tripartite division of forces for the Salmous to Sousa stage of our return journey as he had for the previous leg. He dispatched the bulk of the army, the camp followers, the baggage train, and the elephants, under the command of Hephaistion and Krateros, toward Sousa on an easier, slower, coastal route along the Persian Gulf. He sent the fleet, under Nearchos's command, on a parallel sea route along the same coast. This time, however, he didn't schedule any intermediate rendezvous until the final meeting at the outskirts of Sousa. Finally, he set off with his elite troops, including the Companion Cavalry, on a harder, more mountainous, ostensibly faster inland route through Persepolis. This group left a couple of weeks after the winter solstice, right after Alexandros confirmed with his own eyes that Nearchos and the fleet had in fact sailed off.

At the Karmania and Persis border, we were met by Orsines, the satrap of Persis. He brought supplies and gifts, as expected, and accompanied us toward Persepolis. When we reached the ancient capital of Pasargadai, located only twenty-five miles from Persepolis, Alexandros visited once again the tomb of Kyros, the founder of the Persian dynasty. Following a detailed inspection, he decided that the tomb had been looted since his last visit. He vented his outrage upon Orsines, accusing him of either committing the sacrilege himself or permitting others to do it while he was satrap. Naturally, Orsines pleaded his innocence but to no avail. When we reached the remnants of Persepolis, the imperial capital that had been burned down by Alexandros six years earlier, Orsines joined the ranks of Persian satraps executed by Alexandros.

The city itself was a pathetic sight. The remnants of the palace complex looked exactly the same as when we left after the great conflagration. Some distance from the ruins a few new government buildings and a new temple to Ahura Mazda had been erected. These were but a pale, pitiful echo of the grandeur that had once stood nearby. Nevertheless, Persepolis was still the capital of the Persis satrapy, the ancestral homeland of the Persian tribes, and it required a new satrap. Alexandros chose Peukestas. He liked the veteran Macedonian commander because, in addition to being one of the three men who had jumped in to save him during the Mallian melee, he was unique among the Macedonian commanders in not opposing Alexandros's Persianization policy. In fact, after becoming satrap of Persis, Peukestas dressed exclusively in Persian attire and became fluent in the Persian tongue.

After a two-week stay, during which Alexandros had no more success forcing the magoi headquartered in Persepolis to stage a proper coronation ceremony anointing him the new, legitimate emperor of Persia than he'd had before we'd left, we resumed our march to Sousa. We reached the outskirts of the city eight weeks after our departure from Salmous. We were met by Abulites, the satrap of Susiana. He brought along not only gifts but also his young son.

This time the excuse was that Abulites should've sent provisions to the Gedrosian desert, which was complete nonsense. Abulites met the fate of his colleagues but, in a telling escalation of Alexandros's psychopathic cruelty, on this occasion he personally ran through the young son in front of his father's eyes before having Abulites killed by his henchmen.

****

Barsine shook her head and laughed. "Nah, he'll go to Roxane first."

"That's not true, Barsine. You were his first one. You've got this, hands down."

"I assure you I wasn't his first, Apame, even if I was the first among those of us here in the harem. But Roxane was the most recent. My money is on her."

Roxane, hearing her name, turned to Apame. Her grasp of either Persian or Greek remained tenuous. Hearing the translation, she turned beet red. But she didn't disagree. "I hope so," she beamed in passable Greek.

Barsine, Thais, and Roxane, the three favorites in the eunuchs' betting pool, plus Artakama and Apame, neither of whom had drawn any wagering interest among the participating punters, were seated in their usual spot next to the pond. They were watching the children playing at the other end of the meadow, chasing one another, squealing, and trying to skip pebbles across the surface of the water. It was the start of spring, the most glorious time of the year in Sousa. For a short time, the harem paradeisos really lived up to its name.

Apame spoke up. "If I were you, Thais, I'd bet on myself."

Thais, who didn't like mixing talk of money and sex, tried to change the subject. "Barsine, your children have grown so much."

"Shush! They're not my children; they're the serving women's children. Except for little Herakles, of course."

Thais laughed. "Yes, yes, of course. I forgot."

Barsine smiled. "It's easy to forget. Especially when it's just us girls chatting. But now that Alexandros is likely to visit very soon, I worry somebody might slip up and let the truth out in his presence."

"Don't you think he already knows? After all, everybody in the harem, including the eunuchs, has figured it out by now. The children look just like you and Alexandros is not a stupid man. Maybe he's chosen to go along with your little fairytale to protect your reputation."

"You've got it wrong, Thais. It's the other way around. My reputation doesn't need protecting. I was married to the father of my first four children when I had them. It's Alexandros's pride that needed salving. How would it look if he fathered a child with the widow of his former enemy? Don't you know he only cavorts with virgins?"

They looked at Thais to see how she would react. The famous hetaira paused for dramatic effect. Then, unable to maintain an expression of outraged dignity, her face cracked into a wide smile. All five of them burst into uproarious laughter. Thais held up a finger, trying to say something, as waves of uncontrollable merriment washed over her. "Yes, that's certainly true," she agreed when she finally caught her breath. "That's why he picked me."

The explosive volume of hilarity caught the attention of the children, who came running over. "What's so funny?" Amastrine, who was the oldest, asked.

"Oh, it's nothing, honey. Aunt Thais just made a funny joke. Go back to playing."

Amastrine blushed at the mention of the hetaira's name. She was old enough to be aware of her "aunt's" profession and smart enough to know that if the women were laughing this much, there must've been something naughty about the joke. And, of course, she was right. Obediently, she headed back to the other end of the meadow, holding six-year-old Herakles by the hand and herding the three older children in front of her.

"I worry about her," Barsine said when the children were out of earshot.

"Why?" Apame was puzzled. "She is a gorgeous girl." She paused. "Just like her mother."

"That's exactly why. She's sixteen — a very dangerous age for a beautiful girl, especially if she happens to be held in a harem."

"I'm sixteen, too, you know," Apame said quietly.

Barsine was nonplussed but recovered quickly. "Did you know I was fifteen when I had her? I mean, when one of my serving women had her? So, you've got nothing to worry about."

Thais, trying to help, jumped in. "No wonder you look so good, Barsine. I've always wondered how a mother

432

of five children, including a sixteen-year-old, can look as great as you do."

"Well, you should've seen me when Alexandros's soldiers captured me. Hard to believe that was ten years ago."

"Was that how you ended up in the harem?" Apame asked.

"Nah, I was already in Dareios's harem before then. The ownership of my body, and my children, simply changed hands."

"This is way too depressing," Artakama interrupted. "At twenty-three, I feel like an old maid. No wonder no one is putting any money on me."

"You're disqualified," Barsine said in a maladroit attempt to reassure her. "You're my sister, so how could Alexandros go to you instead of me?"

"That doesn't even make any sense. And besides, it wouldn't have to be Alexandros. I'd be happy with someone else."

"Who?" Thais asked.

Artakama looked like a child caught with her hand in the cookie jar. "Never mind."

Barsine returned the conversation to safer ground. "I'm afraid Roxane is the winning bet. I know men and they always go for the newest and youngest trinket in their collection."

They basked in the sun and speculated idly about the outcome to the eunuchs' pool. In the end, they all turned out to be wrong.

******

Our camp outside the walls of Sousa sprang up overnight. We made it extra-large to accommodate the rest of our people arriving later. Alexandros chose not to remain in his command tent at the center of the camp. Instead, he, his top-ranking officers, bodyguards, and a couple of battalions of select infantry entered the city and took up quarters in and around the palace. He didn't visit the harem. There were many administrative matters to address and, while Alexandros had a healthy libido, in his case ambition always took precedence over indulgence. The harem could wait.

The fleet, led by Alexandros's favorite admiral, arrived as scheduled. Nearchos, who continued in Alexandros's good graces, took up residence within the city walls, leaving his sailors behind to tend to the ships. A few days later, the bulk of the army, led by Hephaistion and Krateros, marched in. The troops were bivouacked in tents already waiting for them, while the two commanders joined us in the palace.

At first glance, things couldn't have been better. The weather was delightful; food, wine, and luxuries of all kinds abundant; women aplenty, even if the gates to the harem remained barred; and Alexandros the acknowledged emperor of Persia, pharaoh of Egypt, king of Macedonia, hegemon of mainland Greece, and possessor of unimaginable wealth and resources. And yet, he was discontented.

Every day, his Persian courtiers washed him, dressed him in finest royal attire, shaved his face, trimmed and coiffed his mane, scented his body, and attempted to apply kohl around his eyes, which he always refused. "Don't want to start looking like a dandy," he'd say, without a hint of irony. And then, he would take his seat on the throne, as everyone, except the Macedonian commanders and bodyguards, fell to the hard granite floor of the apadana and paid him homage. Then, after he graciously permitted everyone to rise to their feet, he would confront another interminable day of petitions, complaints, administrative headaches, and recalcitrant clerics.

He was still bothered by the festering issue of the magoi. Despite the fact that the previous emperor was dead, that he had conquered the country by force of arms, and that he now controlled all four imperial capitals and possessed the imperial tiara and scepter, the stiff-necked priests refused to recognize him as the new, legitimate emperor. The clerics were intractable, irritating, and – by this point – largely irrelevant. Unfortunately, Alexandros was superstitious. He remained disturbed by the divines' ceaseless imprecations against him. In reality, he had all the powers of an emperor and the magoi could do nothing about it, except beg for the assistance of their god, Ahura Mazda, whose influence was questionable, given his failure to stop Alexandros thus far. He considered killing the magoi en masse but his instinctive desire to get along with all the local deities got in the way. He wanted to make peace with Ahura Mazda, or at least negotiate some kind of truce, and killing all of his earthly representatives seemed an ineffective way to go about it. Each morning, seeing several white-clad charlatans standing at the back of the apadana, he gave the matter some further thought, threw up his hands, and pushed off a final resolution until another day.

The administrative problems were more difficult to ignore. Running a huge empire took a lot of work. Alexandros was happy to delegate as much responsibility to local bureaucrats and officials as possible. However, certain decisions couldn't be handed off, foremost among them the appointment of satraps for each province. There were a lot of vacancies and, for some reason, few volunteers vying for the appointments. As a result, Alexandros spent many hours trying to find loyal and competent administrators and, in the meantime, making mundane decisions in their stead.

He was also worried about the army. Quantity was not the issue. Despite a high attrition rate, the size of the army kept growing. The problem was quality. Once upon a time, the overwhelming majority of his troops had come from Macedonia. They had been, and remained, the best fighters in the world. And he'd had a special bond with them. He knew most of them by name, could ask about their families, and considered their lives precious. They, in turn, had believed in him, trusted him, and had been willing to follow him anywhere. But all that was in the past. Many of his Macedonian veterans had died. An even greater number had been left behind on garrison duty. And the rest were getting old, jaded, and mutinous. The murders of Parmenion, Philotas, and Kleitos had broken the bond between Alexandros and his oldtimers and veterans and the march across the Gedrosian desert, with its incredible and unnecessary loss of life, was the final straw.

Alexandros was determined to mold the new recruits into a fighting force every bit as good as the original invasion force had been, but it was no easy task. Alexandros's new army was a polyglot mélange of races, ethnicities, tribes, social classes, and levels of civilization. To bring them up to snuff required a large number of competent junior officers capable of communicating with the recruits and gaining their trust. Until the newcomers were fully trained and integrated, Alexandros wanted to entice the remaining Macedonian soldiers back to the banner.

The final concern gnawing at Alexandros was quite counterintuitive. He had one subordinate who had performed loyally and exceptionally well for the past twelve years – his regent in Macedonia. Antipatros had not only safeguarded the original kingdom but also maintained iron control over the many city-states of the Greek mainland and the Peloponnese. This was no mean accomplishment, given the armed uprisings, endemic unrest, and Greek propensity for internecine disputes. The more Alexandros thought about it, the more suspicious he became. Things couldn't possibly be as rosy as they appeared. Something was afoot. Antipatros had to be planning a coup. And, when it came to his regent in Pella, Alexandros's paranoia, which was doing just fine on its own, was assiduously stoked by the letters his mother had managed to smuggle out, despite Antipatros's and Kassandros's guards and spies.

Sitting in his chambers in the Sousa palace, Alexandros came up with a solution to each of these problems. Although he hated managerial work, he was as decisive, incisive, and propulsive in dealing with administrative issues as he was in commanding his troops in battle. His first decision was to replace Antipatros with Krateros as regent in Macedonia. Next, he ordered the 30,000 Persian youths, who'd been getting educated, indoctrinated, and trained at the School of Pages for the past three years, to be brought to Sousa in order to assume the duties of junior officers for the non-Macedonian contingents. But he saved his best idea for last: With one masterstroke he would cement his legitimacy in the eyes of the magoi; turn his senior commanders, most of whom were Macedonian, into senior commanders of the new, integrated army; convince the Macedonian rank-and-file soldiers who were still young enough to be useful to stop contemplating mutiny and yearning for Macedonia and start thinking of the Persian Empire as their new home; and assure a steady supply of loyal, reliable, capable young recruits for years to come.

******

While Alexandros struggled with intractable issues of empire, I had plenty of time to contemplate my own cosmological, chronoscientific, and carnal conundrums. Having waged a mostly unsuccessful fight against the shackles of the Prime Directive, I didn't feel exactly liberated from, but perhaps a little more flexible in my understanding of, this edict that had circumscribed my life since the beginning of my journey through this ancient world. I had tried and failed to save men's lives at the Hindu Kush and at the Oxos River and I had contemplated premeditated murder in the aftermath of my friend Kleitos's death. The inertial tendencies of the temporal stream had stymied my efforts but those episodes had enlarged the subtlety and nuance of my thinking. Now, here in Sousa, the scope of my cogitation narrowed once again to the point of my penis.

Artakama lived within walking distance of my current lodgings. By now, it was no longer the Prime Directive but only the walls of a harem and the strictures of the times that prevented me from joining the woman I loved and starting a family with her.

I awoke one morning in a particularly turgid state, with a persistent thought coursing through my mind. *After scaling all those fortified walls, am I going to let this distaff wall defended by eunuchs stop me?* I set off forthwith toward the harem gate, armed with a large bag of coin.

Stopped by the guards, I demanded to see the principal eunuch. After letting me cool my heels, Dilshad showed up, decked out in all his unctuous glory. "Sir, are you here with a message from the emperor?" he politely inquired.

"Do you know who I am?"

"Yes, sir. You're Ptolemaios, one of the emperor's bodyguards. I've seen you before."

I nodded. "That's correct. And I do have a message for you but I need to convey it somewhere more private."

Without hesitation, Dilshad ushered me into the guardhouse flanking the gate and chased the eunuchs on duty away. We sat down across a table from each other. "Here we are, sir. No one can see or hear us in here."

"I need to see one of your inmates," I said quietly.

Dilshad grew tense. "Which one?"

"Artakama."

Dilshad exhaled. "Well, at least it's not one of the emperor's women. Of course, they're all the emperor's women but you know what I mean. Nevertheless, as you well know, the inmates are not permitted to have any contact with the outside world."

"Of course, I understand. However, I was told that it's possible to purchase a pass." I pushed a couple of gold darics toward him."

"Sir, I'm offended. The idea that I can be bought for a couple of darics!" He sounded genuinely outraged.

I added a couple of additional coins.

"Sir, are you trying to buy a pitcher of wine or what?" He shook his head but the vehemence of his outrage abated somewhat.

I dipped into my bag and doubled the number of coins on the table.

Dilshad raised his hands in an ambiguous gesture. "Sir, we do have one or two serving women here who might be willing to bring you a pitcher of wine."

The game was growing tiresome. "I need a specific woman to be the wine bearer," I said. "Name your figure."

"Do you wish the wine pouring to be one-sided or mutual?"

"Oh, for crying out loud. There will be no wine pouring. I simply wish to speak to Artakama. Now, this is all I've got, take it or leave it." I emptied the contents of the bag on the table.

For the first time, Dilshad cracked a smile. "You should've said so at the outset, sir. I'll make the necessary arrangements. Present yourself at the postern gate at sundown and wait there quietly. Do not knock."

"I didn't know there was a postern gate."

"Very few people do. However, now that you know, I'm confident you'll find it. Just make sure no one sees you while you're looking. Now, if you'll excuse me, I have other duties to attend to." He grabbed the empty bag from my hands, swept the coins into it, and rose from the table. Then he stopped, as if struck by a new thought. "And, by the way, a second bag of equal value to this one is due upon delivery."

He spun on his heels and disappeared without a further word.

******

Artakama stood in the courtyard of the visitors' compound, unable to move. I walked toward her, a small package in my hands. It had been more than six years since last we saw each other but nary a day passed during all that time when I didn't think of her.

Finally, the spell broke and she ran to meet me. "My liege, is it really you?"

I smiled. "Yes, my dove, in the flesh."

The endearment brought her up short. "Is that the fashionable new way of addressing women on the outside?"

"It's a word I reserve only for you."

I held out my package toward her. It was a spectacular gold necklace wrapped in a colorful chiton. She brushed the presents aside. "Seriously, my liege, please don't toy with me. It hurts too much when you leave."

"Who said anything about leaving? I just got here."

She hesitated a moment longer and then, I could see in her face, she decided to throw caution to the wind. She took my hand. "Let's go to one of the rooms where we can have more privacy."

"I thought this entire compound was empty."

"A couple of women live here but they won't bother us. Now, c'mon!" She pulled me along with surprising strength.

We entered a small room furnished with nothing more than some carpets, pillows, trunks, and a large bed in the corner. The only light was provided by an oil lamp. She embraced me as soon as I had closed the door. "I dreamt about you every night."

I smiled. "It's funny you say that. I thought about you every day."

She kissed me on the lips and this time I kissed back. "I'll get you out of this place," I whispered.

She placed her hand behind my neck and kissed me again. "And where will you put me?"

I caressed the small of her back. "I'll keep you with me wherever I go." Then I thought of our death march across the Gedrosian desert. "As long as we can do it safely."

She laughed. "Are you quitting the emperor's service?"

I was taken aback. "No, why do you ask?"

"In the past six years, how many days would it have been safe for me to be traveling with you?"

She had a point and I had no answer. So, I kissed her instead, letting my hands wander farther down her back. She pressed herself against me. I could feel her hardened nipples through the thin fabric of our clothes. It occurred to me that she could feel a lot more than that. As if reading my thoughts, she grabbed my buttocks and pulled me against her, to the point of discomfort. I wiggled a little, searching for a more congenial conjunction, but to no avail.

She seemed to relish my distress, crushing me with all her might, matching me wiggle for wiggle. "As long as you visit me more than once every six years, I don't care."

She was going to say something else but I silenced her with another kiss. She didn't seem to mind, sighing contentedly. I was mentally removing her clothes and leading her to the bed, congratulating myself on my perspicacity in finding a chink in the Prime Directive allowing me to breach the citadel, when an unbidden thought invaded my brain. *My escape hatch is due to appear in less than four years. It will be a one-person escape hatch.*

I did lead her to the bed but I stopped her when she tried to shed her chiton. "Let's just kiss and caress."

She gave me a look I couldn't read in the dim light of a single oil lamp. "You're a strange man, Ptolemaios. I don't think I'll ever understand you."

We spent the night kissing, caressing, and, most of all, talking. It must have been close to dawn by the time we fell asleep. We were awakened by insistent knocking only a few minutes later, or at least so it seemed. "Wake up, Artakama!" a female voice commanded. "Dilshad is at the compound entrance and he wants you out right now."

"Who is that?" I whispered.

Instead of answering, Artakama called out to the person on the other side of the door. "That's fine, Apame. Please tell Dilshad we'll be right out."

Apame was waiting for us in the reception room. "Dilshad says you can't come out together. Artakama, you have to get back to your suite first. You, sir, may leave a little while later. Dilshad also said something about a bag."

After a quick, chaste separation, during which everything we yearned for was left undone and unsaid, Artakama walked out without a backward glance.

I turned to Apame. "You've grown a great deal since last I saw you in Marakanda."

She turned red. "Thank you, sir. I'm sorry, sir, but I don't remember you."

"Oh, please forgive me. The only time I saw you was right after you were handed over by the Massagetai following the death of your father. You were a young girl then and you must have been in a terrible state of shock, caught up in inexplicable events, amid scary strangers, fearing for your life. It would've been impossible for you to know any of our names, with the possible exception of Alexandros. My name is Ptolemaios; I'm a friend of Artakama's."

She smiled. "So I've gathered."

"You spoke no Greek the last time. How did you manage to pick up the language so quickly?"

"The ladies here in the harem are very good teachers," she said modestly. "But now, sir, I think enough time has passed; it's probably safe for you to go."

I would've enjoyed speaking to her longer but I understood the delicacy of her position. "It was very nice to speak with you, Apame. I hope we get a chance to speak again in the future."

She nodded. "Don't forget the bag."

Apame's reminder was superfluous. Dilshad, guarding the exit from the compound, could've been easily mistaken for Kerberos. I handed over the bag. He counted the contents and kept the bag.

After the bag disappeared in the folds of his tunic, he led me to the gate. "Please do not hesitate to call upon me, sir, should you wish to visit again."

****

Somewhat suspiciously, a couple of days after my visit with Artakama, Alexandros suddenly remembered the ladies of the harem. During a private visit to discuss military matters, he asked me out of the blue what I thought he should do with them.

After swallowing hard, I managed to stammer, "Why ask me, sire?"

There was a twinkle in his eyes. "You seem to have a good instinct about such matters, Ptolemaios."

I fought to regain my equanimity. "Perhaps you should summon the principal eunuch to report on the conditions and developments since your last visit."

"Sounds like a good idea, my friend. I think I'll do just that."

****

When Dilshad showed up, Alexandros, Hephaistion, and I happened to be discussing the ongoing refusal of the magoi to recognize Alexandros as the legitimate new emperor.

Informed of the eunuch's arrival, Alexandros let him cool his heels in the antechamber. When he was finally ushered into the throne room, the emasculated potentate of the feminine fiefdom prostrated himself and remained on his ample belly, awaiting permission to rise. Alexandros let him wait, winking at Hephaistion and me.

Once back on his feet, Dilshad commenced his meticulously prepared briefing. His plan was to discuss each of the ranking inmates, going in order of precedence, at least as perceived by him. He started with the late Dareios's mother Sisygambis who was, amazingly, still alive, and sharing an apartment in the harem with her two granddaughters, Stateira and Drypetis. (In response to Alexandros's question, Dilshad confirmed that the third grandchild, Ochos, had been taken away when he reached puberty. Dilshad claimed not to know his current whereabouts.)

Before he could proceed to the next ranking household, Alexandros interrupted again. "Tell me, eunuch, why did you start your report with Sisygambis and her two granddaughters?"

"Your celestial brilliance, she is the mother of the former emperor and the two young ladies are of royal Persian blood."

With a flash in his eyes, Hephaistion was about to light into the eunuch for the impudence of his answer. Reading his friend's mood, Alexandros stayed the diatribe by placing a hand on Hephaistion's arm. "Tell me, eunuch, how do the magoi view these two young women?"

"I beg your forgiveness, your celestial brilliance, but some magoi still regard them as the daughters of Dareios and therefore of royal blood."

"Well, of course, they are daughters of Dareios. He may be dead but he's still their father. Tell me, Dilshad, how old is Little Stateira now?"

"She's not Little Stateira any more, your divine highness. She's twenty-one. And Drypetis is nineteen."

"You know what, Dilshad? Go back to the harem now. You can finish your report next time. Inform Sisygambis that Hephaistion and I are coming to visit her daughters later today. Don't make a big deal about it. I don't want anyone else to know we're coming. And I certainly don't want us to be mobbed by a bunch of demanding women. You've got that?"

Dilshad gave me a meaningful look before answering Alexandros's question. "Yes, your celestial brilliance, I have just the place. I'll come back to collect the two of you midafternoon and take you in through the postern gate. The two young ladies will be waiting for you in the visitors' compound." He cast another glance at me. "I'll make sure there's no one else around during your visit." Hearing no reaction from Alexandros, he added with a leer, "And of course the young ladies will be prepared to accommodate all your wishes."

"We're only coming to talk, you idiot. Now get out!"

As soon as the old eunuch was ushered out, Hephaistion rounded on his friend. "What's gotten into you? Why didn't you let him finish his report?"

"I've had an idea. Suppose I marry Stateira. That'll shut the magoi up, don't you think? I'll be marrying a woman with royal Persian blood, the daughter of the guy who, they think, is the last legitimate emperor. So, that will make me the next legitimate emperor in their eyes, right?"

"Brilliant, Aniketos, that's just brilliant."

"And if she turns out to be a dog, maybe I can marry Drypetis, who's just as royal as her sister and maybe better looking."

"Or you could marry them both. Persians believe in many wives."

"Let's not go crazy now, Hephaistion. I already have one wife in Roxane. And then there is Barsine, who's not my wife but is the mother of my son. And you never know what the future holds. I may need to marry some other women. So, one royal Persian bride will do. Let's go have a look and I'll pick out the one I like better."

And so it was that the first woman visited by one of us was Artakama but that didn't count in the betting pool. And besides, no one had put any money on her in any case. The visit by Alexandros and Hephaistion was not exactly what the punters had in mind either but, there being no better solution, the pot wound up getting split between those who'd put their money on either Stateira or Drypetis.

****

"Well, what do you think?" Hephaistion asked as soon as they were safely beyond the harem walls.

"I thought they both looked great; nice wide hips; seemed eager and fertile. And I liked the fact they'd been studying Greek."

"So, which one are you picking?"

"I guess I've got to go with Stateira. She is the older of the two and she seemed intelligent enough, although neither one said too much."

"Which proves they've got some sense."

Alexandros laughed. "Tell you what I'm thinking, my friend. Why don't I marry Stateira and you take Drypetis? No sense letting someone else grab the prize. And, speaking of which, locate Ochos and make sure he never marries anyone."

"You want me to cut his balls off, Aniketos?" It wasn't clear whether Hephaistion was joking but Alexandros took him at face value. "No, there's no need for that. Just make sure someone buries a sword in his belly."

******

As Alexandros contemplated the upcoming double wedding ceremony, his creative juices really started to flow. When Dilshad returned to complete his report, Alexandros was ready with another brilliant idea. "I want a list of every

452

woman in the harem between the ages of fifteen and thirty. I don't need a lengthy report on any of them. Just their names, parentage, and age. Can you do that off the top of your head or do you need more time to put together a list?"

"If you wouldn't mind, your celestial brilliance, I'd rather go back, do a careful census, and get a scribe to write it all down on a scroll. I wouldn't want to get any details wrong."

"That's a good idea, Dilshad. In fact, when the list is done, just send the scroll. No need for you to come back."

When the scroll arrived, Alexandros staged a drinking party in the palace. These banquets were almost a nightly occurrence but, at this one, there were two departures from the usual routine. First, only Macedonian commanders in good standing with Alexandros were invited. And second, after everyone was nicely lubricated, Alexandros had a special announcement. He unrolled Dilshad's scroll and explained that every man in the room would marry one of the women on the list at a mass wedding two weeks hence. "I'll be marrying the first name of the list, who happens to be Stateira." With a flourish, he wrote his name next to hers. "Hephaistion will marry the next lady, who happens to be Drypetis." He made a notation. "Alright, who's next?"

No one rushed up to be inscribed in the scroll of marital bondage. Alexandros took the time to explain what he was up to. "This is a list of all the voluptuous, well-bred, fecund young ladies we've been holding in the harem. They are a wasted asset. We have to feed, clothe, house, and guard them and we're getting nothing in return. At the same time, I need commanders who are happy, who are seen as members of Persian nobility, who are able to communicate with their Persian-speaking colleagues, junior officers, and ordinary soldiers, and who are producing many future fighters for our army."

Suddenly, every man in the room wanted to ask some questions but Alexandros hushed them with a raised hand. "Just to make myself clear, nobody leaves this room tonight until his name is inscribed next to the name of a lady on this list. And," he added with a wink, "Nobody leaves Sousa until his wife is carrying a future soldier in her belly." Then he glanced at me. "If any of you have had a chance to meet any of the women currently in the harem and wish to marry them, speak up and we will try to accommodate your preference. Otherwise, we'll just go in order of seniority and assign you to the next name on the list."

I jumped faster than any other man in the room and before my brain could intervene. "I'll take Artakama, sire!"

While the rest of the men in the room were hesitating and adding their names, I whispered in Seleukos's ear. "Do you remember that girl they brought to us in Marakanda?"

"You mean the daughter of the dead Spitamenes and his Massagetan consort?"

"Yes, exactly. I'm surprised you remember her. Anyway, I had a chance to speak to her recently. Although she's still only sixteen, she's all grown up. Perhaps not a beauty but she's very bright. I think you'd like her."

Seleukos gave me a long, appraising look. "Alright, Ptolemaios, I'll take your word for it." He added his name next to Apame's on the scroll.

Barsine, who was thirty-one, and Thais, whose age was indeterminate, were not included on Dilshad's list, thus avoiding any possibly awkward moments.

Most of the senior commanders, who'd never met any of the women in the harem, were happy to let the Fates choose their new mates. And they were too busy imagining the pleasures awaiting them to give another thought to leaving Alexandros and returning home to Macedonia. In due course, most of them managed to impregnate their new wives and, perhaps to their own surprise, found themselves better able to relate to their new, multicultural, polyglot troops. The non-Macedonian junior officers and ordinary soldiers, in turn, found new respect and acceptance for their senior Macedonian commanders.

****

Alexandros added one more enhancement to his grand mixed martial and matrimonial matchmaking. It occurred to him that what was a good idea for his senior commanders would work even better for his restive Macedonian veterans and old newbies. He had his agents round up all the unattached female camp followers, local ladies of easy virtue, Sousa strumpets, and respectable young girls and women from throughout the satrapy. They were brought in and offered the chance to marry rich Macedonian soldiers. Very few refused.

By the time the day of the great wedding feast rolled around, Alexandros had arranged for thousands of marriages. It was his hope that the Macedonian rank-and-file soldiers who were not hopelessly disenchanted, were still vigorous and able to fight, and horny enough to let their libidos guide their thinking, would embrace their new brides, forget about Macedonia, and adopt the Persian Empire as their new home. In addition, because he was a farsighted leader, he thought about the myriad splendid young soldiers these unions would produce.

****

Inevitably, there was a complication. Alexandros, unwilling to rely on the spiritual expertise of a harem-bound eunuch, had the chief magos of Ahura Mazda brought in for consultation. He had only one question for the haughty divine: "Tell me, priest, will you and your fellow magoi finally recognize my legitimacy if I marry Dareios's oldest daughter?"

"My views are not important, sire," the magos temporized. "I only serve Ahura Mazda. As for my fellow magoi, yes, it will make a difference to most of them. And, if the marriage is blessed by male offspring, most of them will recognize the oldest boy as the legitimate heir apparent. But, of course, there will be some who will remain unpersuaded."

Alexandros was not amused. "How can they continue to deny my legitimacy and the legitimacy of the offspring of my marriage to royal Persian blood?"

"Well, you see, they deny the legitimacy of Dareios. They believe he was a usurper who took over the throne after the last two legitimate emperors, Artaxerxes Tritos Ochos and Artaxerxes Tetratos Arses, were murdered. So, obviously, Dareios's daughters are no more legitimate than he was."

Alexandros reached for the hilt of his sword. "This is preposterous!"

The cleric quickly raised his hand. "Sire, I may have a solution. Emperor Ochos's youngest daughter survived the massacre and is still living in your harem. If you were to marry her, I believe even the objections of these holdout magoi would be overcome. Her name is Parysatis. I believe she must be around sixteen years old now."

Alexandros solved the problem in the locally acceptable manner. On the wedding day, he married both Stateira and Parysatis.

******

The marriage ceremonies were conducted outdoors, on the palace parade grounds, in accordance with Persian custom. Chairs and tables were set up in long rows. The bridegrooms sat on one side of the tables, looking at empty chairs on the other side. The front row of tables was occupied by the leading men of Alexandros's army, who sat side-by-side in order of precedence, with Alexandros occupying the first seat, Hephaistion the second, followed by the rest of the eighty or so senior commanders. The remaining countless rows of chairs and tables for the thousands of ordinary Macedonian troops filled most of the well-trodden mustering field.

At the start of the ceremonies, all the men rose to their feet, raised chalices of wine, recited the ritual prayers, sang the prescribed paeans, sprinkled a few drops of wine on the ground and drank the rest. After placing the empty chalices on the tables, they turned around to face the aisle between the tables. In the meantime, the blushing brides were led into the aisles to meet their husbands, almost always for the first time.

Each man took his intended by the hand, kissed her, and escorted her to the seat across from his own. When all were seated, Alexandros climbed onto a small dais and led the men in reciting the marital pledge to their brides. At the conclusion of the pledge, they were all deemed married. Great quantities of food and wine were consumed to seal the deal.

As daylight began to fade, Alexandros bid the couples to rise and approach the registration tables at the exits. He told the men to take their chalices as wedding presents to remember this day. At the head table, these drinking vessels were made of solid gold. At the remaining tables, they were made of electrum, silver, and various alloys of precious and base metals but even at the lowliest tables the men received a beautiful and valuable memento. Alexandros also told them that they would receive a cash bonus equal to a year's pay at the registration tables. The men rose and, holding hands with their new brides, started to depart, still walking in orderly lines. After a short but perhaps uncomfortable wait, the impatient newlyweds had their marriages duly recorded, received their bonuses, and then wended their way home to make the marriages official.

******

By the time the army marched out of Sousa, many of the new brides were pregnant, as ordered. One of Alexandros's wives would become pregnant as well but it wouldn't be either Stateira or Parysatis. Roxane would manage to beat them both to the punch, although not quite yet.

As for the thousands of other marriages, most lasted less than two years. A few, however, endured for life, including Seleukos's marriage to Apame. With respect to my own marriage to Artakama, all I can say is that the strictures of the Prime Directive were shredded, along with much else, in the course of our second night together.

Chapter 19 – Back to Babylon

Not long after the weddings, it was time to move on. Alexandros's next destination was the de facto principal capital of his new Persian Empire, Babylon, but the rapidly approaching summer months were not an ideal time for a visit, Hanging Gardens or no Hanging Gardens. He decided to emulate what so many Persian emperors had done before him and spend the hottest part of the year in the coolest of his four capitals, Ekbatana. However, he chose a somewhat indirect route to get there, for reasons that he kept to himself.

Our first stop was to be a large city on the banks of the Tigris River called Opis. Most of the army would get there overland, under Hephaistion's command. They were to march east until they reached the Tigris, then make a left turn and follow the river north to Opis. A select few, including most of the Companion Cavalry and several battalions of Silver Shields, would get to cruise, under Alexandros's personal command, on the flotilla of vessels brought to Sousa by Nearchos. We were to sail a short

461

distance down the Choaspes River to the marshy upper end of the Gulf of Persia, then over to the mouth of the Tigris, and finally upstream to our rendezvous point at Opis.

This time around, the baggage train, most of the camp followers, and all the wives and mistresses were to stay where they were, in Sousa, pending further orders from Alexandros. As a result, all those newlywed brides with whose charms the men had barely had time to gain a passing acquaintance and whose faces they would surely not recognize if they chanced upon them in the market square, were left behind. On the other hand, all the old, lame, disaffected, and mutinous Macedonian oldtimers were told to march to Opis with Hephaistion.

Once we had all arrived at Opis, Alexandros called an assembly of the disenchanted oldtimers, who had already suffered a blow by being excluded from the Sousa nuptial tomfoolery, and gave them the bad news. "You have served me loyally and well, you have won many battles and achieved great things. You have earned my gratitude and the gratitude of your homeland. Now, the time has come for you to reap your rewards." Big cheer. "I have listened to the requests and demands you have been making and I'm pleased to tell you that the time has come." The word 'demands' struck a slightly jarring note but the men were still listening. "Many of you will soon get to see your homes, your wives, your children, and you will arrive as the richest men in your districts." There was hesitant applause, the men wondering where this was leading. "I have great news for you: You're going home!" Instead of the expected cheering, Alexandros heard heckling. "But wait," he yelled, "there is more. Each discharged oldtimer will receive a bonus of one talent of silver."

The bribe didn't mollify the most cantankerous of the oldtimers who did their best to start a riot. The commotion attracted the younger veterans and old newbies who came running to the oldtimers' assembly. After hearing of the separation bonus, some of them decided that a talent was worth more than a chintzy chalice, a stingy wedding present, and a Persian trollop combined. They wanted to accept the offer that had been rejected by some of the oldtimers. In truth, the Macedonian soldiers, old and young, veterans and newbies, had been growing more and more disgruntled. Regardless of what Alexandros said, their inclination was to add his latest decision to their growing pile of cumulative grievances. They didn't like Alexandros's ever-rising royal Persian airs; they didn't like his increasingly more pointless, reckless, costly, and crazy marches to the ends of the Earth, which brought lots of death and suffering and very little by way of loot; they were getting tired of their unremitting lives of soldiering; and most of all, they were scared because, slowly but surely, they were getting outnumbered in Alexandros's army by mercenaries from all over Greece, and worse, by Persian soldiers, and worst of all, by savage barbarians. The rioting spread through the rapidly growing horde of Macedonian soldiers like wildfire.

Alexandros was furious. As was his wont lately, he flew from outlandish beneficence to murderous outrage in the blink of an eye. He dismounted from his horse and, accompanied by his personal bodyguard, dashed among his troops, pointing out the loudest hecklers. Anybody he singled out was seized by the bodyguards and killed on the spot. By the time he regained control of his emotions, thirteen of his beloved Macedonian soldiers lay dead.

A shocked, deathly, minatory silence descended on the assembly. Alexandros, as if seeing for the first time what he had done, stopped, turned around, remounted, and rode back to his tent. He realized that he'd mismanaged the discharge of the superannuated oldtimers. However, he still retained his touch as a master manipulator of his soldiers' psyches. He hid in his tent for three days, although he dispensed with the pretense of fasting and repenting. On the contrary, he staged nightly feasts to which only Persian nobles and courtiers were invited. At the end of each night, he made a point of letting the leading Persians kiss his cheeks, keeping the flaps rolled up to assure that anyone standing outside had a good view of the proceedings.

When Alexandros emerged from his tent three days later, grizzled veterans standing around outside, their cheeks streaked with tears, rushed up and begged for forgiveness. Alexandros, no mean actor in his own right, shed a few tears himself. The soldiers withdrew all their complaints but one: Their feelings were hurt because Alexandros had never invited any of them to kiss his cheeks. After prolonged deliberation, Alexandros relented and let as many of those present as time would permit step up and kiss him.

After this, the veterans marched back to their portion of the camp, singing joyful paeans of victory. Alexandros watched with a smile. Those Macedonian soldiers he wanted to keep would continue to fight for him with renewed vigor. Those he wanted to discharge would leave content, basking in his love and approval. There was another feast. This time, the Macedonians received the best seats.

Immediately after the feast, Alexandros implemented his plans. The reason he had come by way of Opis was that this was the logical parting point for those going west, toward the Hellespont, and those heading east, toward Ekbatana. He met with Krateros and Polyperchon and handed them two scrolls. One scroll contained their written orders. They were to lead the discharged oldtimers back to Macedonia, with Krateros in command and Polyperchon serving as his deputy. He gave them ten days to get the men ready for the long march. The second scroll was for Antipatros. They were to hand it to the regent upon their arrival, with the seal intact, to guarantee its authenticity.

******

Once the discharged oldtimers were on their way, Alexandros and the rest of the army set off toward Ekbatana. The journey was uneventful, although it took until the start of summer to get there. The stay in the summer capital was even more boring, with no battles to fight, no satraps to execute, no women to inseminate, no worlds to conquer. Alexandros was climbing the walls.

He spent most of his time drawing up plans for his invasion of the western Mediterranean, with Carthage as his first target and the other non-Greek cities and territories within easy reach of the Mediterranean coast to follow. Having turned the Aegean into a Greek sea, his next ambition was to do the same for the entire Mediterranean basin. The problem was that, with his grip on reality gradually receding, it was difficult to tell, even for Alexandros, what was feasible and what mere fantasy. Although he was only thirty-two years old, his physical health was not what it had once been. All those hardships, serious injuries, and bouts of heavy drinking had taken their toll. He lived to conquer and felt almost a religious duty to fulfill his destiny but, in those rare moments of honest self-reflection, he saw glimpses of mortality.

He considered having the harem transported from Sousa to Ekbatana but, by the time the slow harem convoy made it to Ekbatana, the summer would be over and it would be time to go to Babylon. *I'll have them moved to Babylon in the fall*, he thought.

He staged a lavish festival in honor of Dionysos instead. It lasted for many days and included athletic contests, theatrical performances, and nightly feasts with much food and drink. Halfway through, Hephaistion contracted an intestinal illness, which quickly grew worse. He became deathly ill. His physician told him to cut out hard-to-digest foods and stay away from alcohol. Initially, Hephaistion followed his doctor's orders and his health improved. As soon as he felt better, he returned to the next feast and consumed many servings of greasy, spicy food, which he washed down with prodigious quantities of uncut wine. The next morning, he was sicker than ever.

Alexandros, who was watching some athletic contests, received a message that Hephaistion had taken a turn for the worse. He hurried back to see his friend but, by the time he arrived, Hephaistion was dead.

Alexandros was disconsolate. This time his mourning was not a show. He retreated to his chambers in the palace, barred the doors, and refused to see anyone. For two days, he neither ate nor drank. His grief knew no bounds. And then he became angry.

When he emerged from seclusion, his first act was to have Hephaistion's unfortunate physician killed. Next, he did something truly extraordinary. He had the temple of Asklepios in Ekbatana razed to the ground.[20] To tear down

---

[20] Asklepios was the god of healing. Every Greek city of any size had a temple to him, which functioned as a kind of hospital. Sick and injured people came to the temple, brought offerings, and slept in the temple precinct or in the temple itself until they either got better or died. The

a temple of a god was an act of breathtaking sacrilege. For someone as superstitious and religion-obsessed as Alexandros, it was unimaginable. It did, however, illustrate the depths of his grief, the heights of his anger, and perhaps his growing delusions of divinity. He may have reached the point of considering himself an equal of Asklepios, if not his superior.

Hephaistion's embalmed body was sent to Babylon, along with Alexandros's instructions for the funeral arrangements. In an indication of the grandiosity of Alexandros's plans, it would take until early spring of the following year for the preparations to be completed.

In the meantime, to keep himself busy, Alexandros planned and executed a military campaign against one of the violent tribes living in the mountainous terrain of western Media, which had given much trouble to previous Persian emperors, including Artaxerxes Tritos Ochos.

---

priests of the temple accepted the offerings and attended to the supplicants according to their unscientific, superstitious ways. Their remedies consisted mostly of prayers and sacrifices on behalf of the sufferers. For real medical treatment, patients sought the help of physicians, although the line between shaman and doctor was not clear-cut. Physicians professed to be followers of Asklepios but mostly didn't practice their profession in the temples, leaving that area to the priests. The sick and injured, on the other hand, often consulted physicians and made offerings to the priests, just to be on the safe side.

Those emperors had found it easier to pay an annual tribute, in return for which the tribes agreed to stay in their mountain fastnesses.

Not long after Hephaistion's death, tribal representatives showed up in Ekbatana to collect their annual tribute. Their timing proved to be unfortunate. Alexandros sent the representative home and promised to deliver the requested subsidy in person. True to his word, he showed up, at the head of his army. It took him about two months to exterminate the troublesome tribes to the last man, woman, and child. Alexandros dedicated his "victory" to the memory of Hephaistion.

****

The reluctant march of the oldtimers proceeded slowly. Their route either took them across deserts or skirted them. Spring had turned to summer and the oppressive heat was not conducive to rapid marching.

When the discharged oldtimers reached Kilikia, on their way to the Hellespont, Krateros called a month-long halt to give the troops a chance to rest up. While in camp, he received news of Hephaistion's death and of Alexandros's reaction to it. It got him thinking.

He took the newly-arrived news bulletin to Polyperchon and waited until his deputy finished reading. "Do you remember when Alexandros dispatched

Polydamas to Ekbatana with two messages, one for Kleandros and the other for Parmenion?"

Polyperchon looked up. "Yeah, what about it."

"Well, we're carrying two messages too. One with our orders and one for Antipatros. Have you ever wondered what's in that second scroll that we're not supposed to open?"

"Sure, but I guess we'll find out when we get there."

Krateros showed him the second, sealed scroll. "Maybe it would be better to find out now, lest we run into some unpleasant surprise when it's too late to retreat."

Polyperchon thought it over and then, without saying a further word, took out his dagger, heated it in the flame of an oil lamp until it was nice and warm but not too hot, and then, ever so carefully, lifted the seal, doing his best to keep both the parchment and the impressed wax disk intact.

******

In the Pella royal palace, Antipatros was visibly agitated.

"What's up, father?" Kassandros asked.

"Here, read this." Antipatros tossed the scroll to his son. "This arrived from Krateros this afternoon."

Kassandros's face reflected a storm of raging thoughts. He was reading the same scroll that Polyperchon and Krateros had read and then carefully resealed in Kilikia. In contravention of Alexandros's wishes, they sent it on to Pella by messenger, rather than delivering it by hand. The intention of the orders was unmistakable. Upon arrival in Macedonia, Krateros was to take command of all Macedonian troops, take control of Macedonia, Thrake, and Thessaly, and assure the freedom of Greece. Antipatros was relieved of command of all Macedonian troops and relieved of his posts as Alexandros's regent in Macedonia and deputy hegemon of Greece. He was ordered to set out immediately on a recruiting trip through Macedonia and Thrake, enlist at least a brigade of fresh Macedonian and allied troops, and to report, with the new brigade, to Alexandros in Babylon with all possible dispatch.

This latest set of orders was simply the culmination of a blizzard of orders, reports, and rumors arriving in Pella for years. Antipatros was well aware of the fates of Philotas, Parmenion, and his own son-in-law, Alexandros of Lynkestis. He knew all about Alexandros's growing megalomania, his denigration of Antipatros's victories and achievements, his assumption of Persian attire and customs, his increasingly frequent outbursts of irrational behavior, and his pretensions of divinity. Most germane for their immediate discussion was his ongoing purge of satraps.

After mulling the matter over for a couple of days, father and son came to a decision. Kassandros would go to Babylon, by way of Kilikia. Antipatros would stay where he was, pleading ill health.

****

Two months later, Krateros, Polyperchon, and the discharged oldtimers were still in Kilikia. They hadn't moved an inch. Kassandros arrived at their camp, in disguise and under cover of darkness, in late fall. He claimed to be a messenger from Alexandros. The soldiers on sentry duty didn't recognize him. They did recognize his Macedonian accent, however, which served as his passport. After searching and disarming him, they escorted him to the command tent. Krateros and Polyperchon were seated, engaged in throwing knuckle bones with some of the other commanders. Of all those present, only Krateros recognized Kassandros after a single glance. The young man warned him, with a subtle gesture of his hand, not to say anything.

Krateros nodded. "There's a private message I must receive, gentlemen. So, if you'll excuse me."

Everybody stood up and started to make their way out. Krateros pointed to Polyperchon while looking at Kassandros.

"He can stay," Kassandros said.

The three of them sat up the rest of the night. By dawn, they had the outline of a plan. But it would require some time, and much work, if the plan was to be successfully executed.

One result was that, when the plan was finally implemented, six months later, Krateros, Polyperchon, and their oldtimers were still encamped outside Tarsos in Kilikia. Antipatros was still in Pella, still regent of Macedonia and deputy hegemon of Greece, his hold on the Macedonian home guard stronger than ever. Kassandros, in the meantime, had traveled incognito throughout the major cities of the empire, taking the temperature of various satraps and garrison commanders.

******

Alexandros's first order of business, upon his return to Babylon, was Hephaistion's funeral. Although Hephaistion's corpse still looked as fresh as the day he died, thanks to the expertise of the Egyptian embalmers, Alexandros was anxious to pay his respects to his dead comrade by staging the most elaborate funeral the world had ever seen. The funeral pyre was finally finished. It took up a good portion of the large plaza in front of the Etemenanki. It was five stories tall. Its architecture echoed the gigantic ziggurat behind it. At the bottom level, massive trunks of cedar supported the next, somewhat smaller level, which featured carved ebony elephants. The third level, which rested on the elephants' backs, boasted a bestiary of creatures real and imaginary, from lions to dragons and from eagles to griffins. The penultimate level consisted of captivating caryatids whose heads kept aloft a small wooden temple. The bier that would hold Hephaistion's corpse was ensconced within the pillars of the temple. Of course, from where we stood, it was hard to see the temple, much less anything within it, but we had been told the bier was there.

Where did they get all this wood? was my first thought upon seeing this massive yet ephemeral monument. *All the forests of Babylonia – admittedly a counterfactual concept – wouldn't have been enough to build this pyre. They must've ranged far and wide to collect all this kindling.*

On a cool, crystal clear, early spring morning, the ceremonial precinct around the Etemenanki and the Processional Way beyond it were filled to overflowing by mourners and gawkers. It seemed as if every inhabitant of Babylon turned out. Certainly, the entire army was present and accounted for, lined up, phalanx by phalanx and squadron by squadron, on either side of the funeral pyre. Directly in front stood Alexandros, all the closest friends and companions of the deceased, all the important and mighty personages of the empire, and suffocating squads of clerics, officiants, seers, and charlatans. Behind the pyre stood swarms of women, expected to ooh and aah, sing, keen, and ululate at the appropriate moments. Lost somewhere in the crowd was Hephaistion's widow Drypetis, whom he'd hardly known.

Immortal Alexandros

A great deal of ritual preceded the actual moment of cremation. Finally, a couple of priests stepped forward and fastened a rope across the chest, under the armpits, and behind the back of the shrouded corpse, which had been resting in an elaborately carved, open coffin. Once the rope was tied behind the dead man's head, the shrouded bundle began to rise into the air, hoisted by a system of pulleys jutting out from the roof of the temple. As it ascended, plaintive hymns rose from the top of the pyre to the heavens. It turned out that the caryatids holding up the small temple were hollow, sheltering within their cavities the best female singers of the Greek world that unlimited funds could import.

When the corpse reached the level of the temple, a couple of workers, dressed as priests, guided it to the waiting bier. Once the body was in place, the workers discretely descended to the ground using ladders concealed within the center of the pyramid. The singers then made their way down, one by one, continuing to sing as they went, stopping only when they hit bottom and scurried away from the coming conflagration.

The last of the singers barely made it to safety when Alexandros lit the pyre. Within seconds, the flames reached for the sky, nicely perfumed by tons of incense, exotic oils, and aromatic spices strategically spread throughout the blazing mountain of timber.

The inferno burned well into the night, long after all the mourners had dispersed to various feasts and banquets. The important people gathered in the imperial palace, where Alexandros presided over a solemn gathering of senior commanders, courtiers, clerics, sycophants, and social climbers. Great quantities of food and wine were consumed, followed by the usual salacious entertainment provided by scantily dressed dancers, acrobats, and contortionists. The night ended with discreet couplings in adjoining chambers and tableaux of conspicuous degeneracy in the main hall.

We were truly back in Babylon.

Chapter 20 – On to Immortality

Kassandros walked into the Great Hall of the Babylon Palace on a warm, end-of-spring day. Alexandros, who was in the middle of another interminable weekly audience, didn't notice his arrival.

He'd been busy during the three months since Hephaistion's funeral. The ladies of the harem had been transported from Sousa to Babylon during the winter and were awaiting the return of their husbands and paramours with varying degrees of eagerness. Alexandros's three wives and two concubines, Roxane, Stateira, Parysatis, Barsine, and Thais, kept him hopping night after night. Unlike his Persian predecessors, he hadn't had much practice juggling so many concupiscent balls at once and he found keeping it up a challenge, especially after evenings spent in heavy drinking. He had, however, succeeded, at long last, in getting Roxane pregnant. We all expected that the two Persian wives would follow suit in short order, thus assuring a good supply of royal offspring. None of us knew, at that point, that Roxane's child would turn out to be

Alexandros's only legitimate heir. Barsine's son Herakles was seven and a half years old and a delightful child, but he would always be viewed as a bastard. Alexandros rarely had time to visit him.

The emperor's days were a hectic whirl of activity. For example, he had a bit of unfinished business with his former treasurer. Harpalos, and his 6,000 mercenaries and 5,000 talents of silver, successfully reached Peiraieus, the port of Athens, but there his luck ran out. The Athenians, rightfully concerned about Alexandros's reaction, refused to admit him into the city. Harpalos retreated to Megara in western Attika and resorted to the usual method of changing the Athenians' minds: he bribed Demosthenes and a few other leading citizens. The Assembly reversed its decision and admitted him but not his mercenaries. Harpalos left his soldiers near Megara and took the precaution of hiding most of his money. He arrived in Athens with only 700 talents, which still made him incredibly rich. (It had taken only a gold chalice and twenty talents to bribe Demosthenes.)

When Alexandros received word of Harpalos's whereabouts, he sent a brief note to the Athenians. Harpalos was promptly arrested and thrown in jail, pending further orders from Alexandros, and his 700 talents confiscated. Harpalos, who was still a lot richer than any jailer, bribed his way out of prison, made his way back to his troops and the rest of his money near Megara, and proceeded to march into the Peloponnese. However, he discovered that no amount of money was sufficient to persuade any city on the peninsula to take him in. Left with no other choice, he sailed for Krete, perhaps hoping eventually to find sanctuary in Kyrene, on the north coast of Africa. Alexandros's agents caught up to him on Krete and killed him.

There were other, more important things, that kept Alexandros busy. He had progressed beyond simply making plans for future conquests and started to take concrete steps. He dispatched small expeditions to the Mediterranean, Black, and Caspian Seas. Their assignment was to collect intelligence for our upcoming campaigns. Any payoff from these reconnaissance missions would take time but Alexandros strove to be patient, contrary though that might've been to his natural instincts. After all, it would've been almost unseemly for an immortal god to appear to be in a hurry. Unfortunately, the one immediate result these spies and agents produced was not intelligence but consternation in the places they visited. Given Alexandros's track record, no city wanted to be the next stop on his itinerary. As a result, they all hurried to send ambassadors with lavish gifts, offers of submission, proposals to erect shrines in his honor, and pledges to do whatever would make him go somewhere else.

Alexandros, restless as ever, decided to launch a small expedition into the Euphrates delta. He had been told that some of the marsh people who lived in that area didn't view themselves as his subjects. He found and killed as many of them as time permitted during his brief excursion out of town. By his next audience day, he was back on his throne in the Great Hall, listening to a long line of ambassadors and other important people desperate to have their say.

Kassandros watched in astonishment as dignified men representing the leading cities of Greece prostrated themselves in the presence of his former schoolmate, paid him extraordinary homage, and generally behaved as if worshipping a living god.

Finally, the endless stream of ambassadors, supplicants, litigants, and sycophants began to ebb and Alexandros noticed Kassandros at the back of the line. With a quick, whispered command, he dispatched a bodyguard to grab him and drag him to the front.

It had been eleven years since they'd laid eyes on each other. Alexandros was twenty-two then, the charismatic leader of an army that loved him. He was about to launch an invasion of the greatest empire the world had ever known, intending to liberate the Greek cities of Ionia from bondage. By any rational calculation, he had no chance of success. What he had instead was preternatural confidence, a belief in his own destiny, and a genius for military leadership. Kassandros was twenty-four then, the immature, spoiled, untested son of Alexandros's most trusted general.

"Where is your father?" Alexandros barked, in lieu of greeting.

Kassandros, who had remained on his feet, didn't blink. "My father is in Pella, sire, serving you as your regent. He sends his regrets but is unable to travel all this way, due to his age and health."

"Why isn't Krateros serving as my regent? Weren't my orders explicit enough?"

"Sire, Krateros sent your orders ahead but he himself had not yet arrived in Pella when I set off in response to your command."

Alexandros exploded. "It's been more than a year since Krateros left with the discharged oldtimers. How long does it take to travel to Pella?" He was seething. "Clear the hall! And place this insolent young man under guard!"

The emperor's weekly audience was done for the day.

******

Alexandros dispatched agents to track Krateros down and haul him back to Babylon. The agents carried new orders for Polyperchon, commanding him to get to Pella as quickly as possible and arrange for the delivery of Antipatros to Babylon, in chains if necessary. At the same time, however, he relented with respect to Kassandros. He ordered his release from custody and invited him to attend a banquet scheduled to be held at the palace a couple of nights later.

Kassandros used the time to visit his two younger brothers, Iolaos and Philippos, who had come over to Asia at the start of the invasion, serving as pages to Alexandros. They had received several promotions since. Iolaos, in particular, had been appointed cupbearer to the king, making him responsible for all wine arrangements at the royal banquets.

After the reunion with his brothers, Kassandros looked up a couple of friends from their Mieza days, including Perdikkas, Nearchos, Seleukos, Lysimachos, and paid courtesy calls on several other leading commanders. He stopped by my chambers as well. After some small talk, he tried to gauge my feelings toward Alexandros. I politely sidestepped his questions and ushered him out the door.

On the night of the banquet, Kassandros arrived early, angling for a seat as close to the head couch as possible. He needn't have bothered. Once the guests were well into their cups, Alexandros invited Kassandros to join him on the head couch and, while plying him with wine – delivered by Iolaos personally – cross-examined him at length about conditions in Macedonia.

By the end of the banquet, Alexandros felt lousy. Philippos the Physician, who was in attendance, told him that he'd had too much to drink, should return to his bedchamber, and sleep it off. Alexandros, unable to walk, was carried to his bed by several attendants.

When he finally awoke in middle of the following day, he had a high fever and was violently sick. Philippos was summoned once again but, it turned out, he'd left town at dawn. Alexandros, with the help of some aides, managed to get up, take a bath, and put on clean clothes. By the evening, he felt a little better and had something to eat. His fever spiked immediately. His aides put him to bed but he was unable to tolerate the sheets and the heat in his room. He was carried back to the bath house and placed next to the cold-water pool, where the air was moister and cooler than in his bedchamber. He lapsed either into sleep or unconsciousness.

The next morning, he felt well enough to be carried back to his room and put in bed. He ate nothing. He took a few sips of undiluted wine, supplied by Iolaos the Cupbearer. That evening, he asked to be carried back to the bathhouse, where he spent the night.

He continued to be carried back and forth between his bed and poolside for the next three days. His fever continued to increase and his condition to deteriorate, with frequent bloody diarrhea, dark urine, vomiting, muscle spasms, convulsions, and loss of consciousness.

By the fifth evening after the banquet, it was obvious to everyone, with the possible exception of Alexandros, that he was dying. He attempted to carry on his usual activities, such as religious rituals and military briefings, but it was just a farce, since he was delirious most of the time.

Two days later, he lost the ability to speak. He gave his seal ring to Perdikkas, so that documents could continue to be sealed and the routine business of administration kept going.

Somewhere along the line, the troops started to suspect that Alexandros was dead. The relatively few Macedonian veterans who were still left in Babylon, perhaps 500 of them, began to gather around the palace to find out what was happening. Getting no satisfactory answers, they demanded to see their leader.

Eleven days after the banquet, Perdikkas, taking charge, moved Alexandros's bed into a small audience chamber not far from his bedroom. This room had the advantage of a door at either end. The aides attending Alexandros propped him up in his bed, in the middle of the chamber, and made him look as presentable as possible. Then, they allowed the soldiers to stream into the audience chamber and walk by his bed. Some of the warriors paused momentarily to say a word or two. Alexandros was too weak to speak, to raise his hands, or to move his head. His eyes were open, most of the time, and would occasionally track the soldiers walking by. He even blinked a few times. Whether the blinks had any significance was impossible to tell. The tough, battled-hardened veterans were in tears, almost to a man, supporting one another as they walked out lest they fall to their knees.

After the veterans left, Alexandros's top commanders gathered in the audience chamber and spent the night holding vigil around his bed. Alexandros slept fitfully. With the arrival of dawn, he woke and rallied for a moment.

One of commanders asked him: "To whom do you bequeath your empire, sire?" Alexandros managed to whisper one more sentence: "To the strongest."

Those were his last words. He lapsed into unconsciousness, with his eyes wide open. His breathing slowed and rattled as he was no longer able to clear his windpipe. It got to the point where a minute would go by between breaths. Finally, he stopped breathing altogether. A different commander stepped forward, closed his eyes, and placed a gold daric on each of his eyelids.

Alexandros had joined his colleagues, the immortal gods of our imagination and primeval memory.

****

I struggled to disentangle my emotions. Alexandros was a complex man who'd changed over time. I found him impossible to understand. But the loss of any life is tragic and certainly the loss of a person who'd played such an important part in my life, who'd affected the fates of so many other people, and who'd altered the destinies of nations, deserved a moment of heartfelt mourning and respectful remembrance. On the other hand, by the end of his life, he'd become a monster. So, despite my best efforts, there was a tinge of relief mixed in with my grief.

My thoughts turned, as they so often did at the most inopportune moments, to the Prime Directive. *This man, who would've been killed at Granikos eleven years earlier but for my inadvertent, indirect intervention, used that extra time to alter history. After Alexandros, the world will never be the same. The ramifications of his actions will reverberate down the millennia. He's truly immortal, although perhaps not quite in the way he imagined.*

My own adherence to the Prime Directive had 'evolved,' to use a polite euphemism, over the twenty-one years since I first arrived in this ancient world. But, instead of regretting what couldn't be fixed, I resolved to make the best of it.

Alexandros was dead but his funeral games were about to begin. This time, I wouldn't simply stand idly by.

Immortal Alexandros

Author's Note

Faithful readers have asked me why this series is called The Ptolemaios Saga when Ptolemaios himself seems to play a secondary role in the first four books. To which I always reply, "Just wait; our narrator is about to come into his own."

Book Five will deal with the fight among Alexandros's surviving commanders, known to history as 'the Successors,' to take control of the empire he left behind. Ptolemaios will play a leading role during this epic struggle.

In the meantime, I hope you've enjoyed reading the series thus far.

September 1, 2021

Alexander Geiger

Additional Materials

Additional materials, including sources, illustrations, maps, battle depictions, an author's blog, and descriptions of upcoming volumes, are available at AlexanderGeiger.com.

Alexander Geiger

Acknowledgements

The author wishes to express his gratitude to the following individuals who kindly read (and, in some cases, re-read) the manuscript of this novel and offered numerous helpful suggestions and corrections, ranging from fixing typographical errors to pointing out infelicitous phrasing to urging a restructuring of plotlines: Kathy McGowan, Alan Unsworth, David Schwarz, George Rifkin, Jeffrey Johnstone, Nadine Gibbons, R. Philip Giles, William Mezick, Sheldon Miller, Carol Benderson, and Joseph Marinaro. Special thanks to Scott Schmeer of The Fierce Pixel, LLC, for the cover design. And endless love and thanks to Helene Geiger who not only did all of the above but has also put up with the author, supported him, and kept him alive for the past forty-nine years.

Any remaining mistakes are attributable solely to the obduracy of the author.

Immortal Alexandros

About the Author

The author is a history buff who has always wished he could travel back in time to visit some of his favorite historical figures, places, and events. The entire Ptolemaios Saga is an account of one such extended trip, intended to witness the dawn of the Hellenistic world. The men and women who lived, strived, fought, and loved during this seminal age didn't know their ideas, exploits, and accomplishments would reverberate all the way to the present day but, boy oh boy, did they leave a mark. Imagine being able to see, through the eyes of Ptolemaios Metoikos – who was actually there – all the adventures, sights, and colorful figures of that vibrant, memorable, and thrilling era. It's the author's hope that you will enjoy the ride.

In real life, the author is a graduate of Princeton University and Cornell Law School and a retired commercial litigator. He lives with his wife in in Bucks County, PA.

Please email all comments, questions, suggestions, or requests for author interviews and appearances to Alex@AlexanderGeiger.com.